...ren Booth is a Midwestern girl transplanted in the ..., raised on '80s music and repeated readings of *...ver* by Judy Blume. When she takes a break from the ... of romance, she's listening to music with her nearly ...wn kids or sweet-talking her husband into making her ...ocktail. Learn more about Karen at karenbooth.net

A TODAY bestselling author **Tessa Radley** has always ...d reading. It started with fairy tales, and it never stopped. ...sa keeps a towering TBR pile of books on her desk, ...ther on her nightstand… there's even one on the dining ...e. During Tessa's writing day, Cleo-of-the-China-blue-...s is her constant (and constantly complaining!) feline ...panion. Regular beach walks with her darling dog, ...y, are a favourite form of exercise—you can catch ...res on Tessa's Twitter feed, @tessaradley. To find out ...e about what she's reading and writing, join Tessa's ...sletter at www.tessaradley.com

Discover more at millsandboon.co.uk

A CINDERELLA SEDUCTION

KAREN BOOTH

A TANGLED ENGAGEMENT

TESSA RADLEY

MILLS & BOON

First Published in Great Britain 2019
by Mills & Boon, an imprint of HarperCollinsPublishers,
1 London Bridge Street, London, SE1 9GF

A Cinderella Seduction © 2019 Karen Booth
A Tangled Engagement © 2019 Tessa Radley

ISBN: 978-0-263-27187-4

0719

MIX
Paper from
responsible sources
FSC™ C007454

This book is produced from independently certified FSC™
paper to ensure responsible forest management.

For more information visit: www.harpercollins.co.uk/green

Printed and bound in Spain
by CPI, Barcelona

A CINDERELLA
SEDUCTION

KAREN BOOTH

For Piper Trace. Every book I write has your
delightfully crazy fingerprints all over it.

One

The room was pitch-black and perfectly still, except for the ring of Daniel Stone's cell phone. He rolled over in bed and blindly slapped his hand on the nightstand, fumbling for the device. He didn't bother checking the caller ID. Despite the five-hour time difference between London and New York, his mother never worried she might be calling too early.

"It's 5:49 in the bloody a.m.," he croaked, pushing himself up in bed. He switched on the lamp. The bright light shot across his room, and he squinted hard until his eyes adjusted. "What could possibly be so important?" The second of April, it was still dark out. His three dogs, Mandy, Buck and Jolly, were asleep at the foot of the bed.

"Are you going to see spaces for the new store today?"

His mother always jumped straight into business. She'd been this way as long as he could remember, but ever since his brother, William, had passed away, it was even more impossible to keep her content.

"I meet the real estate agent at nine. Two spaces to see today. I'm hopeful." That was a lie. Daniel was anything but optimistic, but he had to keep up the charade. It had been his idea to forge ahead with his mother's long-held dream of a New York location of Stone's, the family's wildly successful department store chain based in the UK. He'd hoped it might finally make her happy. So far, it was doing nothing but making Daniel second-guess himself. He'd been in Manhattan for three weeks now and he'd only come up empty-handed.

"You'll ring me when you've had your look?" she asked.

"Don't I always check in?" Daniel hated that she still had so little faith in him. He'd worked for the family his entire adult life. Then again, he'd spent those years playing second chair to his brother. That changed a year ago, when William's black Aston Martin hit a slick of oil on a road outside London and went careening off a bridge. The Stone family was no stranger to tragedy, but this one had hit especially hard.

Daniel's father now spent his days and a considerable chunk of the family fortune sailing the world. No boat was fast enough, no stretch of ocean too dangerous. He was currently somewhere off the coast of West Africa. His mother despised her husband's new hobby and had become equally reckless with the family business. Daniel felt as though he was babysitting them both, an unfair situation given that they still felt he needed to prove his worth.

"I trust you're prepared for the Empire State fashion show this evening?" she asked.

His mother was the micromanaging sort of boss. Never mind that he was thirty-four and this had become wearisome. "I am."

"Taking a date?"

"I've been busy." Daniel was not in New York to make

friends. He certainly was not in America for romance. Women only made life complicated. No, he was here to prove to his parents that he had things well in hand and it was time for them both to retire. William might have been the golden boy, but Daniel refused to be the black sheep because of the argument he and his brother had had the night of the accident.

"I'll take that as a no then. Now, please tell me you remember your marching orders for this evening."

"I track down Nora Bradford and convince her to design a line exclusive to Stone's."

"I can't emphasize enough how important this is. Eden's has not done right by her and her designs. She's too talented to be selling an entire line of her gorgeous garments in a second-rate department store."

Daniel choked back a grumble. He hadn't realized his mother still had an ax to grind with Eden's until he'd already begun his initiative of opening Stone's New York. If he'd know this much, he never would've suggested it.

"It's not second-rate. I've seen it."

"You're wrong. And you know how much I despised Victoria Eden. The woman was vindictive."

Victoria Eden, the founder of Eden's, had given his mother her start in retail years ago, grooming her to be the manager of the Eden's flagship store in Manhattan. Eden's had locations all over the world, and Stone's, a business founded by his grandparents, was dying on the vine. His mother had been sent to New York to learn the secrets of Eden's. But when Victoria found out, she not only fired his mother, she got even with his family by convincing suppliers to stop selling to Stone's. It nearly crippled their company. A family feud was born.

"I'm aware."

"Our move into New York has everything to do with

destroying Eden's. It does make me sad, though, that William isn't here to be a part of it."

Daniel slumped down in bed. Jolly, the English bulldog that had belonged to his brother, crawled her way closer, curling up at his hip. Daniel gave her a scratch behind the ear, but she growled. She wasn't always affectionate with him. Even Jolly thought he didn't quite measure up to William. "Our best strategy is to focus on being Stone's. May the strongest survive," he said.

"The Eden sisters are no competition. Those three know nothing about running a department store. One of them has been off in the south of France her entire life, doing nothing."

Daniel closed his eyes and pinched the bridge of his nose. "I need to take the dogs out. I'll ring you later."

Daniel said goodbye and shuffled into the kitchen to put on some tea. With the kettle heating up, he strode into the living room. Through the tall windows, he watched the sun begin to creep up over the horizon, illuminating the edges of the lush green tree line of Central Park, tucked neatly inside the hard city landscape. This was a million-dollar view, the sort of vista most people only dreamed of.

Still, something was missing. He probably felt that way because it wasn't London. There was nothing tying him to this luxury high-rise or this impossibly busy metropolis. The sooner he found a location for Stone's, got the store opened and staffed, the sooner he could head back to England and whatever future he could manage to build.

For the fifth time in as many days, Emma Stewart stared into the mirror, scrutinizing herself and her attire. Was this dress chic enough for the Empire State fashion show tonight? It was flattering. Tasteful and tailored. The gray midweight crepe fabric had a beautiful drape. Plus, she had on somewhat daring shoes—black Manolo Blahnik pumps that her half sister Sophie had instructed her to buy. The ensemble was befitting a woman with an executive position at Eden's department store. But would it make the cut in a room full of designers, celebrities, fashion editors and models? That, she did not know.

Emma took a final skeptical turn in front of the mirror, gathered her long brown hair and reached back to unzip the dress. It was just going to have to do. The fact of the matter was she was comfortable wearing gray. She might someday be a bolder, sexier version of Emma Stewart, but not today. She wasn't ready. It didn't matter that she now had a net worth of over a billion dollars, owned a swank apartment overlooking Central Park, and was CFO of the largest department store in the city. Three months ago, Emma's checking account held thirty-four bucks, she was renting a tired one-bedroom apartment in New Jersey, had a fleet-footed brown mouse for an uninvited roommate, and was a junior CPA at a tiny accounting firm. She wouldn't be at ease in a dress that might make her the center of attention, mostly because she'd never been the center of anything.

She tucked the dress inside a garment bag in order to take it to work. She and her half sisters, Mindy and Sophie, were not only attending Empire State, they were going to get ready together, at Eden's. Sophie had arranged for a hair stylist and makeup artist, which was perfect, since Emma had time for neither this morning. She was going to be late if she didn't get out the door. Putting her hair up in a ponytail, she bothered only with sunscreen, a light coat of mascara and lip balm, and dressed in her usual work attire—black trousers and a silk blouse. To mix things up, the blouse was royal-blue. She also decided to stick with the sky-high pumps she planned to wear that night. Twice daring counted for something, right?

Out in the hall, she waited for the elevator, mentally running through the workday ahead. She'd been at Eden's for three months now, and the days weren't getting any easier. It was a bizarre situation to begin with—in late December, Emma had been called to the reading of Victoria Eden's will. Emma had known Victoria Eden only as her cousins' grandmother, and the owner of Eden's, the largest department store in the city. Turned out that Victoria Eden was also Emma's grandma. Emma's mom had had an affair twenty-seven years ago with her sister's husband. Everyone kept it a secret, especially from Emma. But Victoria Eden blew the top off this powder keg when she left one-third of her empire to the third granddaughter nobody knew about—Emma. The other two-thirds of the store went to Sophie and Mindy Eden, women Emma had always believed were her cousins. In truth, they were her half sisters. Emma still wasn't sure what to make of that. She'd grown up an only child. She'd always wanted siblings, but this was a lot to grapple with at once.

Finally, the elevator dinged. Emma glanced down at her pumps as the door slid open, but then her sights landed on someone else's shoes. A man's shiny black wingtips to be exact, leading to charcoal dress pants on ridiculously long legs. The hem of a suit coat led to a trim waist, under which was a crisp white shirt over a broad chest and shoulders, all topped off with a tousled head of thick brown hair swept back from the forehead of a man she'd never before had the good fortune to run into.

Icy blue eyes connected with hers. The man didn't say a word. He merely cleared his throat and pressed his hand against the elevator door as it threatened to close.

Emma hopped on board while a flush of heat washed over her. "I'm sorry. Morning. On my way to work. Too much on my mind." She added a casual laugh for good measure.

The towering man said nothing in response, folding his hands in front of him and staring straight ahead at the doors.

"Are you on your way to work, too?" she asked.

The man glanced over at her and nodded. "Yes."

Ooh. A British accent. "Have you lived in the building long?" She'd been in the building for nearly two months now and had made friends with almost none of her neighbors. Not that she hadn't tried. She brought pumpkin muffins to the couple who moved in down the hall from her. They seemed…bemused. Emma realized her tragic mistake as soon as the wife said, "How sweet. Homemade and everything." She should have brought something from Dean & Deluca or Zabar's at the very least. Next time, it'd be chocolate truffles and a bottle of champagne. Emma was capable of faking her way through this world if she simply put a little thought into it.

The man shook his head. "No." He raked his fingers through his hair.

Emma had another four or five questions queued up in her head, one of which was whether she could smell him some more. His cologne was intriguing—warm and woodsy. Unfortunately, the doors slid open and he stepped aside. "Please," he said. If he was that good with single-syllable words, Emma could only imagine what might happen to her if he chose to utter an entire sentence in her presence.

Emma scurried off the elevator to the right and the main lobby, but the British mystery man strode left through the entrance to the parking garage. She looked longingly as he disappeared from view. Maybe she could get her driver to meet her in there next time. She might be missing out on a whole slew of handsome men.

Or perhaps she should just get to work and stop thinking about handsome men. Eden's was her entire future, one she'd never dreamed she could have. There was no room for distractions now.

After twenty minutes of stop-and-go Manhattan rush-hour traffic, Emma's driver dropped her at Eden's. Lizzie, the receptionist in the administrative offices, hardly let her step off the elevator before speaking. "Mindy and Sophie are waiting for you in Sophie's office. They want to talk about Empire State."

Emma forced a smile. "Thanks. I'll head in." Simply hearing the name of the big charity fashion show made her nervous again. Their grandmother had apparently attended the event every year. Tonight would be the debut of the three sisters, Mindy, Sophie and Emma, as the new faces of Eden's department store.

"Emma. Good morning." Sophie sprang up from her desk, swung her long, strawberry blond hair over her shoulder and gave Emma a hug. She was wearing a gorgeous navy blue dress and killer red heels. Sophie was the epitome of put-together, and quite frankly, everything Emma hoped to be someday.

"Hey, Em," Mindy offered, unsubtly eyeing Emma from head to toe. Mindy was wearing a plum-colored pencil skirt and short peplum jacket. She didn't have a wardrobe as funky as Sophie, but she always looked impeccable. "I see we went with black pants again."

"I was in a rush. I just grabbed what I knew would look good." Emma stood next to Sophie's desk rather than sitting. She didn't want to be here for long.

"Is that your dress for tonight?" Mindy asked, pointing to the garment bag Emma was still toting.

"Oh. Uh. Yes."

"Sophie and I would like to see it, please. No more keeping it a secret."

Emma walked over to Sophie's coat tree and hung up the dress, unzipping it from its bag. She pressed her lips together tightly, preparing herself for what these two might say. Anything was fair game. They worked in an industry built on first impressions and style, and she wasn't doing great on either front. But, and this was a big but, Sophie and Mindy had grown up in a household where money was never an issue, where they were encouraged to dress in any way they saw fit. Emma, however, had grown up buying her clothes at discount stores, and had been preached the value of blending in.

"Well?" Emma stood a little straighter, holding the dress up and steeling herself for the onslaught.

"No way," Mindy said. "It's terrible."

Sophie shot Mindy a look and got up from her desk again, rushing over to where Emma was standing. "Oh, I don't know. Gray is a hot color this season." She took the hem of the dress in her hand. "I think the problem is that this isn't really an evening dress. And it's not very fun. This is a fun night. It's a night for standing out."

Emma had been afraid of that. "It's not my fault that I'm not up to speed on the fashion world. Up until three months ago, I was working in an accountant's office and had no money."

"You know you can't tell anyone about that," Sophie said, holding her finger to her lips.

Oh, right. The family fable. Soon after Emma's inheritance was announced, Mindy and Sophie had concocted a story to explain Emma's absence from the public lives of the Eden family. They owned up to the poor behavior of their father, but not the fact that the truth had been hidden from Emma for her entire life and she'd lived with very little money. They felt it might reflect badly on their grandmother, and in turn, the store. Emma was to tell everyone that she'd spent her formative years with a private tutor in France, then moved back to the States to quietly pursue her education in finance. It wasn't that far from the truth, except that she'd lived in New Jersey and been home-schooled. Emma would have fought the lie, but it made it easier to exist in this world of money and power. It was a shred of a pedigree, and she'd take what she could get.

"Don't worry. I won't say anything."

"Anyway, that dress is a snooze fest. You need to find something else." Mindy crossed her legs and bobbed her foot impatiently.

"I'll go down to jewelry and find a necklace to brighten it up," Emma said.

Sophie scrunched up her face. "I'm not sure that will be enough."

Emma wasn't going to stand here and endure their criticism. She did not want to appear weak or foolish in front of her half sisters. She still wasn't sure they had her best interests in mind. "I'll pick out a different dress then. Surely we have something in the store that will work." Head held high, Emma marched out into the hall, but she felt anything but confident. There was too much sheer embarrassment coursing through her veins.

She darted into the safety of her office and flipped on the light. This had been her grandmother's office when she was still alive. Every time Emma walked into this room, she was reminded of what might have been. What if the family secret had come out when she was a little girl? She would have had a chance to know her grandmother. She might have known her father. She might have been a completely different person, the sort of woman who had no problem picking the right dress for an event like tonight.

But no, all of that had slipped between Emma's fingers and she hadn't even known it was there.

Sophie appeared in the office doorway. "May I come in?"

"I don't want to turn this into a big thing, okay? I'll figure it out." Emma sought the comfort of the chair behind her desk, putting a big piece of furniture between herself and her half sister.

"I know that. But why don't you let me come with you?"

"I'm a grown woman. I can pick out my clothes." Emma didn't want to sound defensive. The truth was that she needed help. She at least needed someone to tell her she didn't look ridiculous.

Sophie took a seat in an available chair. "You know, the first time our grandmother took me to this event, I was a wreck. I had no clue what to wear. I really needed Gram to point me in the right direction."

"Well, she's not around to help me, is she?" Emma hated that tone in her voice, but it came from a very deep place. She'd been robbed of the relationship with her family.

"She's not. And I'm sorry about that. But I'd like to help. I've been to this event four times now. I can help you find the perfect dress."

Emma didn't want to admit it, but this was what she'd been waiting for—the smallest of opportunities. A door opened. Plus, the clock was ticking. "I don't know when I'll have time. My schedule is hell, and I hate doing things at the last minute. I'm a planner. I don't like surprises."

Sophie stood. "Don't worry about that. I need to run down to the designer department this morning, anyway. I'll find a few things and you can pick from those. Sound good?"

"Just don't go too overboard, okay? I'm not a showy person."

"You don't have to be showy to be a showstopper." Sophie looked at her phone, which she always had in hand. "Meet me in the private fitting room in two hours."

Emma didn't have a great feeling about this, but what choice did she have? She couldn't go to this event looking as if she didn't belong. She desperately wanted to stop being the proverbial fish out of water. "I'll be there."

Two

After a morning of crunching numbers, Emma found herself with Sophie in the private fitting room reserved for Eden's most important customers. Emma had never tried clothes on in such a lavish setting. The room not only had a lovely sitting area with elegant upholstered slipper chairs in silvery velvet, it had especially flattering lighting, and came with a valet who took drink orders. For Eden's wealthiest and most influential clients, this was their shopping experience—an oasis tucked away in a quiet corner of an otherwise bustling department store.

The valet appeared with two flutes of champagne.

"Really?" Emma asked, when Sophie offered her a glass. "It's the middle of the day."

"I'm hoping we'll have a reason to toast and celebrate. I wanted to ask if you'll be one of my bridesmaids."

Emma could hardly believe what she was hearing. "Really?" As soon as she'd said it, she realized how inappropriate and knee-jerk her response was. If she didn't want to feel like an outsider in this family, she had to stop assuming that role. "I mean, yes. Of course. I would love it. Such an honor."

Sophie grinned and held out her glass. Emma clinked it with hers. "Perfect. I still need to figure out who's designing the dresses, but I'll let you know."

Emma was in a state of delight and shock. Custom designed bridesmaids' dresses? "Sounds wonderful."

Sophie sank down onto one of the chairs, her skirt billowing in a poof. "It's funny, but I think of Gram every time I drink champagne."

"What was she like?" Emma sat in the chair opposite and took a small sip. It was so delicious. The bubbles tickled her nose.

"Gram was amazing. My idol, really. I loved her to pieces. But she rubbed some people the wrong way. She could be a ruthless businesswoman."

Emma pushed back any sadness over not having known her grandmother. "All women have to be ruthless at some point, don't they?"

Sophie eagerly nodded. "If they want to be a success, yes."

"Speaking of which, I happened to notice that our exclusive arrangement with Nora Bradford still hasn't been renewed."

Sophie frowned. "I know. They're dragging their feet. You know, we lost two of our exclusive designers in late December, right before you started. If we lose Nora, it would be devastating."

"Why do you think this is happening?"

"People aren't treating us the way they did when Gram was in charge."

Emma took another sip. "Sounds like we need to get a few things in line."

"I'm working on it. I'll need your help at some point. For now, I'm hoping the dress I picked for tonight might help. It's in the fitting room."

"Dress? Singular?"

"I know I said I'd give you some choices, but this one is perfect. It just came in this morning. It's one of our Nora Bradford exclusives." Sophie shooed her into the fitting room. "Go on. Go look."

Emma ducked inside the dressing area. On the hook was a dress she wouldn't have dared to choose. Ice blue, strapless and sparkly and daring. It was so far outside her comfort zone it was in a different zip code. And maybe that was exactly what she needed.

Wasting no time, she shed her work clothes and slipped into the garment. "Can you help with the zipper?" she called.

Sophie poked her head inside and her face lit up. "That's it. That's the dress. It's even better than I imagined. Now suck in your breath."

With a quick zip, Emma was squeezed in. She looked down at herself. "I don't know. I've never worn a strapless dress before and there's all this fabric." She fussed with the strips of pale blue organza that made up the skirt. If she stood still, her legs were hidden, but the second she moved, the strips swished open like streamers in the breeze. "What if I trip? And I can barely breathe." The bodice was holding her tight, all the way down to her hips.

"Oh, there is no breathing in a strapless dress. Not if you want it to stay up all night. And really, you look incredible. It's perfect for your body. You look sexy and glamorous."

"I do?" If it wasn't for the freckles on her cheeks and

the earrings she wore every day, Emma wouldn't have even known it was her.

"Yes. And the best part is I've instructed the department manager to keep the rest of the inventory off the showroom floor until tomorrow morning. You'll be the only one at Empire State wearing this."

Emma studied herself in the mirror, dropping her head to the side and swishing the skirt. The dress looked like magic. Maybe this really was the right choice. "Okay. This is the one."

Sophie grinned with pride and clapped her hands on Emma's shoulders. "I don't want you to be nervous about tonight. You'll be amazing. And I'll be there the whole time, okay?"

Emma felt so much better than she had that morning. "Thank you for helping me. And thank you for asking me to be a bridesmaid. That means a lot to me."

"Of course. You're my sister. It only seems right that you'd be a part of my wedding."

Emma had never felt so optimistic. Sophie was making such an effort to include her. Emma was starting to feel like a real part of the Eden clan, less like a person who was unwittingly plopped down in the middle of it. She would get what she'd missed out on during her twenty-seven years in the world—a close relationship with siblings, the camaraderie of an extended family. She felt sure of it now.

From the bench in the corner, Emma's phone buzzed. "Oh, shoot. I have a call." Back to reality.

"I'll help you out of the dress. Then I need to get Lizzie to order me some lunch."

Emma changed and raced upstairs. One of Eden's personal shoppers steamed the gown and delivered it to her office, along with a pair of strappy silver Blahniks Sophie had picked out. The dress was the only thing Emma looked at as she finished up her call. The fabric, the style, the price tag—it all seemed unreal, as if it wasn't meant for her.

Mindy appeared in Emma's office doorway around three. "The hair and makeup people are here, but we have a problem. Sophie's sick."

"Is she okay?"

Mindy shook her head. "A stomach bug or something she ate. I sent her home. I don't see any way she can come tonight. Looks like it's just you and me."

Great. The sister who hates me. Emma felt queasy herself. Her security blanket was gone. "Oh. Okay."

"We need to leave right at five or we'll get stuck in traffic forever. I'll send in the hair and makeup people."

Emma was now not only nervous, she was dreading tonight. Before she had time to think about it, a man and a woman invaded her office with brushes, hair clips, a curling iron, and every shade of lipstick and type of hair product you could imagine. They wheeled her across her office in her chair and parked her in front of a full-length mirror they'd brought.

The male stylist took her hair out of the ponytail and tutted. "I'm Anthony. This is going to take a while."

The makeup artist at least offered a smile. "I'm Charity. It's going to take me some time, too."

"Oh. Okay. Well, I'm Emma."

"We know," they answered in unison.

Charity dug through a case of makeup, picking up tubes and examining the colors. "I'm going to cover your freckles, if that's okay." She pointed to Emma's cheeks.

"I like them."

Charity shook her head. "I don't think they'll photograph well. There will be paparazzi tonight. You want to look good."

Emma hadn't taken the time to think about the fate of

her freckles, and definitely not photographers. "Do whatever you need to do."

The duo went to work, tugging and dabbing, prodding and pulling, spraying and spritzing. Emma kept her eyes closed whenever possible. They were doing too many things that she would never do to herself.

"Voilà," Anthony said a good forty-five minutes later. He was like Michelangelo presenting a masterpiece.

Emma opened her eyes and blinked several times. If it wasn't for the same clothes she'd worn to work, she never would have known it was her. Her hair was tugged back in a dramatic updo, she had long false lashes and smoky eyes. She looked fantastic, practically ready for the cover of a magazine. So this was what it was like to be glamorous.

"Wow," was all she could say.

"Emma, you are a stunning woman if you put some work into it," Charity said.

Perhaps that was her problem. She hadn't been trying hard enough. "Thank you so much. Both of you."

"Call us anytime."

Not wanting Mindy to be angry with her, Emma closed and locked her office door and dressed. She called in Lizzie to help with the zipper.

"You are so lucky," Lizzie said, looking at Emma with eyes full of wistful envy. It was a bizarre feeling. Emma and Lizzie were more alike than she and Sophie or Mindy.

"Maybe we can figure out a way for you to come with us next year."

"Really?"

Emma nodded. "In fact, I promise to do whatever I can to make it happen, okay?"

Lizzie grinned from ear to ear. "Wow. Something to look forward to."

Mindy walked in wearing a supershort magenta dress

with a plunging neckline and sky-high Christian Loubou-
tins with the signature red bottoms. She surveyed Emma's
new look. "They did wonders. You hardly look like yourself at all."

Gee, thanks. "You look great, too."

Lizzie rushed out of the room when the reception phone
started to ring.

"Hey, so, I need a favor from you tonight," Mindy said,
digging through one of her prized Hermès clutches. "I
have a friend meeting me there, so I won't be able to spend
much time with you. But I don't want you to tell Sophie."

"Does this friend happen to be the guy that Sophie
doesn't like?"

Mindy pursed her lips. "His name is Sam, okay? He's
in town for a few days and I really want to see him. And
yes, Sophie hates him. But that's her problem, not mine.
It has something to do with her fiancé, Jake."

Emma was tempted to ask what was in it for her to keep
the secret but decided against it. She needed to forge a connection with Mindy, somehow. "Okay. My lips are zipped."

"Awesome. I owe you one."

Well, that was something. "No problem."

Mindy's phone beeped with a text. "My driver's here."

Downstairs, they climbed into the back of a black
stretch SUV. As they whizzed through the city, Emma
tried to ignore her nerves. She tried to ignore that little
voice inside her head that said that every last person at
this event was going to know she didn't belong. There was
only so much refinement she could fake. What if someone asked her where she went to school and she forgot the
canned story Sophie and Mindy had cooked up about private school in France? What if someone asked about her
family and she accidentally blurted the truth, that until

three months ago, she was the deep dark family secret? Even worse, what if no one asked her anything at all?

As the driver pulled into the line of limousines and black town cars, Emma could see the paparazzi's camera flashes popping like crazy. *The red carpet.* Emma's stomach wobbled. She wasn't practiced in the art of posing for cameras. She didn't know how to hold her head at the right angle or slant her leg to make herself look skinny, or even how to properly plant her hand on her hip. This could be a disaster.

"Anything I need to know about this first part?" she asked Mindy.

Her half sister eyed herself in a compact mirror, them clamped it shut. "Follow my lead. You'll be fine."

Mindy climbed out of the car first and Emma followed. A woman with a clipboard was checking names, but she took one glance at Mindy and knew exactly who she was. "Mindy Eden. Nice to see you. Who do you have with you tonight?" the woman asked, her tone syrupy.

"My sister Emma."

A deep crease formed between the woman's eyes. "I thought your sister was Sophie."

"Long story," was all Mindy said, patting the woman on the shoulder and waving Emma ahead.

Emma stepped onto the red carpet, her heart thundering in her chest. She followed every move Mindy made, mimicking her stance and posture, every elegant quality Emma did not possess naturally. The paparazzi were quite taken with the couple in front of them, but then a few spotted Mindy and she quickly became their focus.

"Mindy! Over here!"

"This way, Mindy!"

Emma didn't know what to do, so she hung back, letting the photographers focus on her sister. Mindy smiled effortlessly, turning her head just so, shaking her shiny red tresses with all the confidence in the world. She was such a pro. Emma felt like a kid standing on the edge of the pool with water wings.

"Who's with you tonight?" a photographer asked.

Mindy cast her sights at Emma. Emma worried that Mindy might throw her under the bus and pretend she didn't know her.

"My youngest sister, Emma, of course." She reached for her hand, and before Emma knew what was happening, a million flashbulbs went off as she stood next to Mindy. These strangers were taking her picture and saying her name.

Emma! Emma!

Mindy stepped back and left Emma at center stage. She smiled, willing her face to be relaxed and natural. She planted her hand on her hip in what she hoped was the appropriate place.

Why are we just meeting you now, Emma?

She hadn't prepared for questions. "I've been living in France. Just came back to the States to help my sisters run Eden's."

Who are you wearing?

"Nora Bradford, of course. The gown is an Eden's exclusive. It'll be available in the store starting tomorrow." She glanced down for an instant and knew that if she didn't move, they'd miss the most dramatic part of the design. Hands on her hips, she turned in a circle, the skirt flying up and showing off her legs. She was nearly blinded by flashbulbs when she'd completed the three-sixty.

"Let's get out of here," Mindy mumbled in her ear.

"Did I make a mistake?" Emma asked nervously.

"It was fine. You just can't give them too much."

She and Mindy strolled the remaining length of the

red carpet and stepped into a lavish room already packed with people. Emma's eyes were still adjusting from the bright lights of the cameras to the moodier party atmosphere, but she could see enough to know that beauty was everywhere.

Mindy tapped Emma on the shoulder. "Sam's here." She waved across the room, and sure enough, a tall and handsome man with jet-black hair waved back. "I'll see you later."

"Wait," Emma blurted. "Will I see you at our seats?"

Mindy was distracted by her quickly approaching guy. "I'll be with Sam. Not sure where I'll see you. My driver will take you home. You have his number?"

Emma nodded. Mindy's driver had taken her all over the city before she had a driver of her own. "I do."

Just like that, Mindy was gone. Emma turned to the crowd, unsure what to do. She disliked being by herself. If Sophie had been able to come, Emma still would have been the person nobody knew, but at least she wouldn't have been alone. In this big room filled with fabulous people, she felt insignificant. Like a speck of dust floating around everyone's head, unnoticed.

A waiter walked by with a tray topped with glasses of champagne. Emma snagged one and took a long sip. Then another. She scanned the room, and for an instant, she wondered if she'd already had too much to drink. Either that or an optical illusion was walking into the room. Her heart nearly stopped beating. It was Mr. Brit from her building. Sure, he'd been less than friendly in the elevator, but she was now officially intrigued. His accent alone had been enough to interest her, but was he somehow involved in fashion? Perhaps a wealthy investor? Hopefully, he wasn't one of those men who habitually dated models.

She studied him as inconspicuously as possible, sucking down the last of her champagne. Damn, he looked good in a tux. Ridiculously good. Like it had been sewn around his broad shoulders. His light brown hair was a bit of a tousled mess, but she liked that about him. It made him seem human. Everything else about him was a little too perfect—the five o'clock shadow, the kissable lips, the way he could see over the top of nearly everyone in the crowd. For a moment, she imagined herself combing her fingers through his bed-head hair and allowing her hands to get completely lost.

But the best thing about Mr. Brit was that he seemed to be alone. Just like her. Did she have the nerve to approach him? They did have a slight rapport. There was at least a starting point for a conversation. And she still had the questions she'd cooked up in the elevator. She could likely hold her own for a good ten minutes.

As if he sensed she was watching him, he turned his head. Their gazes connected. Emma would've looked away if he didn't have her so locked in. His eyes were like a tractor beam designed to pull her across the room. And maybe that was precisely what she needed to do.

Three

If Daniel wasn't mistaken, he hadn't merely laid eyes on one of the most beautiful women he'd ever seen, she was coming his way. He never played coy, so he made eye contact again, but still his pulse raced. She was stunning—floating through the room as if her feet never touched the floor. Her dark hair was swept up and back from her face, accentuating her graceful neck. He hadn't pondered kissing a woman in that region for months. Now it was all he could think about.

"Hello." She had an air of self-assurance that was simply breathtaking. This was a woman who was accustomed to taking what she wanted.

"Hello yourself."

"We've got to stop meeting like this."

Taken by surprise, he couldn't help but laugh. What a confident way to greet a stranger. "Clever." He held out his hand. "I'm Daniel." He stopped short of offering his last name. No one knew he was in New York scouting locations for Stone's, and he intended to keep it that way. Luckily, few people in the States knew him by sight. In London, it would be a different matter.

She slid her long, delicate fingers against his and shook his hand, sending ripples of warmth through him. "Emma." She let go, leaving his palm tingling.

"So, tell me, Emma, what brings you to an event like this?"

She looked up at him from beneath a fringe of dark lashes that brought out the sheer sexiness of her brown eyes. "My job. I work for Eden's."

A waiter walked by with champagne, which gave Daniel a moment to decide how best to proceed. This gorgeous woman who'd managed to find him was employed by the company his mother considered the enemy. "Can I interest you in a drink?"

"Yes, please."

Daniel took two flutes and handed one to Emma. "To new friends?"

Emma shook her head. "You can't toast with a question. To new friends." She clinked her glass with his.

For the first time in three weeks, Daniel wasn't so eager to get home to London. He also found himself dismissing his commitment to staying away from the fairer sex. "Hear, hear." He took a sip, studying her rosy-pink lips as they curved around the glass. "What do you do for Eden's?"

"Number crunching, mostly."

The lights in the room flashed off and on. Emma looked up, then returned her sights to him. "I guess we have to find out seats?" The crowd began moving toward the double doors leading into the adjoining room.

Something in Daniel's gut told him he was an idiot if he

let Emma get away. They were just getting started. "Did you come alone?"

"I didn't, but my date ditched me."

"Date?"

"My sister. I mean my half sister. It's complicated."

"I see. Well, if I'm not being too forward, where are you sitting?" he asked.

A sheepish smile crossed her lips. "My seats are in the front row. I have an extra if you want to join me. My other sister wasn't able to make it."

"I'm sorry to hear about your sister." But he wasn't sorry he would be sitting with Emma. "And I'd love to join you." He didn't have to tell her that his seat was also in the front row. He'd let her think she was giving him a thrill.

They made their way inside and found their seats along the runway. Daniel subtly surveyed the rest of the front-row attendees, and spotted Nora Bradford, the designer he had to speak with before the end of the evening. He'd have to find a time to break away from Emma, which was a real shame, but for now, he would enjoy himself.

"You haven't told me what you do, Daniel," Emma said.

He couldn't afford to tell her the truth. He had no idea of her stature at Eden's or to whom she might end up speaking. "I'm here in the city looking at some real estate for my family's business." Not a lie. Not a lie at all.

Emma nodded, her eyes wide and eager. "Sounds exciting."

"Not as exciting as meeting you."

Emma smiled and shied away, looking down at her lap and running her fingers over her evening bag. The crowd had filled the room, the conversation at a steady din, broken only by the introduction of a thumping beat of dance music. The lights went down and the volume grew louder, the bass reverberating in Daniel's hips and thighs. Or perhaps that was Emma's effect on him. He had an amazing vantage point sitting next to her, one where he could admire the dips and valleys of her collarbone and shoulders. She had exquisite skin. Touchable and shimmery. How badly would he jeopardize his family business if he asked an Eden's employee out for dinner?

The models began to strut down the catwalk, which would normally catch Daniel's attention, but Emma was the real attraction. She leaned into him. "Isn't it exciting?"

"It is." He found himself smiling, of all things. That was not his usual reaction when forced to attend an event like this.

"This is my first time coming to one of these."

Utterly charming—those were the words the came to mind. "I never would've known. You seem like an old pro."

She reached over and swatted his thigh with the back of her hand. Now the grin on his face felt as though it might never leave.

Emma studied the models and applauded, her enthusiasm for fashion seeming so genuine. Her face was full of wonder as she followed each new design down the runway. Watching her became Daniel's primary source of entertainment, especially as she pointed out her favorites.

"Ooh. I love that one," she whispered in his ear. The hint of warmth from her sweet breath brought every nerve ending alive, like flipping on a switch.

"It's lovely." *You're lovely.*

She repeated this exercise over and over again, muttering comments into his ear whenever she found a particular design detail interesting. As the show went on, she seemed to become even more comfortable with him, leaning in closer. The conversation continued, and he found it was easier to hear her if he slung his arm across the back of her chair. She placed her hand on his thigh, sending signals straight to his groin. He wanted her. He wanted to take her home. But he had work to do after the show was over. Important work he couldn't afford to miss.

When the designers and several models made their final procession, Emma was one of the first in the audience to shoot to her feet and applaud wildly. Daniel was even more entranced. He loved her lack of inhibition. He was intrigued by the possibilities of getting Emma into his bed.

"I take it you enjoyed yourself?" he asked as the music died down and the crowd began to filter out of the room. From the corner of his eye, he saw Nora Bradford walking away. He couldn't let her out of his sights, but he wasn't ready to excuse himself from Emma. He needed her number. He deserved a little fun while he was in New York. No strings attached, of course.

"It was amazing. The clothes were incredible. It's definitely been the most exciting part of my job to date."

Daniel wasn't sure how much he should dig into Emma's life at Eden's. He dreaded learning anything that might indicate she was not a woman to pursue. He wanted her, but he wouldn't risk everything to take her to bed.

"One more drink?" he asked, unwilling for this to be goodbye.

"Yes. Please." Emma answered instantly and smiled widely, momentarily numbing him to his sense of duty to his family business. Daniel knew where a second drink might lead, or at least where he wanted it to go, and that was not a good idea. He had unfinished business tonight. And it didn't involve the stunning woman from Eden's department store.

Emma worried for more than a moment that she'd answered too quickly. Daniel was all suave sophistication, and she'd been nothing but goofy with excitement during the fashion show. She wasn't sure what had come over her, except that she felt different right now. For the first time, she felt as though she could be comfortable in this world. More importantly, she could hold her own with a handsome man like Daniel.

"Shall we?" Feeling a bit invincible, she hooked her arm in his and snugged him close to her.

The look he cast down at her shook her to her core. So confident. So pleased. So hot. "Please."

Emma took a step and her shoe caught on the carpet. It twisted right off her foot and she stumbled forward.

Daniel kept her from falling with a strong hold on her arm. "Are you okay?"

Embarrassment heated her cheeks, but she was determined to make a graceful save. A little hiccup was not going to ruin her evening. "I'm great. Just need to get my shoe." She reached down to hook her finger into a silver strap, but as she bent at the waist, she felt a pop behind her. Cool air hit the center of her back. She still needed her shoe, so she crouched to grab it. In a rush, the cold spread down her spine. *The zipper.*

She let go of Daniel's arm, righted herself and immediately flattened her back against his chest, clutching her dress to her bosom with one hand and her shoe in the other. The fine wool crepe of his tuxedo brushed against her bare skin. Her zipper had split wide-open. The only thing that was keeping the dress on was that impossibly tiny silver hook at the very top and the few inches of bodice before the skirt started.

"Everything all right?" Daniel grasped her shoulders from behind and looked down at her.

Emma's chest was heaving. Panic coursed through her veins. Of course something disastrous would happen. "My zipper. I think it broke." She knew one thing as soon as those words came out. The humiliation of this scene was going to last her entire lifetime. She'd have to start taking the stairs in her apartment building. She might have to move.

Daniel pushed her shoulders forward ever so slightly. "Indeed it has."

That small breach of the space between them told her exactly how bad it was. Daniel could see far more of her than was reasonable for the first few hours of their acquaintance. Her bare back. Her skimpy panties. "Do you think you can fix it?" Luckily, most people had made it back out into the reception area. The few still milling about didn't seem to notice. "I can't walk out of here with half a dress."

He pulled her a little closer and lowered his head. "No. But we could stay in here with half of your dress." His breath was warm against the slope of her neck.

She craned her head, looking at him over her shoulder. His lips were so close, achingly within reach. If they were somewhere quiet and private, this mishap could've been the perfect icebreaker. Her clothes were already half off. Might as well go all the way. "As fun as that sounds, I'm still going to need to walk through that room at some point."

"Hold on. Let me see if I can do anything." He waited as a few people walked past, then he made more space between them.

Emma tried very hard to not think about how much he was essentially studying her naked back and every inch of lacy undergarments that went with it. "Well? How bad is it?"

"From where I'm standing, the view is spectacular." He traced his finger along one edge of the zipper, his warm skin brushing hers. It had been so long since a man had touched her like that, and certainly no man as sexy and handsome as Daniel.

"You get bonus points for flattery." *And for making me dizzy.* "I'd still like to know if the dress can be saved."

"The two sides of the zipper aren't attached anymore. It's just the hook holding it together."

Emma didn't know a lot about garment construction, but she did know that there was no saving that stupid zipper. "What do I do? I didn't bring a jacket or coat."

"I did." Daniel stepped back and shrugged his shoulders out of his tuxedo jacket. Emma got a much better sense of his body now that it was hiding under fewer clothes. If she wasn't so deathly embarrassed, she might be daring enough to invite him home. He placed his jacket on her shoulders and held her shoe and handbag as she slipped her arms inside.

"This is so nice of you."

"Think nothing of it."

Emma sat in a chair and worked her foot into her shoe. "I'm not accustomed to such chivalry." Not even close. Her only real boyfriend had been the sort of guy who didn't want to share his umbrella in the rain.

"Still care for a drink?"

Emma stood, well aware that whatever magic she'd managed to conjure this evening would evaporate if she was the woman walking around in a broken dress and tuxedo jacket. "It's probably best if I head home." She could hardly believe the words. He was too amazing. She was missing her chance. Hopefully, she'd have another, perhaps run into him in the building again.

He nodded. "I understand. There's someone I need to track down, anyway. Let me walk you to your car, though."

Emma pulled out her phone and sent a text to Mindy's driver, who said he could be out front in a few minutes.

The disappointing end of this evening was unimaginable, but she was determined to steal a few more lovely moments with Daniel. "That would be nice."

"Don't worry. I won't let anything bad happen." He placed his arm around her shoulder and walked her through the double doors.

They wound their way through the crowd. Several people gave her funny looks, but she did her best to hold her head high. Daniel's presence certainly made it easier. He ushered her outside, where the red carpet photographers were lying in wait. As soon as she was spotted, the flashes started going off. Yet another thing she had not bargained on.

Emma squinted as the bright lights made it hard to see. A black SUV pulled up to the curb and Mindy's driver rounded the back of the car, waiting for her on the sidewalk.

"That's my ride," she said.

Like the perfect gentleman, Daniel escorted her to the waiting car, and Emma climbed into the back seat. As soon as she was inside, she started to remove his jacket.

He held up his hand. "Please. Keep it."

"No. It's okay. I know you have to go back in and find someone." She had to wonder who he was meeting. Surely there were hundreds of women in that room who would love even a moment with Daniel. Still, Emma was immensely grateful for the time she'd had with him, even with the way it was ending.

He slid his hand onto her shoulder and gave a subtle squeeze. Even through the suit fabric, it was wonderful. "I'm the only person who has seen the state of your dress. When you arrive home, I'd like you to be able to retain your dignity."

She smiled. "That's so sweet."

"Oh, I have my reasons. If you keep it, it'll give me an excuse to see you again."

Emma's face flushed so quickly she was surprised she could still sit up straight. "You're forcing me to hold your jacket hostage?"

He leaned in even closer. Good God, she wanted him to kiss her. She found herself puckering just to extend the invitation. "Part and parcel of being a gentleman."

The car behind hers honked. She jumped. Daniel grimaced and looked back.

"I should go," she said, hoping he'd protest.

"I'll need your number if I'm going to see you again."

His voice was a bit desperate and that was when the realization hit her—he didn't recognize her from their building. Looking back at the first thing she'd said to him tonight, she was shocked by her own brazenness. That had been a far bolder gesture than the real Emma would have ever made.

"So you *really* don't know who I am? I don't look the slightest bit familiar to you?"

"I'm so sorry. Should I know who you are?"

She laughed quietly, but it was more born of sad resignation than happiness. He hadn't noticed the everyday Emma. Not at all. She leaned over and placed a kiss on his cheek. She desperately hoped that wouldn't be the extent of things between them, but if it was, at least the end could be on her terms. She'd either be bold Emma and go to his apartment, or she'd be her old self and leave the jacket with the doorman and attempt to hide from Daniel forever. First, she needed time for her ego to feel a little less bruised.

She reached for the door handle. "Don't worry, Daniel. I'll find you."

And just like that, the driver pulled away from the curb

and sped off into yet another magical big city night. Emma wrapped her arms around herself and sat back in the seat, looking off through the window, wondering what was ahead for her and her slightly-less-mysterious Mr. Brit. Romance? At least a real kiss? Or was tonight as good as it would ever get?

Four

Mindy Eden knew she had to make a change. She nudged Sam Blackwell, trying to wrench him from his peaceful post-sex slumber. Yes, they'd had a white-hot night after they'd skipped the Empire State fashion show, but Sam took chances Mindy wasn't always comfortable with. In the elevator on the way up to her apartment last night, he'd slipped his hand under her skirt while a couple from her building rode along with them. He'd blocked any view with his jacket strategically draped over his arm, and she'd nearly had an orgasm while he pleasured her. It was fantastic, but it was not right. Mindy didn't like herself when she was like this, making rash decisions and not caring about consequences.

But Sam did that to her. He made her do stupid, stupid things. All the more reason to make a pre-emptive strike. "Sam. I think you should go." She shook his shoulder again. He rolled away from her, his breaths quickly becoming soft and even.

Simply saying that she wanted him to go made her remorseful. She didn't really want him to leave. She wanted him to stay, for real, just spend a day with her. But she'd learned by now that expectations like that were foolish with Sam. He was always on to the next thing, hopping on his private plane and jetting off to another corner of the world. There was always more money to be made, another deal to strike. She worried there might even be other women. How could there not be? With his square jaw, dark eyes and thick tousled hair, he could have any woman he wanted. Never mind the billions he had in the bank. For most women, Sam would be impossible to resist, even if he were penniless. She had no proof he was romancing anyone else. It was more a hunch, a little voice at the back of her head asking one simple question—*Why do you trust this guy?*

Her sister Sophie certainly didn't trust him. Neither did Sophie's fiancé, Jake. Sam had a reputation for being an unscrupulous businessman. He would do anything to succeed. He had a knack for finding other people's weak spots and taking advantage. In Mindy's case, her weak spot was her neck. One brush of Sam's lips and she was putty in his hands. It took very little effort for him to get her into bed. She'd learned that hours after meeting him, five months ago.

Knowing he'd wake up at the prospect of more sex, she slid closer to him, pressing her breasts against his broad back, cupping his firm shoulder with her hand and rubbing his calf with her foot. "Sam. Please wake up," she whispered against his neck. She tried very hard not to inhale his smell, but she couldn't resist. She liked it too much.

He rolled to his back, a cocky smile crossing his lips while his eyes remained shut. "I don't usually perform sex on demand, but in your case, I'll make an exception."

"That's not what I was asking." Her nipples grew hard at the mere suggestion, heat pooling between her legs. She wanted him. Again.

He reached around and grabbed her bottom, giving it a gentle squeeze. "Then maybe *I* should ask. I want you, Min. One more time?"

Mindy knew she had to be strong. "I don't think that's a good idea. I don't think we're a good idea anymore, Sam."

He opened his eyes, a flash of dark sexiness that was a verifiable shot to the heart. "What's wrong? Didn't we have fun last night?"

Mindy sat up in bed and pulled the rumpled sheets against her chest. "We did have fun. But that's all we ever have and I should be focusing on work. I blew off an important industry event because of you last night. You're a distraction."

He propped himself up, his elbow on the pillow. "You need a distraction. You work hard and are in an impossible situation." Under the covers, he caressed her inner thigh, starting at her knee and moving north, the tips of his fingers dangerously close to her center. He knew exactly how to manipulate her.

Still, she ached for more of his touch. She ached for all of him—body and soul. That was the problem. All he offered was the former, never the latter. "I know how hard I work. I eat stress for breakfast, lunch and dinner." It was the truth. Before she'd inherited one-third of Eden's, she already had a wildly successful company of her own, By Min-vitation Only, an online greeting card and invitation design and printing service. Although she'd hired an interim CEO for BMO, she was still involved in the day-to-day, all while performing her duties at Eden's. She could be stretched only so far.

"I offered to get rid of the obligation you don't want."

She shook her head. "And I told you no. Don't you dare sabotage Eden's. Sophie and Emma would never forgive me."

"Why? You'd all lose some money, but you'd also all be out from under the burden of that business. Plus, it's a drop in the bucket compared to what you'd be left with. The real value of Eden's is the building and the land it sits on."

This was an argument Mindy had wholly embraced six months ago, when Gram died unexpectedly and Mindy knew she and Sophie were set to inherit the business. But the terms of the will were such that the heirs, Mindy, Sophie and Emma, had to run the business together in good faith, for two years. Mindy might be driven to protect her own best interests, but she couldn't turn her back on her sisters. She couldn't thumb her nose at her grandmother's wishes.

"We've been through this one hundred times." She climbed out from under the covers and grabbed her silk robe from a hook on the closet door. "Logic says you're right, but I have to be a good person. That means working like a dog for two years and hopefully being able to sell my interests in Eden's to my sisters when that time is up. I might be stuck, but it's not forever."

"Why be stuck at all?"

"Because I'm loyal to my family."

Sam shrugged and threw back the covers. The sight of his naked muscled form made her breath catch in her chest. "You worry too much about what other people will think."

Again, Sam had a talent for zeroing in on Mindy's weaknesses. She did worry about what Sophie thought. She wasn't so sure what to make of Emma. She wasn't sure she could trust her to do a good job at Eden's. Mindy and Sophie had known her for only a few months in the context of sisterhood and partnership. Emma had largely been a disappointment. She didn't have a nose for big business strategy. She certainly didn't have a nose for fashion.

Mindy's phone rang with the ring tone she'd assigned to Sophie. "I have to get this. If my sister is calling at seven in the morning, something's wrong." She lunged for her cell as it buzzed on the nightstand. "Soph, hey. Two seconds, okay?" She pressed the button to mute the call.

"I'm going to hop in the shower. Join me when you're done?" Sam casually placed his hand against the jamb of the bathroom doorway, flaunting his unbelievable body. She didn't need to touch him. She could see how hard he was.

"Give me a minute and I'll be there."

"Don't be long. I need you, Min."

I need you, too, Sam. Precisely the reason she had to make a change.

Daniel didn't wait for his alarm clock the morning after Empire State. He'd hardly slept at all. Visions of sexy, enchanting Emma tormented him. She was a feast for the senses, beautiful, sweet smelling and impossibly soft to the touch. If he could afford to put any time at all into seduction, he might pursue her with everything he had. But there was no room for distractions while he was in New York, and especially not of the female variety. Daniel had a real talent for finding women who at best made his life impossibly complicated, and at worst, broke his heart. His family was counting on him. He had to prove that he could fill the void left behind by William.

Still, it was tough getting Emma out of his head. She'd surprised him at every turn last night. From the moment she so boldly introduced herself, she'd been nothing but refreshingly candid and at ease. She did not put on airs or try to impress him. She hadn't boasted once of her family lineage or about important people she knew. He still wasn't sure what to make of her, especially after her parting comment: *Don't worry, Daniel. I'll find you.* How, exactly, would she do that?

The sun was beginning to peek between the drapes and the dogs were beginning to stir. There was no point in pretending he'd get any sleep at all, so he tossed back the covers and dressed for his morning walk with the dogs. With all three on their leashes, he took the elevator down to the lobby and made his way across the street to Central Park. They completed their usual circuit, then Daniel made his last stop at a newsstand a block away. Call him old-fashioned, but he didn't enjoy reading the news on a computer screen or tablet. He preferred the feel of real paper. He didn't think twice when reaching for *The Times*, but the large print of a tabloid made him stop short.

Retail Royalty Romance!

There, beneath the juicy headline, was a picture of himself and Emma as she placed a kiss on his cheek. Shock and heat coursed through him in equal measure as he was confronted with the visual evidence of one of last night's most memorable moments. He read the headline again. The British press had long referred to the Stone family as retail royalty. He was outed now. His mother was going to lose it.

He wasn't about to read more out on the street, so he paid for his purchases and rushed back to his building, dogs in tow. Daniel rushed into the waiting elevator and jabbed the button for his floor, willing it to travel faster. He peered at the picture on the front page again. He was *leaning* into the kiss, his hand at Emma's waist. Despite the fact that it hadn't been on the lips, the photograph was nothing less than sexy. Of course it was—she was too stunning for words.

Inside his apartment, he tossed his keys aside and let all

three dogs off their leashes. They bolted into the kitchen for water. Daniel took his papers and plunked down on the sleek black leather sofa in the living room. He flipped to the full story inside. It took only a few words for him to learn why Emma had been so flabbergasted that he hadn't known who she was.

She was one of the Eden heiresses. A beautiful billionaire. He wasn't the only member of a royal retail family. They both were. *Bloody hell.*

He studied the other photographs. One was of her on the red carpet, spinning her skirt up in the air like a model, revealing her lithe legs. There was a second one of himself with Emma during the show, apparently snapped by someone with a camera phone. His arm was slung across the back of her chair. Her legs were crossed, that unforgettable dress cut dangerously high up her silky thigh. He saw how focused he was on her as she whispered in his ear. If this was any other woman on the planet, he might not feel so stupid about how distracted he'd been by her. But Emma was trouble. She was an Eden.

How had he managed to not only meet the one woman he had no business spending time with, but also let her run off with his tux jacket? He hadn't simply waded into treacherous waters with an Eden heiress, he'd found a stretch of shark-infested sea.

His phone buzzed in his pocket. It was certainly his mother. She'd stopped reading the papers after his brother's accident, especially when the press figured out that William, and Daniel's former fiancée, Bea, had been having an affair. Their mother had been too embarrassed, and unwilling to believe it. But she had plenty of people at the Stone's office in London feeding her information. It was now time for damage control. "Hello, Mum."

"It looks as though you had a good time at Empire State."

"You've seen the papers."

"Was this a calculated move on your part?"

"It wasn't, but seems like an awfully good stroke of luck."

The other end of the line became eerily quiet, so much so that Daniel wondered if the connection had been dropped. "I fail to see how this could possibly be good," she finally said. "The Eden family is poison."

"I'm not sure of that. Emma is lovely. And she undoubtedly knows quite a lot about her family's business." All of that was the truth, but he was well aware he was covering his own ass.

"So you're after information?"

He hadn't known until moments ago that it was an option, but it wasn't a bad idea, especially if it meant spending time with Emma. "Seems like I ought to try, doesn't it?"

"Do you think she'd actually trust you? How do you know she won't lie to you?"

"I don't. But I'd like to think I'm a good judge of character."

"One could argue that you're a bit blind when it comes to women, Daniel."

He bristled at the suggestion. He hadn't been blind to the fact that William and Bea had fallen in love behind his back. He'd only been stupid enough to hope his own brother would do the right thing and back off. "This is just business. Information is power. You know that as well as anyone."

"And you've handed it to the enemy on a silver platter. You've blown your cover. Everyone knows you're in New York scouting locations for Stone's. There's no telling what the Eden sisters will do to try to stop us."

Daniel's shoulders tightened with every damning detail she launched at him. He knew his predicament. He didn't need her constant reframing of the problems. "We should have been up front about it from the beginning. If you're going to compete, better to do it out in the open where everyone can see."

"This isn't a competition, Daniel. It's war."

He shook his head. How his mother loved to cling to her Eden's grudge. "It doesn't matter what you call it. Stone's will succeed. I promise you that."

"I'm not sure you're in a position to make guarantees."

He wasn't, but he'd never admit defeat until he'd run out of options. Right now, he had many directions he could take this, and he intended to do exactly that. "Everything is proceeding according to plan."

She tutted on the other end of the line. "Alright then. But stay out of the papers. At least until we've signed a lease."

"I'll do my best, but you know how the press is."

"Yes, dear. I do."

Daniel hung up the phone, relieved his mother had forgotten about the most pressing task from last night—speaking to Nora Bradford. Daniel had been unable to track her down after seeing Emma off in her car. He couldn't afford to call her office and leave a message. Someone would figure out what he was up to. He was going to have to find a different way.

He began pacing in his living room. He needed to formulate his next several moves. If anyone asked, he was going to have to hedge his answers about Stone's opening their first US store in New York. As for Emma, pursuing her even for a fling would do nothing but create problems. But as he thought about her naked back, the channel of her spine and those lacy panties she'd been wearing last night, he couldn't deny that he wanted her. Perhaps there was some truth in the value of keeping your friends close. And your enemies closer.

Emma stared off at the city as she rode in the back of her black Escalade on the way to work. Her inability to focus was surely from no sleep after Empire State last night, and that was all because of Daniel. He was everything she'd never been able to find in a man—easy on the eyes and a true gentleman. It was hardly fair that his rich British accent came in a package six feet and several more inches tall. His manner and pure refinement made him seem too good to be true. But *someone* had saved her from a lifetime of embarrassment last night, and she had the tux jacket back at her apartment to prove it.

When she arrived home last night, she'd considered grilling Henry, her building's doorman, for Daniel's apartment number. She'd considered showing up on his doorstep, returning his jacket and asking him to undo the tiny hook that was holding up her dress. She'd fantasized about loosening Daniel's tie, unbuttoning his crisp, white shirt and spreading her hands across his broad chest...

But she had done none of those things.

He had gone to meet someone, presumably another woman. Never mind that Emma wasn't a woman who took charge, especially not when it came to unbuttoning. Her history with men was limited and disappointing—she'd gone to bed with only one, and he'd been such a jerk about her inexperience, telling her that a woman should know what to do without needing to ask him. Emma wasn't a mind reader. She'd only wanted someone who could be patient with her.

Plus, she was foolishly glossing over the most upsetting revelation from last night. Daniel hadn't recognized her from the elevator in their building. He'd taken notice only once she was wrapped up in a ten-thousand-dollar gown, and made up by two professionals who'd devoted an hour to the pursuit. But everyday Emma, with her freckles and propensity to babble when she got nervous? He hadn't noticed her at all. That told her all she needed to know. Daniel the mysterious Brit would never let her take off his shirt. She was out of his league.

The Escalade rounded the corner onto Thirty-Seventh Street and pulled up in front of Eden's. A cluster of people with cameras were waiting by the central revolving doors.

"What the heck?" she muttered to her driver, Gregory. "I wonder if they got a tip about a celebrity shopping at the store this morning."

"I don't like the looks of this. Do you want me to drive around to the south entrance, Ms. Eden?" Gregory asked.

Emma waved it off. "No. It's fine. They're not interested in me."

Gregory exited the car and rounded to her door as she hopped out onto the sidewalk. The photographers swarmed her. All she could see were cameras and arms and faces.

Emma! Emma!

Are you and Daniel Stone dating?

Did you know he's opening a store in New York?

They barked their questions, shouting her name. Gregory begged them to stand back so she could get into the building unscathed. She shuffled across the sidewalk in heels, while everything they'd just said hit her. Dating? Mr. Brit? It had to be. How many Daniels had she been seen with? Exactly one.

Gregory blocked the photographers from getting into the store while Emma ducked through the revolving door. Duane, the hulking head of Eden's security, was lumbering toward her, hitching up his belt and looking frazzled.

"Ms. Stewart. I'm so sorry. I chased two photographers away from the south entrance, but I had to stay and deal with the shoppers lined up to get into the store."

"Shoppers?" Emma kept walking toward the executive elevator bank, Duane at her side. "Do we have an event this morning?"

"So you don't know?"

"Know what?" Was she really so out of the loop that the head of security knew more about the goings-on in the store than she did?

"You're the event, Ms. Stewart." Duane jabbed the button to call the elevator. "You. Your dress. Your date last night. Those women outside are lined up to buy the dress you wore to Empire State."

With a ding, the doors slid open, but Emma was frozen in place. "I'm sorry. What did you say?"

Duane held the elevator and ushered her on board. "It sounds like you need to see the papers. I need to get back to the crowd outside. Only five minutes until the store opens."

"Papers?" Emma muttered to herself as she made the short ride upstairs. The instant she stepped off the elevator, Lizzie popped up from her seat. "Mindy and Sophie are waiting for you."

At this point, this came as no real surprise. Thank goodness Duane had given her a heads-up. "Is this about the photographers downstairs?"

Lizzie nodded. "And the tabloids."

It was all starting to come together. Sheer horror shuddered through her. Had someone managed to get a photo of her dress split wide-open? That was *not* the fashion statement her sisters had hoped for her to make. For the second day in a row, she marched into Sophie's office.

"Feeling better?" she asked Sophie. Emma was legitimately concerned, but she was also stalling. She didn't want bad news to end the spell of last night.

"Something I ate. I'm sorry I left you in the lurch with Empire State."

Mindy, who was sitting in a chair opposite Sophie's desk, crossed her legs and tutted. "I am not the lurch."

Uh. Yes you are. Emma wanted to say it so badly as she took the other chair. "You did leave me alone in a room full of hundreds of people."

Mindy slid a newspaper from Sophie's desk and casually tossed it into Emma's lap. "You didn't seem to have any problem making friends."

Emma could feel the deep crinkles forming on her forehead. There before her was a photograph of her kissing Daniel on the cheek. She could see her own fingers curling into his biceps. How one photograph could convey so much longing, she wasn't sure. Hopefully, it was only her interpretation and not the way the rest of the world saw it. "Wait a minute. How long have you two known about this? Why did nobody call me?"

"We were strategizing," Sophie said. "Trying to figure out what Daniel Stone is up to."

"Up to? What does that mean? You know him?" Emma tried very hard to squash down her hurt feelings. Mindy and Sophie were a unified front and Emma was the third wheel.

Mindy turned to her and shook her head. "You really don't know who he is, do you? Or *what* he is, to be more exact? He's a Stone."

Confusion whirled in Emma's head. "I'm sorry. A stone?"

Sophie bugged her eyes as if she couldn't believe Emma was so dense. "Stone's of London. Department store? The biggest in Europe? They're the reason Eden's was never able to get off the ground overseas."

"I've never even heard of it. This guy is part of the company?" Her vision returned to the paper and she opened it up to the main article. As she read, the weight of this hit her. "Oh. Wow. They think he's opening a department store in New York?"

"Why else would he be here?" Sophie asked. "Jake did some digging and found out that Daniel's been looking at commercial real estate properties. His agent is Charlotte Locke. She's the sister of one of Jake's closest business associates."

"He's been looking at big properties," Mindy added. "Definitely big enough for a department store."

"What does this mean? Could they put us out of business?" It would be just Emma's luck that she would essentially win the life lottery by meeting a guy as sexy as Daniel, only to have everything crumble to dust in her hands.

"They could not only put us out of business, that's likely their sole aim. Daniel's mother hated Gram. My guess is he cozied up to you last night for information," Sophie said.

"But I approached him."

"You did?" Mindy asked, incredulous.

"He lives in my building. I recognized him from the elevator. Don't forget that I was all alone in a room full of five hundred strangers." Emma sank back in her seat. "There's no way he talked to me because I'm associated with Eden's. He didn't even know who I was." She picked at a spot on her pants. "I don't even think he recognized me at all. That's how memorable I am. Apparently."

"He's playing dumb," Sophie asserted. "He's up to something. I know it."

Lizzie poked her head into Sophie's office. "Sorry to interrupt, but there's been a run on the designer department downstairs. We've completely sold out of the dress Emma wore last night."

"Hey. That's something." Emma sat a little straighter, proud of herself for doing something positive for the store.

"Also, Emma," Lizzie continued. "Daniel Stone is on the line for you."

Emma's heart was now residing in her throat. Apparently today was capable of getting exponentially more bizarre.

"Like I said. Up to something." Sophie seemed entirely convinced of her theory.

Emma still wasn't buying it. If he did know who she was, he'd done a convincing job of being nothing but a gentleman who didn't remember her. "What do I do?"

"Take the call," Mindy said. "We'll put him on speaker in here."

Emma shook her head. She'd had enough of Mindy and Sophie treating her as if she had no autonomy. "I'll take it in my office." She got up from her chair and met Lizzie at the door.

"You can't keep this from us," Sophie pleaded. "If you talk to him, we need to know what you're talking about."

"You two sent me into that fashion show on my own and I'm the reason there are women buying up Nora Bradford dresses downstairs. I've earned the right to speak to Daniel on my own. Trust me, I'm not going to let him do anything bad to Eden's." She turned to Lizzie. "Please put him through."

"Right away."

Emma hurried into her office, her mind and body buzzing with anticipation and excitement and more than a little worry. What if Daniel really was cozying up to her to get information about Eden's? What if he was out to destroy them? She didn't have time to think about the what-ifs. She had to answer the phone. "Good morning." She feigned as much confidence as she could.

"Good morning, Ms. Stewart."

Emma sat back in her chair, relishing the way the sound of his voice made her feel lighter and warmer. She could get used to hearing him say those four words, especially if he whispered them across the pillow. "Calling about your jacket? I told you I'd get it to you."

"I'm phoning because I embarrassed myself last night. Now I know what you meant when you asked if I knew who you were. I'm sorry I didn't realize you were one of the Eden heiresses."

Emma laughed quietly. "That's not how you should have known me. I'm by far the lesser known of the three. Most people have no clue who I am, Mr. Stone."

"Please call me Daniel."

"Only if you call me Emma. And like I said, most people don't know who I am."

"I'd say that's their loss." His voice was low and even a bit gravelly. Emma's mind flew to the photograph of their kiss on the cheek. She should have gone for it and planted one on his very sexy mouth, especially if those were the kinds of words that were going to come out of it.

"It's okay. I prefer to hang back."

"That's not what your dress suggested."

"It's not my habit to let my zipper split open at a fashion show."

Now it was his turn to laugh. She realized how much she loved the sound, which was not a good development. Mindy and Sophie might be right. What if Daniel Stone was up to no good? "I just happened to be the lucky bloke who witnessed it."

Heat bloomed across her face. It felt as if her cheeks were on fire. "That was a one-time occurrence, hopefully.

Just like I'm hoping that you hiding your true identity from me won't happen again."

He cleared his throat. "You didn't tell me your whole story, either."

"I told you I work for Eden's. That much is true." She still felt that way, like she was an employee and not a real part of the team. Not even her newfound wealth made her feel like an Eden. While Mindy and Sophie continued to tell her what to do and micromanage her, she would always feel like that.

"You own a third of the Eden empire. You're far more than an employee. I could ask what your motives are. After all, you approached me."

Motives. That was the most pressing question between them, wasn't it? Was Daniel Stone up to something nefarious? The mere thought of answering his question made Emma's heart thump harder. "You want the truth?" She could hardly believe she'd offered.

"Always." His British accent and smooth delivery were chipping away at her resolve.

"I approached you because I was all by myself and you were by far the most handsome man in the room."

"I see."

"Does it disappoint you that it wasn't because you're a Stone?"

"Not at all. I always enjoy knowing where I stand." He was playing things quite close to the vest, which not only made Emma nervous, it made her curious.

"Don't we all?"

"I suppose that's true."

The gears in Emma's head were turning. She had to find out where she stood with Daniel. She had to find out what he was up to. If she played her cards right, Daniel Stone might end up being a real boon. It could give her the chance to learn more about an important competitor's plans. It would help her prove her worth to Mindy and Sophie, all while spending time with the sexiest man she'd ever met.

"I do feel as though I owe you the favor of returning your jacket in person. After all, you did rescue me last night." She smiled, lazily drawing her fingertips back and forth across her collarbone. If Daniel were to show up at her office right now, she'd have a hard time containing herself.

"It's what a gentleman would do."

"Is that what you are, Daniel? A gentleman?"

"I'm whatever you need me to be."

Emma doubted that greatly. "When can I bring you your jacket?"

"I could come by your office? Maybe take you to lunch?"

Emma could think of nothing better, but she also didn't want Mindy and Sophie breathing down her neck. They were deeply suspicious of Daniel and his motives. Emma was concerned, of course, but she'd have been lying if she said that wasn't partially eclipsed by a deeper desire to see where their flirtation might lead. Mindy and Sophie both had exciting men in their lives, so why couldn't Emma? "I have a very full day today. Why don't I bring it by your place this evening? Does seven work?"

"Even better. If you give me your cell number, I can text you the address."

If Daniel was embarrassed by the fact that he hadn't known she was one of the three Eden heiresses, what she was about to say next was going to be a bit more painful. "I already know your address, Daniel Stone."

"Been doing a bit of your own detective work?"

"It wasn't hard. I live two floors below you."

Five

London traffic was considered some of the worst in the world, but Daniel was starting to think New York might have it beat. He pulled back the sleeve of his suit jacket to consult his Rolex. Six fifty-five. He was going to be late.

If Emma was a prompt person, and something told him she was, she would be waiting on his doorstep by the time he arrived. Between his tardiness and other missteps, he'd be surprised if Emma would wait for very long. Perhaps he'd arrive home only to find his jacket hanging on the doorknob of his apartment. One could argue that he hadn't been a *complete* ass. He'd rescued a woman in distress with his coat. He'd walked her to her car. He also hadn't realized she lived in the same building. If ever there was a sign that he was preoccupied with work, that was it.

"Sorry we're so jammed up in traffic, Mr. Stone." His driver made eye contact via the rearview mirror.

"Not your fault."

"At least it's not raining, right?"

Indeed, it had rained for much of the afternoon, but the night was clear and beautiful. At least his walk with the dogs later this evening would be a good one. "So right."

Another fifteen minutes and his driver pulled into the parking garage of his building. Daniel quickly bade him farewell and rushed to the bank of elevators, only to be stopped by Henry, the doorman.

"Mr. Stone. There's a problem. I tried to call you, but we must not have your correct cell number down here at the desk."

"Problem?" Daniel had already pressed the button for the elevator.

"Your dog walker never showed."

"What?"

Henry shrugged. "I'm just glad you got here. Hopefully, your apartment won't be too much of a mess."

Daniel blew out an exasperated breath. "Thank you, Henry. I appreciate the information. Remind me tomorrow morning to get you my mobile number."

"Will do."

The elevator dinged to announce its arrival and Daniel stepped on board, worrying twice as hard about what might be waiting for him upstairs. An angry Emma and an epic dog disaster? He arrived on his floor and the doors slid open. Emma was sitting on the leather-upholstered bench next to the elevator, his jacket draped over the seat next to her.

"I'm late. I'm so sorry," he said.

She rose to her feet, her eyes warm as they quickly found his. He felt stuck for a moment, grappling with the realization that he'd run into this woman in the building and hadn't noticed her. He was losing his touch.

"It's no problem. I tried to wait by your door, but the

dogs kept barking." She gathered the jacket and looped it over her arm. "I didn't have a chance to have it cleaned. I hope that's okay. It's a beautiful jacket. I see that it has a Stone's label."

"Indeed. We carry only our store brand for menswear. It has quite a cult following." Daniel reached for the jacket, admonishing himself. He had no business sharing this information. He really had no business hoping the garment might smell like her. "This is perfect. Thank you."

Emma turned back to the elevator. "Okay, then. I guess I'll see you around the building? Maybe next time you'll remember me."

The dogs began to bark. They must have gotten a whiff of him. Pulled between his urgent obligation to them and wanting to at least make slight amends with Emma, he grabbed her arm. "No. Please. Don't go." He turned toward his own apartment. "Come with me? The dogs will quiet down once I'm inside. I'd like to talk."

A clever smile crossed her plump, raspberry-pink lips. All he could think about was convincing her to break every zipper she owned. "Sure. I love dogs."

"Brilliant." Daniel opened his door, doing his best to calm his canine trio and keep them from jumping on his guest. "Slow down. It's okay. Daddy's home."

"That's so cute. Daddy." Emma snickered and closed the door.

Daniel had never once gone for cute. "I'm so sorry, but apparently the dog walker didn't show up today. Is there any chance you'd accompany me to the park for a few minutes so we can talk?"

Emma crouched down and Jolly went straight to her. "I have a few minutes, then I need to go."

Of course she did. She likely had a date. A woman like Emma did not sit home alone. Daniel deposited his laptop bag on the table in the foyer and grabbed the leashes from the hook. "We'd better get going then, shouldn't we?"

The instant they were in the confines of the elevator, he remembered meeting Emma the first time. Perhaps it was a recollection of her perfume, but the memory of her, and his poor behavior, rushed into his mind. "I'm so sorry I didn't recognize you the other night. I do remember meeting you. I held the elevator door, right?"

She pressed her lips together. "That was me."

"I'm so sorry. If you'd been wearing an evening gown that day I might have recognized you last night."

"You didn't find it strange I said that thing about how we had to stop meeting like that?"

He laughed. "I thought you were being a cheeky American."

"Just my attempt at being clever."

He reached out and touched her arm. "It was clever. Honestly, it works in either situation, strangers or someone you know. Of course, a line like that is always better delivered by a beautiful woman." He had no idea what had come over him. Only the old Daniel said openly flirtatious things and threw caution to the wind. He had to keep himself under control. "I'm sorry if that was forward."

"You've seen my undies. I don't think there's such a thing as forward at this point."

Heat bloomed in Daniel's chest, spread down to his waist and kept going, wrapping around his hips and thighs. Why had he not kissed her last night? He'd been a fool for not taking his chance, especially at a time when he hadn't known she was a member of the family his mother was dead set on destroying.

It was simply a beautiful night. The sidewalks were damp from the rain earlier in the day. The clip-clop of the horses drawing carriages around the park managed to rise above all other noise. She and Daniel crossed at the corner and walked one of the sweeping asphalt trails that meander through Central Park. She should have been happy to be with him, but once again, her nerves had returned. It'd been easy to convince herself earlier that she was capable of flirting with Daniel and gathering information about his business, but confronted with him in person, she knew how silly that notion was. She wasn't capable of being ruthless or heartless about anything. She simply wanted to get to know him, but she knew that anything she asked could be misconstrued as prying.

"Lovely night," he said, breaking the silence between them.

"It is." She frantically searched her mind for something else to say. She wanted to ask if there were nights such as this in London, but she didn't want him to know that she'd never been. Perhaps it was best to talk about the dogs. "What are their names?"

Daniel stopped near a bench while the dogs explored and marked some nearby shrubs. "The two Corgis are Mandy and Buckingham, Buck for short. The miniature English bulldog is Jolly." The second her name crossed his lips, the dog waddled over to Emma.

She crouched down to pet her. "She's adorable."

"She used to belong to my brother."

"How could he give up such a sweet dog?" Emma scratched Jolly behind the ears.

"It wasn't his choice. He was killed in a car accident."

Emma couldn't believe she'd put her foot in her mouth so badly. She should've been smart enough to at least look into Daniel's history after their phone call. She should've researched the Stone family and figured out who she was dealing with. This new world of hers was more conniving than she found normal. Everyday people did not need due diligence before a walk in the park. "I'm so sorry for your loss. When did it happen?"

"Not quite two years." They resumed their walk, deeper into the park.

"Was he older or younger?"

"Older by two years. My only sibling. He was the golden boy, so it's been an adjustment. There's no living up to William or his memory."

Emma could hear the pain in his voice. It went deep. "I'm sure that's not true."

"You haven't met my mother." Daniel cleared his throat. "What about you? Two sisters, right? Sophie and Mindy?"

So he *had* done his research. What if Mindy was right? What if Daniel did have ulterior motives? What if last night had been a trap and she'd walked right into it? "Half sisters. We have the same father. It's a long story." She was fairly certain that if Daniel had snooped, he would know the sordid details that were out there to be found. Everything else, the hush money paid to her mother for years, was well hidden.

"So I understand you're CFO for Eden's. That's far more important than a number cruncher." Every new detail he revealed made her more nervous.

"True."

"And how is the store doing since your grandmother passed away? Victoria Eden's memory must cast a very long shadow."

They'd officially arrived in uncomfortable territory for Emma. She didn't want to talk about this. She couldn't risk giving away a single secret. "We're doing our best. What about Stone's? I didn't realize you were considering a foray into the American market."

He nodded, looking down at the ground. "It's early days. No telling what will happen."

His answer was all evasiveness and that put Emma even more on edge. Spending time with Daniel and getting closer to him could be playing with fire. Sophie and Mindy had warned her. Unfortunately, the part of Emma that had the nerve to wear that dress last night was still dying to get out. She was so tired of playing it safe. She wanted a little fire in her life. And if she was going to get burned, she might as well do it with a scrumptious man like Daniel. "How long are you here in New York?"

"Three months, I think. I don't love it, but I'm learning to like it."

With any other man, that would be a strike against him. Emma had little patience for men who didn't stick around. Her father had certainly done that to her mom. But perhaps this was her safety net. She could have a fling and it wouldn't matter what happened. It would eventually end. Was the new Emma capable of getting close and not getting attached? The old Emma was not.

Too many conflicted thoughts were going through her head right now. She needed time and space to think. She liked Daniel a lot. But she wasn't sure it was a good idea to tempt herself. "I should probably head upstairs."

"I'll walk you. I don't like the idea of you walking the park alone at night."

Just when she'd been seeking distance in the name of her sanity, he offered more time together. More to the point, he was doing that chivalrous thing again. She had such a weakness for it. They turned back, but out of nowhere, Jolly bolted ahead. Her leash slipped from Daniel's hand. The bulldog scrambled off under the bushes.

Daniel took off after her, with the other dogs leading the way. "No! Jolly!"

Emma joined the pursuit.

Daniel arrived at a park bench and crouched down, peering behind it. "She loves to put me through my paces. I think she sometimes wants to remind me that I'm not her true master. Only my brother could fill that role."

Emma couldn't help but notice the bitter edge to Daniel's words, but there was a larger task at hand now, namely a small bulldog needing to be coaxed from out of the bushes. Emma got on all fours and made eye contact with Jolly. "Come here, sweetie. I won't hurt you." She snapped her fingers. Jolly took a small step, then shrank back.

"I'm worried she doesn't like living with me."

Emma snapped her fingers again and made a kissing noise. The dog took two steps this time, so Emma puckered up and made the noise again. Slowly, Jolly crept out from her hiding spot. Emma didn't move until the dog nudged her hand with her nose. "That's a good girl." She scooped up Jolly and tucked her under her arm. "Maybe I'll carry her inside."

Daniel stared at her in amazement. "How did you do that? The last time this happened, it was a half hour ordeal."

Emma relished her minor victory, even if once again Daniel had seen her in a less than ladylike position. "I worked for a dog groomer one summer." As soon as the words left her mouth, she worried that the answer made her seem too unrefined.

"Where did you come from, Emma?"

The question made her heart race. She wanted to tell him everything about her history, and how her father had left her and her mother dangling by a thread. Then again, she didn't. She refused to play the role of victim. After all, she had the entire world before her right now. Anything she could ever desire was at her fingertips. Maybe even Daniel. "Does it matter where I came from? I'm here right now."

He smiled and their gazes connected. Every bit of the electricity from last night was zipping back and forth between them again. "I…" He stepped closer. "I'm sorry. I'm sorry that I didn't remember you from the elevator."

"We hardly spoke."

"I remember it now. You made an effort. And I didn't. For that, I'm deeply sorry."

She touched his arm, the fabric of his suit jacket soft and smooth under her fingers. Her eyes were drawn to his face and not just because his eyes were so entrancing. There was so much more to admire, like his full lips and the way one side of his mouth wanted to twist higher than the other when he was amused. "I don't want you to feel bad, Daniel. Apology more than accepted."

He grinned and reached for her hand. Emma's pulse picked up, beating in double time. "You know, you aren't helping me at all. I thought it might be easier to ask you on a proper date if I was some way in debt to you."

A proper date? Emma had more than a few improper thoughts going through her head right now. "I'm the one who's in debt to you. If you hadn't given me your jacket, I might have left last night wrapped in a tablecloth."

"It could have been the biggest fashion statement of the entire event." Warmth radiated off him as they were again drawn closer. His fingers were wrapped snuggly around hers, his face close enough that she could see the darker flecks of blue in his incredible eyes.

"Maybe. Of course, I could ask *you* on a proper date. And then you wouldn't need to worry about needing a reason." So bold Emma really did exist. She just needed a bit of encouragement.

He scanned her face like he was searching for answers.

Just as she'd already learned to expect, the right corner of his mouth went up. "And what about a reason for asking if I can kiss you? Do I need one of those?"

"A person can always ask." Emma bit down on her lip in eager anticipation. Was she going to get the kiss she should have had the sense to claim last night? "No guarantees on the answer. Although I'm definitely leaning toward yes."

His lips spread into a full smile, his breathtaking eyes crinkling slightly at the corners. "Yes?"

"I'll take it one further. Yes, please." Emma couldn't wait. Jolly tucked under her arm, Emma rose up onto her toes, leaning into Daniel. Her mouth met his and her body sprang to life. Her face tingled, her chest flushed with heat, her lips were nothing but hungry. When his lips parted and his tongue urged hers to do the same, she tilted her head even farther to the side, wanting everything she could get from him. The buzz of the city and the fresh smell of rain faded into invisible recesses as their kiss became the most powerful, living, breathing thing around them. His hand slid to the small of her back and Emma arched into him. She could already imagine how they would fit together in bed, and even though the idea intimidated her, just like she'd recently made so many other leaps, she wanted to jump ahead to that right now.

From under her arm, Jolly yipped. Emma was brought back to earth, reluctantly pulling her lips from Daniel's. "I don't think she likes us kissing."

His chest was rising and falling with each breath. She loved seeing that she'd gotten his pulse racing. She wasn't sure she'd ever had that effect on a man. "This would definitely be easier if I didn't have the dogs with me. I could take them back upstairs. Or you could come with me."

As tempting as his offer was, this was all moving too

fast. She wanted Daniel. But they'd known each other for a scant twenty-four hours, and their true identities for an even shorter amount of time. Plus there was the larger looming question of intentions. What were his? She wasn't sure she knew her own.

"I have a big day at work tomorrow. I should go." Everything Mindy and Sophie had said was ringing in her ears. Could she trust Daniel? Should she even be speaking to him? Her body and her mind warred while she struggled with the question. There was a chance she couldn't trust her sisters, either. They had their own agenda, and although it was undoubtedly intertwined with Emma's share of Eden's, they could throw her under the bus at any moment.

Daniel pressed his lips together and nodded. "I understand. I have quite a lot to accomplish tomorrow, as well. I'd still like to take you out if you're open to the idea."

Emma's heartbeat was beating so fast she wasn't sure how she was still standing. He wanted to see her again. "That would be lovely. What were you thinking?"

"I'm sure you've heard, but the English National Opera is performing *La Bohème* on Broadway over the next six weeks. It's opening Thursday night and I'm certain I can get us tickets. I've known the director for quite some time."

Emma pulse picked up again, sheerly out of nervousness. No, she hadn't heard. All these years living in close proximity to the city and she'd never seen a Broadway production, let alone the opera. Of course, she wasn't about to admit that. She couldn't imagine Daniel would be drawn to a woman whose world was as small as hers. Once again, she was going to have to fake it until she could make it. "That sounds lovely. I'd love to go."

A confident smile crossed his face and Emma had to

wonder what it was like to walk around the world so self-assured. "Excellent. I'll secure the tickets."

What was the saying about playing with fire? That was how it felt to be with Daniel. He was unafraid to make an overture and kiss her in the middle of the park. He wasn't shy about asking her to the theater, all while there was a very good chance he intended to destroy her family's business. Despite his seeming sense of obligation to her, in the real world, Daniel owed her nothing. In some ways, that should scare her more than anything, but it also made the notion of Thursday night that much more thrilling.

"I can't wait."

Six

Daniel was not going to be late to pick up Emma for the opera. He gave himself plenty of time to jog down the two flights of stairs to her floor. Thinking about tonight, he was filled with the most puzzling mix of wariness and elation. Surely those two feelings were never meant to comingle in a sensible person's mind at one time, and he'd been feeling that way for two days. He'd tried to distract himself from thoughts of Emma by focusing on work, which was the perfect illustration of the push and pull in his life. He was drawn to Emma, but everything about her, her family and her career stood in direct opposition to his life.

Still, he was moving forward. Somehow. He'd found a space he quite liked for the New York location of Stone's this week. His real estate agent, Charlotte Locke, was negotiating terms. If all went well, that would be sewn up soon. And he was moving forward with the date he'd asked Emma out on, even when he knew it wasn't a smart idea. Sometimes things don't make sense until later, he'd told himself. He had to listen to his gut, and it was telling him he'd miss out if he didn't at least test the waters with Emma.

He knocked and folded his hands before him, his heart beating fiercely in anticipation.

"Hey." Emma opened the door only a moment later, seeming flustered, almost panicked. "You're a little early." Her hair and makeup were perfect, but she was not dressed for a night out. She was wearing a short satin kimono-style robe, tied at the waist.

Daniel was mesmerized. "I'm sorry. Am I?" He fished his phone from his pocket and glanced at the home screen. Indeed, he was five minutes early.

Emma waved him in. "It's okay. I just need to finish getting dressed."

He trailed her into her apartment, enjoying the view of her bare legs and feet. "I'll just sit on the sofa and wait. Please don't rush on my account."

Emma turned to him and it was impossible not to notice the gentle swell of her breasts as her robe gaped slightly. He glimpsed just enough to make him wish he'd been unable to get tickets to tonight's performance. "Can I make you a drink?"

He held up his hand. He needed to stay on top of things this evening. "I'm fine, thank you."

"Okay. I just need a few minutes. Make yourself at home." With that, Emma ambled down the hall and disappeared.

Daniel took the opportunity to explore her apartment. It was beautifully decorated in a neutral color scheme of snow white and creamy gray, with the occasional pop of pale pink and gold metal accents. Either Emma had a very refined sense of personal style or she'd paid a king's ransom to an interior designer. The apartment looked like a jewel box, straight out of a magazine.

He knew very little about Emma, and this trip through her abode wasn't providing many clues. There were no family photos, no real personal effects. He'd done a quick internet search since their visit to the park, but hadn't learned much, other than that Emma's place in the Eden lineage had been kept a secret for years. She'd been shipped off to France, apparently, to study in quiet, probably because of her father's affair. It was as if Victoria Eden had been hiding her granddaughter in an ivory tower. All the more reason not to trust Emma, however beguiling and gorgeous she was. But Daniel was certain he had everything in hand. He wouldn't let Emma get too close. He certainly wouldn't let her within the vicinity of his heart.

"I'm ready." Her voice was right behind him. Apparently she was light on her feet, like a cat.

Daniel turned and decided he couldn't care less about attending the opera. Emma was a vision in a sparkling black dress with skinny straps and a neckline that flaunted the same maddening view as her robe. Her skin shimmered as it had for Empire State, the light dancing off the enticing contours of her collarbone and cleavage. He didn't want to go anywhere. He wanted to stay here and kiss her again, let his lips roam everywhere. "You look beautiful. Like a princess."

"Thank you. Like retail royalty? If you believe what the tabloids say." She smiled and stepped closer, brushing the shoulder of his tux jacket. "You don't look too bad yourself."

"No need to worry about the tabloids this evening. I've made arrangements for us to duck into the theater through a back entrance without detection."

Disappointment crossed Emma's face. "Back entrance? That doesn't sound like much fun."

"It's the one a president or dignitary would use. I'm certain it's quite nice."

"I was hoping we'd end up in the papers again. Just like the other night, I'm wearing a Nora Bradford. She's one of Eden's exclusive designers. I'll earn big bonus points with my sisters if I can create another run on the store."

"Surely you realize it's not in my best interest to help Eden's." Nor was it in Daniel's best interest to help Eden's as pertained to Nora Bradford. He'd been unable to reach her, and his mother still didn't know about it.

"Of course not. But you can help *me*. The store and I are not synonymous."

She not only had an excellent point, Daniel felt the same way. His family was important, but he and the business were not the same thing. Still, his stomach churned at the prospect of going through the main entrance of the theater. He'd purposely avoided the red carpet at Empire State, although that had been for naught since he still ended up in the tabloids. "I'm sorry. I'm just not a fan of photographers or the media. They've treated me and my family badly in England." They'd been especially brutal once they figured out his brother and fiancée had been having an affair. It was too juicy for them to let it rest, so they'd kept the love triangle of his deceased brother, himself and the woman who'd betrayed him in the headlines for months.

"I don't want you to do anything you don't want to. I just…" Her voice trailed off.

"What is it?"

"My sisters. I'm trying to prove to them that I'm a real member of the team. That I can contribute."

Again, she was hitting all the right notes. It was exactly

the way he felt about needing to prove himself to his parents. "You seem more than capable."

Emma shook her head, her eyes filled with a worry that tugged at his heart. "It doesn't matter. Mindy and Sophie are thick as thieves and they treat me like I'm an idiot sometimes. They see me as the outsider."

"But you're a blood relative."

She arched her eyebrows at him. "You've done your research."

"I have." He could admit that much. Didn't everyone do a Google search on anyone they might take on a date?

"Then you should know that Mindy and Sophie didn't know I was inheriting part of Eden's until the day our grandmother's will was read. I'm still earning their trust. They're still earning mine, for that matter."

"It really means that much to you? Going through the main entrance of the theater?"

"Unless you're worried that people will think we're dating. I wouldn't want to embarrass you." Her leading inflection did nothing but put him on the spot.

"The tabloids don't care about facts. They'll say whatever they want."

"As someone who's spent her entire life invisible to the public eye, I'm enjoying my moment in the spotlight. But if you'd prefer we hide, I'm okay with it."

Indeed, the Edens had hidden Emma away. It wasn't fair to her. She couldn't help that she'd been the product of an extramarital affair. He drew in a deep breath, realizing he wanted only to please her. He could stomach a few moments standing before the paparazzi and whatever headlines resulted from it. Just this once.

"We'll go in through the main entrance and see what happens."

"Really?" Emma's excitement was its own reward. Her cheeks colored in radiant pink. "Thank you so much."

"Of course." He'd forgotten how wonderful it was to make a woman happy. Would he have the chance to please Emma in other ways? He hoped so.

Daniel's driver was waiting for them downstairs in the parking garage.

"Why don't you ever have him pick you up out front?" Emma asked.

"Same reason I wanted to take the side door at the theater. It's a habit now. I do anything to retain my privacy."

"I see."

His driver had them to the theater quickly. It seemed like New York traffic was conspiring against him—whenever he had somewhere to be, it was nothing but gridlock. And when he was in no rush to confront what was awaiting him, like the chance of photographers, it was smooth sailing. They waited their turn in the line of limousines and town cars, but he could already see camera flashes going off. Opening night was always a big affair.

As soon as Daniel climbed out of the car, his pulse picked up and he waited for his stomach to sour. But then he reached for Emma's hand, her fingers slid against his palm, and a pleasant wave of warmth overtook him. He could do this. He had an extraordinary woman on his arm.

One photographer spotted them and the flashes started. Daniel and Emma weren't even on the red carpet yet and they were already a focus. Emma squeezed his hand. He wasn't sure if she sensed his trepidation or was expressing her own excitement. It didn't matter. He only knew that he wanted more. When they took center stage, the questions began.

Are you officially dating?

How did you meet?

Emma, what are you wearing?

Emma took a single step toward them and let go of Daniel's hand. "It's Nora Bradford, of course. We love her at Eden's." She turned to let them photograph the back of the dress while she peeked over her shoulder like a veteran of the red carpet. If he were inclined to enjoy this sort of thing, he'd be loving it right now. Watching Emma was the most fun he'd had in weeks. It was the photographers he disliked so greatly. "It's beautiful, isn't it?"

Daniel, is Stone's opening in New York?

How will the stores compete?

What do your families think?

Daniel had to admit that last question was an excellent one. He wasn't about to answer it. His mother had expressed more than enough concern. He was sure her sisters felt the same way. Emma snugged herself tighter against his arm, smiling for the cameras and smartly ignoring the latest batch of questions. The photographers moved on to the couple behind them, a Hollywood actress and her husband, and Daniel tugged Emma into the theater.

"That wasn't so bad, was it? I think it's exciting." Indeed, she looked nothing short of exhilarated, her cheeks flushed with color and her eyes bright. "Thank you for putting up with that. I appreciate it."

"I'm just glad it's over." He didn't want to think about how what Emma had just done might end up dashing his hopes of signing Nora Bradford to Stone's. Forget damage control with his mother. She was going to hit the roof. For tonight, he wouldn't worry about it. He would instead enjoy his time with Emma.

They took their seats in the theater, the front row of one of the side boxes with an excellent view of the stage. Emma was perfectly at home here, among the women in evening gowns and men in tuxedos. However hidden away she'd been for much of her life, she'd surely been exposed to the finer things.

"These seats are amazing," Emma said. "I can't wait for the performance to start." Once again, he was taken aback by her enthusiasm. She enjoyed life, no matter how routine the moment. He could learn quite a lot from her.

The house lights went down. The orchestra began to play, exquisite music filling the theater. Emma turned her sights to the stage expectantly, practically sitting on the edge of her seat. When the curtains opened, she reached for Daniel's hand and squeezed hard.

He'd seen *La Bohème* many times, but never like this. Not with someone like Emma who so plainly appreciated it on a different level. Just like at Empire State, she openly displayed her enjoyment of the spectacle before her. Daniel had a difficult time keeping his eyes on the stage. It was much more beautiful and enchanting to watch it reflected in Emma's face, her eyes darting from side to side as she followed the performers, her luscious lips parted as she got caught up in the music.

And she wept, softly and sweetly, squeezing his hand tighter and letting the tears fall. Emma Stewart was a singular woman. She appreciated beauty in all its forms. She seemed to have nothing but the warmest of hearts and the most generous nature. If he wasn't careful, it wasn't a question of whether he would fall for her, but rather, how fast.

Daniel was intensely quiet on the ride back to their building. Emma was still composing herself after the performance. She hadn't wanted to embarrass him with her tears, but there was no holding any of it back, especially not at the end, when the music was so achingly beautiful and Rodolfo realized that Mimi had died. Though tragic, the story of poverty, sacrifice and love was wrapped up in such a spectacle, she couldn't have held back her emotion if she'd tried.

"I'm sorry about the tears. It was my first time seeing *La Bohème*. I guess I just got caught up in it." She didn't want to make an admission of her naivety, but she wanted to be honest with him. She didn't like always pretending to be something she wasn't.

He nodded, but she could see that look of surprise on his face. "That explains a lot. But there's no need to apologize. A lot of people cry."

Deep inside her was a desire to tell him more. She didn't like pretending to be something she wasn't, even when she knew her money and pedigree were part of what made him want to spend any time with her.

His driver dropped them in the parking garage. As they walked inside, she prepared herself for the awkward moment to come, when Daniel thanked her for accompanying him for the evening and then found a way to absolve himself of more time together. Perhaps this was the natural progression between a man like him and a woman like her. They were from different worlds. Warring families. But the fighter in her was unwilling to give up hope. She liked Daniel. She liked being with him—he had a way of making her feel like she was the only woman in the world. His focus was always on her. She'd never experienced that before. With anyone.

"Thank you for a lovely evening," she said, as the elevator opened.

Daniel waited for her to board first. She nearly choked on the quiet as the doors slid shut. He pressed the button for her floor—confirmation that there would be no invitation to join him upstairs. She was about to crumple in defeat when he turned to her with a gaze so intense it nearly knocked her over.

"It's you I have to thank, Emma. Tonight was extraordinary. I felt like I was seeing the performance for the first time, too. It's amazing to see the world through your eyes."

The elevator dinged and the doors opened. She had only seconds to act. She took his hand. "Don't go upstairs."

Daniel didn't take his eyes off her, but he thrust out his arm to keep the elevator open. "Are you sure?" His voice was soft and low. Intoxicating. "If I come over, I'll just want to kiss you again."

Her heart fluttered in her chest. "Good." Without a second to waste, she tugged him down the hall to her door. She felt like it was okay to breathe again until his eyes narrowed on her face. He set his hand on the side of her neck and ran a thumb across one cheek. That one innocent touch sent zaps of electricity through her. "You have freckles. How did I not notice that before?"

Her makeup had failed her. "I shouldn't have cried at the opera. It washed away my foundation. I must look horrible."

He shook his head. "You're stunning. It's okay to cry. It's beautiful. It's real. And moving."

Now her heart was thundering so much harder. He'd asked her the other night where she'd been hiding, but she was inclined to ask the same of him. He gathered her into his arms, pulling her close. She rose up onto her tiptoes. His kiss was soft and patient. A spark started a slow burn, his lips parting slightly, his tongue teasing when it touched hers. The anticipation might kill her. Not only had she never wanted a man the way she wanted Daniel, she hadn't known until that very moment what it was like to be desperate for someone and be in his arms at the same time. She was starving for more of him. All of him.

Emma fumbled with her keys, dropping them on the floor. Daniel bent over to pick them up, and she smoothed her hand across his broad shoulders, dying to know what his skin felt like, wanting nothing more than to touch him.

He opened the door and handed her the keys. She cast them aside on the foyer table, along with her clutch. Then she found his arms wrapping around her waist, and she clasped the sides of his face, his light facial scruff tickling her palms. He kissed her—sensuous and slow, a pace that was pure Daniel. Emma was already on fire, consumed with desire. She wanted him out of his tailored tux. She wanted him to tear off her dress. She threaded her hands inside his jacket and urged it from his shoulders. He loosened his tie with one hand, but didn't let go of her with the other, his hot fingers curled into the bare skin of her back.

"I need to know if you want this, Emma."

Yes was waiting on her lips, but she was struck with a terrible case of nerves. Like everything else in her life, she was searching for a way to belong where she was, right now in the arms of the sexiest man she'd ever met. She absolutely wanted this. She wanted him more than anything, but she was scared of how he'd see her. She didn't want to be shy and inexperienced Emma. She wanted to be a woman who could rock his world. "I do want this. I want you. Let me take off your suit. I want you to take off my dress."

"I sense hesitation."

Blue light from the city filtered through the living room windows and pooled on the foyer floor. She looked deeply into his eyes. Even that much felt bold. It wasn't daylight, but she wasn't shying away. If she did nothing else right, let her confront him with this. Let her be honest and trust that he wouldn't think less of her. "I have to tell you something."

"Please." His voice rumbled with concern.

"I'm worried I might disappoint you."

He unleashed his off-kilter smile. He shook his head, tugging her closer and kissing her tenderly. First her lips, then her jaw, and finally—blissfully—her neck. "Nothing about you is disappointing."

Emma swallowed hard. Did he really feel that way? Was it the truth? Or had she merely done a good job of convincing him she was something she wasn't? His roving lips on her neck weren't helping her sort any of this out. "I've only been with one man, Daniel. Ever."

He reared back his head, vision narrowed. "Did your family actually lock you up in a tower somewhere? I don't see how dozens of men haven't at least tried to seduce you."

It was both surprising and oddly reassuring to know that Daniel saw her that way. "Not a tower. A small apartment. And my mother was especially good at keeping tabs on me."

"I know the feeling."

She sensed that he did. "I've never enjoyed myself with a man. I never reached my ultimate destination, if you get what I mean."

"Never?"

This conversation had already gone so much further than she'd intended. She should be feeling humiliated right now, but she wasn't. Something about Daniel made her want to be an open book. He made her want to bare her soul *and* her body. "Not with him."

He slid his hand down the back of her left arm, then locked his fingers with hers. "You've never had an orgasm?"

Heat flushed her face, but she refused to be embarrassed. "I have. Many times. By myself."

A knowing look crossed his face. "So you know what you like?"

"I think so. I'm sure there's a lot I've been missing out on, though."

He got serious again, the crease between his eyes deepening. "Emma, you couldn't disappoint me if you tried. Tonight has been incredible."

However much she'd wanted him a minute ago, that desire was tenfold now. She reached back and pulled the clip from her hair, letting her hair fall down onto her shoulders. Daniel sucked in a sharp breath and she knew she was not only on the right track, but this was the only way she wanted to go. She tightened her grip around his waist. "I want you to show me what I've been missing."

A lustful groan came from the depths of Daniel's throat. "I will." He slipped the thin strap from her shoulder. She shuddered with anticipation. He pressed a kiss to her bare skin, and she tilted her head to the side, silently begging him to kiss her neck again. Daniel claimed the stretch of skin with his mouth. His kisses were wet and hungry. Heat pooled between her legs. "Just do what feels right. Do what feels natural."

She anticipated no problem with that. Daniel was so sexy, her body was giving her hundreds of cues. Heat coursed through her veins. Her skin was alive with electricity. She turned her back to him and twisted her hair to the side. "I've heard you're good with zippers."

"I'm terrible. I can't promise you'll ever be able to wear this dress again."

She smiled as he unzipped her, his breath warm against the back of her neck. "That's okay. I've already been seen in it." Her pulse picked up when she realized that, unlike the other night, she was free to let her dress fall. He undid the tiny hook at the top and she pulled the garment from her shoulders, letting it flounce to the floor.

Daniel placed his hands on her hips and flattened himself against her back. She could already feel his erection, hard against her bottom. He smoothed his palms around to her belly, pulling her into him while he dragged his fingers up her torso. Her nipples drew tight just waiting for his touch.

He kissed her neck again. "It's so sexy that you didn't wear a bra tonight," he muttered into the sensitive spot behind her ear. He cupped her breasts with his sizable hands, enveloping them and squeezing.

She felt light-headed as pleasure and excitement had her heart racing again. "The dress did the dictating."

"Bravo for the dress." He rolled her nipples between his fingertips. Emma clamped her eyes shut, sinking back against his chest as currents zipped from her breasts to the tops of her thighs. He slid one hand down her midline and into the front of her panties. His fingers spread her delicate folds. "You're so wet." His breath was warm against her ear. He gently nipped her lobe.

"I want you," she gasped, as he found her apex and began rubbing in small circles. He knew precisely what he was doing, his fingers driving her straight toward her peak. She felt it zeroing in on her, building so fast she could hardly think straight. "I'm going to come…"

The words had hardly left her lips before she knocked her head back and the orgasm slammed into her, hard. It felt so impossibly good, waves of blissful heat washing over her. Still she was a bit mortified that it hadn't taken much to bring her there. She turned in his arms, grabbed both sides of his head and brought his lips to hers, threading her fingers into his hair. "That was amazing. I'm sorry it happened so fast."

"Don't apologize. That's just the beginning." He reached down and scooped up her legs, lifting her into his arms. "Which way to your bed?"

She pointed to the hall and he strode to her bedroom, taking charge, every inch the confident man she was so immensely attracted to. She coiled her hands around his neck, still reeling from the pleasure he'd delivered. He ducked into the darkness of her room and placed her feet on the floor. Emma took both his hands and walked backward to the bed. Her calves met the mattress and she raced to start on his shirt. He caressed her bare shoulders while she freed the buttons, then pushed the crisp cotton down his arms. Being able to smooth her hands over his firm chest was the best reward. His muscles were hard and defined, even better than her brain had imagined. But there was more waiting for her, so she unhooked his belt, the hook and zipper on his trousers. They dropped to the floor and Daniel took her hand, pressing her palm against his erection. His body was telling her just how primed he was. She'd made him feel like that.

She pressed harder and he groaned, but she wanted to touch him for real, not just through his boxer briefs. Pure instinct taking over, she shimmied them down his hips and took him into her hand. She wanted to feel every inch of him. Her thumb smoothed over the head, silky smooth. Daniel groaned again. She slid her fingers along his length and began to stroke from base to tip, matching the tension coiling beneath his skin with her firm grip. He kissed her with abandon, mouth open and craving. He needed her. She felt it in every inch of him that she touched. She sensed it in every kiss and subtle moan.

The pressure was building between her legs again and she ached for him to touch her. She placed a knee on the bed and, wanting him to truly see her, stretched out on her back, her body on full display. She wanted him to see that she was his for the taking.

He reached down and curled his fingers into the waistband of her silky panties, tugged them down her legs and tossed them aside. She expected him to stretch out on the bed next to her, but he watched her instead. She squirmed against the sheets, rubbing her head back and forth. It felt like she was on fire.

"Do you have a condom?" she asked, kicking herself for not thinking this through and buying a box ahead of time.

"I do." He reached for his pants and opened his wallet. "A gentleman is always prepared."

Emma sat up, her heart racing. "Come here. Let me put it on."

He grinned and handed over the packet, standing between her knees. Their gazes connected as she rolled it on. Her fingers didn't fumble. It was like she was a different person. She felt him get harder in her hand. She'd never wanted anything as badly as she wanted Daniel. She lay back on the bed and spread her legs for him. He lowered his beautiful body onto her, positioning himself at her entrance and then slowly driving inside.

Emma raised her knees and he sank down until his hips met the back of her thighs. He felt so impossibly good, filling her completely. He lowered his torso against hers, resting on his elbows, but putting a delicious pressure against her center. His thrusts were pure magic, his hips rotating with every pass. She might not last long the second time, either. They fell into a kiss that had no logical end. Passionate. Unafraid. It was like they'd done this hundreds of times together, but the newness was there, too. It was a feeling unlike anything she'd ever experienced.

Daniel's breaths were getting shorter, his thrusts longer and deeper. He pushed back with one arm and lowered his head, drawing her nipple into his mouth. Emma wrapped her legs around him, muscling him closer. She felt like her entire body was about to burst. She was poised. Muscles tight and inching closer to release. And she gave way, ecstasy washing over her in a colorful array of light. Daniel followed, his torso freezing in place, deep moans coming from his incredible mouth. He took several more slow passes, his hips delivering aftershocks of pleasure to her.

As her heart rate slowed, he collapsed next to her, pulling her into his arms and kissing the top of her head over and over again. Emma was overcome with a powerful realization, one she hoped wasn't born of too much naive optimism. On paper, she and Daniel did not belong together. But alone, away from the rest of the world, they might be perfect.

Seven

Daniel woke to a feeling he hadn't given into for a very long time. He was daring to wonder what came next with a woman. Here in her bed, sheets tangled around them both, he wasn't thinking about any work he had to do today. He was instead wondering if they could go out to dinner. He was wondering if she might want to come over. He was at ease with her already, and she was more than comfortable with him. He'd loved every minute of seeing her open up to him physically last night. She'd picked up on his cues and given herself fully to him. He hadn't banked on the emotional side of that. He felt connected to her. Fast. Exactly what he'd feared.

He already knew he couldn't let his mother continue to believe he was trying to extract information about Eden's from Emma. The small bits he'd learned thus far would remain under lock and key. Still, he had to devote some time to thinking through how this might possibly work. Was there a happy middle ground? Or was he fooling himself because he was in bed with a beautiful woman?

Daniel's arm was pinned under Emma's shoulders, and he was starting to lose the feeling in his fingers. He carefully tried to unthread himself from her, but that was enough to make her stir.

"Are you awake?" she grumbled. "It's still early." Her morning voice was soft and velvety, just like her. She rolled over and faced him, settling her head on his chest. "You smell nice in the morning."

Such a funny and sweet thing to say. It made something in the vicinity of his heart swell. He shook his head, trailing his fingers up and down her back, bringing back memories of their night together and the ways they'd pleased each other. "You smell nice, too. I should get up, though. The dogs will surely want to get out."

Emma sat up, her wide eyes popping open. She didn't bother to cover herself, baring her luscious curves to him. "I can't believe we forgot."

How adorable was it that she'd used the word *we*?

"It's okay. I snuck upstairs after three to let them out and to grab some different clothes. They don't like it when I don't come home at night."

Emma arched her eyebrows and narrowed a skeptical stare at him. "Does that happen a lot?"

"Not at all in New York."

A wide smile bloomed on her face. She leaned down and kissed him on the cheek, then swatted his leg. "Good. Come on. I'll go with you." She hopped out of bed and traipsed over to her dresser, fishing out some clothes.

He was inclined to let the dogs wait a few more minutes just so he could enjoy watching her flit around the room naked. But he couldn't let responsibility get too far away from him. He was doing enough of that already. "You don't have to come with me if you'd rather sleep."

Emma tugged on a pair of black leggings and a white tank top. "I love your dogs. I like being around them." She zipped up a gray hoodie. "I like being around you."

"I like being around you, too." Again, Daniel was wading in deeper. The depth didn't scare him so much as his own enthusiasm for going there.

When they arrived upstairs, the dogs were raring to go, especially Jolly, who was running in circles. Emma got her on her leash while Daniel took care of Buck and Mandy. Minutes later, they arrived in the park. Emma took his hand and he led the way on the loop the dogs preferred. He was struck by how this was all so normal. So calm. Of course, things might change when they ended their walk at the newsstand. Daniel cringed at the thought of what the papers might say. Hopefully, there had been more interesting tabloid fodder in attendance last night.

They came to a stop so the dogs could mark some bushes. Jolly was sticking to Emma's side. "She likes you a lot. A lot more than she likes me."

"She doesn't realize that you made a sacrifice by adopting her. She's probably still waiting for your brother to come back."

He wondered if that was true. "Probably. I think my mother's wondering the same thing."

"What happened? When he died? It clearly caused some problems in your family. I can hear it in your voice."

Daniel cleared his throat. He'd never had his chance to tell his side of the story. He'd kept it all bottled up inside for two years. "William and I had an argument the night he got into the accident. I was quite angry and told him that he was no longer my brother."

Emma held her hand to her lips. "Wow. What made you say that?"

"He was having an affair with my fiancée, Bea, and I found out about it. We'd always competed with each other and they'd dated once or twice before she and I started going out. I don't know if she just liked the idea of playing us off against each other or what, but that's what happened. So those were the last words I said to my brother. My mother never forgave me. She's convinced that William wouldn't have crashed if he hadn't been so upset."

Emma shook her head. "No. I'm sure that's not what happened. And of course you were upset. Your brother betrayed you."

"But there's no winning that argument. He's gone now. I will always have regrets."

Emma scooped up Jolly and looked her right in the face. "You and your dad need to get things worked out. You both miss the same person."

Daniel smiled. She was truly amazing. Just then, his cell phone rang. He pulled it from his pocket. The caller ID said it was Charlotte Locke, his real estate agent. He wasn't sure he should take this call with Emma nearby.

Emma put Jolly back down on the ground. "It's okay if you need to answer your phone."

"It'll just be a moment. I'm so sorry." Daniel handed her the leashes and distanced himself. "Hello?"

"Daniel. It's Charlotte. Do you have a minute? We need to talk."

Daniel watched Emma with the dogs. They were already hopelessly head over heels for her. Mandy and Buck were practically climbing over each other to get to her, while Jolly circled her ankles. Their tails wagged with endless excitement. "Of course. News on the lease?"

"I'm afraid not. I'm not going to be able to work with you any longer."

"What? We're in the middle of a negotiation." Daniel couldn't believe this. Charlotte was one of the top agents in the city and he'd still come up empty-handed. He'd never get Stone's off the ground with someone else. "Why now?"

"A long-time client has asked me to stop working with you."

"Excuse me?"

"I'm sorry. I can't explain further."

"Can you tell me who the client is?"

"I'm sorry. No."

Daniel was reeling. Who would cut him off at the knees like this? As he eyed Emma, he couldn't help but suspect this could be connected to Eden's. The conclusion made his stomach lurch, but the history between their families made sabotage likely. "Can you at least refer me to someone else? You told me you have a great relationship with this landlord."

Charlotte cleared her throat. "I do. And I'm sorry, but I can't. But you have plenty of resources, Mr. Stone. I have no doubt that you'll land on your feet. Have a good day." Before Daniel could utter another word, Charlotte had hung up.

Daniel jammed his cell phone into his pocket. His blood was on the brink of boiling. If he were in London or Paris right now, he'd have no problem finding a new agent. Now he was starting over from scratch.

"Everything okay? You look terrible." Emma approached, the dogs not so much leading the way as staying by her side.

It was such a shame. He liked Emma a great deal, but the suspicions going through his head right now were exactly why he had no business becoming involved with her. When he was younger and felt indestructible, he would've thumbed his nose at his gut feelings. He'd ignored the signs with William and Bea and it had destroyed his world. "Actually, everything isn't okay. It appears my real estate agent has left me. I'm wondering if you know anything about this."

"How could I?"

"Then perhaps your sisters?"

"You think they got your agent to dump you? They would never do something like that." Her eyebrows popped up as a realization crossed her face. "So you really are opening a Stone's in New York. This isn't early days or you just exploring your options. You're doing this."

"You had to know that. I don't for a minute believe you are naive enough to think I'm spending time in New York looking at real estate for anything else."

Emma reared her head back. Jolly growled at him. "Wow." She shook her head slowly, looking him square in the eye. "You could have just been up front with me. You hedged your answer and I took you at your word. Now I'm thinking that was a foolish move on my part."

Daniel's anger was quickly replaced by guilt. He'd skirted the issue when asked. That much was true. "I thought we were toying with each other."

Emma shook her head. "I don't play games, Daniel. Maybe other women have done that to you, but not me. Maybe your old fiancée did that to you, but that's just not my style." Emma collected the dog leashes and placed them in his hand. Her touch sent an ache right through him. She began to walk away.

"Where are you going?"

She turned around, walking backward. "To talk to my sisters. If you're right, this has to stop now."

"And if I'm wrong?"

"It won't be the first time you've had to apologize to me."

Emma called Sophie as soon as she was back in her apartment. No answer. Next, Mindy. Voice mail. What in the world was going on? Had those two really resorted to cutting Daniel off at the knees? She'd told him they wouldn't do such a thing, but she worried she might be wrong. She had to get to the office right away to track down her sisters.

She got into the shower. "This is so stupid," she muttered to herself. "What kind of families feud with each other?" She placed a foot on the stone ledge meant for shaving her legs and aggressively scrubbed, suds splatting against the glass walls of the shower enclosure. "It's not like we're the Montagues and they're the Capulets. We're not even the Hatfields and the McCoys. If we're fighting, we're talking about who might sell the most perfume and designer shoes. Why does anybody need dirty tricks to do that?"

She shut off the water, stepped onto the plush bathmat and wrapped herself up in a fluffy towel. Swiping at the fog on the mirror with her hand, she looked at herself. If what Daniel had accused her sisters of was true, this was worse than stupid. It couldn't continue. It didn't matter how much money was on the line, she wasn't about to be a part of underhanded tactics.

And then it hit her—what if it wasn't true? What did Daniel's assumption say about him? It certainly demanded that she look at last night through a different lens. But she didn't want to do that. It had been too amazing. She wouldn't let circumstance color her view of something she'd enjoyed so much.

Her phone buzzed with a text. She flipped it over on the bathroom counter. The message was from Duane, head of store security for Eden's.

Customers lined up for the dress you wore last night. Have Gregory text me when you arrive.

She did a quick search on her phone. Sure enough, she and Daniel had hit the tabloids again.

An Eden Princess and Her Enemy Prince.

There was that word again, the one she hated so much— *enemy.* The story focused on the hatred between the families and the businesses, and how unlikely a pair Daniel and Emma were. The reporter surmised it would never last. Emma knew the odds were stacked against them, but she at least wanted her chance. She and Daniel looked nothing but right in the pictures, holding hands on the red carpet, smiling at each other. Daniel was so handsome it made her entire body tingle, especially when she thought about the things they'd done together in bed. That was the happy ending she'd wanted, not the nightmare of the last half hour.

When Emma arrived at Eden's, there were twice as many photographers outside as last time. Duane had them cordoned off to one side of the store entrance with the sort of metal barricades the city put up for parades. Meanwhile, customers were standing in an orderly line marked off by velvet ropes and brass stanchions—a line that went all the way to the corner of the block and wrapped around the building.

"Wow," Emma said. "Looks like we're selling some dresses today." This was a better reaction than she'd hoped for. The public didn't care about family feuds. Why should anyone else? If there was any evidence that Mindy and Sophie should be listening to her, this was it.

Her driver, Gregory, glanced back over his shoulder.

"Duane wants us to wait until he can escort you to the door."

"I see him." Emma opened her own door and all hell broke loose.

The photographers ran out from behind the metal barricade and descended on her. They weren't asking questions, just setting off flashbulbs in her face, while the people in line shouted her name. *Emma! Emma!* Duane got to her at the same time Gregory did, and the two men shielded her, rushing her to the door. Gregory dropped back and Duane followed her inside.

"This is crazy." Emma neatened her hair and headed straight for the elevators. "I want us to sell dresses, but this seems a bit much."

Duane was breathing hard. "People love a budding romance."

Romance. Duane was capable of focusing on the positive. Why wasn't everyone else? "Thank you for dealing with all of that. No big media events for me for a while. Hopefully, things will go back to normal." She stepped onto the elevator.

Upstairs, the offices were exactly that—normal. It was like any other day. Lizzie was on the phone, writing something down. She gave Emma a quick wave. Down the hall, Mindy's office door was closed, her light off. She often arrived late, so that was no big surprise. Ever the workaholic, Sophie had her door open and her desk a verifiable mess, but she was on a call, her back turned away. Emma dropped her things in her own office and waited patiently for Sophie to finish.

"Knock, knock." Emma rapped on the door frame. "Do you have a minute?"

Sophie looked up. "Well, if it isn't Princess Emma." She waved the newspaper in the air, then handed it over. "Nora

Bradford's office called. They're pleased. In fact, they're agreeing to our terms for the new five-year license. I just need you to work out a few points on the financial side and get them to sign off on everything."

Emma was welling with pride. This was a big development. "Oh, fantastic. I'm happy to take things over from here."

"I have to say thank-you. Nora was so happy I think I convinced her to not only design my wedding gown, but the bridesmaids' dresses, as well."

"Oh, wow. That's amazing."

Sophie stuffed some papers into a folder. "It really is. I'd been unable to pull that off on my own."

"Nice job with the press, Ems." Mindy's voice came from the doorway. For once, it wasn't full of ire.

"I'm thinking we should get you to host a celebrity pop-up in the store," Sophie said to Emma.

"Great idea," Mindy said. "Ooh. Yes. Next week. I don't think we should wait."

"You want me to host a pop-up?" Emma had attended only one of these events, where Eden's asked a notable person in fashion or pop culture to curate a collection of favorite items from the store for an exclusive invite-only shopping night. Only Eden's biggest spenders would be in attendance.

"Yes, you. Like Mindy said, we should strike while the iron is hot," Sophie said.

"Uh. Okay. Fine." Emma officially no longer knew what was going on in her world.

"Speaking of hot, we need to talk about Daniel Stone," Mindy said. "A date so you can show off a Nora Bradford dress is one thing, but you cannot be dating him for real. He's going to chew you up and spit you out."

"She's right," Sophie added. "Plus, things will get really awkward once we start discussing strategy to squash Stone's New York."

Emma's stomach sank. Was Daniel right? "Did you guys get Charlotte Locke to drop Daniel as a client?"

"What? What happened?" Sophie asked.

"Daniel was dropped by Charlotte Locke. So now he's starting from scratch with looking for a location for Stone's. He thinks we were involved."

Sophie pursed her lips. "If we were going to interfere, that would have been the logical place to start."

"So you didn't do it?"

Sophie pressed her hand to her chest. "Not me. Mindy? Anything you need to tell us?"

Mindy shook her head. "No way. I'm fine with Stone's moving into New York. If they want to compete with us, let them try. At least it might make things interesting around here."

Emma rubbed her forehead, playing mental catch-up. She had no idea who had sabotaged Daniel, but it wasn't her or her sisters. That was all that mattered right now. "Sophie, is there any way you can do me a favor? Can you reach out to Charlotte and see if she'll reconsider? Just in the interest of good sportsmanship?"

"You want us to help him?" Sophie's voice was incredulous. "No way. Not a Stone."

"Just as a sign of goodwill. That we're willing to fight fair."

Sophie planted her elbow on the desk and her chin on her hand, looking over at Mindy. "Thoughts?"

"We don't want the papers thinking we sabotaged him. But we still need to talk about Emma and Daniel." Mindy cast a stern look at Emma. "Are you going to keep seeing him?"

"I'd like to."

Mindy closed her eyes and shook her head. The implication was that Emma couldn't possibly be any stupider. "You do realize there are other men in the city, right?"

"I know. But I like him. A lot. We get along great. We had an amazing night last night."

"Did you sleep with him?" Sophie asked, her voice reaching a superhigh pitch.

"Have you seen him?" Mindy interjected. "Of course she did." She turned to Emma, her eyebrows drawing together in concern. "Please tell me you at least had sex with him."

Heat flushed Emma's face. Memories of last night flooded her mind, every last one white-hot and unforgettable. "I did."

"Oh, boy," Sophie said, making it sound as if Emma was a lost cause.

"It was just one night." Except that it was so much more. She knew that the instant she'd tried to be dismissive. They'd made a connection last night, one she was inclined to fight for, even with outside forces trying to push them apart. "If you could just make that phone call, Sophie, that would be great. I'd like to at least be able to tell Daniel that we never set out to screw him over."

As soon as Emma left, Sophie called Jake to have him fix the Charlotte Locke situation. "Everything should be back to normal very soon," Sophie said to Mindy when she hung up the phone.

"I'm worried about Emma."

"Me, too." Sophie tapped her fingers on her desk. She did so whenever she was feeling uncertain. She said it helped her focus. Right now, it was making Mindy even more upset. Sophie's ten-carat Fred Leighton engagement ring glimmered, a reminder that Sophie had the world at her feet right now—her dream job and her dream guy, Jake Wheeler, a man as rich as he was handsome, funny and charming to boot. Come October, they would be married.

And now Emma was taking center stage with splashy headlines dubbing her Princess Emma, while she seemed to be pursuing the impossible—a romance with a member of the Stone family. Meanwhile, Mindy herself was in perpetual limbo, professionally and personally. She spent her days trying to perform her duties at Eden's while keeping her own company afloat. And as for her guy, Sam was more a pipe dream than a dream come true. Sam was not a man you pinned down. He was always the one doing the pinning.

Mindy crossed her legs, bobbing her foot so forcefully that her Christian Louboutin pump popped free from her heel and dangled on her toes. There was too much pent-up frustration coursing through her body right now. Her mind flew to Sam, the man who had no problem helping her unwind. She desperately wished he was in town. No matter his commitment to business, he always made himself available for a midday tryst. "I realize Emma has done some good things for the store, but I'm sure this Daniel Stone thing is going to blow up in our faces. She's so impressionable and you know she's caught up in the excitement of being in the papers. I can totally see her falling for the handsome guy and selling us down the river."

"I'm worried, too, but what are we supposed to do? We have to believe she's on our side."

"Why?"

"She has a fortune tied up in being on our side."

Mindy shook her head, unconvinced. "She knows what it's like to have nothing. That scares the crap out of me."

"Are you listening to yourself? She came from nothing.

She's not going to throw this away. And you agreed with her that there's no reason for us to interfere with Stone's. They think they can move in on our home turf and beat us at our game? Let them try."

"I worry she's too naive. Daniel will deceive her and we'll have to pick up the pieces of our business *and* her heart."

Sophie pressed her lips together. "I think she's doing her best in a tough situation. She likes him. She feels she can keep work and fun separate. We have to trust her. We can't tell a grown woman what to do with her personal life." On the desk, Sophie's cell phone buzzed with a text. She turned it over and a goofy smile crossed her lips. "Oh. Jake's here. We're going to look at a few possible wedding locations." She leaped from her chair and opened her office door.

Jake walked in, looking as ridiculously handsome as ever in a killer suit. He came bearing a gift, too—a fragrant bouquet of bright pink flowers. "Hello, gorgeous." He placed a soft kiss on Sophie's lips.

"Peonies. You shouldn't have."

"I wanted to."

"They're beautiful." Sophie beamed like the smitten bride-to-be. Mindy had always looked forward to the day her sister would get married, but as the oldest, she'd assumed it would be her turn first. "I'll get these to Lizzie so she can put them in some water."

Jake grinned as he watched Sophie walk away. "Hey, Mindy." He strolled over and leaned down, pecking her on the cheek.

"Thank you for straightening out the Charlotte Locke situation."

"I still don't know who got to her, but things are back to normal for Daniel Stone. You could have left him flapping in the wind, you know. Someone with pockets that deep will find a new agent."

"I know. But it's the principle of the thing. We don't want it to look like we'd play dirty pool." Only members of the Stone family employed such low-down, backhanded tactics. The Eden family remained far above the fray. "Plus, we're trying to keep Emma happy. She and Daniel Stone are quite the item."

Jake nodded. "So I saw in the tabloids."

Sophie reappeared in the doorway. "Ready?" she asked Jake.

"Always," he answered.

"See you later?" Sophie asked Mindy.

"Of course." She watched as her sister and Jake wandered down the hall. Sometimes, it looked like they were walking on air.

Mindy's stomach was an anxious tangle right now, and Jake's mention of not knowing who had prompted Charlotte Locke to make her move was eating at her. Why did she find herself wondering whether it might have been Sam? Probably because he was not an Eden, and if anyone was known for stooping to low levels, it was him. This certainly had the hallmark of a Sam move, but it didn't make sense. His aim had always been taking down Eden's, not propping it up. Her only course of action was asking him straight up if he had anything to do with it.

She crossed the hall to her office to grab her prized gray Birkin bag. She had to stop by the By Min-vitation Only office, and with Sophie away for a bit, this was her best window of opportunity. Plus, she preferred that her visits be unannounced. Her interim CEO, Matthew Hawkins, seemed to have a real talent for doing whatever he wanted to do, regardless of any precedent set by Mindy. The last time she'd dropped by, he had them completely reworking one of the production lines. She couldn't let Hawkins put his stamp on her business. It was still her ship to steer.

"I'm heading over to the BMO office," she said to Lizzie, breezing past her desk. She pressed the elevator button and studied their irreplaceable receptionist as she juggled a call, signed for a delivery and arranged Sophie's flowers. As soon as she hung up the phone, Mindy had to ask, "Lizzie, when was the last time you got a raise?"

She blew her spiky bangs from her forehead. "It's been more than a year. My last performance review was supposed to happen the day after your grandmother passed away. It sort of fell between the cracks."

Mindy was horrified. "You're kidding."

Lizzie shook her head. "It's totally understandable. We were all in shock when she died, and Sophie was more than a little busy then. It's not a big deal."

The elevator arrived and Mindy held it. "First thing I'm doing after I get back from lunch is fixing that. You're too valuable to be treated like that. I'm so sorry that happened."

Lizzie smiled, but it was more relief than happiness. "Thank you so much. I'll see you when you get back, Ms. Eden."

Out on the street, Mindy donned her Chloé sunglasses and greeted her driver, who opened the Escalade door for her. She pulled out her phone and looked at the time. If she was going to confront Sam, this was the time to do it, away from the microscope of Eden's. She pulled up his name on speed dial. He answered after only one ring.

"This is a sexy surprise," he said.

Damn him. Everything about him—his voice, his words—made her weak. He always knew how to make her smile, how to bring her to her knees. "Do you have a minute? I need to ask you a question."

"I always have a minute for you."

"Where are you, anyway?"

"London. I have a meeting, then I'm on to Frankfurt and Prague."

"Big deals in the works?"

"I hope so. I'm investing enough time and money in them. Just some real estate. A possible tech acquisition." Sam didn't worry about carving out a niche. It was more about having a nose for profit.

"Speaking of real estate, do you know Charlotte Locke?"

"Of course. I know all three Locke siblings."

"Do you know anything about Daniel Stone? Because Charlotte was his real estate agent until she dumped him early this morning, and everyone thinks Sophie and I were behind it."

"Are you calling to share this bit of news, or are you calling because you think I did it? Because I did."

Her hunch had been correct. Mindy blew out a breath and shook her head. "Great. This puts me in a terrible position. You know that, right?"

"I never want you in a bad position. I only want you in the best possible ones. Preferably ones with a good view." Everything Sam said somehow led back to sex. When she wasn't angry with him, she liked it quite a lot.

"I don't understand why you would do that. You're the one who's always scheming for the demise of Eden's. Why go after our competition?"

"Have you really not figured out what motivates me, Mindy?"

"Aside from money and sex, no. I haven't figured you out. At all."

"I want what you want. You told me you felt trapped by Eden's, so I thought of ways for you to get out. You told me you were committed to succeeding with your sisters, so I did what I had to do to take your competitor out of the way. It's very simple, Mindy. I just want you happy."

"I don't believe you. You always think about yourself first."

"It's not my job to convince you. But it's the truth."

Her mind was running a million miles a minute. Was that really true? Did he actually care? Most of the time, he seemed so blasé about everything, especially her. It wasn't like Mindy to make demands, but something told her it was time to put everything on the line. She did not want to keep sitting idly by, letting her heart be subject to the whims of a man she wanted badly. "If you want me happy, you won't go to Frankfurt or Prague."

"Where would you like me to go instead?"

"Come back to New York. And when you get here, come straight to my apartment. Even if it's the middle of the night." Her heart was pounding like a bass drum, not knowing how he would react.

"And how long am I staying?"

Mindy gnawed on her fingernail. It was time to ask for everything she wanted. "Until I figure out what in the world I should do with you."

Eight

Daniel was just as shocked by Charlotte Locke's second phone call that day as he'd been by the first.

"We're still full speed ahead with the lease negotiation?" He tapped a pen on the mahogany desk in his home office.

"Yes. I should know something in a few days. There are quite a few layers of bureaucracy with the property management company. And I'm sorry about the confusion earlier today. My other client is, well…" Charlotte hesitated, as if she felt the need to parse her words. "I'll say they're particular. And not easy to please. I hope you can understand that I had to show loyalty. There's a lot of family history mixed in. It makes everything more complicated."

If ever there was a situation Daniel could relate to, it was one where family history made everything hopelessly tricky. He only hoped that Emma wasn't somehow involved. "I'm glad to be back on track."

Daniel said goodbye to Charlotte and got off the call. He waited for some sense of relief to settle in, but it showed no signs of coming. He was just as torn up and conflicted as he'd felt that morning. His conversation with Emma was still fresh in his mind. She'd insisted that she didn't play games. That was a refreshing idea. If it proved to be true.

His phone rang again and he was dismayed to see it was his mother. Luckily, he hadn't had to tell her about losing his agent for a few hours. "Hello, Mum," he said.

"Hello. Have we got an update on finding a space?"

He hadn't told his mother about the lease, since she would only give him a hard time if he began negotiations and they failed. But it would be nice to deliver good news for once. "I do, actually. I just got off the phone with the agent. Lease negotiations are under way. We should know something next week if all goes well."

His mother let out a squeal on the other end of the line. "Wonderful. Simply wonderful. Which one is it? The last one you sent pictures of?"

"That's the one."

"Oh, good. It's perfect. Only five blocks from Eden's. I'd like to be able to go head-to-head with them."

"That's not why I chose it. The architecture of the building is lovely. It needs some work, but it has enough history that it will make sense for the store."

"Well, I'm glad we're moving forward. Now what's the latest with Nora Bradford?"

Daniel cleared his throat, his stomach uneasy. No matter what might happen between Emma and him, he wasn't sure he was cutthroat enough to steal a designer from Eden's. "I've been wondering if we shouldn't go in a different direction. Perhaps focus on some new up-and-coming designers. Someone fresh and exciting who we can get for a good price."

"I saw the papers, Daniel. Miriam in my office showed them to me. You're still seeing that woman and she's still wearing Nora Bradford dresses for all the world to see."

"Emma and I went to the opera. I told you we've developed a friendship. It's nothing more serious than that. Trust me, I know what I'm doing."

"I don't like wondering where my own son's loyalty lies."

Oh, how Daniel could have turned the tables on her. She'd shown so much more loyalty to William than she'd shown to him. She'd simply refused to believe the stories about William and Bea. "You don't have to worry."

Of course, Daniel was nothing but worried right now. He felt as though he was teetering atop a house of cards.

"I want Nora Bradford. If you won't get her, I will."

"I'll work on it, okay? I'm also going to send you information about some other choices. Designers that will still bring customers into the store. In the end, that's all that matters."

"Fine. I'll look at them, but I don't want to play around."

"Neither do I."

Daniel got off the phone and ran his hands through his hair. The sooner he could get his mother to retire, the happier he would be. The question was when? Not any time in the immediate future, he feared.

A knock came at the door and Jolly tore off, barking like crazy. Mandy and Buck were close behind. "Shush!" he snapped. Jolly quickly obeyed the order, although she looked as though she resented it greatly.

He took a peek through the hole in the door. There through the fish-eye was Emma. The universe did not make a habit of sending him happy things, and he knew he shouldn't be having this reaction, but there was a smile a mile wide across his face. He opened the door.

"Emma. This is…" He watched as she crouched down and Jolly hopped up and down on her stubby rear legs, tail wagging.

Emma looked up at him, her eyes like a beacon in the middle of a dark night. "What? A surprise?" She straightened back to standing.

"I hate to be so unoriginal, but yes."

"I came to tell you that neither of my sisters had anything to do with Charlotte dropping you. Have you heard from her? Sophie made a phone call to try and sort things out."

So he had been wrong. So very wrong. He reached for her arm, his pulse pounding. "She did call me. All has been fixed. I'm so sorry I assumed you or your sisters might be involved. I jumped ahead and I shouldn't have done that without more information. I hope you'll accept my apology."

"I do. Of course I do."

He was still so in awe of her generous nature. "Thank you."

"I have to be honest. I wasn't entirely certain that my sisters hadn't done it. I'm still learning to trust them. It's not easy. And this whole thing about the feud between our families? Is it just me or is it a little crazy?"

Daniel smiled. How they could be of the same mind so often, he didn't know. "I agree. In this day and age, it simply doesn't make sense."

"I guess that's what happens when there's so much money on the line, huh?"

"And pride. Don't forget about that."

Emma nodded in agreement. "So I think the question is, what do we want to do about it?"

"In terms of business?"

She shook her head. "No, Daniel. In terms of us. I like

you. I like you a lot. And it's more than just last night, although last night was spectacular…" Her voice trailed off and Daniel watched as color rose in her cheeks. She was thinking about him the same way he'd been thinking about her. He was sure of it.

He took her hand and pulled her closer. "Last night was unbelievable. I hate the idea that we'd only get to do those things once." He could feel his own body temperature spiking. Every nerve ending was crackling with electricity.

"I agree. I totally agree. Can we find a way to put everyone else's baggage off to the side? It doesn't seem fair to either of us."

It seemed an impossible task. Daniel's entire life revolved around his business and his family, but he knew the same was true for her. Maybe they could do this. He wanted to try. "Agreed." He realized there was another component to their short relationship that wasn't working, at least not for him. "I have a request of my own to make, though. Can we please stay away from the press?"

"The hubbub about Eden's starting to get to you?"

"Honestly, no. I know how hard it is to come by a boon like that. You find a means of creating excitement and you seize it."

"So then what is it?"

"What has been in the newspaper twice will quickly become five times, then ten. Then we'll reach the point where even taking the dogs across the street will become an ordeal. We'll be living in a fishbowl, and trust me, it's no way to live."

"That's what you were trying to tell me last night, before the opera, isn't it? Was this after your brother's accident?"

"It was." Daniel's nightmarish memories sprang to life again, of trying to outrun reporters and photographers on the streets in London while they shouted questions at him about

William and Bea. He didn't want to think about those things now, not when he had Emma here. "I don't want to talk about it. Not now. Not while I have the chance to kiss you."

He placed his hand on her hip and slid it around to the small of her back. He was prepared to pull her forward, but he didn't have to do a thing. Before he had the chance to think, Emma had dropped her handbag on the floor and threaded her hands into his hair. She kissed him eagerly, backing him up until his spine met the wall.

"Is it bad if I say I've been thinking about this non-stop since last night?" Emma yanked his shirt out of the waistband of his jeans. Her fingers scrambled to undo the buttons.

"Not at all. I'd be lying if I said I hadn't been thinking about the same exact thing." Jolly yipped at Daniel's feet. "Somebody's jealous."

Emma leaned into Daniel and kissed him. "Is there somewhere we can be alone?"

"Absolutely." He took her hand and led her down the hall to his bedroom, closing the door behind them.

She perched on the edge of his bed, bouncing once or twice. "Nice." She was a vision too sexy and beautiful to believe. In a silvery-gray silk blouse and form-fitting black skirt, she was sheer sophistication with an edge. Exactly what he liked.

She reached down and pulled a sleek black pump from her foot, placing it on the floor. She did the same with the other. How he enjoyed watching, and waiting to see what she did next.

"Well?" she asked, popping the top button of her blouse and trailing her fingers down the edge of the placket. Her knuckles grazed the top of her breast. A growl worked its way through his throat. He wouldn't have thought it possible, but he wanted her more now than he had last night.

He approached her and stood between her legs, letting her finish getting rid of his shirt. She smoothed her slender fingers across his abs. The admiration on her face was a great reward for all the hours he spent in the gym.

She looked up at him, seeming uncertain, as if she was waiting for him to tell her what she should do next. "You're thinking," he said. "Don't think too much. Just do what you want to." With a reassuring nod, he encouraged her.

She kissed his stomach, dragging her tongue across his skin as she unbuttoned his pants and pulled them down his legs. He dug his fingers into her silky hair, gently curling them into her scalp.

The tension in his hips was growing, the ache for her making him restless. He wanted to be in her hand, her mouth, inside her. As if she knew what he was thinking, she tugged his boxer briefs down and took his erection into her palm. She wrapped her fingers around him and he felt himself get harder with just that single touch. Then she lowered her head and took just the tip into her mouth, rolling her tongue over the smooth skin. Daniel's mind went blank. Rational thought was gone as she took him between her lips, sucking and licking. He touched her shoulders, the fabric of her blouse soft and sensuous against his hands, but what he really wanted was her naked. He leaned down and kissed the top of her head, urging her to let go of him.

She parted her lips with a pop and peered up at him. "Did I do something wrong?"

"You did everything right. Now I want to get you out of that blouse. And that skirt. And everything else."

Emma stood so Daniel could undress her. "Sure you don't want me to help?" she asked.

He shook his head, as he busied himself with unbuttoning her blouse. "No. This is the fun part."

"*This* is the fun part?"

He laughed. She really loved that sound. It even came out with a tinge of his wonderful accent. "It's the fun before the real fun."

He undid the final button and slipped his hands under the fabric and onto her shoulders. Just that one touch made her ready to give in. She dropped her head to one side as he dragged the sleeves down her arms. Then he dropped to his knees before her, and tugged her skirt and panties down in a single motion. Goose bumps dotted her skin when he looked up at her, and his blue eyes somehow darkened.

He smoothed both his hands over the upper part of her inner thighs, and with his fingertips, spread her wider. He lowered his head, and before Emma knew what was happening, he was pleasuring her with his tongue, rolling it in delicate circles over her apex. She clamped her eyes shut, quieting her mind and letting her body take over. It felt so good, and she willingly gave in to the heavenly sensations.

Once again her peak was barreling toward her. Perhaps it was just being with Daniel that had her so sensitized to his touch. Hot tension sizzled up her thighs. She took one hand and threaded her fingers into his hair, while with the other caressing her own breast through the lacy fabric of her bra, her nipple already tight from everything Daniel had aroused in her. The orgasm rolled over her slowly this time, growing in intensity, and Daniel followed the cues of her moans, changing his speed, playing her body like he was a master musician and she was his instrument.

Daniel sat back and looked up at her, grinning like he was pleased with himself. He had no idea. She dropped to her knees and kissed him with abandon, wrapping her fingers around his erection and stroking firmly.

"I need you now, Daniel. I'm not done yet."

He lunged for the bedside table drawer and pulled out a condom, quickly rolling it on. Emma kissed him again, hungrily, and urged him to his back, right there on the bedroom floor. She straddled his hips and lowered herself onto his body. Again, she was overwhelmed with how perfectly he filled her. How well they fitted together. She rocked back and forth as Daniel moved his hips. She liked how connected they were right now. It was like they were one.

Emma realized she still hadn't taken off her bra, so she reached back and unhooked it. Daniel's hands immediately went to her breasts, plucking at her nipples, bringing her back up to speed.

"I love this view of you," he said.

"I love *all* views of *you*."

He smiled and dragged one of his hands from her breast, down her midline, and settled his thumb against her apex. The man did not neglect this one part of a woman's body and she was so happy for it. He knew exactly how to make her feel her absolute best, sexy and adored all at the same time. She sat back a bit, resting her palms on his thighs and lifting her body higher with each pass. This gave Daniel an even more effective angle with his hand, and he brought her right to the brink.

His eyes were closed now, his mouth open, head to the side, breaths choppy. He was so handsome, she just had to watch, and the expressions on his face gave her enough clues to know when he was about to give way. She held tight, waiting for him, and when he began to squint, she let go. They both came at the same time, and that was an experience even better than she'd ever imagined. Colors and music swirled in her head while the ecstasy rushed through her body, every inch of it from her toes to the top of her skull. She pitched forward and collapsed on his chest, letting her full body weight rest on him.

He wrapped his arms around her and they kissed. And kissed again.

"That was unbelievable," she said.

"It was. Nothing like some floor sex to remind you you're alive." He took a playful nip of her neck.

"Very funny."

"But seriously. Let's get up into bed."

She climbed in under his fluffy duvet and he joined her after a quick trip to the bathroom. "I really am sorry I ever doubted you." His hand traced up and down her hip, soft and sensuous. He was so gentle when he wanted to be, and so commanding if that was his mood.

"It's okay, Daniel. Really." She cupped her fingers around his shoulder, feeling every hard contour. "There's a lot of bad blood between our families. It makes perfect sense that you would suspect my sisters. I just need you to know that it wouldn't be me."

A smile bloomed on his face and he rolled to his back. Emma smoothed her hand over his firm chest. "I do know that. My gut was telling me it couldn't have been you."

She cozied up next to him. It meant so much to have someone see the good in her. Many days, she felt invisible to the two people whose opinion she cared about most—Mindy and Sophie. But Daniel was stepping into the arena. She cared what he thought of her, and how he saw her. "I knew you were a good guy, Daniel. That's why I wanted so badly to be able to prove you wrong. I think it's time for us to turn our backs on this silly feud between Stone's and Eden's."

"Is there an opt-out form I missed?"

She playfully swatted his arm and leaned over to kiss him softly. "No. I'm just saying that we can say we won't play those sorts of games. We're the newest generation of both businesses, right? I want to find a way to get past the negativity. I don't see the point in it."

A deep crease formed between his eyes. He seemed leery at best. "Have any ideas how to do that?"

"We focus on the good. We focus on helping each other."

"You really think your sisters and my mother will be okay with that?"

"I'm not saying I'm going to come work for you or anything. But if it's the context of us dating, is anyone entitled to their opinion?" She quickly realized what she'd just said. "I'm sorry. I… I don't want to assume. This is only if you want to be dating."

He laughed quietly. "After the last few days, I don't want to be *not* dating you. Let's put it that way."

Her cheeks puffed up with a smile so fast it made her face hurt. "Good. Because I have an idea of how we can keep tearing down these walls."

"Tell me. Please."

"I have to host an evening shopping event at Eden's. I want you to be my date. Hold my hand and don't let me be nervous. Just like that night at Empire State."

"And you think your sisters will be okay with this?"

"As far as I'm concerned, they have to be. What choice do they have? Are they going to tell me I can't date you? A woman makes her own choices." There were more words about to spill out of her mouth. Did she have the nerve to say them? Something told her that she could make this leap with Daniel and it would pay off. She'd never felt this confident with a man before. It was exhilarating. "And I choose you."

From behind the door, there was a small bark. "Jolly," he said.

"Let her in."

"You sure? She might try to chase me out of bed."

Emma tossed back the comforter and tiptoed around the bed to the door, letting the dog in. She scooped up Jolly and climbed back under the covers next to Daniel. "It's time you two made some strides forward in your relationship."

Daniel narrowed his stare, full of skepticism. "I'm not going to talk about my feelings with her, if that's what you're suggesting."

Emma shook her head. She'd seen this advice on one of those reality shows about people who train difficult dogs. "It's a trust thing. She needs to see that I like you." She gave Jolly a scratch behind the ear, then leaned closer to Daniel and kissed his cheek.

"That's it?"

"It'll take time." She did it again. And again. Eventually, Jolly curled up between them and got comfortable.

"Now we have a dog between us, which is putting a serious damper on my plans for the rest of the night."

"The floor is always available. Or my place."

"Either one. Both. Whatever you want." His eyes scanned her face. How she could feel both exposed and comfortable at the same time, she wasn't sure.

"You're amazing. You know that, right?" he added.

She smiled and kissed him again, relishing the contentment that came when Daniel was being sweet. "You're the one who's amazing. I'm just being me."

Nine

Five days. Emma and Daniel had enjoyed five magnificent days together. No drama. No problems. Not even any gossip in the tabloids. Just five days of spending every nonworking moment together. A lot of their time had been spent in bed, but they'd done other things, like go out to dinner, and of course, they took many long walks in the park.

They switched back and forth between her place and his, but they spent each night together. Jolly still refused to give them much privacy, but she was being more consistently sweet to Daniel. Progress. Emma made a point of kissing him every time the dog was around. It seemed to be helping.

Emma had to wonder if things could really be this simple between her and Daniel. Had it been as easy as deciding they didn't care to participate in the feud? For now, it seemed to be working.

A big test was awaiting them, though. The night of Emma's pop-up at Eden's had arrived. She was about to burst. Not out of excitement. Out of the worst-ever case of nerves.

Daniel squeezed her hand in the back of the car on the way to Eden's. "You're trembling. Is everything okay?"

She nodded. He did have a way of calming her. "I'll be fine once I get going. I'm just nervous about talking to customers and sounding knowledgeable and like I know what I'm doing. My sisters have put all of this ridiculous pressure on me because of the Princess Emma stuff in the papers, which I guess is my fault. They're sure we'll have a huge turnout tonight. I just want it to go well."

Emma looked down at Daniel's hand wrapped around hers. How she loved his hands. He might spend his days pounding away at his laptop, but there was something so deeply masculine about them. There was nothing better than having his hand at her back, especially when she felt unsure of herself.

"Are you sure you aren't nervous about me being there? About me finally meeting your sisters?"

She didn't want to feel anything less than excited by the prospect of Daniel meeting Mindy and Sophie. Tonight was supposed to be a step forward, for both her relationship with Daniel and the future of the family feud she hoped they could eventually end. But she never really knew how Mindy and Sophie would react to any given situation. They could be cordial, but aloof. She certainly couldn't see them being overly welcoming, even though Emma had told them ahead of time that Daniel was coming.

"I'm excited for them to meet you. I think they'll see things differently after they do. And at least they'll get to see what all the hubbub is about."

"Hubbub?"

A flash of embarrassed warmth hit her cheeks. "Well, you know. Sisters talk. Especially about men." She'd only had a taste of those sisterly moments with Mindy and Sophie, but she'd greatly enjoyed every one.

He nodded. "I see. I only had a brother. And there was far more punching than talking."

Emma disliked that tone in his voice when he talked about William. She could feel his pain when it bubbled to the surface. "You never confided in each other?"

"We did at times. Say if one of us was in a battle of wills with our mother. But most of the time, it was nothing but strong-willed, head-butting sibling rivalry."

"Do you think that had anything to do with him pursuing your fiancée?" Emma still couldn't imagine the betrayal he must have felt at that.

Daniel was quiet and looked out the window.

"You don't have to answer that if you don't want to," she added, feeling desperate. Why she'd decided to dive into this topic, she didn't know, other than she only wanted more of him. She wanted to know everything. "I'm just trying to understand what happened. A betrayal like that is hard to comprehend."

He turned back to her. "It's good for me to talk about it. I don't think I can boil it down to one thing. I'm sure that part of it was jealousy over me getting engaged first. Our mother certainly expected him to be married first. She was merciless about it at the Christmas before the accident. She said he was behind and he'd better catch up. But that's how she got us to be better at everything. She'd pit us against each other."

Emma shook her head. "I'll never understand why anyone would torment someone with such an arbitrary idea, especially a loved one. Her own son, no less. My mother's head is full of rules that have no basis in anything other than the way she sees the world. That's why I never dated.

She had me so convinced that all men were terrible and it wasn't worth risking your heart for one."

"Certainly that had to do with your father."

"I'm sure. I mean, she'd gone and fallen in love with her sister's husband." The rest of the story sat perched on Emma's lips. She and Daniel had grown so close and she wanted to keep going. But that meant he had to know that part of what he believed to be true was in fact a lie. "I need to tell you something."

"Anything. Anything at all."

His voice was so measured and calm, she knew she could tell him. "You should know that I didn't grow up in France. Mom and I lived in a small house in New Jersey. She was paid by my father to stay quiet. And so she did. For my entire life until the day my grandmother's will was read."

"She never told you?"

Emma shook her head. "She told me my father was a deadbeat and that he'd walked away from her before I was born. It's not entirely a lie, but it's also not the truth. He was living right here in Manhattan. I could have had a relationship with him."

"Where did the story about France come from?"

"Sophie and Mindy made it up. It was already bad enough that people found out our father had cheated. So they made up that story to make it seem like the family had known about me all along, and that I'd been taken care of. They were worried the truth would hurt the store and the Eden name."

"I'm so sorry. That's dreadful."

"I went along with it because it made me feel less like a fish out of water. People were quick to accept me. I should have told you earlier, but there was never a good time. And things have moved so fast between us. I didn't want to ruin it. I hope I haven't ruined it now."

Daniel put his finger under her chin and raised it so he could look right at her. His eyes were so caring and warm. "You couldn't ruin it if you tried. It's funny, but we're so alike. We both love our families deeply, but we've suffered because of it."

Emma was so wrapped up in the combination of his face and his words that it was hard to think straight. She loved the moments when they were on the same wavelength. They made her feel nothing less than incredibly lucky that she'd met Daniel at all, let alone had the chance to be with him. "You're so right."

The car pulled up in front of Eden's. A small cluster of photographers was waiting for them outside. She turned to Daniel just as her driver was about to open the door. "You sure you want to do this? We can drive around to another side of the store and bypass this altogether." They'd discussed this back at her apartment and he was adamant that they should make one more exception on the night of her pop-up.

"This is where they're expecting you. You're the star tonight. This isn't about me."

"I still want to know that you're comfortable with it. I know this is difficult."

"As long as you're on my arm, I'm bulletproof."

Emma felt a verifiable squeeze right in the center of her chest. She leaned closer and kissed him on the lips. When she pulled back, she found words circling in her head. Three little words to be exact—*I love you*. But it was too early for that, wasn't it?

Or was it?

She didn't have time to think, let alone say it. Gregory opened the door, and the sounds of the city, traffic and car horns, along with the shouts of the photographers, rushed in.

Emma! Emma!

Over here!

Daniel!

She'd never get used to the idea that the press cared about her, although they clearly did, or at least they liked her with Daniel. Perhaps it was just a sign that people loved controversy, but Emma wanted to put an end to that. There wasn't anything salacious about what she and Daniel were doing—hot, yes, but not wrong. So they'd decided to thumb their noses at some decades-old history. What was the big deal?

She and Daniel came to a stop in the middle of the sidewalk and obligingly posed for a few photographs. He looked as handsome as ever, in a charcoal-gray suit with white shirt and no tie. She loved the little peek of his chest. It left her eager for what might come after the event, when they could go back to their building and be alone. She'd worn a fun navy-blue cocktail dress with a full, knee-length skirt and a low neckline, which Daniel said he liked best on her. In a nod to Sophie, she'd gone with crimson-red Blahniks. It felt like an adventuresome choice.

Emma squeezed Daniel's hand in a steady pattern as the flashbulbs went off. She wanted to remind him that she was thankful for his willingness to endure the public eye. This was hard for him. She knew that. She leaned in and pressed a kiss to his cheek. The flashes went off twice as fast, and she sensed how easily this could turn into a feeding frenzy. Daniel tugged on her arm, and into the revolving door they went, out of one pressure cooker and into the safety of Eden's.

Waiters were on hand with champagne. "Hello, Ms.

Stewart," one of them said. "Mr. Stone." They'd clearly been briefed by staff on who would be attending.

"Hi, guys," Emma said. She'd never get used to deferential treatment, however much it made her feel special.

"Where to?" Daniel asked.

"Straight up to the second floor."

They stepped onto the escalator together and began their ascent. As they rode higher, Daniel's shoulders tightened. Was he that uncomfortable to be at Eden's?

"Is this your first time in the store?"

"Actually, it's my third or fourth time since I've been in New York."

"Oh, really? Spying on us?"

Daniel shook his head and they stepped off the escalator onto the floor that carried the various lines of women's casual wear. The entire department had been condensed into half the normal space, and the open area sectioned off with swaths of sheer silvery fabric hanging from the ceiling, like a glamorous circus tent. Reginald, Eden's creative director, was busy putting the final touches on the displays with his team. Shoppers would be arriving any moment.

"I was merely checking out the competition," Daniel said. "Can you blame me?"

"And? What do you think?"

"It's great."

"The whole thing?" She knew there were parts of the store that fell short. She, Mindy and Sophie were working on it. "You can be honest with me. You won't hurt my feelings."

"Your menswear department is lacking. It needs to be brought into this decade at the very least."

From out of the corner of her eye, Emma spotted Mindy and Sophie walking toward the pop-up shop from the back of the store, where the bank of executive elevators was.

"I want to hear more about that at some point. If you're willing to share."

"I'm more than happy to tell you where you're missing the mark. As for ways to improve what you have, I might need some convincing." He smiled slyly, telling her he was only playing with her.

She leaned in and kissed him. "Something tells me I can find a meaningful form of persuasion."

"I can't wait for that."

"For now, I need you to meet my sisters. I hope you're ready." *I hope I'm ready.*

Again, he took her hand, and that was enough to ward off her trepidation. Mindy and Sophie walked toward them in unison, Mindy showing off her enviable legs in a short emerald-green dress, and Sophie showing hers in a sexy black above-the-knee sheath. They both smiled, their teeth gleaming white, their long red tresses bouncing past their shoulders. They were an intimidating sight, nothing but brute beauty and confidence, but Emma found herself clinging to optimism. Maybe this would all be okay. Maybe today, Sophie and Mindy would welcome with open arms the man Emma cared about so much.

"Finally, we meet Daniel Stone." Mindy was the first to greet him with a handshake, her voice only lightly tinged with skepticism. "I'm Mindy. This is my other sister, Sophie."

Despite Mindy's wary edge, Emma was pleased that she had introduced Sophie as her *other* sister. Maybe she was finally starting to see Emma as a true part of the family.

"Daniel," Sophie said. "It's nice to meet you. Welcome to Eden's. I hope you have good intentions in visiting the store. And in dating Emma."

Emma nearly choked. This was not Sophie's usual disposition. Not even close.

"Sophie, be nice," Mindy muttered, casting a look over her shoulder. Invited members of the press were filing in.

"I'm sorry, but these are legitimate concerns, and Gram taught me to take any threat to the survival of the store quite seriously." Sophie was now artfully mumbling out of the side of her mouth, as a few reporters strolled past and seemed quite interested in the scene unfolding. "Knowing who his mother is, I'm guessing Daniel has been put on the spot far worse than that."

"Oh, I have," he said.

A reporter waved at Sophie and she politely returned the gesture. Then she sucked in a deep breath, forced a smile and looked Daniel square in the face. "More than anything, I need to know that you're going to be kind to Emma. Because if you aren't, if you're playing at some other game, Mr. Stone, there will be problems."

"That's really what this is about," Mindy said, patting Daniel on the shoulder. "If you hurt her, you'll have three angry women on your hands, not just one. Trust me, no man wants to go up against the Eden sisters."

Emma swallowed hard. She wasn't sure she'd breathed once during that exchange. It was a tad horrifying to watch her sisters launch thinly veiled threats at Daniel. They were behaving like glamorous mobsters. But after having felt left out so many times, it felt good to know they had her back. It didn't matter to them that Daniel was handsome and wealthy and powerful. They would take on a man who didn't treat her well.

The crowd had grown significantly as the first wave of shoppers and members of the media arrived.

Mindy patted Daniel on the shoulder again. "You don't have anything to worry about. If you're a decent guy, everything will be fine."

Daniel turned, looking down at Emma. "Then I truly

don't have a thing to worry about. I'm more than a decent guy."

"That's the spirit," Mindy said. "Now if you'll excuse me, I have a boyfriend to track down and shoppers to schmooze with."

"Yes. We should be spending time with our customers," Sophie said. A large gathering of their guests had assembled inside the pop-up. "It's your night, Emma. You lead the way."

And to think Emma had worried about chatting with shoppers. That was going to be a piece of cake compared to what they'd just experienced with Sophie and Mindy. "Time to get to work." She tugged on Daniel's hand. "You coming?"

"For you? Of course."

Daniel downed another glass of champagne to take the edge off. He wasn't surprised that Sophie and Mindy had questioned his intentions. It was more a shock that they'd done it so fiercely. Still, he would've been lying if he'd said he didn't enjoy watching Emma, Mindy and Sophie in action. He kept to the periphery of the pop-up, observing the interactions of the shoppers and the three sisters. They mingled with customers, they chatted and encouraged purchases. One thing was certain—everyone seemed to be thoroughly enjoying themselves. They couldn't snatch up items fast enough. This had been a brilliant idea on Sophie Eden's part. One he might have to steal and adapt for Stone's.

Of course, Emma was the main source of his attention, but he did enjoy observing the dynamic between the sisters. Despite the confrontational approach she'd taken in meeting him, Sophie was the peacemaker, a bridge between Emma and Mindy. Mindy was the watchful eye, the hawk who made sure everyone was okay.

Emma brought unbridled enthusiasm to the table, especially when speaking with their customers. She certainly didn't act like a woman with billions in the bank. She was warm and gracious, and they were all suitably charmed. Born a Brit and having lived in England his entire life, Daniel was well aware of the allure of royalty. You got swept up in it, even when you knew deep down that notions of one family being more important than another were nonsense. He despised the press, but they'd been so right about one thing—Emma came off exactly like a princess, graceful and warm and utterly breathtaking. He only hoped the tabloids didn't decide to tear her off her pedestal. In his experience, they loved to love you, until they decided that ripping you to pieces would sell papers.

Daniel's phone buzzed in his pocket. Emma was preoccupied with a woman and her male companion, so he distanced himself from the crowd as well as he could, though there were people everywhere at this point. He wound his way past the other guests, down one of the wide white marble-floored aisles between departments. He didn't want to be that person—the one with his nose in his phone while standing in the midst of a crowd.

He had a text from Charlotte Locke.

Lease terms accepted. Sign papers Monday 2:00?

Daniel read the message twice. This was good news. To the Daniel of a few weeks ago, the one who'd never laid eyes on Emma Stewart, this was a fantastic development. Everything he'd worked for, everything his mother wanted. The space was perfect. It was time to make his move.

But he found his thumb hovering over the keyboard, unable to type a reply to Charlotte. Why was he hesitating? What was holding him back? He heard Emma's exuberant laugh over the din of the crowd and turned to see her smiling and tossing back her hair. No matter what they'd agreed to, it still seemed unlikely that this wouldn't come between them. Eden's was her whole life, a tether to the one thing she'd said she'd always wanted to be a part of—a family.

If he did things right, the existence of Stone's New York would threaten that. And if he failed, the amount of his family's money down the drain would be devastating. It would give his mother more than enough reason to put off her retirement another five or ten years. Daniel didn't think he could live through that. He couldn't deal with her constantly breathing down his neck. It was too much part and parcel of living in the shadow of William.

He and Emma were going to have to talk about this, in depth, before he could sign the lease. He wasn't going to pull the rug out from under her that way. It had nothing to do with Mindy's and Sophie's threats and everything to do with wanting to treat Emma with the respect and courtesy she deserved. He had to let her know that he was about to do something that would turn up the heat. He just had to find the right time, and fast. Perhaps a getaway was in order. Something romantic, if only for a few nights. Today was Thursday. They could leave Saturday and return Monday morning in time for him to do what his job and his family required.

He tapped out his response. Great news. I'll be there Monday. Thx.

He further distanced himself from the crowd and sent his mother a text. Lease is a go. Signing Monday. More soon. That should be enough to keep her happy. At least for a little while.

He stuffed his phone back into his pocket as a towering man wearing an all-black ensemble of suit, shirt and tie approached.

The man held out his hand. "You must be Daniel Stone. Sam Blackwell."

Daniel was stuck for a moment. According to Emma, Sam had played a role in convincing Charlotte Locke to drop him. "Ah, yes. Mr. Blackwell."

"Please. Call me Sam. Our girlfriends are sisters."

"That's not our only connection now, is it?"

Sam's dark eyes lit up. "I know. I'm sorry about that. All's fair in love and war, right?"

"It's not really my style, but we all have our methods." Daniel's upbringing demanded at least a veneer of politeness, but he could see why Sam rubbed so many people the wrong way.

"I can tell you the sisters feel that way. These three take their business very seriously. Does make me wonder what exactly your end game is. The business rivalry has to be a bone of contention. Or are you just getting your fun while you can?"

Daniel bristled at the suggestion, even when he understood exactly why Sam was asking the question. "Emma and I enjoy each other's company greatly. That's all we care to focus on."

"I think Mindy's still figuring her out. They've definitely butted heads a few times."

Daniel felt a deep need to defend Emma, even when he knew she was strong and didn't need rescuing. What was there to figure out about Emma? She was open and loyal, resilient and big-hearted. "Emma's had a difficult life. She wants to claim her role at Eden's and in that family. It hasn't been easy for her to find a place between two sisters who've known each other their entire lives. She's been forced to play a lot of catch-up."

"Emma has been more than compensated for any hardships. She's a billionaire. She'll never worry about money ever again. She grew up in a French chateau with lavender fields and a private chef. It's not like she's suffered."

"That's not entirely accurate." Daniel was surprised at the force with which those words left his mouth, but it was worse than inaccurate. It was an outright lie.

"Oh, really? Are you saying I don't know the whole story?"

Daniel wasn't about to share a single detail with Sam. He had no way of knowing if Mindy chose to share the same things with Sam that Emma had shared with him. "Perhaps you should ask Mindy about that." Daniel shouldn't have let himself get angry, but his protective side had taken over. He was beginning to despise the way Emma's family had treated her.

"That's all you're going to say?"

Daniel cleared his throat. He saw no reason to answer. "You'll have to excuse me. I'm going to check on Emma and see if she needs anything."

"Yeah. Not a bad idea. I should see if Mindy will let us get out of here any time soon."

Daniel took long strides to get to Emma. She glanced over at him as he approached and their gazes connected, her brown eyes as inviting as ever. Would there ever come a time when he wouldn't feel that zap of electricity between them? Emma grinned, then returned her attention to the customer she'd been speaking with. "Thank you so much for coming this evening. I hope your daughter enjoys the perfume."

The woman left and Daniel took his chance, smoothing his hand across Emma's back and tugging her against his side. "How much longer?"

Emma surveyed the remaining customers. "An hour?

Maybe less if people make their purchases." She looked up into Daniel's eyes. "Why? Are you bored?"

"No. I'm just eager to get you home."

An effortless smile crossed her sumptuous lips. "Home? Does that mean my place or yours?"

"Whichever place makes you most comfortable."

"What did you have in mind? TV? A walk with the dogs?" She ran her slender fingers along the edge of his jacket lapel.

How he loved it when she was being playful. Everything felt more exciting. He leaned down and settled his mouth on her ear, inhaling her sweet perfume. "I want to get you out of that dress. I want to leave you gasping my name."

"I could use some unwinding."

He kissed the side of her neck. "Don't worry. I'm on it."

Daniel stayed by Emma's side as she chatted with the remaining big-roller customers, every minute an exercise in patience. He wanted her so badly right now it felt as if the seconds were ticking by impossibly slowly. Every subtle brush of their skin, every knowing glance was torture.

He tried to stem the tide by staying in the moment, but that only brought to mind what his family would say if they could see him, spending time on enemy territory and feeling, quite honestly, like an invading army. Ever since the night of the opera, he'd thought once or twice that perhaps his parents would change their minds about the Edens once they'd met Emma. But after meeting Mindy and Sophie, he knew it was going to take a lot. They were just as entrenched and invested in the hatred as his side. What a waste.

"I need to check something in my office," Emma said, when it was finally time to go. Eden's employees were cleaning up and restocking the pop-up, which would remain open the next day for the general public. Mindy and

Sam had long since left. Sophie was making her way to the escalator with her fiancé, Jake.

Daniel hoped her sisters had taken the time to tell her she'd done a good job or congratulated her for what had clearly been a successful evening. "Tonight was incredible. Well done," he said, when they reached Emma's office upstairs.

She walked behind her desk and hit a key on her computer keyboard. "Do you think it went well?"

"Are you kidding? It was unbelievable. It's a fabulous concept, but I think you did a particularly bang-up job. Your sisters should be more appreciative."

"So you noticed. They didn't say a thing to me."

"I wondered about that. I don't like it. Not one bit."

She shrugged her lovely shoulders and scanned her computer screen. She shook her head.

"Everything okay?" he asked.

"Yeah. I was just looking for an email. I get them on my phone, but sometimes my work messages don't always make it through."

"Hopefully, it'll be there tomorrow morning." He didn't want either of them to have to think about work anymore. They'd both had enough of that for tonight.

"It better be. I've been waiting for it for a while."

Emma was holding something back from him. He could hear it in her voice. These were the moments when Daniel most sensed the ways the businesses could come between them. "I meant what I said. You did a fantastic job and your sisters should tell you so."

"They work hard, too. We're all working our butts off. I'm sure I need to be better about telling them the same things." She waved it off. "It's fine. I don't need constant reassurance. I'm confident that I did a good job tonight."

Once again, Daniel felt a need to protect Emma from

the forces around her—the store, which had her hemmed into obligations, and her sisters, who weren't appreciative enough. He knew exactly what it was like to be in that situation. "You did better than good. You were a star. It's no accident that you've garnered so much media attention. The press can't take their eyes off you." He found his pulse pounding in his ears. This was what she did to him when they were alone. "*I* can't take my eyes off you." *I love you* nearly escaped his lips. He sucked it back in, his head reeling. It had come out of nowhere, a force of nature, like a summer storm that swooped in and leveled everything in its path.

"You are too sweet to me, Daniel Stone. If you aren't careful, the world's going to find out that you're not the cutthroat businessman everyone thinks you are."

"I vote that we keep that secret between you and me."

"As long as you make it worth my while, I can keep my mouth shut."

Another wave of heat rolled over him. They might not make it home. "I like it better when your mouth is open." He claimed her lips with his, giving in to every sexy thought Emma had provoked in him this evening. His hand slid to her hip, his fingers curling into the soft flesh of her bottom as their tongues wound together, hot and wet. Emma leaned back against her desk and he gathered the skirt of her dress, dragging the fabric up until his hand found the silky skin of her inner thigh.

She bowed into him, moaning against his mouth. "Yes, Daniel. I want you." She reared her head back, eyes frantically scanning his face. "The door."

Daniel needed no further instruction, crossing the room in two long strides while he cast aside his jacket. With a click of the lock and a flick of the light switch, they had the privacy he'd been so desperate for all night. "Don't move."

He rushed back behind her desk where she was sitting, legs dangling off the edge. "Tell me you'll leave the shoes on."

The large window behind him glowed with light from the city. She grinned. "I'll leave the shoes on."

He unbuttoned his trousers and let them fall to the floor. His pelvis was buzzing with electricity. Just like every other time with Emma, he was so hard so fast that he wondered how there was enough blood to circulate through the rest of his body. He needed her so badly he ached. He unbuttoned his shirt while Emma reached down and took his erection in her hand. Her fingers were cool against his overheated skin.

"Mmm," she hummed, resting her chin on his bare chest and stroking firmly.

"You're going to drive me mad." He could hardly keep his eyes open. Her touch felt so impossibly good.

"Then take off my dress." She scooted forward and hopped off the desk, pulling her hair to one side and presenting her back to him.

"I plan to." He urged her closer to the window, dragging down the zipper.

"Daniel. Somebody will see."

He slipped her dress from her shoulders and pushed it to the floor. Emma covered her breasts with her hands, looking back at him, questioning.

"Don't you trust me?" he asked. "No one can see us up here. We're all alone."

She nodded. "I do trust you. Implicitly."

"Good." He pressed the full length of his body against hers, his chest to her back. He gathered her hair and kissed her neck, her shoulder, then down the channel of her spine as he tugged her silky panties from her legs.

Emma stepped out of them, now wearing only those sexy heels, leaving her beautiful naked form before him.

She turned and he gripped her rib cage with both hands, his thumbs pushing up on her full breasts. He lowered his head and sucked her nipple into his mouth, swirling his tongue. He loved the way she reacted to him, the way the pink bud gathered and tightened. He loved how sweet she tasted. He couldn't get enough of the soft moans that escaped her lips. All he could think about was being inside her. All he wanted was to make her writhe with pleasure.

He let go of her nipple, giving it a few quick flicks with his tongue before turning her toward the window. He could see their reflections in the glass, could see the anticipation on her face, her mouth slightly slack and her eyes dark with desire. She liked that this felt a little dangerous, and that made him even more turned on. He reached down for his trousers and pulled a condom from his pocket. He'd brought one in case they ended up at her apartment. He hadn't taken the time to consider they might not make it home. He rolled it on and positioned himself behind her, urging her to bend forward, and pulling her hips closer. Emma reached out and placed one hand against the window, gasping as he slipped his fingers between her legs to make sure she was ready for him.

"You're so wet," he muttered.

"That's because I want you."

He drove inside her, his eyes clamping shut as he gave up all rational thought and sank into the magnificent warmth of her body. He reached around with both hands and caressed her breasts, teasing her nipples with his fingertips. The noises that left her lips told him he was doing everything right, but he knew he could do better, so he slid one hand down her belly and found her apex, spreading her folds with his fingers and rubbing in determined circles.

"That feels so good," she muttered, moving against him.

He opened his eyes, unable to decide what to look at

first—the creamy skin of her bottom as he drove his hips into her, or the reflection of her full breast in his hand, her mouth gaping and her eyes closed. Once again she was a feast for the senses. Everything he ever wanted in the most tempting package.

The tension was wrapping tight around his hips, the muscles of his groin aching for release. Emma's breaths were shorter now, the moans deeper and almost continuous. Her muscles were starting to tighten around his length, pulsing stronger with every thrust. He knew she was close. He only hoped he could hang on until she came. He was right at his peak, carnal forces threatening to push him over the edge, when Emma called out, "Daniel."

He grinned for an instant before the orgasm slammed into him, enveloping his body in so much warmth and bliss he could hardly support his own weight. Emma pulsed around him, prolonging the pleasure. This had been so worth waiting for. Emma straightened and turned, pressing her chest against his and kissing him hard.

"That was a surprise," she panted.

He smiled with the best sense of pride imaginable. "I want to keep you on your toes."

"Or in heels." She kissed him again, her lips soft and tender against his. "You're unbelievable. You put up with my sisters and my work event and then you seduce me in my office. I'm trying to think of a time a guy has ever been so generous with me, and I know for a fact that it's never happened."

Again, he was proud of these feelings he was able to build in her. Probably because he knew very well by now that this was a two-way street. She was uncovering so many things in him that he'd long thought were gone— hope and happiness and, quite possibly, love.

"Let's go away," he blurted.

"What? Where?" Her face was full of surprise.

"Bermuda. I have a beautiful house there, right on the beach. It's quiet and warm, and most importantly, we can be alone. It's only a two and a half hour flight from New York. I'll charter a plane."

"Really?" There was that sound he adored—Emma's bubbly excitement.

"Yes, really. I know that neither of us can get away for long. Two nights? This weekend?"

"I suppose Mindy and Sophie would be okay with that."

"You work hard, I work hard, and I want us to be able to spend some time together away from things like the press and your sisters. It'll be just the two of us. We can swim and take naps and make love all afternoon." Simply saying the words ushered in the most beautiful fantasy he could imagine. He might not ever want to come back.

"You sure you'll be able to pull the trip together so quickly?"

He had to show up on Monday afternoon to sign the lease. He had to have the chance to break the news to her before he made that one crucial move. "If you can make it work, I will make it happen."

She drew a finger down the center of his chest. "I'll make it work."

Ten

The morning after Emma's pop-up, Mindy opened the door of her apartment to pick up her daily copy of the newspaper. It didn't stay in her hands for long. She read the headline and it promptly slipped from her fingers and fell to the floor. "Oh no." The ugly words practically screamed at her from the front page.

Eden Family Hid Heiress: Princess Emma a dirty secret.

Her heart started pounding, her mind racing. The press had found out. They knew what Mindy and Sophie had wanted so badly to keep hidden, Sophie especially. This was enough to take down more than the store. It could destroy the entire Eden family. The affair that produced Emma would be all anyone would ever remember about their father. The fact that he and Gram had paid Emma's mother hush money for years? That would be their shared legacy. Not Eden's department store. The story would always be tainted by sex and money, the only things anyone seemed interested in these days, anyway.

Mindy bent down and picked up the paper, closing her front door and forcing herself to read. She knew every bit of the tale, and most of what the story said was true, although there was certainly conjecture. She didn't know for sure that Emma had ever lived in a mouse-infested house. Mindy supposed she should have asked. She should have spent some time getting to know Emma a bit better. For the moment, she had to figure out where the press had gotten this story in the first place. How had anyone known to dig? Emma was supposed to be the media's princess. Now she'd been reduced to a dirty secret.

Mindy marched into the kitchen and quickly made coffee. Today was going to require a lot of caffeine. This story could very well mean that her own business could be ruined. Gone in the blink of an eye. In the age of tabloid firing squads and internet witch hunts, she knew exactly how damaging a story like this could be.

Coffee made, she rushed back to her room, two mugs in hand. Sam was sound asleep in her bed. She set down his cup and, holding the other, sat on the edge of the mattress. She hoped her movements might wake him, but Sam slept like the dead. Maybe it was the sex. He did have a real talent for wearing her out. And he always wanted it. Always.

She drew in a deep breath and studied him. With his eyes closed in peaceful slumber, he was remarkably nice to look at. Long and muscled, with touchable, jet-black hair that held a slight wave. He was her beautiful problem. She wanted him more than almost anything, but time and again, he'd proved how adept he was at disrupting everything. If he wanted to make trouble, he did. With aplomb. Something about that newspaper article was telling her that he'd done it again.

"Sam. Wake up."

He rolled to his back and his bracing blue eyes popped

open. This was already a good sign. He was usually impossible to rouse without the promise of sex. "Let me guess. There's a story in the newspaper."

She smacked his arm. "So you are behind this." She tossed the publication across the bed and it landed in the center of his chest.

He lifted his head and ruffled the pages, squinting to read. "Oh, wow. That's quite a headline, isn't it?"

"It's horrible. How am I going to explain to Sophie and Emma that you were behind this?" Mindy didn't fear her sisters' ire so much, as she'd been trying to convince them that Sam wasn't a bad guy. This would do more than set back her efforts. It might be the final nail in the coffin. It might be confirmation that she needed to cut Sam loose. For real this time. No second chances. Or third or fourth.

"So don't explain it. It's not your job to prevent this from happening. Sophie and Emma bear just as much of the brunt of this secret as you do. Just tell them there must be a leak in the store."

"There isn't a leak. Sophie will never believe that. She trusts everyone implicitly. Besides, no one knows about this. Just me, Sophie and Emma."

"That's not entirely true. You told me some of it and I heard the rest from Daniel Stone."

A strange mix of shock and vindication rushed through Mindy's veins. She and Sophie had been so sure that Emma's involvement with Daniel would backfire on them all. Sure, Sam had fired the shots, but it appeared that Daniel had given him ammunition. "I can't believe she told him. She was under strict orders to keep her mouth shut."

"Orders? Is Emma not an equal partner? It seems to me like you and Sophie spend an awful lot of time telling her what to do." Sam rolled to his side and propped his head up with his hand. His splendid naked chest was on full display, the sheet dipping temptingly low, beneath the trail of hair under his belly button. For a moment, Mindy forgot what they were talking about.

"She doesn't always know what she's doing. She's new to this whole world. She knows nothing about running a business. If we don't guide her, it'll be a disaster."

"I'm not sure that's true, either. She seems to have a natural affinity for enticing the press. That's not an easy thing to accomplish."

Mindy crossed her arms. "Will you stop reminding me how amazing Princess Emma is? Whose side are you on, anyway?"

A cocky smile crossed his lips. "I knew you were jealous. That's why I leaked the story. I thought it would make you happy to have her knocked down a few pegs. I can guarantee there will be no more princess stories. It'll all be about poor, sad Emma."

Was Mindy jealous? Was that her problem? Was that why she'd been so hesitant to trust Emma and her choices? "She's still my sister. I don't want her dragged through the mud. Nor do I want my entire family and our name becoming a disgrace."

"You sure you feel that way about her?"

Mindy couldn't have said that for certain in January, when Emma was new at the store and new to the family, back when Mindy and Sophie were still reeling from learning they had to share the four-billion-dollar inheritance three ways rather than two. But seeing her on the cover of the paper this morning, all Mindy could think was how this was going to shake Emma's confidence, just when she should be on top of the world. It wasn't fair. Mindy knew what it was like to be on top and have things go upside down. That's what had happened to her when she'd been forced by their grandmother's will to work for Eden's and set aside her own company.

"Part of me wants to protect her. Of course. Sophie and I both feel that way. We're still getting to know her, though. It's a ridiculous situation."

"One you can thank your father and grandmother for."

Mindy pressed her lips together tightly. "I know. They messed up. Big time." Any realizations she was coming to right now about Emma were quickly being overshadowed by the larger looming problem. Sam needed to go. She was sleeping with a man who made a lot of assumptions and was in no way scared to act on impulse. He kept thinking he would make her happy, and all he did was make her situation worse.

"Sam. I don't think we can be together anymore. I don't think it's going to work. Sophie doesn't like you. Emma might never speak to you after she finds out what you did. And I can't help it. My family is important to me. They might drive me crazy sometimes, but I can't alienate them for a guy."

"Is that what I am to you? Just some guy?" Sam tore back the sheet and climbed out of bed. "I put multiple business trips on hold so I could be with you. I went to that silly event at the store, and listened to you come home every night and complain about your sisters. Do you not understand that I don't do that for just anyone?"

"I'm supposed to be impressed that you'd be willing to hang around for two weeks?" Mindy could never have a future with Sam if he was going to treat her like an inconvenience. The things she'd asked of him were perfectly reasonable. She wouldn't be told any different. She stood and tightened the tie on her robe. "You need to go."

"You tell me to go and I'm not coming back. Ever."

Mindy absorbed every word he said, knowing exactly

how determined he would be to keep his promise. There would be no going back. She bit on her lower lip before mustering the strength to push him all the way out of her life. "I know. My sisters need me more than I need you." Even she was surprised by how harsh her words were.

"Have it your way, Min. Good luck with your dysfunctional family."

She walked out of the room, waiting until she got into the hall to let the tears stream down her face. Mindy didn't cry often, but this hurt. Sam Blackwell had an inexplicable hold on her heart. He was going to be impossible to forget.

Daniel woke to the sound of Emma's cell phone ringing in the other room.

"Emma. Darling." Half-awake, he pressed a kiss to her bare shoulder. "Your phone's ringing. Shall I get it for you?"

She pried one eye open. "What time is it?"

"A bit after seven."

"It has to be Mindy. She's the only one who calls me this early." The ringing stopped. "Oh, good. She gave up." Emma scooted closer to Daniel and nudged his chest with her nose. "I'm not ready to get out of this bed."

From the foot of the bed, Jolly yipped. "Someone's not happy we're snuggling without her." Daniel was about to evict Jolly from the room when Emma's phone rang again.

"Ugh." She threw back the covers and grabbed a T-shirt of Daniel's, which was slung over the back of a chair. "I'd better see what she wants."

Daniel took this as his cue that their day had begun. He climbed out of bed and dressed in another of his T-shirts and a pair of track pants. The instant he stepped out into the hall, he heard the distress in Emma's voice.

"Oh my God. Are you serious?"

Daniel rushed to her side, placing his hand at the small of her back. When Emma turned to him, her forehead was wrinkled with worry, her eyes tormented.

"What's wrong?" he whispered.

"Okay. I'll be in as soon as I can," she said into the phone. "We'll meet at nine?" She nodded. "Yes. Bye." Emma pressed the end button and pinched the bridge of her nose with two fingers, her eyes clamped shut.

"What's going on?" he asked.

"There's a story in the paper this morning."

"About last night?"

She shook her head. All color had drained from her face. "About me. My past. Everything my father and grandmother did to hide me from the world. The lies. The money. Everything."

Daniel's stomach lurched. If he was responsible for this, he'd never forgive himself. "Do they know who fed this information to the press?"

"That was actually Sophie calling, not Mindy. She said Mindy confessed it was Sam. He's had it in his head for months that if he messes things up for the store, it'll get Mindy out from under the obligation."

Daniel had to come clean. He couldn't drop this bomb on her in Bermuda. He already had a big enough one waiting. He hated having any at all. "I talked to Sam last night. I slipped about New Jersey. I don't think he knew."

Emma's eyes became as large as saucers. "No. Daniel. Mindy and Sophie can't know that I told you anything. I never should have said anything. I was supposed to keep it a secret."

"He was trying to say that it didn't matter that you've had a hard life, because you inherited so much money. I had to defend you. I'm so sorry."

Emma walked away from him, pacing the living room,

bare feet padding across the hardwood floors. "Sophie has been saying for months that she doesn't trust Sam. I can't believe Mindy said anything. She's always harping on me to keep my mouth closed." She pressed the home button on her phone and the screen came to life. "I have to see what the paper says. It's just going to make me upset, but I need to know."

Daniel reached out for her arm. "Do you want me to read it first?"

"If I'm going to be an embarrassment to the store and my family, I'd like to know exactly what I'm up against." She scanned the screen.

Daniel read over her shoulder. *That headline*. A dirty secret. A sob left Emma's lips and she sank down onto the couch.

"Let me see." He took her phone from her. Despite everything, the first photo brought a smile to his face—of him and Emma in front of Eden's last night. She was radiant as always, but the affection that had grown between them was plain as day. As fake as the tabloids could be, that picture was real. His mother was going to see that picture. She would know he hadn't shared the full scope of his relationship with Emma.

"Well?" she asked.

"It's everything you told me. But you didn't tell me that your mom home-schooled you to keep you away from people. You didn't tell me that she hid the money from you."

Emma buried her head in her hands. "Oh, God. That's in there?"

He put his arm around her shoulders, desperately wanting to comfort her. "This is why I hate the press."

"I want to hate them, but they're telling the truth."

"I'm still sorry this happened. And I'm sorry your

mother lied to you all those years. No one should ever be treated like that."

She lifted her head, staring off into space. "I don't blame her. I don't. Of course she didn't trust my dad. He bribed her to keep their child a secret. So that's why she hid the money. She was so worried that he would stop paying and somehow manage to ruin her if she dared to speak out."

No wonder Emma had once had so little trust of men. Her father, the most important man in her life, had acted so horribly toward her and her mother. "I'm so sorry. But you have an amazing life now and a wonderful job and more than enough money to live off." *And there's us.*

Emma looked at him, shaking her head. "My amazing life is never going to be the same. Every time I go to a party or work or even just walk through the lobby of our building, everyone's going to know the smallest details about the worst things that have ever happened to me. They'll know that I don't really come from wealth and power and influence. I'm just a girl who grew up with nothing and stumbled into an inheritance. I hardly know what I'm doing at work most of the time. Sophie and Mindy know it, too."

Daniel pulled her into his arms. He'd never had to worry about the things she had, and he wished he could take her pain away. "If anyone thinks any less of you because of this, they don't deserve to know you or have you in their life. There are plenty of people who don't care about the money or the designer dresses or the fancy parties. You don't have anything to live up to, Emma. You're perfect just the way you are."

"You didn't notice me at all until I was wearing a ten-thousand-dollar designer dress and so much makeup I could hardly hold my head up."

Daniel wasn't making anything better. She wasn't wrong on that point. "And I feel like an ass for it. I know I apologized then, but I'll apologize again. I'm sorry. I came to New York for business and nothing else." Just thinking about his state of mind when he'd arrived made him realize just how much Emma had changed him. He didn't recognize the man he was about to describe. "I was trying to find a way to live up to my brother's memory, and now I'm sitting here telling you that trying to live up to anyone else's expectations is pointless. I understand that you don't want to disappoint your family, but you can't forget that in a lot of ways, your family let you down."

A tear leaked out of her eye, followed by another. She tried to blink them away, and she looked up at the ceiling as if she could hold it all in. "I just want to find a place where I belong. A place where I can be me."

He wrapped her up in his arms, rocking her back and forth and pressing his lips to the top of her head. "You can belong with me. I always want you to just be you."

"No fancy designer gowns?"

He kissed her temple. "I'm fine with whatever you want to wear. Or not wear. Totally up to you."

She laughed quietly, resting her head on his shoulder. "Thank you. That makes me feel a little better. I don't know what I would do without you."

"I feel the same way." With those words, Daniel knew that this trip to Bermuda tomorrow had to be more than just the sharing of a few uncomfortable truths. He couldn't let Emma slip away. He loved her. "I'd say the timing of our trip tomorrow couldn't be any better."

"Yes. I need a vacation now more than anything." She sat back and wiped the tears from her eyes. "Thank you for talking me off the ledge. Thank you for everything."

"Of course."

"Unfortunately, I need to get into the office so my sisters and I can have it out."

"You can blame it all on me."

"Something tells me that's not how it went down."

"Everything will be okay. It will all work out. I promise." He knew he had no business making assurances like that, but he would have done anything to make it all okay.

She sighed heavily, her shoulders dropping. "Maybe. Hopefully. What are you going to do today?"

"Work. Run an errand or two."

"Stay out of trouble."

"I will." He smiled, hoping it wasn't considered trouble to go shopping for a ring.

Emma called Duane and let him know ahead of time that she was on her way to Eden's. He got rid of any photographers by having Lizzie feed them a fake tip on her way into the building, stopping and whispering that she'd seen Emma down the block at Starbucks.

Emma was immensely thankful to be able to walk quietly into the store. Her life plan from now on involved zero red carpets, minimal publicity and avoiding attention whenever possible. Princess Emma was dead now. The media had killed her.

Up on the executive floor, Emma stepped off the elevator and Lizzie bolted out of her seat, but Emma already knew what she was going to say.

"I know. I know. They're waiting for me in Sophie's office. Did I get a call from anyone at Nora Bradford's?"

"No. Not this morning."

"Shoot." Emma was tired of stressing about this. Eden's had agreed to Nora's conditions. Why was the paperwork delayed?

"I'll put them right through if they call." Lizzie stepped out from behind her desk. "I'm so sorry about the tabloid story."

"Thank you. Me, too."

"If it helps at all, it doesn't make me think less of you. In fact, it makes me like you more. You could have told everyone from the beginning. It would have been fine."

"It doesn't make you look at Eden's differently? My grandmother? My father?"

Lizzie grimaced. "Yes. I suppose that left a bad taste behind."

Tell me about it. "I'd better go speak with my sisters." Emma hustled into her office, set down her bag and checked her email. Nothing there from Nora Bradford's team. As soon as she was done with Mindy and Sophie, she was going to have to make another call.

She pushed back from her desk and strode into Sophie's office. "I'm here. Whether you like it or not."

She was so over everything right now. All she could think about was getting to Bermuda with Daniel. She so looked forward to forty-eight hours of getting lost in him and shutting out everything else.

"That's a terrible attitude," Mindy said. "But I get it."

"It was Sam. Just so you know," Sophie said by way of interjection. "He fed the story to one of the reporters at the pop-up last night."

"Nice. Real nice," Mindy said. "You're just a ray of sunshine lately, aren't you?"

"She deserves to know the truth. Your boyfriend is a jerk. He's the reason we're in this predicament."

"He's no longer my boyfriend, so you can stop referring to him that way. I kicked him out of my apartment this morning." Mindy chewed on her thumbnail.

"For good?" Sophie asked.

"It's over. Done. I don't want to talk about it."

Emma and Sophie looked at each other, silently agreeing that this was a good thing. Mindy didn't seem too overly broken up over it. Emma took a seat. "I don't think it's all Sam's fault. Daniel slipped and said something about France not being the whole story."

"So you *both* told your boyfriends the story that we promised to keep a secret between the three of us." Sophie crossed her arms and sat back in her chair, shaking her head. "This makes our whole family look so bad. Both Dad and Gram would be horrified to know that this came out."

Emma dug her nails into the heels of her hands. Looking bad was one thing, living an entire life on the receiving end of a family secret was another. Neither Mindy nor Sophie seemed to grasp that. "I don't know how they would feel about it. I never really knew either of them." This was still very much the elephant in the room whenever their dad or grandmother came up in conversation. Emma had been robbed of those relationships.

"Why are you spending so much time worrying about what Dad and Gram would think?" Mindy shot a look at Sophie. "They're both dead. Why don't you spend some time thinking about how Emma must feel? She's the real victim in this."

Sophie sat frozen. So did Emma. How could anyone have ever known that Mindy would rush to her defense?

"It still reflects badly on the family and on the store. It makes us all look horrible," Sophie said.

"Of course it does. But we can't stuff the genie back in the bottle. We can't undo what's been done. We have to figure out what our next step is. We have to move on." Mindy sucked in a deep breath, as if she was getting ready to unleash even more. Perhaps her breakup with Sam had put her that much more on edge. "Emma, you should know that neither Sophie nor I was close to our father. Whatever you're thinking you lost out on with him, it didn't exist. He wasn't around for us, and when he was, we were nothing but a disappointment to him. Especially me."

"Mindy…" Sophie started.

"No. Soph. It's true. Dad thought girls should only be sweet and quiet, and I was neither of those things. I was serious. I was focused on school and career. He hated every guy I ever dated. He was always needling me to look for good husband material. Whatever that's supposed to mean. Clearly, I haven't learned much." Mindy shook her head and closed her eyes for a moment. For the first time, Emma saw real pain on her face.

"He definitely had dysfunctional attitudes about women," Sophie said. "Gram always fought him on it, but I think it was his way of rebelling against a mother who was just larger than life."

"He showed our mom zero respect." Mindy said, turning to Emma. "He showed your mother no respect. He simply wasn't a nice person. So you didn't miss out on anything where he's concerned. I promise you that. I loved him, but only because he's my dad. It has nothing to do with any true affection for the man."

"I… I had no idea," Emma said, unsure if this made her feel better or simply made her sad. It certainly made her heart go out to both Sophie and Mindy.

"If you think about it, Gram gave him his just deserts when she wrote you into the will, Emma," Mindy continued. "She'd made a promise to keep his secret, but she also made sure that at least part of it came out when she died. But the three of us never promised to be the steward of those lies. And we made a mistake when we tried to do that. It's even worse that we made up something else."

"I felt like it was the best thing for the store," Sophie said. "We were already struggling, and the second Gram died, all signs were pointing to the store going right along with her."

"I know, and I backed you up at the time, but it was a mistake. We covered up Emma's history, and she's our sister. We can't treat each other like this. We have to be a unified front or we're going to fail. If we care at all about honoring Gram's legacy, we need to own up to everything that came out and focus on the store. If we can't be real with people, I have to wonder what we're doing."

Emma wasn't sure she'd taken a breath at all in the last several minutes. Not only because she'd just been handed a lot of information to unpack, but because she'd had no idea Mindy felt this way about any of it.

"I thought you hated the store," Sophie said to Mindy.

"I don't hate it. I love the store. I just don't love the timing. If this had happened five years from now, I might have been more settled with my own business. But that's not how things happened. And the reality of it is that if it had gone on for five more years, that would have meant all that time Emma would have been living without what was rightly hers."

"I hadn't thought about that," Sophie said.

"The thing I figured out this morning, as I was looking at the man I stupidly fell for, is that you two are the only people in the world I can really trust," Mindy said. "That's the way it should be. We're sisters. There is no stronger bond than that. And we have to stick together. No more secrets. We keep everything out in the open."

"How does this strike you, Emma?" Sophie asked. "It's your story that's all over the papers today. You have to decide which version of your history you want out there. Even if it damages the Eden name, you're still the one who has to live with it."

Several weeks ago, Emma might have been tempted to

go on clinging to the lie. It made life easier. But it wasn't right. She was who she was, and as bizarre a journey as her life had been thus far, as much as it had caused her pain, she wouldn't have traded it for anything. "Keeping secrets is too much work. I don't see any point in hiding any of it anymore."

It was quiet in Sophie's office for a good minute or more, all three of them nodding and thinking. "Okay, then," Sophie said. "That's settled. If anyone asks, we say it's all true."

"Did you really live in a house infested with mice?" Mindy asked. "I'm so sorry if that's the case."

"We did have a few mice for a few weeks one winter. It wasn't a big deal. The neighbor brought her cat over and that was the end of that." Emma disliked that look of pity on her sisters' faces, but she was going to have to live with that. She'd likely get that treatment a lot in the coming weeks as people got used to the real version of her past.

"So what's the story with Daniel?" Sophie asked. "I mean, I know you guys are having fun, and he's super-hot, but how long can you continue seeing the guy who still wants to open a store that will become our biggest competitor?"

"I don't know. He hasn't said anything about Stone's New York. I know he's still looking at spaces, but nothing has been decided. Maybe nothing will come of it."

"I don't want to be the bearer of bad tidings, and I'm not the person to dole out relationship advice, but in my experience, a man will always pick business first. Always. And with his family in the mix? It doesn't matter how much he likes you. He will eventually hurt you," Mindy said.

"That's the only reason we said anything to him last night," Sophie said. "We don't want you to get hurt."

Emma didn't have much of a stubborn streak, but she

was certainly a willful person. She wasn't willing to give up on her and Daniel yet. She wanted to see if they could beat the odds. Find a way to make it work. "We're going away tomorrow morning. To Bermuda. For the weekend."

"When did this happen?" Mindy leaned forward and rested her elbows on her knees, seeming more than a little interested.

"Last night. After the pop-up. He said he wanted to get away from the spotlight and the businesses and spend some time together, just the two of us."

"Interesting." Mindy sat back, crossed her legs and bobbed her foot.

"What does that mean?" Emma asked.

Mindy shrugged. "It means it's interesting. Either he's being sweet or he's up to something."

"Like what?" Emma asked.

"Could be lots of things," Sophie said. "The history between our two families says that anything is possible."

Emma refused to believe she was going to end up being a cautionary tale. "I trust him. I'm not worried about it." That much was true, even when there was a voice in her head telling her that if Stone's New York happened, the odds were stacked against them. Could they truly ignore the rivalry between the stores? She didn't know the answer to that. It was like she and Daniel were inching forward in the dark, trying to find answers, while there were so many obstacles lurking in the shadows. She just had to believe in him. That was the only thing that made any sense. He wouldn't have asked her to get away with him if he didn't truly care about her.

"I need to get some work done." Mindy got up from her chair.

"Yeah, me, too." Emma followed her to the door.

"Hey, Emma," Sophie said. "I noticed that we still don't

have the Nora Bradford agreement. We have to have it by the end of business today. I want to be able to walk into the office on Monday morning knowing that we have our most important designer signed for the next five years."

Emma swallowed hard, but held her head high like the entirely confident businesswoman she was still trying so hard to be. "Don't worry. You'll have it." She ducked out of Sophie's office and went in the opposite direction from Mindy, muttering to herself, "Even if I have to go over to Nora Bradford's office and camp out in the lobby all day long."

Hours later, Emma finally got the returned call she'd been waiting for. Nora Bradford's head of operations was on the phone.

"I'm so glad you called," Emma said, relief washing over her. "I don't know if there's a holdup in your legal department or what, but we still don't have the signed paperwork on the new licensing agreement. The old one expires on Monday and I think we'd all sleep a lot easier if we had everything in hand today. If we can get it done before five, I can arrange the first payment."

"Emma, I'm sorry, but we've had a change of direction. We aren't going to be signing the agreement."

"New direction? What in the world are you talking about? I thought this was a done deal."

"It was a done deal. But Nora got an offer from a different retailer a few days ago and it was just too good to pass up. They really rolled out the red carpet for us."

Emma was about to make a crack about how she had walked the red carpet for Nora Bradford, twice, but she felt like she was going to be sick. "Different retailer?"

"Yes. I'm afraid so. We're going to be working with Stone's."

Eleven

Emma couldn't believe the name she'd just heard. "I'm sorry. Did you say Stone's?"

"Yes. They're expanding into New York and the terms were too generous to pass up. Plus, it was probably time to make a change. Nora appreciates everything Eden's has done for her and we all loved your grandmother, but her passing was the end of an era."

An era I never knew. "Is there anything we can do to change your mind?"

"No. I'm sorry. I believe Stone's is making the announcement this afternoon. But please tell your sister that Nora is still willing to design her wedding dress."

"Oh. Okay." Like Sophie would want to wear a dress of betrayal on her wedding day. Emma hung up the phone, but she didn't have even a second to think before Sophie was yelling for her.

"Emma! Mindy! Get in here!"

Emma straightened her skirt, her mind a jumble of horrifying thoughts—the worst of which was that there was a very good chance her boyfriend had deceived her. She rushed into the hall. Mindy appeared, and they arrived at Sophie's door at the same time.

"What's going on?" Mindy asked.

Sophie held her finger to her lips and pointed at the flat screen TV on the wall, tuned to the twenty-four-hour business news channel. Mindy and Emma stepped inside and the three sisters stood shoulder to shoulder as the anchor, a woman who looked to be straight off the runway, spoke. "If you're just tuning in, we have major news in the retail world today. It appears that the rumors about Stone's department stores of London moving into New York are true. They seem poised to take down the legendary Eden's, which has been a fixture in Manhattan since the 1980s. They have also announced an exclusive licensing agreement with fashion designer Nora Bradford, known for her red carpet gowns and wedding dresses."

"Holy crap." Mindy pointed at the screen, then turned to Sophie and Emma. "What the hell, you two? I thought Nora Bradford was a done deal."

"I just got off the phone with them," Emma said. "I don't know what Stone's offered them, but it was enough to make them jump ship."

"When were you planning to tell us this?" Sophie's voice was so thin with distress it sounded like it might shatter.

"I told you. I just got off the phone with them."

"No. I mean when were you going to tell us that your boyfriend was screwing us over?"

Daniel. Everything she'd refused to believe was coming true. "I had no idea. He didn't say a thing. We tried very hard not to talk about business."

Sophie shook her head, tears streaming down her face.

"Everything Gram worked so hard for. Down the tubes. It's all my fault. I'm CEO."

Emma didn't want to think about whose fault this really was. Had Daniel really betrayed her like this? She didn't want to believe it could be true. She pulled Sophie into a hug, and Mindy quickly had her arms around both of them. The three bowed their heads.

"We'll get through this," Mindy said. "We'll sign another designer even better than Nora. Or we'll start doing more private label clothing. Or both. Or we really ramp up our plans for the women's shoe department. There's always a pivot we can make. Always. And as for Stone's, maybe this is good. Maybe this is the kick in the butt we need."

The anchor was talking again, and the sisters watched. "Reporters spoke to Margaret Stone outside of her London home just minutes ago."

"Ms. Stone, what does this mean for your son's relationship with Emma Stewart, CFO of Eden's department store?" The reporter jammed the microphone in Daniel's mother's face.

Margaret Stone laughed as if Emma were a bug on someone's shoe. "Daniel had his fun, but I knew it was over when he let me know last night that our lease was ready to sign. It was never going to last. She's an Eden, for God's sake."

"Have you talked to your son?"

She smiled. "I have. He couldn't be more pleased with today's developments."

Emma truly felt as though she'd been punched in the stomach. She staggered back until she had no choice but to plop down on the couch. She stared up at her sisters in utter disbelief. Everything they'd warned her of was coming true. She really was naive when it came to business, and apparently even more so when it came to love. "I don't know what to say. I'm just floored. By all of this. Am I an idiot for not wanting to believe that Daniel could do this?"

Mindy looked at her with the pity she'd come to hate so much. "No. Honey. You're not an idiot. But this is what we worried would happen. When we said we didn't want you to get hurt, we meant it."

Sophie sat on one side of Emma and Mindy sat on the other. "What are you going to do?" Sophie asked.

"I have to go talk to him. Right?"

"Yes. You have to confront him and take your chance to tell him to his face he's a jerk," Mindy said. "Otherwise you'll always regret it."

The thought of saying that to Daniel made it feel like her heart might crumble to dust. "So that's it, then."

Sophie patted her hand. "It'll be okay. I promise. You have Mindy and me. We're here for you. Even if it's the middle of the night and you need us to bring you ice cream."

"Or something stronger," Mindy added. "And Sophie's right. We have to stick together or we won't succeed. I don't think any of us has any interest in failing."

"So you don't blame me for this?" Emma asked.

Mindy stood and reached for Emma's hand to help her up. "We've all made mistakes that hurt Eden's. Especially me. We just need to know that Daniel Stone is done. No more trusting him. We know you like him, but that ship has sailed."

Emma walked to her office, numb. Seeing her desk and her office window brought to the forefront the memory of the pop-up night and all that had happened between them here. It had been more than passionate abandon. Daniel had seemed like he had such an incurable weakness for her. It had been an intoxicating thought. For the woman who'd worried whether she could be the kind who could turn Daniel Stone's head, she'd proved she not only could be, but that she was. And that had all happened after he knew the truth of her past. He didn't care that she'd come from nothing. He cared about the Emma of here and now.

Or so she had been foolish enough to think. She'd thought they could set aside business and bad blood between families. She should have been smart enough to realize those were the two things that drove Daniel and her the most. There was no compromise to be made, however badly she'd wanted to think there was.

She glanced at her phone and for an instant considered calling Daniel to tell him she was coming over. But no, he didn't deserve a heads-up. He deserved to be blindsided. Just as he'd done to her. She sent her driver a text, shut off her phone and rushed downstairs to go home.

Daniel stared at the television in disbelief. He would have missed this nightmare if a friend hadn't sent him a text congratulating him on signing the lease for Stone's New York. His mother. She just couldn't wait. She simply couldn't trust him. He watched as reporters caught up to her outside his family's London home. He cringed at her first answer, but the second truly made him want to retch. *He'd had his fun? It was never going to last?*

He had to get Emma on the phone right away, but he also needed to speak to his mother and get her to shut up and stop talking to the press. Every time she opened her mouth, she made it so much worse for him. As soon as Emma found out, she'd think the absolute worst of him. He sent her a text to buy himself ten or fifteen minutes.

I have some news I want you to hear from me. Can I come by your office?

He waited but got no response from Emma. His stomach rolled with the uncertainty. Did she already know? He didn't have time to worry further.

His mother answered the call without so much as a hello. "I guess you've seen the news."

Daniel wanted to scream. "What in bloody hell are you doing? You announce the lease before it's signed? You go to Nora Bradford behind my back?"

"You gave me no choice. You were never going to sign Nora. You were trying to curry favor with that woman you're seeing."

"Emma, Mother. Her name is Emma. And you don't know that to be true." Except that it was true. Emma was precisely the reason he'd tried to get out of enticing Nora Bradford to leave Eden's for Stone's. "This is a big problem for me. You've put me in a terrible situation. I can't talk about it now. I need to speak to Emma before she finds out what you did. But you and I need to have a conversation about my role in the company. I won't have you undermining me like this."

"We can talk about it on Monday after the lease is signed. How about dinner?"

"What?"

"I was thinking I should pop over for this momentous occasion."

"No. I do not need your supervision. I have everything in hand."

"So you don't want to see me?"

Daniel grumbled over the phone. How she loved to lay on the maternal guilt. "I'm only saying that you don't need to make the trip. It seems silly."

"Okay, well, I'll be there, silly or not. I want to see you and the new store. I know you're upset, but you'll see that this was everything we needed to do. You'll meet another woman. There are always more women."

Not like Emma. Daniel heard a knock at his door. The dogs ran right over and started barking. "I have to go." He ended the call and tossed his phone onto the table, rushing for the door. "Enough. Sit," he said to the dogs, which immediately piped down and followed instructions. Even Jolly.

Daniel opened the door. The sight of Emma nearly mowed him over. She was breathtaking beautiful, but there were ragged edges to her now. She knew what had happened. He could see it on her face. He felt the disappointment radiating off her. "Please. Come in. I tried to reach you."

"You did?" The dogs were begging for her attention, and Emma crouched down to pet them all.

"I sent you a text."

"I didn't get it. I turned off my phone after I saw the atrocity on TV. What in the hell happened, Daniel? Have you been lying to me this whole time?" She stood and smoothed her hair back, a deep crease forming between her eyes.

"No. Of course not. The Nora Bradford thing was my mother's doing."

"But did you know she was pursuing her?"

He couldn't lie. He couldn't hide anything else from her. "I did."

Her shoulders dropped in disappointment. "How long? How long have you known?"

"Since before I met you. I was sent to talk to her that night at Empire State. But we hardly knew each other then, and I knew you were tied to Eden's. I couldn't say anything. Plus, it was just an idea then." He reached for her, but she turned away. The disappointment that registered in his body was so deep it went down to the soles of his feet.

"An idea to hurt Eden's."

"Yes. My mother's idea, mind you. Not mine."

"Does it really matter? The net effect is the same. This is a huge hit for our store. Sophie and Mindy are so upset."

"Please tell me they aren't angry with you. I'll talk to them if you need me to. I'll tell them you knew nothing about it."

"Actually, they're being nothing but supportive. They resisted the temptation to remind me that they'd told me exactly what you were going to do. They told me you would ultimately betray me and I didn't believe them. That's how stupid I am."

Daniel ran his hands through his hair. "I didn't betray you, Emma. I swear I didn't know about actually signing Nora Bradford, and my plan was to tell you about the lease this weekend during our trip."

"So you were planning to sweep me off my feet with your private plane and your getaway, just so you could tell me that I'd better prepare myself for the fight of my life? How did you think that was going to go over, exactly? Did you think I was going to congratulate you? Be excited?"

He drew in a deep breath. He'd really done a horrible job of thinking this through. "I guess I hoped you might handle it like every other conflicted moment we've had together. I hoped that you'd decide that you liked me more than you hated my business."

"This is more than your business. It's your family, too. You stand by them, and I have no choice but to do the same with mine."

He refused to believe that this had to be an impasse. They had to find some way through this. "So you'd rather be loyal to Sophie and Mindy than me? Even after everything the Eden family has done to you? For your entire life?"

"What choice do I have? These are ties that I don't want broken. They're ties I've wanted my entire life. Plus, you cannot preach to me about family loyalty. I know that comes first for you. Even after your mother has treated you terribly. Even after your brother betrayed you. You cling to the Stone name exactly like I'm clinging to my own."

"I don't want to cling to my name if it means I'm going to lose you."

"I heard what your mother said about me. Do you think there's ever any coming back from that? If I'm going to be with a man, I need his family to accept me. To welcome me. I've spent my entire life feeling lost. Searching for the place where I would belong. I'm not going back to that. We would never overcome it."

"What are you saying, Emma?" He held his breath. It would mean moving forward, and he didn't want to do that without her. He didn't just sense that his heart was about to break, he felt it.

Tears were streaming down her face. "I'm saying that there's no future for us, Daniel. And if there's no future, we're done. I can't merely have fun with you. I can't sleep with you and pretend like it doesn't mean something. Aside from maybe that first night at Empire State, I don't think we were ever only having fun. There has always been a serious undercurrent between us."

"That's part of what I loved so much. We fell into sync. So quickly."

"And that's what makes this ridiculously hard." She looked down at her hands as she wrung them together. When she looked back up at him with those warm brown eyes he adored, he knew she was about to deliver a crushing blow. "Because the truth is that I love you. I know it sounds silly, but it's the truth. I've had those words waiting on my lips many times and I never had the nerve to say them."

Everything in his body went impossibly still. "So you're saying them now?"

"I don't want to regret this any more than I already do. Our cards should all be out on the table. Let's leave nothing unsaid."

Daniel swallowed back the emotion of the moment. He dreaded telling her his true feelings, only because he knew she no longer cared to return them.

"Goodbye, Daniel. I really do wish you the best." She kissed him on the cheek and reached for the door. "But you should know that my sisters and I are committed to kicking your family's ass."

Twelve

After a weekend without Emma, Daniel's greatest fear was that the emptiness would be permanent this time. At least it was familiar. He'd felt exactly like this after William died and Bea left. His father had given himself over to the despair, while his mother defied it, tightening her chokehold on the family business and Daniel. Meanwhile, loneliness, guilt and doubt brewed a toxic cocktail in Daniel's head.

He hadn't been doing that much better when he arrived in New York, but at least he had a charge to distract him—opening Stone's New York. This morning, he'd get back on course and sign the lease. The trouble was, his heart didn't want to go there. His heart was too hung up on Emma.

He rolled over in bed and that made the dogs stir. He waited for a growl from Jolly, but it never came. Instead, she crept toward him until her nose nudged his hand for a pet. He pulled her nearer and ruffled her ears. This one remaining piece of his brother's life was so special to him, but it had taken Emma to bring them closer. That was what she did—she made everything and everyone around her better.

She'd helped him see the joy and beauty around him, perhaps because she'd spent so much of her life going without. She'd shaken him awake, turned him from a man who ignored a stranger's conversation in the elevator to someone who could face things he'd been avoiding for years, like the press. She showed him that the world wasn't a dismal place. It could be so beautiful, especially with her in it.

His chest ached just thinking about her. Although his longing was so much more than physical, it manifested itself as pain. Chronic agony. Whoever said that love hurts had been absolutely right. He'd thought he'd loved Bea, but he hadn't. Not like this. What he had with Emma was once-in-a-lifetime. Irreplaceable. If he had any chance at all of living a happy life, he had to get her back. But he didn't see how that was possible. Not with their families standing between them.

He glanced at the clock. The signing had been moved to ten o'clock by the property manager, so he had only a little more than two hours. His mother was due to land at the private airstrip at JFK in an hour. Charlotte would be on hand to sign the paperwork. He'd worked to reach this milestone. He'd wanted it. But he couldn't help but think that his name on that dotted line would be like signing the final death decree of his romance with Emma. She would never take him back then. Perhaps it was best to get it over with. He had to pick himself up and move forward. Somehow.

He slogged through his normal morning routine of tea and walking the dogs. He didn't stop by the newsstand. He was done with that. He couldn't stomach the thought of showing up and seeing Emma splashed across the front page. No matter what they said about her, good or bad, it would hurt like hell. He followed it up with a shower, but skipped the shave. His mother despised his five o'clock shadow. If he had to be unhappy, she might as well be, too.

He dreaded having to take her to task at dinner this evening, but it had to be done. It wasn't merely to make his professional life better. She needed help. He was certain she still hadn't truly mourned William's death. He needed to help her see that it was time to stop. And take a breath. At the very least, she needed to loosen the reins and give him full autonomy in New York. And once he returned to London, they needed to devise her exit plan from the company. If she wasn't willing to do that, he wasn't sure what he'd do. Quitting would mean walking away from his family. He didn't have that in him, however miserable he was.

Daniel's driver met him in the parking garage and got him to the store in record time. He looked out the window for a glimpse of their new building, but as they approached, he saw that his worst nightmare was waiting for him—the press. Photographers. All of them waiting outside.

"Is there another entrance?" he asked.

"Aside from the loading dock, I don't think so. It's probably not open, anyway, since the building is empty."

Daniel pressed his lips together. He'd do this. He'd live. "Okay. Thanks. I've got my door." He jumped out and straightened his suit coat. "Morning," he said, marching forward while people shoved cameras in his face and shouted questions at him. He didn't stop, didn't want to look, and certainly didn't want to listen. They were asking about Emma and it nearly killed him.

He rushed through the glass doors into the grand and empty space. Charlotte was waiting for him, along with the representative from the property company.

"Hello, Charlotte," Daniel said. "Thanks for taking care of this."

"My pleasure." She shook his hand and introduced him to the landlord. "Everything look good?" she asked Daniel.

He turned and surveyed the sprawling main floor. It was just as amazing as he'd remembered it, Carrara marble everywhere—floors, arches and pillars. Vintage art deco chandeliers hung from the twenty-foot ceilings. There were very few spaces like this in New York anymore. He was lucky to have found it, but he didn't feel that way. "Yes. Let's hope my mother agrees."

"It looks as though she's just arrived," Charlotte said, nodding toward the entrance.

Daniel turned and watched as his mother climbed out of her stretch limo. She was wearing a pale blue Chanel suit, black pumps and oversize sunglasses. Her light brown hair was in a perfect bob, not a strand out of place. She immediately walked up to the members of the press who had gathered, took off her sunglasses and began regaling them with some sort of tale. He had no idea what she was saying, but they were laughing while they snapped their pictures. The next thing he knew, she was waving them all in.

"In we go, everyone. Take as many pictures as you like. Of course, it'll look quite different once my son and I have gotten our hands on it." She made her way over to Daniel. "Hello, darling. How are you?" They kissed on both cheeks. "You look skinny."

Of course he did. He'd been too distracted by Emma to ever think about food, and since losing her, he'd had no appetite. "Nice to see you."

She tapped her sunglasses against her chin as she looked high and low, getting her first full view of the new store. "The space is wonderful. I love it."

Daniel was relieved about that much. He'd gotten this one thing right.

One of the photographers stepped toward them. "Mr. Stone. Ms. Stone. Can you turn around for some pictures?"

"Why didn't you tell me you were inviting the media?" he asked out of the side of his mouth. "Shouldn't we wait for those favors when the store actually opens?"

"Because all publicity is good and you're a hot property right now." She spoke through her perfect smile as they posed.

"No I'm not. And I don't like the idea of being paraded around."

"Daniel? Is it over between you and Emma Stewart?" one of the reporters asked.

His heart sank at the mere mention of her name. "I'm not discussing that today."

The photographers finished taking pictures of them and returned their attention to the store. In one corner, a camera crew was setting up.

"Smart of you not to answer the question," his mother said. "I think it's probably best if we ignore the question of the Eden girl and pretend like it never happened."

"Daniel? Are we ready to sign?" Charlotte asked.

"Yes. Indeed," his mother answered. She strolled over to the small table where the paperwork was set out.

Daniel didn't move. His feet simply wouldn't go. He didn't want to ignore anything about Emma. He didn't want to pretend like it had never happened. He'd been happy with her and he wasn't willing to let go of that.

"Daniel. Come on," his mother said. "We'll sign it together."

He managed to pick up his feet, but every step felt wrong. Putting his name on those papers might put a solid wall of concrete between Emma and him, but not signing wouldn't mend his heart. He'd still be the sad and empty version of himself, and he didn't want to be that man anymore. He wanted to be his best self and he was that only with Emma.

He walked up to his mother and Charlotte. "I'm not signing." His words echoed in his head, but they felt right. It felt good to get them out of the way.

"Don't be silly," his mother said.

"Is something wrong?" Charlotte asked.

"I need a moment with my mother, if that's alright." The press in the room had figured out that something was amiss and were closing in, just like they loved to do. "And I need you all to back off," he said to them sternly. "Please."

"You're embarrassing me." His mother's jaw was firmly set.

"I'm sorry. Truly. I am. But this was never the right thing to do. I wanted this for you because you wanted it. I thought it might make you happy. But I can't see this through because it all started out of hatred."

"It's business. Nothing else."

He shook his head. "No. I'm not buying that. It's more than that and you know it. You want to show the world that you're invincible and that we won't let the bad things knock us down. But this is a distraction from the real work that needs to be done. You and I and Dad are never going to get past William's death until we stop worrying over the family business and get back to the business of being a family."

"You're my son and my employee, and I expect this of you."

"You're my mother and I expect you to want me to be happy." There would be hell to pay for what he was about to say, but hopefully, she'd one day see that this was all for love. A love that could not be bought, or negotiated, or replaced. There was only one way out of this. "I'm not signing. I'm quitting. Effective immediately."

Mondays were never Emma's favorite day of the work-week, but today was especially bad and she'd been in the office for only two hours. It was going to be a long day. Being at Eden's was like attending a funeral. There was an overriding sense of doom, a dark cloud overhead. She felt responsible. She'd let Daniel into their world, even when everyone told her to keep him out. She'd been naive and stupid. She'd been everything she'd never wanted to be. Princess Emma was a fool.

Mindy appeared at her door with a newspaper in hand. "Got a minute?"

"Whatever you're about to tell me, whatever's in that thing, I don't want to hear it. Especially if it has anything to do with Stone's or Daniel." Her voice cracked. It might be a while before she'd ever be able to say his name again without wanting to cry.

Mindy walked right in and dropped the paper on Emma's desk. "Pratt Institute. Student fashion show. We should go. Maybe we can get in on the ground floor with some promising new designers."

"Look at you. Actually wanting the store to be successful."

She shrugged. "I work best when everything is falling apart. I have no idea why."

Emma skimmed the story while Mindy sat in an available chair. "Friday?"

"Unless you have other plans."

Emma twisted her lips into an unhappy bundle. "You know I don't have plans. I have no life outside of work. Just like before."

"Precisely. We're two peas in a pod. We could go out for a drink afterward. Flirt with handsome men. It'll be fun."

Emma blew out a breath through her nose. "The first part sounds okay. I don't need to go out and flirt with anyone. I'm done with men."

"Too soon, huh?"

"Yes. And you've only been broken up from Sam for a few days yourself. Are you really ready to start meeting people?"

"It's easier when it's the third or fourth time you've broken up." She tucked her hair behind her ears. "But no, I'm not really ready. I like to tell myself I'm ready. I'm not."

"Okay. Good. I was starting to worry that I might be acting like a wimp."

"You aren't. I get it." Mindy got up from her chair. "So Friday? Do we have a date?"

"Can I get back to you? I might not be up to it."

Mindy waved her closer. "Come here. Give me a hug."

For a moment, Emma wondered if she was in a parallel universe where Mindy was the caring, sensitive one. Still, she gladly took the embrace from her sister. The trouble was, the instant she was in Mindy's arms, tears began to roll down her cheeks.

Mindy smoothed Emma's hair and rocked her back and forth. "Everything will be okay. I promise. I know you were head over heels for him, but I promise you there will be other guys."

She couldn't imagine any man ever matching up to Daniel. He made her a stronger version of herself. She'd felt invincible with him. Probably why she'd been so convinced that their obstacles didn't have to be a problem. "I don't want another guy."

"The cards were stacked against you two. Sometimes

things happen that way. Too much family history. Too much money and business in the mix."

"Yeah. You're right." Emma took in a deep breath, but she still wasn't convinced. Hopefully, time would help her get there.

"You want to grab lunch?"

Emma stood back and shook her head. "No. I think I'm going to run back to my apartment and eat something there. I need some quiet." What she really needed was time away from Eden's, if only for a few hours.

"Okay. I'll see you later this afternoon."

Gregory drove Emma back to her building. She hoped that eventually it would again feel like coming home. Right now, it felt like a trap. She was terrified of running into Daniel. She didn't want to fall apart. She wanted to be whole again.

"Ms. Stewart," Henry the doorman said. "I'm wondering if you can give me Mr. Stone's mobile number. He forgot to give it to me and his dog walker hasn't shown up."

"And he's not home?"

Henry shook his head. "He won't be back until later this afternoon."

Emma dug her phone out of her purse but thought twice about it. It was silly, but she hadn't had a chance to say goodbye to the dogs, and she loved them. "I have a key. I'll walk the dogs."

"You sure?"

She nodded and smiled. "Yep."

Upstairs, the dogs started to bark as soon as she put the key in the door. She scrambled inside and they ran around her, circling her legs and jumping "Shh. Shh." She crouched down and showed all three some love. She was going to miss them. At least Daniel had some company. He needed that, all alone in the city.

She went to get the leashes from the hook but was drawn to step into the living room. She loved his place, possibly more than her own. It smelled like him. It felt like him. It was warm and cozy and made her feel secure and comfortable. Just seeing his sofa brought back memories of watching movies and laughing and not making it to the end before clothes started coming off. They'd been so consumed by each other that the outside world had mattered very little to her. That had been her solution for moving forward with Daniel—keep everyone and everything else out. But the forces of the outside world had crept back in.

She couldn't stay in his apartment any longer. It simply hurt too much. She hooked up the dogs and got them downstairs and across the street. The sky was clouding over and rain was threatening, so she quickly started on the shortest of Daniel's routes, the dogs leading the way. Even the park no longer held the allure it once had. It would always make her think of him—their first real kiss, the moments of getting to know each other, the instances when she'd felt like he might be the only thing she ever needed. Of course, that wasn't true. That wasn't reality. She needed her family. Her sisters.

A raindrop fell on her nose. And another. She looked up, to find gray storm clouds swirling. "Come on, guys, we need to get going." They walked double time as the rain began to fall softly.

"Emma!" The voice was somewhere behind her. The press had tracked her down in the park. This was the last thing she wanted to deal with. She started to run, but between her heels and Jolly's little legs, she could go only so fast.

"Emma! Stop! Please!"

She ground to a halt, the dogs just as surprised as she was, looking back at her. She turned around and there was a vision she'd feared she'd never see. Daniel was running toward her. She stood frozen until the dogs took off in his direction, Emma following along, clutching their leashes.

She and Daniel were both out of breath when they got to each other. The rain was coming down hard, but it was warm, and he was such a heavenly sight it made her heart flutter.

"Your dog walker didn't show up," she said. "I didn't want them to destroy your apartment."

"I know. Henry told me. That's why I came looking for you. We need to talk."

She fought back the optimism that wanted to walk through the door he'd just opened. "Is there anything left to say? I don't want us to torture each other."

"I quit my job."

She blinked back the rain that was starting to roll down her forehead. "You what?"

"I quit my job. I refused to sign the lease. I couldn't do it. I couldn't hurt you like that."

Thunder clapped overhead. "We need to get out of the rain. You'll ruin your suit."

He shook his head and took her hand. "You think I care about this thing? I don't. I only care about you. I'm not going anywhere until you tell me what you're thinking."

Her heart was heavy right now. She appreciated his sacrifice, but it wasn't right. "I don't want you to give up your family because of me, Daniel. That's not what I wanted."

The raindrops had weighed his hair down in the front. He dragged it back with his fingers. "I didn't give up my family. I gave up my job so I could do a better job of being *in* my family. It wasn't working. I need to be a son, not an employee."

She took his hand and led him under a tree to shield

them from the rain. She was still struggling to understand what he'd done. "You did all of this to apologize?"

He didn't let go of her fingers, just held on tighter. "Apologize. Make amends. Turn over a new leaf. I don't want to go another minute without you, Emma. I don't think I can move forward until we see where this goes." He swallowed so hard she could see his Adam's apple bob up and down. His face was dotted with raindrops. His suit was drenched. "I love you, Emma. I think I loved you from the minute you walked up to me and made me laugh."

Her heart was now flying circles in her chest, but she had to know one thing. "I told you I loved you the other day and you didn't say it back."

"I know. I was stupid. The words were there, but I wasn't thinking straight. But I realized this morning that the most important thing to me has always been loyalty. And loyalty is so much more than an act. You have to have it in your heart." He stepped closer and set his fingers on Emma's chest, right at the base of her throat. "You have the most loyal and generous heart I have ever known. I need you in my life. Will you take me back? Will you give me another chance?"

Emma scanned his handsome face, her heart pounding. What was she waiting for? He was everything she'd ever wanted, everything she'd once only dared to wish for. "You were brave enough to tear down the wall between us. I want nothing more than another chance. I love you. That's not going anywhere."

"Good. Because I'm not going anywhere, either."

"What about London?"

He smiled and tugged her closer. "What about it? I can visit it anytime. But for now, as long as I have you, my home is in New York."

All she could do was wonder if this was real. The only

thing that was putting her in the present was the rain and his eyes. They told her that Mindy was right. Everything would be okay. It had to be. She'd come too far for it not to be. "I thought you didn't really like it here."

"I know I said that, but I met the most incredible woman and she makes me see things in a whole new way."

"She sounds awesome." Emma smiled.

"She's better than awesome. She's a princess." He gathered her into his arms, and Emma pressed herself hard against the solid plane of his body. She kissed him without hesitation and he did the same. There was no more wall between them. He'd torn it down. This was their new beginning. Even in the rain, his warmth poured into her, or maybe that was love that made her feel so wholly content, from head to toe.

"Can we go inside now?" she asked.

"I thought you'd never ask. I'm dying to get you out of those wet clothes."

Epilogue

Emma looked out the airplane window at the stretch of pale sky and wispy clouds. Far below was the deep cobalt churn of the Atlantic. "How much longer until we get there?"

Daniel finished off his glass of champagne and shook his wrist to consult his watch. "An hour? We should be starting our descent soon."

He took her hand and she looked down at their entwined fingers. Her heart was galloping just like it did every time she started to think about what was waiting for them when they landed—Daniel's mother and father. He wanted the unthinkable to happen. He wanted Emma to spend time with his family.

He'd only recently started speaking to his mother again. He'd let her cool off for a good two months after quitting his job. But now that she had unofficially halted any plans for Stone's New York, he wanted to begin the pro-

cess of mending fences, and that apparently meant pulling Emma into the family fold. Hence the trip to London.
On the family's private jet, no less. She hoped that was a
sign they might accept her. It seemed doubtful you'd send
a plane for someone you didn't like, although Emma was
still getting used to the funny things rich people did. Even
though she was one herself.

"What if they don't like me? What if your mother kicks
me out of the house?" She'd asked him these questions several times over the last week or so, but once more didn't
seem excessive.

"We've been through this. You'll win her over."

"I hope so. It means a lot to me to have her approval."
Emma didn't want to pin too much on this trip, but it was
another test. There was no doubt about that.

"If you don't, it doesn't matter. I love you and I approve
of you and that's all that matters."

"If you say so." She sucked in a deep breath, reminding herself that everything he said was true. "She's going
to ask about Eden's, isn't she? Should I tell her we aren't
doing well? That the store is teetering on the brink?" The
loss of Nora Bradford had been a big one. Sophie was worried, but she was also focused on her wedding. Mindy was
strategizing, while trying her hardest to stay away from
Sam. Emma was busy keeping things moving forward,
and she wanted to do exactly that with Daniel.

"You tell her the store is doing great and you change
the subject."

"She's going to ask about the menswear line." This was
Daniel's new venture. He'd curated everything in the men's
department at Stone's over the last several years. That was
part of the reason it was their most successful department.
"She's going to want to know where you plan to sell it."

"And I'll tell her I don't know yet. Plus, this is a test run for me. It might flop."

As if anything Daniel ever did could be considered a failure. "Or it might be a huge success."

"One can only hope. If not, I'll look into something else. I have plenty of ideas up here." He tapped his temple.

Emma leaned over the center armrest and kissed him softly. "Such a handsome place to keep ideas."

He smiled, his eyes half-closed. "I try."

Sometimes when she looked at him, she needed someone to pinch her. Being with him was still so much like living in a dream. "Do you think she feels like you're trying to push her?"

"If she does, it's only because I am. I never imagined that quitting would finally get her to truly pay attention to what I want, but it has."

Daniel had double-downed on his love for Emma when he'd left his family's company. He'd been the one who made the big sacrifice. Yes, his job had been making him crazy, but she knew very well that it hadn't been easy for him to walk away, even though he tried to make it seem as if it had been the only logical course of action. He could have taken the situation in any number of directions, but he'd chosen the one that led back to her, and she couldn't be any more thankful.

But it bothered her that she hadn't found a way to make a similar overture. A grand gesture. Yes, she'd moved into his apartment, but that was only because the dogs were more comfortable there and he had an even better view. Otherwise, she'd had to do very little other than love him, which was impossibly simple. It was so easy it was like breathing.

"Daniel?"

"Yes?"

"Do you believe in fate?" Emma had wondered a lot about this over the last few weeks while she'd been mulling a way to show Daniel just how much she loved and adored him. She had a question tumbling around in her head, but she worried how he would react. They'd been together for only three months. Plus, there were certainly things about Daniel that were old-fashioned, or at the very least steeped in tradition. She didn't want to push him too far outside his comfort zone. He'd been pushed around plenty.

He sat back in his seat, seeming deeply contemplative. "I never really thought about it. I mean, I know now what it feels like to be with the right person, and it does seem like awfully good luck that we met, but there was some other force at work when you walked up to me at Empire State and struck up a conversation. Especially considering that I'd been a complete ass to you the day before."

Good. That was exactly what she thought. Hello, same wavelength. "So we set these things in motion. We have to take steps to get what we want."

"Yes. Exactly. I don't want to live in a world where I don't have some say in what happens."

She had a great deal of what she wanted—a job she loved and two sisters she grew closer to every day. There had been a time in the not-so-distant past when none of this would have seemed possible. She didn't want to be greedy, but she wanted it all. She didn't feel like waiting to make it happen.

Emma scooted forward in her seat and looked at Daniel. "You know I love you, right?"

He cocked his head to one side, his eyes narrowing. "Yes. Of course. I love you, too. Why do you ask?"

She took both his hands and pulled them into her lap. "I just want you to really know. I don't ever want you to question it."

"Please don't tell me you're dying of an incurable disease."

"What? No."

He breathed a sigh of relief. "Good. I was starting to wonder."

"I just need you to know that you're the only person I want to be with. And I felt like I needed to say this before we landed in London. Before we went to see your parents. Because I know we've already had two beginnings, but it feels like right now is another one." She scanned his face, still awfully nice to look at when he was so confused. "I want you to marry me, Daniel. It doesn't have to be tomorrow or next week or even next year. But someday. I want you to know that I don't want anyone else. You're all I'll ever want or need." Emma was so proud of getting out the words, even if she'd rambled.

"Emma." His shoulders dropped and her stomach felt like it went right with them. "What in the world am I going to do with you?"

"Are you mad?"

He looked…well, he didn't look happy. In fact, he unbuckled his seat belt and got up, stepping across the aisle to where he'd left his carry-on bag. He unzipped a side pocket, took his seat again and placed an ivory-colored velvet box on the armrest between them.

"What's this?"

"Open it." He underscored his invitation with a pop of his eyebrows.

She did as he asked, and inside the box was a ring that knocked the wind right out of her—a glimmering oval, icy-blue gemstone surrounded by diamonds. It was the same color as the dress she'd worn for Empire State. "Aquamarine?"

He nodded. "It is."

"It's beautiful. I don't even know what to say."

"This is my side of the question you asked."

She was both elated and feeling guilty. "Did I ruin your proposal?"

"It definitely didn't go according to plan, but that's okay. I hadn't worked out exactly when I was going to ask. I was mostly bringing it as insurance. If my mother got too horrible, I was hoping I could convince you to stay with a ring."

Emma dropped her head to one side as Daniel took the ring from the box and slipped it on her hand. She waggled her fingers. "It's beautiful. I love it." She pried her eyes away to look at him. "More than anything, I love that we were thinking the same thing."

"Full confession, I've been thinking about this for a while. I bought it before we broke up."

"You did?"

"Yes. Shows you how desperate I was to find a way to keep you. But you know, I'm glad it happened this way. We did this together, just like we're going to do so many other things together." He leaned closer. "Now come here and kiss me."

His lips settled on hers and her eyes fluttered shut. Kissing Daniel was the best, mostly because she always felt reassured that he loved her. And she could show him how much she returned the sentiment.

"What's your mother going to say?"

"Honestly, this might be a brilliant stroke of luck on our part. How can she hold a grudge against an Eden who's about to become a Stone?"

* * * * *

A TANGLED ENGAGEMENT

TESSA RADLEY

For all my wonderfully wild writer friends.
You're all simply awesome!

One

Georgia Kinnear could barely contain her excitement.

Her father commanded the head of the long oval table that dominated the Kingdom International boardroom, a position that granted him an unobstructed view of all present for the Managing Committee's weekly meeting.

Norman Newman and Jimmy Browne had been her father's yes-men for almost three decades—more than Georgia's entire lifetime. Both men served as directors on the board of the luxury goods company, but gossip had it that they'd decided to retire and would not be reappointed at the annual general meeting later today. Not that her father had breathed a word. Showing his hand had never been Kingston Kinnear's style.

If the rumors that had been swirling around Kingdom's cutting rooms and stores all week were true, the annual general meeting due to start in an hour was going to change her life forever...

It was about time!

Her father glared down at his watch. "Where's Jay?"

Jay Black was the original corporate crusader—never late, always prepared, always dangerously well-informed. A rival to respect. Georgia was thankful that no one appeared to have noticed the tension and constant skirmishes she had with him. By unspoken agreement, they both preferred to keep it that way. Their private war. Yet, despite her wariness toward him, taking the opportunity to put the knife in behind his back didn't feel right.

"The copier jammed—he'll be here any moment," she told her father, and tried not to think about how good Jay had smelled when she'd crouched beside him, trying to fix the troublesome machine. Like Central Park on a sunny spring day—all green and woody.

Her father puffed, and Georgia tensed, steeling herself for an outburst.

"That thing has been giving problems all day. I'll get a technician to check it," Marcia Hall said calmly, and her father stopped huffing.

"Thank you." Georgia smiled across at her father's PA of more than two decades. The woman was a saint. Marcia knew exactly how to placate her irascible father, a skill Georgia had never acquired—despite growing up with him and working alongside him since leaving school.

Georgia wished Jay would hurry up.

In an attempt to steady herself, she focused on the larger-than-life photos of celebrities along the wood-paneled walls. Each wore—or carried—Kingdom goods. Totes. Clutches. Coats. Scarves. Gloves. Umbrellas. And, of course, the epochal luggage Kingdom was famous for. Each image was emblazoned with the legendary advertising slogan: "My Kingdom. Anytime. Anywhere."

Her father cleared his throat, and the room fell silent. "We'll start without Jay."

Switching her attention to her father, Georgia said, "Uh, no, let's wait—"

He quelled her interruption with a sharp sideways cutting gesture of his right hand, leaned back in the padded high-backed leather chair and rested his elbows on the armrests.

Her father took his time studying his audience, and Georgia's nerves stretched tighter than a pair of too-short garters. Her left hand trembled a little, and to occupy herself, she smoothed the yellow legal pad on the table in front of her and picked up her Montblanc pen, one of her most treasured possessions.

Norman Newman, the soon-to-be-gone Chief Operating Officer, was seated on Georgia's left, sandwiched between her and her father.

Chief Operating Officer…

She savored the sound of his title. By the end of today, it would be hers.

Together with her sisters, Roberta and Charis, Georgia already sat on the Managing Committee that was responsible for the day-to-day management of the company. An appointment to the Board of Directors would launch her career into the stratosphere. And then she'd join the inner sanctum of the Financial Committee—the ultra-secret FinCo—where all Kingdom International's real decision-making happened.

It was impossible to sit still.

She couldn't wait for her and Roberta to be appointed to the board, couldn't wait to implement the ideas they'd been talking about for years. New stores. New design directions. New global markets. Ideas their father—backed up by his pair of yes-men—had resisted. But that would change now…with the end of Jimmy and Norman's reign.

Kingston would finally have to listen to his two daughters…

Surreptitiously, she stuck her hands under the edge of the table and wiped her suddenly sticky palms down her skirt.

Where *was* Jay? The fashion house's financial analyst had already been appointed to the secret FinCo by her father, which had caused Georgia many sleepless nights. It was time for him to witness her triumph.

The boardroom door opened.

At last!

Even her father turned his head to watch him enter. Tall. Perfectly proportioned and elegant in a dark business suit, Jay moved with easy grace.

Georgia flashed him a wide smile. With his arrival, her over-stretched nerves eased a little. But instead of his customary taunting grin, Jay didn't spare her a glance; his dark head remained bent, his attention fixed on the sheaf of papers in his hand.

"You all know that I am not getting any younger," her father was saying, "but I've always been determined to give Methuselah a run for his money."

A ripple of laughter echoed around the table.

What was this? Georgia went still. Did her father also plan to announce his own retirement today? It was her dream to follow in her father's footsteps, her plan to one day be President and Chief Executive Officer of Kingdom International. But she'd never expected the opportunity to come so soon.

Too soon.

Even she knew that. He couldn't retire. Not today. She'd never be appointed...

She rapidly speculated about who he'd lined up to take his place.

Jay had seated himself in the empty chair to her father's left. She shot him a questioning look across the expanse of polished cherry wood. As the luxury fashion house's financial analyst, Jay was in prime position to have the best insight into her father's convoluted thought process—something that constantly raised disquieting emotions in her.

But Jay's attention was fixed on the stack of papers he'd set down on the table in front of him. Somewhere in that pile were documents that were about to transform her life forever. Yet, suddenly Georgia couldn't stop wondering what else might be in there.

One of her father's infamous surprises?

Did Roberta know something she didn't?

Meeting Georgia's questioning gaze across the boardroom table, Roberta rolled her green eyes—glamorously defined with black-eyeliner—toward the ceiling while her perfectly manicured nails toyed with a pink cell phone. Clearly Roberta thought the comment nothing more than Kingston's idea of a joke.

"I have no plans to retire yet." Her father smiled, and Georgia's pulse steadied a little. "The corner office is far more comfortable than any in my home. My daughters will have to someday carry me out in a box."

There was more laughter. This time, Georgia joined in, the sound high-pitched to her own ears. Of course, her father had been joking. He wouldn't give up his position so easily…

Georgia's attention switched back to Jay, but from this angle, all she could see was the top of his head.

A rapid glance along the length of the boardroom table revealed the mood amongst the other members of the Managing Committee. Since the start of the rumors, Georgia had quietly set up one-on-one meetings with each of them to smooth the coming transition. She was satisfied she had them all on her side. Yet, right now, they all appeared mesmerized by her father.

With one exception…

At the foot of the table, her youngest sister doodled in a sketchbook, locked in a secret world of Kingdom's nascent designs. Charis didn't look like she'd registered a single one of their father's jokes. No surprise there. Meetings were her idea of hell.

Georgia knew her youngest sister would not be interested in an appointment to the board…or whether their father planned to retire. As long as Charis had a pencil and paper, she was in her element.

Again, Georgia tried—in vain—to catch Jay's attention. She willed him to look up so she could figure out what was going on inside that maddening, quicksilver mind.

But he remained stubbornly hunched over the documents in front of him, his espresso-dark hair falling over his forehead.

A wild thought swept into her head.

Was it possible…?

Had her father lined *Jay* up for *her* job?

Old insecurities swamped her. But she weighed the evidence. Only minutes ago, she and Jay had been engaged in a teasing exchange by the copier. Jay had even joked about buying her a cup of coffee when she got the appointment—

No, not *when*, but *if*—

Her breath caught.

He'd definitely said *if* she got the appointment…

Had Jay been trying to warn her?

She replayed that silly exchange. Despite the teasing, he'd seemed a little terse. She'd attributed it to his battle with the monstrous machine. But had it been guilt?

He'd said there was something he had to talk to her about. He must've already known he was getting the appointment she craved.

She stared blindly at the pen between her damp fingers as her thoughts whirled chaotically. *She* was the ideal candidate to replace Norman. She knew it, and so did her father. She'd proven she could do the job over and over in the past couple of years.

The pen slipped under the pressure of her fingertips. Her father couldn't possibly have decided to give *her* job to Jay.

Could he?

* * *

The faster Jay read, the more the words on the page in front of him blurred together. He shook his head, fighting to make sense of the cumbersome legalese.

What kind of prick had drafted this nonsense?

He speared one hand into his hair to push it off his brow. It needed a cut. But he hadn't had time. The past two weeks had flashed past as he'd fought to clear his desk of never-ending fires. And he still hadn't gotten to the bottom of the quiet niggling rumors about Kingdom on Wall Street.

He suppressed a groan as his focus on the black print sharpened. Kingston Kinnear had lost his damned mind. And he couldn't have picked a worse time to go nuts.

In three days' time, Jay was going on leave—his first visit home in years. And he'd made a vow to come clean with Georgia before he left. If he weren't such a goddamned coward he would've done it a long time ago.

Today was already too late…

He hadn't expected his orderly work existence to rapidly turn to crap.

Kingston's retention of a new firm of attorneys to handle "a special project" had seemed harmless enough. If Jay hadn't been so focused on fixing every last crisis before going on leave he might have suspected something clandestine was happening. And maybe talked Kingston out of this insane course of action.

Too late now.

He shuffled the papers back together into an orderly pile, then linked his hands together on top of it as though holding them down would stop the mayhem from escaping. Then he looked up—straight into the pair of Colorado-sky blue eyes he'd been avoiding.

Georgia was smiling at him. She lifted an eyebrow in question and his gut sank into the Italian loafers he wore.

Jay looked toward the head of the table where the cause

of all the trouble sat. Kingston placed his palms on the
armrests of the chair and pushed himself slowly and deliberately to his feet. It was the only chair with armrests,
giving it the appearance of a throne, which, no doubt, was
exactly the impression he intended to convey. Finally, he
straightened the lapels of his hand-tailored suit jacket with
a dramatic touch of showmanship.

The boardroom went so silent that Jay could hear the
whir of the state-of-the-art air-conditioning. At last, Kingston spoke. "While public stockholders own forty-nine percent of Kingdom, I have always enjoyed the comfort of
holding a majority interest and I have been considering the
future of the company for a while now."

Georgia sat straighter. Jay knew she was expecting an
appointment to the board today…

On top of the tower of documents, his hands curled into
fists.

A frisson of electricity zapped around the boardroom.
Even Charis had stopped her frenetic sketching and was
watching her father intently.

For the first time, Jay wondered whether Kingston had
already secretly begun selling off his private stock—it
would explain the recent, unexpected movements in the
stock market.

The old bastard was stringing them all along…

Or did the youngest Kinnear daughter have any idea of
what her father planned? Charis was, after all, the apple of
her father's eye. Jay still hadn't worked out what Kingston
had planned for his youngest daughter. So far, nothing in
the documents he'd speed-read had dealt with her fate. But
Jay had no doubt that Kingston had control of his youngest
daughter's life finely outlined. He rather suspected that this
time even Charis had been kept in the dark.

The tension in the boardroom had become palpable.

Georgia chose that moment to speak. "Roberta, Charis

and I have always been deeply involved in every facet of the company—we are all heavily invested in Kingdom's future."

What a miserable understatement! Kingston expected his daughters to live and breathe the company. And Georgia, even more than her sisters, had made Kingdom her life. There had been moments when her blinkered commitment to Kingdom had caused Jay to despair.

It was Charis who put what everyone was thinking into words. "The obvious thing, Daddy, would be to divide your fifty-one percent share equally among the three of us."

"That would be the obvious solution," drawled Roberta.

Jay braced himself for the firestorm to come.

Finally, Kingston spoke into the silence. "To do so would fragment the company. If I transferred seventeen percent to each of you, it would leave Kingdom extremely vulnerable to takeover."

So Kingston had heard the same rumors he'd been hearing—and hadn't mentioned a word. The first rumblings had surfaced a couple of months ago, but Jay's own investigations hadn't turned anything up. The market had settled down. Then this past week, the stocks had fluctuated, and yesterday the share price had been especially erratic.

"Not if we stood together—we'd still hold the controlling interest." Georgia's knuckles were white as she clutched the pen like a lifeline. Jay discovered that his own hands were clenched just as tightly.

"When have the three of you ever stood together?" scoffed her father.

At the other end of the table, Charis dropped her pencil, and the sound was loud in the large boardroom. "Daddy—"

"So what do you intend to do?" Roberta challenged the old tyrant, talking straight over her sister. "Give everything to Charis?"

"I have three daughters—I must take care of each,"

Kingston said with breathtaking sanctimony. Jay knew the wily old codger had never done anything that didn't serve Kingdom—and himself—best. "But naturally, I will reward my most loyal daughter."

"Don't you mean your favorite daughter?" The edge to Roberta's voice was diamond-hard.

Across the table, the gold pen fell from Georgia's fingers with a thud. "My loyalty to you is beyond doubt." The glitter of hurt in her eyes caused Jay to freeze. "I put in eighty-hour work weeks—heck, I don't have a life outside of these walls. I haven't had a vacation in over two years."

"That's your choice." Kingston shrugged away her plea.

Georgia's lips parted, but she must've thought better of what she'd intended to say. Eyes downcast, she picked up the pen and capped it, and then set it down on the legal pad in front of her.

"You have been unusually silent, Charis. What do you have to say, honey?" Kingston's chilly eyes defrosted as they rested on his youngest daughter.

Charis raised her chin and faced her father down across the length of the table. "Nothing."

"Nothing?" A freeze returned to the blue eyes so disconcertingly like Georgia's in color. "You will be more enthusiastic shortly, my daughter."

Jay felt the hairs on the back of his neck prickle as, taking his time, Kingston's gaze rested on each of his three daughters in turn. "The incentive will be straightforward," he announced. "Whoever proves their loyalty to me first will receive twenty-six percent of the total Kingdom stock—over half my share—and that should be a big enough block to give real power. The other two of you will split the remaining twenty-five percent."

Murmurs broke out around the table. But the three sisters sat like stone.

Jay couldn't bring himself to confront the bruised hurt

in Georgia's eyes. And he knew Kingston had barely gotten started…

Kingston should not have been permitted to torment his daughters in such a cat-and-mouse fashion. Jay forced his hands to relax, smoothing over the stack of papers that contained untold chaos.

"Before you ask, your father has devised a way for each of you to prove your loyalty." He spoke without inflection, not allowing his fury to boil over. "He has a plan."

Two

Georgia's throat closed. Murmurs of surprise swept through the boardroom and then subsided. Across the boardroom table, Jay watched her father through narrowed eyes.

"Jay is correct—but then I always have a plan." Satisfaction oozed from her father's measured tone. "That's how I grew Kingdom from the business my great-grandfather started in a back room into the billion-dollar brand it is today."

"What kind of plan?" Georgia finally found her voice.

Her father didn't even glance her way. "I'm concerned my daughters will be taken advantage of by the unscrupulous money-grubbing sharks that hunt the fashion waters. So I have prepared a shortlist of men able to protect—"

Georgia's breath caught. "A list of men?"

"Protect? Who? Us? *Why?*"

Their father ignored Georgia's and Roberta's squawks of outrage. "The first of my daughters to marry the candidate I have chosen for her will be deemed the most loyal and will be awarded the twenty-six percent holding in Kingdom."

"What?" Georgia and Roberta burst out in tandem.

He was talking as if they weren't even present.

What was going on?

Then it dawned on her. The answer must lie in the documents neatly stacked in front of Jay. He'd still barely spared her a glance.

Georgia had had enough.

Rising in her seat, she pushed aside the clutter of pad, pen, phone and empty take-out coffee cup, and reached across the width of the table. Her feet left the plush carpet and her skirt tickled the back of her thighs as it rode up against her pantyhose. No matter. Modesty was not a priority.

"Georgia!" her father thundered.

So he'd finally noticed her…

She blocked out the familiar angry voice and, with a final heave forward, snatched the block of papers in front of Jay and then slithered back into her seat clutching her prize, her heart pounding in her ears.

Commotion had broken out. But Georgia didn't allow herself to be distracted; she was too busy skimming the pages.

"What the hell is this?" Her eyes lifted to lock with Jay's in silent challenge. He flinched. So he should! "The shares are to be transferred to me and my husband on the day of my marriage…?"

"Marriage?" Roberta was beside her. "Let me see that! I didn't even know you were dating, you secret sister."

Not for the first time, Georgia wished she shared her sister's irreverent sense of humor. "I'm not dating anyone—and I have no intention of getting married." Ever. Georgia's knuckles clenched white around the pages. Not after Ridley. As always, she expertly blocked what she remembered of that disaster out of her consciousness while she did a rapid scan of the thunderstruck faces around the table. Jay's expression was flat, closed off in a way she'd never seen.

Then she appealed for a return to normality. "Jay, what on earth is going on?"

Before Jay could respond, Kingston said loudly, "Georgia, I have chosen a man for you who will do a fine job running the company when I retire."

Panic filled her. "But—"

He held up a hand. "I'm familiar with your dream, and the man I have chosen will match you perfectly."

As Georgia shook her head to clear the confusion, Roberta spoke softly into her ear. "He's about to graft his own vision onto your dream, and then he'll sell it back to you."

"What do you mean?" Georgia whispered.

"Just watch and listen, sister. The master is at work." Roberta sounded more cynical than usual. "Let me see those documents."

Georgia eased her death grip on the papers.

"He will mentor you," her father was saying. "Teach you what it takes."

"You think I need a mentor?" Georgia said faintly. "After all these years? I know the business backward. I know the products, and more importantly, I know the people. I'll head up Kingdom when you step down one day—it's my birthright. And that journey starts today—with the announcement of my appointment to the board."

But her father was shaking his head. "You may be my daughter, but you're not getting a free ride."

A free ride? How could he even think that? But she'd already read the answer in his eyes. He was going to make her jump through hoops—because he didn't believe she could do it. It wasn't just that she was a woman, that she wasn't the first-born son he'd wanted. He would never believe she wouldn't let him down again...

She'd hoped he'd forgotten. Shame suffused her. She should've known... Unlike her, he never forgot a thing!

Nor did he ever forgive.

He blamed her for both the humiliating breakup with Ridley, of which she remembered enough patchy detail to make her swear off dating for life...*and* the horrific car crash that had followed, of which she remembered nothing at all.

"Oh, my God! It even says who you're going to be marrying..." Roberta's voice broke into Georgia's desperate thoughts.

"What?" Her head whipped around.

"Look!" Roberta shoved the papers back at Georgia. "You're going to marry Adam Fordyce."

"Adam Fordyce?" Charis echoed from across the room. "You can't marry Adam Fordyce!"

"That's what it says here, in black-and-white." Roberta's perfectly manicured red nails jabbed at the paper. "That's who Kingston has picked out as your marriage mentor—or perhaps I should say merger mentor? Because that's what this is starting to sound like. I didn't even know you knew him."

This was crazy...

The splintering light from the giant chandelier overhead was suddenly too bright. Georgia touched her fingertips to her temples. Had she gone crazy, too?

A swift glance around the boardroom table revealed that only Jay hadn't reacted. He sat silent and watchful, the familiar gleam of laughter absent from his eyes.

It struck Georgia with the force of a lightning bolt.

He'd known of her father's plan all along...

The betrayal stung. She and Jay clashed often. He infuriated her. He taunted her. The close working relationship he shared with her father concerned her. But despite the rivalry and never-ending mockery, he'd always been honest with her—sometimes brutally so.

Jay had known...and he hadn't mentioned a word about it.

Georgia sucked in a deep breath. She'd deal with Jay—and the unexpected ache of his treachery—later. For now, she had to derail her father's plan. "Of course, I can't marry Adam Fordyce. I don't know him from Santa Claus."

"Unfortunately, he doesn't reside at the North Pole. He lives in Manhattan and he heads up Prometheus," murmured Roberta. "*Forbes* named him one of the top ten—"

"Oh, I know all that! But I've never met the man."

"And trust me—" Roberta was shaking her head "—Adam Fordyce is nothing like Santa Claus. He's the coldest-hearted bastard you'll never want to know."

Charis banged her sketchbook on the table. "That's not true."

Georgia suppressed the urge to scream. "I'm not marrying anyone, and when I do get married, you won't learn about it from a bunch of documents I had no part in drawing up." She shot a killing glare across the table at Jay. "Now, Kingston, why don't you take a few minutes to tell us all what you've been cooking up?"

Her father didn't hesitate. "Adam and I agree it's—"

"'Adam and I agree'?" Georgia repeated, staring at him in horrified dismay. "You've actually discussed this with Adam Fordyce?"

"Oh, yes, we've come to an understanding."

Of course, he had. Otherwise, it wouldn't already be reduced to black-and-white on paper. Jay had known all about it. Adam knew about it. Norman and Jimmy were probably in on it, too. Half the world had known what her father planned for her future…but no one had bothered to fill her in.

Hurt erupted into a blaze of fury she could no longer suppress; it flamed outward, until her skin prickled all over with white-hot heat.

She couldn't bring herself to look at Jay. So she focused

her anger on the one man who she'd worked to impress her whole life. Her father.

"How could you have arranged all this behind my back?"

"Easily!" Kingston's gaze sliced into the heat of her anger like an arctic blast. "You will marry Adam Fordyce."

But, for once, he didn't freeze her into silence. Georgia had had enough. "I told you—I haven't met this man, much less even been on a date with him."

"I've already fixed that." Kingston smirked with satisfaction. "Fordyce will escort you to the Bachelors for a Better Future Benefit on Friday night."

"You're joking!"

"I never joke about business. I've arranged the most important alliance you will ever be part of, Georgia."

He sounded so proud...so confident that she would go along with it.

Why should she be surprised? He'd pulled this kind of stunt before. Except that time, she'd fallen head-over-heels into his manipulative scheme.

Never again.

Even as Georgia reeled from emotions she couldn't find words to express, her youngest sister waded into the fray. "When did you and Adam get so cozy, Dad?"

Georgia finally found her voice. "Let me handle this, Charis. I'm the one he's trying to marry off."

"Not only you." Kingston gave Charis a fond smile. "I've found suitable husbands for all three of you."

A stunned hush followed his pronouncement.

"That's preposterous!" Charis was on her feet.

Her father's face softened. "Charis, the man I've chosen for you is the man I've come to regard as a son over the past two years."

Shock filled Georgia and her attention snapped back to Jay. "You...*you* are going to marry Charis?"

Jay's face was frozen.

Jay and… Charis?

Her sometimes ally, full-time rival…was marrying her sister?

Georgia's stomach churned.

Since Jay had come to work at Kingdom, they'd sparred and argued—or at least she'd argued, while more often than not, he'd simply needled her, provoked her…then laughed at her irritation. He'd unerringly turn up at her office with the take-out coffees she craved, arriving just in time for her to bounce strategies off him. He might excel at pushing her buttons, but Jay was insightful and very, very clever, and all too often his opinions were right on the mark. Despite her distrust, she'd come to rely on his cool level-headedness.

And he'd betrayed her.

Stupid!

She should've known better than to trust one of her father's sidekicks. At least this time, she wasn't infatuated with Jay—or engaged to marry him. Like with Ridley.

Everyone was talking at once. Roberta had drawn herself up to her full height. She looked like some lush goddess. "There's only one thing I want to know. To whom have you dared to barter me?"

But Kingston didn't spare her or Georgia a glance.

Charis's face was pale. She was saying something, but Georgia couldn't concentrate. The sound of her heart pounded fast and furious in her ears and she felt completely incapable of the clear, analytic thought that usually came easily.

All she could think about was that today was supposed to be the best day of her life.

"Father—" Her voice sounded high and thin. Alien. Like someone else's.

She hardly ever called him *Father*—and certainly never at work. It never helped to become emotional. Kingston detested tears, and she'd displayed enough weakness two years ago to last a lifetime.

And her father still held that against her.

She concentrated on the celebrity photos on the wall. Charis had designed most of those carefully crafted products. Roberta had dreamed up the advertising campaigns. And she herself knew the production process from start to finish—how to make sure they made millions from every product launch.

Did her father not understand how indispensable she was to the Kingdom brand? Did he never wonder why he and Norm could find time to play golf so often?

The only way to appeal to his sense of logic was to find a strategic or monetary angle that would make him pay attention.

She drew a breath. "Kingston—"

That sounded better. Stronger. But he didn't even turn his head; all his attention was focused on Charis.

"So, let me get this totally clear. Adam Fordyce is going along with this?" Charis demanded.

As Jay had already gone along with it…

"Oh, yes." Her father actually smiled. "Fordyce is a powerful man and he needs the right kind of wife. And Georgia will be perfect."

Georgia couldn't believe what she was hearing. That's what her father thought of all the years…her whole life… that she'd put into Kingdom? It qualified her to be…what?

The perfect wife?

It was the kind of label Jay, at his most provocative, might have used to needle her…but, tragically, her father was serious.

"And what if we're not prepared to go along with this… madness?" Charis picked up her sketchpad and held it like a shield against her chest.

"If any of you refuses to put Kingdom first—and fails

to show loyalty to me—you'll forfeit the right to stock in Kingdom and immediately have to clear out your desk and be escorted off the premises by security." Kingston's eyes were colder than the ice that covered the Hudson River in mid-winter. "You will no longer be welcome in my business, in my home…or in my life. You will cease to exist."

The air whooshed out of Georgia's lungs, as terror blinded her.

"I'm not going to be a part of this insane scheme, Father." Charis's eyes burned great dark holes in her pale face.

Georgia was startled by the sudden urge to give her sister a hug. Neither of them had ever been the touchy-feely type.

"You can split your stocks between Roberta and Georgia however you choose." Charis stormed past them to the door. "Because… I quit."

Georgia was aware of a ghastly hollow feeling of rejection in the pit of her stomach.

Nothing would ever be enough to make her father proud of her.

Even if she hadn't lost her mind, along with a chunk of her memory, on that disastrous night a little over two years ago when she'd discovered Ridley in bed with another woman.

Even if she'd been perfect.

Unable to help herself, she blurted out, "You don't believe I can run and manage the Kingdom brand, do you, Kingston?"

Roberta leaned forward to murmur, "He doesn't think any woman can run his precious Kingdom!"

But Georgia couldn't summon up a smile. There was only a deep, aching hurt—and endless bewilderment.

What about Jay's role in this? They spent all their working hours arguing, negotiating, talking about every single facet of Kingdom's business, but he hadn't been watching her back. He'd been in on her father's plan...and he hadn't tipped her off.

How could she have allowed him to render her so vulnerable? She'd grown lax and complacent. She hadn't even seen this ambush coming.

"What does Kingston think we've been doing all these years?" she said softly, for her sister's ears alone.

Roberta shrugged. "Who knows? He's always thought women are nothing but pretty decorations."

"That's not true!"

Roberta gave her a long look, and then shrugged again. "At least I had a break from working with him every day while I was in Europe. But you and Charis..." She flipped back her strawberry-red hair with her hand. "I don't know why the hell I ever came back to New York."

Georgia's gaze flickered to her father. But he wasn't paying them any attention. Already on his feet, his face scarlet, he headed toward the exit, chasing after their younger sister with Marcia tottering in his wake.

"Charis!" he bellowed through the open set of double doors. "Get Charis, Marcia. Fetch her back!"

Her father's PA scuttled to do his bidding, and he swung around. Georgia fell back at the ugly fury on his face. "After everything I've done for her!"

It hurt to acknowledge that Charis had always been her father's favorite...

A strange croak sounded.

Georgia stared at her father. Where his face had been red moments before, now it had turned ashen. He clutched at his chest.

Her breath caught. "Father...?"

As she watched, his knees crumpled.

"Jay, help him!" Georgia shoved back her seat and rushed around the table.

Jay got there first, grasping Kingston beneath his shoulders as he sank to his knees on the carpet.

"The resolutions…" her father gasped.

"Stop worrying about the company," Georgia said.

"Who's going to look after Kingdom if—"

"Don't. Don't say it." Fear caused her voice to crack. "Don't even think it."

Kingston Kinnear was immortal—a living legend. He couldn't die.

Her father was struggling to say something.

"Please. Don't talk."

"I'm not going to die." A groan. "I'm more worried about…a takeover."

Georgia bit back her response. She should've guessed he considered himself immortal. "There'll be no takeover. We'll take care of—"

His next moan struck terror into her heart.

"Oh, no!" She dropped down next to him, panic making her breathless. His pasty skin had broken into a sweat.

Then Roberta was beside her.

Their father lay on the carpet. Jay had helped him onto his side and was pushing his jacket open, ripping his tie undone.

"Oh, God, he's having a heart attack!"

Roberta's gasp rooted Georgia to the ground. Her brain stopped working. All she could think was that she hadn't done the first aid course she'd sent the rest of the administrative staff on—because she hadn't had time. She should've done it…then she'd have known what to do—instead of kneeling on the sidelines like some kind of lost soul.

"Roberta, can you get his cuff buttons undone and check his pulse?" Jay instructed her sister.

Jay looked as coolly competent as ever—which only made Georgia feel more inadequate. She was falling apart at the seams, and he was as steady as a rock.

She looked around wildly. "Can anyone help with CPR?"

"He doesn't need it yet—he's breathing." Jay's fingers had moved from her father's wrist to hover over his mouth.

"Oh." She hadn't even known that. Her sense of helplessness increased.

"Call an ambulance," Jay instructed, his hand still over her father's mouth.

Frozen, she couldn't take her eyes off Jay's fingers. Was he *still* breathing? Georgia didn't dare ask.

"Call now," Jay ordered.

Adrenaline surged through her. She shot to her feet and hurried over to where her cell phone still lay on the boardroom table beside the Montblanc pen her father had given her for her twenty-first birthday.

Daddy.

It was a silent scream. The shaking was worse than before, and her fingers fumbled as she attempted to grasp the phone. He hadn't been *Daddy* for decades. *Kingston* at work—which was most of the time. Occasionally *Father.* But never *Daddy.*

The glass face of her phone swam before her. She was crying. Dammit! A tear dripped onto the screen. Her hands were shaking so badly she could barely punch the emergency dial button.

She couldn't fall apart. Not now.

Not when Kingston—the only real parent she'd ever known—was about to die.

Three

Jay paused in the hospital lobby as he spied Georgia's unmistakable silver-blond hair. She was tucked up in the farthest corner of a space that doubled as a coffee shop and gift shop.

If he hadn't been so concerned about her, he might have chuckled. He'd known he would find Georgia in the coffee shop, driven by her craving for the mule-kick of caffeine. *Black gold,* she called it.

He took his time studying her. She'd pulled a short black blazer over that sexy saint-and-sinner vintage YSL blouse. The stark color made her hair look like sunlit-silver in contrast. A coffee mug sat less than three inches away from her right hand. It appeared empty. In front of her, her laptop stood open, and she was hunched down behind the dull silver lid.

Working…even in this time of crisis.

Then his gaze took in her motionless fingers against the keyboard.

No. Georgia wasn't working.

She was hiding, Jay realized. Using her computer to block out the world.

Pity filled him.

She hadn't spotted him yet, so he detoured to the counter laden with bunches of flowers to order a couple of double-espresso shots. He suspected it was going to be a long night.

She looked up as he wound his way through occupied tables, her normally clear sky blue eyes clouded by worry.

The unexpected air of fragility that clung to her tugged at Jay's heart. "May I join you?"

A range of complex emotions flickered in her eyes, including the animosity that often sparkled there. "Would it make any difference if I said no?"

Their intermittent sparring had been going on since the day she'd returned from sick leave after her car accident to find him ensconced in the office beside hers—the office that had belonged to Good-riddance Ridley. His predecessor had done him no favors. It had taken Jay less than a day to realize that she considered him the latest in a series of yes-men hired by her father to usurp the place she one day expected to accede to. A competitor. A threat. He should've handed in his notice and quit then and there, and let her legendary father hire someone else to drive her crazy.

But he'd never been a quitter.

"Tell me to leave, if you'd rather be alone."

She hesitated, and then let out a sigh. "Actually, I'm not sure that I want to be alone." Georgia shut the lid of her laptop and slid it into the black patent leather Kingdom tote perched on the seat beside her. "Roberta's taken Marcia home. And I haven't been able to reach Charis to let her know Kingston…um, father…has had a heart attack."

"We don't know for certain that it was a heart attack." Jay pulled out a chair, sat down and placed the two cups on the table between them, while he searched frantically for appropriate words of comfort. "The EKG looked good. And the first round of blood tests indicated that his enzyme levels were normal—let's wait for the next set of tests before we jump to conclusions."

"There's definitely something wrong." Her expression was bleak. "He collapsed."

Jay wanted to let her drop her head against his shoulder and pull her close into his embrace, until her face hid in the junction between his collar and his ear. There, he knew, she would find sanctuary. She would tremble, and the tears would come…as they had once before…and no one would ever know of her pain.

Except for him.

He'd held her during a night she'd never remembered, during a night he'd never told anyone else about—not even Georgia. On Jay's first day at Kingdom International, he'd promised himself he would never touch her…not until she remembered that night. But she never had. Jay had known he had to tell her about that night, but it had gotten harder to come clean with each passing day he spent working with her.

There was a permanent entry in his monthly task list: *Buy Coffee & Tell Georgia the Truth Today*. Yet, every month he moved that sole uncompleted task forward to the next month. He just couldn't bring himself to do it. Because he was a coward. So this last month, he'd added a second drawn-in-sand deadline to the daily deadline he'd avoided for too long: to tell her the truth before he went on leave. And now that deadline was almost upon him.

But how the hell was he supposed to burden her with the truth now? With her father's life still in danger?

Maybe tomorrow…*if* Kingston's prognosis was good.

Finally, he said, "He's going to be okay."

She glanced around and, apparently reassured that no one at the nearby tables could overhear, she responded, "We don't know that."

Jay nodded, acknowledging the emptiness of his clumsy platitude. "We'll have a better idea once the chest X-rays are done."

She let out a breathy sigh, despair darkening her eyes. She reached for the nearest cup and took a long sip of the richly aromatic liquid before setting it down. "Back in the boardroom, I thought he was dying."

He could tell that soft heartfelt admission to him had cost her.

"Your father is as tough as boot leather."

Jay couldn't bear to see her like this…hurting. She always took care to appear capable and in control. "He's a fighter. He's not going anywhere—and especially not until the annual general meeting has been held."

Georgia choked. "I hadn't even thought about that. When will—"

"Don't worry. Your father has." Back at the office, as the gurney had been wheeled past, Kingston had reached out from under his blanket to grab Jay by the jacket. "I've been tasked with making sure Jimmy and Norman are back at work tomorrow."

The smile he'd half hoped for didn't appear.

"Roberta and I—"

Jay halted her with the shake of his head.

"You're both under enough strain at this time." He thought better of telling Georgia to let up on being the control freak for once in her life. The mocking humor he normally employed to make her examine her decisions—and make sure he kept his distance—would be out of line. "Take whatever help you can get."

Her chin lifted, and she pushed back a silver strand of hair. "Kingston wouldn't."

"You're not your father."

Georgia gave him a narrow-eyed look. She prided herself on being a chip off the old block. It made Jay want to shake her. She was worth ten of the icy man who rarely noticed her—and who certainly never listened to her. She could be so goddamned blind!

Her father could learn a thing or two from her.

"I keep getting nightmarish flashes of what happened. He was ranting one moment, furious as only he can get. The next, he was on his knees. I've never felt so helpless." Georgia dropped her face into her hands. "I can't imagine going to work at Kingdom without him there."

Again, Jay ached to put his arms around her, draw her close. But he knew she'd hate that he'd seen her so vulnerable. So, he did what he knew worked best: he leaned back…and waited.

At last, her hands fell away from her face, and she straightened. Jay could see her silently lambasting herself for showing any weakness.

"Jay, what if he needs surgery?" The words came out in a rush.

"Whatever he needs, he's in the right place to get it." He forced a grin. "His recovery is going to be hell. He's going to be a first-class pain-in-the-ass patient."

"Oh, God." Georgia looked appalled. "You're no help."

"I'm a great help—you couldn't do without me." He winked at her.

That look of haunting helplessness faded to be replaced with a glint of irritation.

Much better. He could tolerate blue sparks of annoyance…anything was better than that desolate little-girl-lost look.

"If you wanted to help, you'd offer to take care of him yourself." She took another gulp of coffee.

"No, thanks. Kingdom couldn't afford the danger pay I'd demand."

She choked.

"But you could hire someone else to do it," he suggested.

She set the cup down. "Then they'd need danger pay!" A flush of shame slid across her face, dousing the spark of amusement that had lit her eyes for an instant. "I shouldn't be joking. Surgery always carries risks. What if…" Her voice trailed away.

Jay instantly stopped grinning. "We don't even know that he's going to need surgery. They're still running tests."

"I know. I know. I shouldn't be jumping ahead. But it's awful being so powerless. All that chaos and then…nothing. I detest this waiting."

Georgia was used to dealing with crises on a daily basis—and solving them. Sitting around like this would be driving her nuts.

"I know this is hard for you," he said softly.

Her eyes flooded with emotion. Jay glimpsed fury…and fear. For a brief moment, her bottom lip quivered. Then she squared her shoulders.

"I've just remembered." Her tone was brisk, the chink of vulnerability vanquished. "You wanted to meet after the annual general meeting. We could do that now. What did you want to discuss?"

He'd planned to tell her about the night that they'd first met.

Placing one hand on top of hers, Jay discovered her silken smooth skin was unexpectedly cold to his touch. Was she in shock?

"Georgia, it can wait." No way was he about to dump that on her now.

Beneath his hand, her knuckles grew rigid. "But—"

He laced his fingers through hers, and cupped his free hand over the top of their intertwined fingers. He'd just broken his promise to himself not to touch her. There was a tightness in his chest.

He gave her fingers a gentle squeeze. "Everything can wait until we have more definitive word on your father's condition."

"You're right." Her hand convulsed under his. "You've been a rock, Jay. Thank you for coming—for asking the doctors all the questions Roberta and I were too scared to voice. And thanks for the coffee."

Her eyes, naked and exposed, sought his; Jay felt the jolt of impact right to his toes. Her thanks made him feel like the worst kind of fraud. But he couldn't bring himself to lighten the mood, to joke about watering down her coffee. He was too hyper-aware of her hand cradled within his larger hand, of the silkiness of her skin, of her unexpected vulnerability—and the shame of his own deceit.

On a soft exhalation of breath, she said, "Most of all, thank you—thank you!—for saving my father's life. I can never repay that."

He didn't want her gratitude. He was a jerk. An utter jerk.

He looked at their hands, linked together. He should never have touched her. Not until she had all the facts. God! What would happen then? After that, who knew if she'd ever let him this close again?

And who would blame her?

Shutting that miserable thought out of his mind, Jay did what he always did—sought escape from a wretched situation in humor.

"I never thought I'd be using Kingston as a dummy model for my first aid refresher course." He cocked an eyebrow at her. "Another coffee?" But he didn't really want to get up, because then he'd have to let go of her hand.

Beep. Shaking her hand free of his, Georgia leaped for her phone, her eyes frantically scanning the text message. When she looked up, the wild panic had returned to her eyes. "He's back from X-rays. I have to go."

That too-brief moment of shared—Jay didn't know what to call it—intimacy? Hell on earth?—was over.

He pushed his unfinished coffee aside. "I'll come with you."

* * *

The following morning, Georgia discovered that Jay had already beaten her back to the hospital coffee shop. Wary, she idled at the entrance, wrinkling her nose at the sharp tang of antiseptic that she encountered everywhere in the hospital, even here.

Toughen up!

Georgia took a breath and approached Jay's table.

Yesterday, he'd betrayed her. *So what!* It wasn't the first time she'd been betrayed; it wouldn't be the last. Today, after seeing the cardiologist, they had business to take care of. Her father would expect nothing less. She was strong. Pure steel. That's how he had forged her.

"I knew you'd turn up here sometime."

Jay gave her an easy smile as he rocked back in the chair and folded his arms behind his head. His light blue business shirt pulled tight across his chest, revealing ridges of muscle Georgia had no business noticing.

"Is your father out yet?" he asked.

She unglued her gaze from his chest and shook her head.

In the bright light of morning, fear still tasted bitter at the back of her throat. The second round of blood tests had been reassuring. It hadn't been a heart attack. Though further tests were being performed right now as a precaution.

"Has Charis been in touch?"

She shook her head again, her stomach winding tighter than a spring. She'd left messages everywhere for her sister. On her cell phone. Her home phone. Her social media pages. At the beach house in the Hamptons. Nothing. And when she'd called Lissa—Charis's best friend—she'd learned Lissa hadn't heard much from Charis lately. Her sister had been too busy with preparing Kingdom's next collection.

All the pressure was getting to Georgia. Normally, she thrived under pressure. The challenge. The cut and thrust of deals and deadlines. But it was nothing like this gut-wrenching emotional tumult she was contending with now.

"She'll come," Jay said.

"I don't know. When she quit, it sounded pretty final to me." Then she realized Jay wasn't talking about Charis coming back to work at Kingdom, but about visiting their father. Perhaps he already knew her sister better than she did. He was going to marry her after all. That caused a maddening twinge in her chest, and made her to snap, "I hope she calls soon—we need her to finalize the spring collection." And Kingston must be missing her…

What if Charis never got the chance to say goodbye?

God. Her father had been so pale…

Georgia had been so angry with him…at his arrogant assumption that he could run her life…force her to marry a man of his choosing. And then he'd collapsed, and her world had fallen apart.

Distractedly, Georgia combed the fingers of her left hand through her hair, and the tiny diamonds on her Cartier watch glittered like dewdrops caught in the sun's first rays. Kingston had recently been talking about getting into watches. She and Roberta had argued against it…

How she wished she could have that time over. She would have been more cooperative.

She looked up to catch Jay studying her. His hazel eyes had taken on the watchful green glint that always meant his brain was working at full tilt. And this time, she was the focus.

"What?" she demanded, instantly on the defensive. She'd never liked feeling like a bug under a microscope. Any way, she wasn't the traitor here.

"Let me get you a coffee."

"Because coffee solves everything?" Despite the under-eye concealer she'd applied, she suspected last night's lack of sleep showed. "Sit—you already have one." She extracted her wallet from her Kingdom Traveler tote and headed for the counter.

She felt antsy this morning, hot and bothered as though her clothes were too tight. They weren't.

Less than two hours ago, she'd finally gone home for a change of clothes. For once, she'd given no thought to what she'd flung on. Clad in the boyfriend blazer she'd worn yesterday, a pair of black wool trousers bought in Paris and her favorite black suede boots, she might appear dismally funereal, but there was nothing wrong with her clothes.

The problem lay with her.

She could feel Jay's eyes boring into her as she waited in line. It made her uncomfortable. Despite his concern, she didn't trust his motives for one moment.

Deep down—or maybe not so deep down—she was mad at him.

Murderously mad.

She accepted that much of Jay's work was highly confidential—he was the in-house finance guru after all—but yesterday it had been her personal life…her future…that he'd colluded with her father about. Maneuvering so that he could marry Charis—to secure himself a major chunk of Kingdom stock. And under the weight of the eternal debt she owed Jay, she was hurt and disappointed and very, very angry with him—the cocktail of emotions was confusing and exhausting. How was she supposed to pretend nothing had happened? Business as usual? Pah! She didn't know how she and Jay were going to be able to work together.

Even though he'd saved her father's life, she was far from ready to forgive him.

It was an impossible situation.

Once back at the table, Georgia set the mug of coffee down and bent forward to slide her wallet into her patent leather tote. Kingdom, of course, but last season's stock, Jay noted as he rocked back in his chair.

Sitting down, she said, "You and I need to talk."

There was a cool edge to her voice and her eyes had an uncanny resemblance to her father's. Yet, something more human, something close to reproach lurked in the blue depths.

Jay winced.

How had she found out? His chest contracted. He was never going to be ready for this confrontation—that's why he'd kept putting it off.

Coward.

"Okay, give it to me with both barrels." He braced himself.

"Your involvement in my father's scheme—" Her voice broke.

For a moment, he failed to absorb the meaning of her words. Then the blood rushed out of his head. She didn't know! He'd been granted a reprieve.

"You should've warned me!"

"Wait—" he demanded.

She warded him off with both hands. "Don't, Jay. No excuses."

He leaned back in the chair, light-headed, his heart jolting inside his chest. "I never make excuses."

No, he only lied to her every damned day.

"I expected better of you, Jay." Her lashes fluttered down, veiling the flash of whatever emotion—anger? Frustration? Both?—that had flickered within, and her silver hair fell forward to hide her face. But Jay was too desperate to allow her to shut him out.

"Georgia!"

She lifted her head and swung her hair back. "What?"

To his horror, Jay saw that her eyes glistened. *Tears.*

That was why she'd looked away. Georgia hadn't wanted him to see how much she was hurting.

"I thought—" She broke off.

The bewilderment that clouded those beautiful eyes almost ripped his heart out. He suppressed the urge to reach for her hand. To touch her. To offer the comfort she didn't want from him.

"Look at me," he demanded.

The look she turned on him was scorching; the tears had been seared away. Jay infinitely preferred her anger to her tears.

Then with a jerky movement, Georgia lifted the mug and took a hasty sip, sputtered and started to cough. Black liquid splashed everywhere as the mug tilted precariously. He reached out and steadied the cup.

When he looked up, Georgia's eyes were streaming.

She glanced around frantically. "Oh, damn!"

Jay pulled a white linen handkerchief out of his pocket. "Here, take this."

"It will stain."

"It doesn't matter."

"Thank you." She took it, her hand brushing his for an instant. She appeared oblivious to his sudden stillness. She wiped her eyes. Quickly. Surreptitiously. As though she feared people might see her crying. When all trace of tears had been wiped away, she turned her attention to the table and dabbed furiously at the spreading pool of spilled coffee.

Head bent, she murmured, "Damn you! I thought there was some degree of respect between us."

The words ripped into his heart. He deserved them—but not for this.

"I didn't expect you to stoop to conspiring with my father to marry me off to Adam Fordyce. Under our rivalry, I thought—"

Jay didn't want to hear more.

He couldn't claim their competition was all in her mind. Hell, he'd provoked her often enough. It had offered great camouflage for his real feelings after all. But he'd *never* colluded against her.

He scooted the chair closer, leaned forward and lowered his voice. "Here's the truth. I couldn't have warned you about his plan involving Fordyce—because I didn't know anything about it myself."

She stopped blotting the tabletop and looked up. He'd never seen her eyes so endlessly blue.

"That's not possible. How could you not have known? He gets you to vet everything that might come back to bite him—"

"—in the ass," Jay finished for her.

Her mascara was smudged, and there was a spark of disbelief in her eyes. His heart clenched. She'd never looked more fragile. Or madder at him.

"I'm not lying to you. The first inkling I had was when I started reading those damned documents after they jammed the copier. I didn't get to see what your father was up to until the Managing Committee meeting was about to start." Jay paused. It was crucial that she believed him. "Your father outsourced his 'special project' to an external law firm he hired because he knew I wouldn't have the time. Because I've spent the past week clearing my desk." And fighting to gather the courage to confess his labyrinth of lies to Georgia. "I'm going on leave, remember?"

"Oh, God. After everything that happened yesterday…" She sighed. "I forgot about that."

Jay could see the wheels spinning in her brain.

"Trust me, had I known about his plan, I would've told your father it was a dumb-ass idea."

She made a choking sound. It was less than a laugh, but the tightness around her eyes eased a little.

"I'd have liked to have been a fly on the wall for that

conversation," she said. "Or maybe not. He hates being challenged. You'd probably have been out of a job."

Not likely. But Jay didn't argue the point. He was too relieved that she was still talking to him. It felt like the sun and the stars had come out…at the same time.

But the spell of brightness would be all too brief. Once he told her—

"Although when you marry Charis, your job will be secure."

His teeth snapped shut so hard at her words that his jaw hurt. "I'm not going to marry your sister."

Georgia took her time examining his every feature. Finally, she appeared satisfied. "And Kingston knows that?"

"We've never discussed it."

Now he wasn't being entirely truthful, though there had never been an explicit conversation. For months, the old codger had implied that Jay's advancement within Kingdom might be fast-tracked if he obeyed certain instructions. And for months, Jay had stubbornly ignored the not-so-subtle nudges to date his boss's youngest daughter. His long-term interest did not lie with the Kingdom, but with something—or rather, someone—else.

Clearly, he should've taken Kingston's ham-handed attempts at matchmaking more seriously—or at least found a way to mention them to Georgia over one of the pitiful cups of take-out coffee he brought her most days—but he'd had no desire to bad-mouth the most important man in Georgia's life. Besides, he'd already stumbled so far down the unholy path of silence that it had become a habit to say nothing at all.

So, here he was—once again—trapped in the quagmire of his own silent stupidity.

"Well, I'm glad to hear that you didn't know."

Like magic the shadow that had hung over him evaporated. "You believe me?"

"Why on earth wouldn't I?" She studied him as though she were trying to read his mind. "You have plenty of faults, but dishonesty has never been one of them."

Jay shut his eyes. All at once, the shadows closed back in, darker than ever. There were so many things he needed to confess. But Georgia was hardly in the right frame of mind to learn about his deception. She had enough on her plate. He'd had the best of intentions to tell her the truth. How he'd met her at a fashion trade show. How he'd comforted her after her fiancé's devastating betrayal, before the crash that took away her memory of their time together. But despite his monthly task list, his daily coffee deliveries, he'd allowed the days of silence to stretch into weeks, the weeks into months, the months into years.

Two damned years.

Too many years to have any excuse. It was unforgivable.

"Look at me, Jay!"

Weary and defeated, he opened his eyes.

"Although there are times I wish you were a little less… blunt," Georgia said as she crumpled his coffee-stained handkerchief in the palm of her hand. She reached for her tote and dropped it inside. "I'll get this laundered for you."

"Don't worry about it." He shrugged. "I've got plenty more."

"It'll come clean."

She'd set her jaw in that stubborn way he'd grown to know far too well.

"And if it doesn't, then I'll buy you another." She swung back to face him, suddenly animated. "Hey, you know what? We don't do handkerchiefs. We do scarves. But no handkerchiefs—not in any of our collections. But we should. And not small dainty female handkerchiefs, but larger man-size ones." Her eyes had taken on fire in the way that they did when she was totally consumed by work.

Always Kingdom.

My Kingdom. Anytime. Anywhere.

Jay suppressed a sigh of frustration as the marketing refrain echoed in his head. It all came back to Kingdom. Every time. Yet, yesterday everything had changed. The foundations of her world had been reconstructed, but Georgia didn't appear to have noticed.

Maybe she never would...

"They'd be white—or maybe not quite white. Ivory. And made from the finest cotton." She paused. "Or perhaps linen, a fine light-as-a-feather linen that both women and men would appreciate. I like that! What do you think, Jay?" Then without giving him a chance to retort that he didn't give a rat's ass about handkerchiefs, Georgia added in a rush, "Perhaps with the Kingdom crown motif printed in white. I like it! I'll speak to Charis. Let's see what she thinks."

Then the light went out in her eyes.

"If she ever comes back to Kingdom."

"Georgia—"

She rose in a hurry. "I hate hospitals. This waiting... this sterilized place...is killing me. I'm going to go check if there's any news."

Jay's heart ached for her. What was really killing her was her corrosive fear that the manipulative son of a bitch who was her father might actually die.

Four

Georgia hurried along the hospital corridor and stopped abruptly in a doorway.

Kingston was already back in his private ward. The luxurious suite belonged in a five-star hotel, not a hospital, with its super-sized television, dining table and chairs, not to mention a seating area complete with a pair of leather couches and a coffee table buckling under the weight of floral bouquets. Propped up on a mountain of snowy white pillows, her father was arguing with a nurse, as was to be expected.

"Give me that!" He struggled to sit up.

The nurse ignored the rude demand and calmly pointed the remote she held at the window. "Mr. Kinnear, you won't be comfortable staring into the glare all day," she said in a bright cheerful tone, even as the state-of-the-art blinds whirred shut.

"I want that blind open!"

Georgia rapidly discovered the reason for her father's disgust: he'd been refused discharge. It only took her a moment to get the cardiologist's number from the nurse and update herself, while her father bickered in the background. Although the tests had indicated nothing of concern, the cardiologist was firm about keeping him for a further twenty-four-hour observation period.

Once she'd terminated a second call to the concierge doctor her father paid a fortune to retain, Georgia cast the nurse an apologetic smile, then waded into the fray.

"Dad, give the poor woman a break!"

The nurse shot her father a long look, muttered something and wisely bustled out.

"Must've recruited her from the marines." Kingston's frustration was about to cause him to rupture a blood vessel. "She won't let me smoke, even tried to tell me it's against the rules. Rules? I've never followed any rules. Now open that damned blind."

Jay was right: anyone who had the misfortune of having to deal with her father while he was incapacitated deserved danger pay. "All the other blinds are open. She's only trying to make sure you're comfortable." Georgia told him. Yet, still she found herself pressing the button on the remote so that the blind lifted. The habit of obeying her father was ingrained bone deep.

He blinked against the bright influx of light. "That's better," he persisted. "The day I lie down and listen to some bad-tempered witch is the day I leave here feet first."

"Kingston!"

But he was already looking past her to the door. "Where is Jay? Call him. Tell him to get his ass up here, will you?"

"He's downstairs. I'm sure he'll be here in a few minutes." Moving to her father's side, she reached out and covered his hand with hers, relishing the warmth of living flesh beneath her touch. He might be impatient, bad-tempered and cantankerous, but he was alive. She stroked his hand. "I'm here."

He shook her hand away impatiently. "I need to speak to Jay."

The rejection pierced her, but Georgia pushed her feelings aside. "You've just had a health scare. Why don't you ease up on meetings for a couple of weeks and take—"

"Ah, good, here's Jay now." He cut her off mid-sentence and sat up.

A wave of energy swept into the ward along with Jay. After she'd been dealing with her father, Jay looked like a glimpse of heaven.

For the first time, she wondered what role he would play in her father's new vision of the company. As her father's confidant—especially if he managed to bring Charis back into the fold as his bride—he'd have untold power.

Would that satisfy him? Or would he want more? He was too clever, too knowledgeable not to know his own worth. She narrowed her gaze as she contemplated him. Tall. Dynamic. Confident. Ambitious. A force to be reckoned with.

"Did you bring the resolutions?" her father barked.

"What resolutions?" she asked Jay.

"Good afternoon, Kingston, glad to hear you're feeling better. Hello again, Georgia."

"What resolutions?" she repeated.

Jay's smile revealed a set of slashing dimples that she couldn't remember ever noticing before. But his smile didn't reach the hazel eyes that saw far too much.

He tapped the leather folio he carried. "Got them right here."

Georgia felt herself stiffen. "Those empower me to run the company while Kingston recuperates, right?"

Jay shook his head, and her blood ran cold.

"Then what are they for?" she demanded.

"They authorize a fresh annual general meeting."

For the board appointments. Nothing ominous in that.

She switched her attention back to her father. She'd had enough of the rumor roller coaster. "Norman and Jimmy are standing down from the board, aren't they?"

"You keep doing your damned job—let me worry about Kingdom," her father snapped.

What was that supposed to mean?

Something dark flashed across Jay's face.

Georgia bit back the torrent of curses that threatened to tumble out of her mouth. "I'm on the Managing Committee—and so is Roberta," she said calmly. "You've taught us everything we know." While they might never have served on the Board of Directors, they were heavily involved in the day-to-day executive management of the company—she pretty much did Norman's entire job already. "Allow us a chance to do what you've trained us to do."

"And where is Roberta now?" Kingston raised his eyebrows. "Shopping? Or preparing to jet off to flaunt herself in the fashion capitals of Europe again? She's certainly not here!"

"That's not fair!" Georgia balled her fists. "She was here most of the night. Then she took Marcia home."

Jay interjected calmly, "I've spoken to Roberta—she's on her way back."

Georgia smiled across at him in gratitude, and a little of her head-crushing tension eased. "I don't suppose anyone has heard from Charis?"

Kingston snorted. "Charis had better not set foot in the Kingdom offices or in any of my stores. She walked out. Call security the instant she's seen."

A chill spread through Georgia. But business was the only language her father understood. Rubbing her arms, she said, "We need Charis to finalize the spring collection designs."

"*I* do not need her. Kingdom certainly doesn't need her." Kingston's eyes blazed. "She's no daughter of mine. Never speak of her again!"

Shock and something close to horror filled Georgia.

He'd meant it.

She crossed her arms over her chest. She'd been so sure he'd get over yesterday's fit of rage. Although his blatant favoritism for Charis had eaten away at her for years, she was stunned at how easily he'd written her sister off without a backward look.

Fear seeped into her. She tightened her arms over her chest, guarding her heart. A quick glance revealed that Jay was watching her. She hoped like hell he couldn't read her terror.

She might be next…

The click of heels in the corridor outside caused her heart to skip.

What if it was Charis? How would her father react?

"About time you arrived," Kingston grumbled as Roberta breezed into the room in a cloud of French fragrance.

Georgia let out the breath that had caught in her throat and her arms fell to her sides.

"Good to see you're as easy-going as ever, Kingston." Bending over the hospital bed, Roberta blew an air-kiss at their father's forehead.

Roberta's makeup was flawless, her lush figure encased in a wrap dress that accentuated every natural asset she had. From the way Kingston was scowling, he'd noticed, too.

"That dress belongs under a streetlamp."

Roberta did a little pirouette. "You think? I think it's perfect."

Kingston's eyes had narrowed to slits. But instead of getting into an argument, he sat up and growled, "Did you bring that pack of cigarettes?"

Georgia opened her mouth to scold him, but Roberta only laughed.

"You need to take better care of yourself," Georgia warned him.

"The cardiologist said I'm as good as new—"

"Not quite! On the phone, he told me that you need some stress-relief strategies." In his fit of rage yesterday, her father had apparently begun hyperventilating. Both the cardiologist and her father's concierge doctor warned it could happen again. "Why not take it easy for a couple of weeks? It will be a good opportunity to test out the succession plan we've discussed—"

"Bah!" Kingston snorted, his tone full of disgust. "You're not running the company."

Georgia stared at him. "I'm more than capable—"

"I will be back in the corner suite on Monday."

The familiar knot started to wind tight in Georgia's stomach. She drew a deep breath, held it for a second and breathed out. One count at a time.

"Can't you at least activate the backup plan we agreed to, Kingston? For the company's sake? What if something really is wrong? What if you become ill over the weekend?" All the possible catastrophes that had been playing through her mind came tumbling out. "And what if they don't discharge you this weekend—and you can't be at the office on Monday?"

"Then I'll authorize Jay to act as interim CEO."

Jay?

Georgia's breath hissed out and she switched her attention back to where Jay stood silhouetted against the window, the Hudson River glittering in the distance beyond.

Her father *was* lining up Jay to take her place as his successor. She wasn't just being paranoid.

Her throat closed up. Had Jay been angling for this ever since his first day at Kingdom? She hadn't been there when he'd arrived. She'd been in the hospital. Being immobilized following the surgery to her ankle had been bad enough, but it had been the concussion and memory loss that had worried the doctors more.

Despite Jay's easy smile, she'd prickled with hostility from the first day she'd arrived back at work. Jay's competence had radiated from him; he made Ridley look like an intern. Slowly, stealthily, he'd become a greater threat than she'd ever imagined. But she wasn't about to let him oust her from the position that would one day be hers.

Jay finally spoke. "I'm afraid I'm not available to serve as interim CEO, Kingston."

Shock caused Georgia to freeze. Jay was refusing her father? He'd had her dream handed to him on a plate and he was turning the chance to run Kingdom down?

Wasn't this what Jay wanted?

Her father and Roberta both turned to look at Jay where he lounged with apparent unconcern against the window.

"What do you mean you're not available?" Kingston raged.

Jay's tone remained level. "I won't be here."

Georgia finally remembered. "He's going on leave."

"Cancel it!" Kingston was struggling to get out of the bed.

Georgia leaped forward. "Father, settle down."

He ignored her, all his attention on the man behind her. "I need you in New York, Jay."

"Kingdom will run just fine without me." The slight upward kink of his lips didn't change Jay's resolute expression. "I'll check my emails and take some calls while I'm away. But I'll be back before any of you notice I've been gone."

I would notice.

The thought caught Georgia by surprise.

Kingston sighed loudly. "Then I'll have to make sure I'm back at work on Monday. Georgia—"

Shutting down her thoughts, she replied automatically, "Yes?"

"Get Marcia to arrange for Bruno to collect me at the usual time, will you?"

Georgia started to object, but then shrugged. What was the point? "Yes, Kingston."

"Oh, and, Roberta, I'm still waiting for that pack of cigarettes."

"Anything else you need?" Roberta asked, her voice saccharine-sweet.

From under heavy eyebrows, he glared first at her, then at Georgia. "A little cooperation from both of you would be helpful."

Roberta didn't flinch. "Ah, loyalty I think you called it yesterday?"

Georgia tensed, waiting for her father to explode.

But the strident ring of Roberta's phone interrupted the storm. Her sister glanced down at the device and pursed her lush lips. Not for the first time, Georgia noticed the fine lines around her immaculately made-up eyes. Roberta was feeling the strain, too. She'd been...different. Distracted. Distant.

"Give me a moment. I've got to deal with this." Roberta was already on her way to the door. "It won't take long."

Abandoned by her sister, Georgia turned to face her father. But she wasn't alone—Jay still lounged against the window, and Georgia was tinglingly conscious of his narrow-eyed appraisal.

"Forget about your half-cocked succession plan. I need you, Georgia." Her father gave her a weak smile. "Fordyce is a damn fine businessman. He's prepared to do a deal—he needs a wife. And he's exactly what our business needs in the long term."

Our business.

Georgia felt her heart melt. Her father needed her. He'd never admitted that before. The urge to do what he wanted—to gain his approval—pulled at her. But she was uncomfortably aware of Jay witnessing their intimate family drama in silence from the window.

So she brought it back to business. "Kingston, you know my views on bringing outsiders onto the board. It's far better to build succession from within the company."

"That's crap!"

"It's absolutely not!" she argued.

"Georgia is right. Internal promotion means far fewer surprises."

Georgia shouldn't have been astonished by Jay's support. After all, her argument for promotion from within worked in his favor, as well as her own. But he'd just turned down a shot at interim CEO…

What did Jay want?

Was he an ally or a foe?

"We've tried developing internal candidates before." Her father's gaze bored into her. "Haven't we, Georgia?"

Shame stained her cheeks and discomfort crawled in her belly. She didn't want to talk about Ridley. Not now. Not ever. "That was different."

"How?" her father challenged.

She certainly wasn't discussing Ridley in front of Jay. "You're missing the point. I can easily—"

Kingston flapped a dismissive hand. "You're not up to running Kingdom."

"At this stage, it would only be for a few days—"

"A few days too long!" He gave a dismissive snort. "I'm not taking that risk."

Then he collapsed back against the pillows and flung a forearm across his eyes. For the first time, he looked old… and beaten.

"I'm only asking you to do one thing for me—put my mind at rest and marry Fordyce." His lips barely moved. He was asking for her help.

How could she say no?

A piercing pain stabbed behind her eyes. The one thing that she'd learned from the Ridley catastrophe was that she was terrible at romance. She'd sworn off marriage—she didn't even date.

Now, Kingston wanted her to marry Adam Fordyce.

No dating—and no romance—required.

Jay was still watching her from his position beside the window, his expression shuttered.

Her gaze slid away from his scrutiny.

Would marrying Adam Fordyce bring her closer to what she'd wanted since she was a little girl, who visited the Kingdom offices and sat and twirled around in her father's high-backed leather desk chair? Her head threatened to explode. Was her father right? Would Adam mentor her and ensure she got what she'd always wanted? Or would he snatch away her dreams forever?

She'd always obeyed her father. But this…? She needed to list the pros and cons the way she always did when she made a decision. But more than that, she needed space… and a shot of black gold.

Grabbing her tote from where it sat on the chair against the wall, she said, "I'm going to get a cup of coffee. Can I get you one, Jay?"

He pushed himself away from the window.

She didn't want him accompanying her. She wanted to think. Alone. "I won't be long."

For once, she didn't want Jay's perspective. This was too personal.

But he didn't take the hint. His smile was easy as he came toward her. "It will give me a chance to stretch my legs—and I need to make some calls."

As she reached the doorway, Kingston called out, "And don't forget to bring me back a goddamned pack of cigarettes!"

Georgia stalked out and resisted the urge to slam the door.

* * *

It didn't take long for Jay to catch up with Georgia. As he came up alongside her, she quickened her pace.

Ducking her head down, she said, "So tell me...honestly...were Norman and Jimmy really going to retire and stand down had yesterday's annual general meeting gone ahead? Was there ever any chance of Roberta and I being appointed to the Board of Directors?"

Jay wished he could give her the answer she so badly wanted to hear. "Who knows what's going on in your father's head—I suspect he'll persuade his golf cronies to stay another term."

They reached the elevator and the doors slid open, revealing an empty car.

Georgia stepped in. "For one glorious instant, I actually believed my father had recognized all the work I've put into the company. I should've known better." She laughed, but the sound held little amusement. "He never had any intention of letting me in—not even temporarily. He wants a man in control." She stabbed a button on the control panel. "Someone like you."

Jay moved in front of the elevator doors and spun around to face her, giving her no choice but to look up at him. He was overwhelmingly conscious of her closeness...the fine grain of her pale skin, the bright blue of her eyes, the familiar scent of her...all the intimate details he had no right to appreciate.

He found his voice. "Not me. I'm not available."

A frown pleated her forehead. "You can tell him that all you like. It's not going to stop him. He'll talk you into it once you get back from vacation—he always gets what he wants. And you'll be married off to Charis before you can say—"

"That's not happening, either!"

"Don't be so sure." Her gaze lifted to focus somewhere

above his head—the floor indicators, perhaps. "He's already convinced Adam Fordyce to marry me."

"But you're not going along with that."

Georgia gave no sign of hearing a word of what he was saying, whereas he couldn't think of anything but her…

"He'll have his way—just wait and see. He never gives up until he gets what he wants. God knows who he's lined up for Roberta. That's going to cause fireworks, for sure." Georgia's eyes returned to lock with his. "Three successors for his beloved company. Three daughters—who come with stock certificates pinned to their wedding dresses—to dangle as carrots."

Georgia was angrier than he'd ever seen her.

"Roberta and I will never have feet big enough to fill his shoes—" She broke off as the elevator car came to a halt. "And besides that, we have lady parts."

How the hell was he supposed to respond to that?

She didn't give him a chance. Brushing past him, she said over her shoulder, "And who can argue with him? He'll only fire anyone who dissents! He's the boss."

Jay strode after her. "Georgia—"

With increasing frustration, he listened to the rapid click-clacking of her boot heels along the hospital corridor. For all his talk, the old man wouldn't be stupid enough to fire her. Kingston's insane scheme had already cost him one of the most talented young designers in the business. Losing Charis was going to create havoc in the coming months. And it was the same with Georgia. She knew too much about the inner workings of Kingdom for her father ever to risk getting rid of her.

The coffee shop loomed up ahead with its racks of magazines, floral bouquets tied with ribbons and the aroma of strong coffee.

It was now or never…

Kingston was going to be fine. Jay hesitated mid-step.

No, not now. She was far too worked up.

Coward.

But he forced himself to commit to some kind of action, saying, "That talk you and I need to have—how about I buy you a drink tomorrow night?"

"What?" She swung around, eyes blank with confusion. "Careful!"

Jay pulled her to one side as an orderly pushed a patient past in a wheelchair.

"The Bachelors for a Better Future Benefit," he reminded her once the pair had passed by, his heart knocking loudly in his chest. He'd been talked into being auctioned off as a dinner date for the charity. "We can meet for a quiet drink afterward." That way, he'd keep the vow he'd made to himself: to tell her everything before he left for Colorado.

"Oh, my God." Her hands covered her eyes. "I'd forgotten all about that. I swear I'm losing my mind all over again. It's like after the crash." She took a couple of sideways steps and sagged limply against the wall. When she dropped her hands from her face, her mascara had smudged, accentuating the hollows beneath her eyes. "Tell me, Jay, do you think I'm crazy?"

It was the first time she'd ever brought up that period missing from her memory. The night they'd met—the meeting she knew nothing about and had changed the course of his life—and the blanked-out days that followed her subsequent car accident on the way to the airport.

"You're not crazy. You're the most sane person I've ever met." It was more than he could handle to see her wilting like this. But he knew better than to touch her, to offer any comfort. He forced a smile. "At least, most days…after you've had a cup of coffee."

Placing his forearm against the wall beside her head, Jay leaned in toward her.

"I need your help…" He kept his voice deliberately light. "I need you to bid on me tomorrow night."

Her eyes snapped wide. "Me? Bid on you?"

He made himself grin—a shark-like toothy grin, and her eyes narrowed suspiciously. *Good.* "Think of it as act of altruism."

"Altruism?"

"You'll be saving me from hordes of—"

She interrupted him with an unladylike snort. "I can't think of anyone in less need of saving."

His grin widened in appreciation. "Afterward, to celebrate your good taste in winning me, we'll share a bottle of French champagne." He lowered his voice suggestively. "Then I'll sweep you off for that incredible dinner you've paid for…"

He was rewarded with a glint of fire in the depths of her blue eyes, and Jay felt a corresponding flame light up deep in his chest. He held his breath. *Down, boy.* He had to tell her the truth tomorrow night.

"You don't need me to bid on you, buddy. You'll do fine and raise plenty all on your own."

"I dare you to outbid everyone," he murmured.

But instead of rising to the bait, Georgia pinned him with a glittery look full of suspicion. "I don't do dares."

"Too risky?" he taunted.

She shook her head, a couple of strands of hair almost whipping against his arm where it rested close to her head. "Too impulsive."

Jay knew he was pushing hard, but he couldn't stop. "Too scared to live a little?"

She froze. "I'm not scared!"

Gotcha. He raised his eyebrows. "You sure about that?"

"Of course!" Georgia gave a dismissive laugh that he might have thought was real if he hadn't made an art of studying her for the past two years. "Why should I be scared to bid on you?"

He let her question hang, watching her, letting it expand to fill the space between them. "Because you're too scared to be swept away on an incredible dinner date with me?"

Her eyes darkened to sapphire. "I definitely don't do dates."

A second later, she gave another careless laugh. She'd recovered so quickly that if Jay hadn't been watching her, he might have missed the flare of panic.

"Your ego is showing, Jay Black. What a hard life, being *such* an eligible bachelor in New York—and having the privilege to turn down an interim CEO position that I would give my right arm for. Why would you worry about a dinner date?"

Jay stared into her eyes which, despite being shadowed by confusion and antagonism, were still the most beautiful thing he'd ever seen. He wanted to tell her those eyes were worth infinitely more than the CEO position she coveted so highly.

"Oh, God. I'd better not forget to arrange where I'm going to meet Adam."

Suddenly, Jay was no longer in the mood to jest. "You're not seriously planning to attend the benefit with Fordyce, are you?"

Georgia stared at him as though he'd grown two heads. "Of course, I am. Kingston's already arranged it."

A primal, possessive response rocked Jay back on his heels. The hand he had propped against the wall curled into a fist.

"I'm sure Fordyce will have no problem finding another date," he said through gritted teeth.

"It's hardly a date. But I can't just dump the man—he's far too important of a player. And I can't let my father down."

"Can't let your father down?" Jay stared at her. "That's a habit you need to break."

"I don't dare, Jay. If he fires me…" Her voice trailed away. "I'm nothing without Kingdom."

Carefully, Jay pushed away from the wall and uncoiled himself, taking a step backward before he said—did— something that he might regret.

Keeping his voice even with great effort, he said, "Why don't we go get that coffee you wanted?"

Five

They took their steaming cups to a sheltered bench Jay had discovered yesterday tucked away in the landscaped gardens surrounding the hospital. Three nurses stood a distance away, clutching their coffees, while half a dozen sparrows tussled like young thugs on the footpath.

A gust of wind shook a drift of withered leaves from a nearby tree.

"Would you like my jacket?" Jay instantly started to slide it off his shoulders.

"No, no. I'm fine."

Dropping her Kingdom tote on the wooden bench, Georgia drew her jacket more tightly around her, and then took a sip of the coffee he'd bought.

"I could get used to this coffee," she said, as she sat down in the washed-out sunlight.

He hadn't brought her out here to talk about coffee. With his free hand, Jay raked his hair off his forehead and sat down beside her.

"The sooner you tell Fordyce that you're not going along with your father's crazy notions of empire-building, the better."

"Maybe it's not crazy. Maybe it actually makes sense."

"Sense? It's completely mad!" Disbelief took his breath away.

"It'll be business—more like a merger than a marriage."

"But you haven't even met the man," Jay protested, seriously rattled now.

She took another sip. Jay noticed how the morning sun glinted in her hair. "That will change tomorrow night."

Desperation pounded through his veins. He wanted to grab her by her shoulders and warn her that she was making the biggest mistake of her life. Leashing his inner turbulence, he sat still as stone. *Reason, not reaction.* "You'd never do business with a company you hadn't done substantial due diligence on."

She didn't even crack a smile. "I'm not stupid, Jay. I'll certainly weigh up every advantage and disadvantage." Her tone had cooled. She glanced down at her watch. "We can't stay long. Roberta will be wondering where I've gotten to—"

"Roberta will call if she needs you." Jay had no intention of allowing Georgia to run out on this discussion. "Forget the business advantages then, and consider the personal aspects. You can't possibly marry Fordyce."

She flicked him a quick sideways glance, then looked away. "I may not have a choice."

His shoulders grew more rigid from the effort it took to stop himself from leaping to his feet. "Of course, you have a choice. No one can force you into marriage."

"It's not that simple."

"It's exactly that simple. Just say no."

"There are plenty of merits to it—even on the personal level." She began ticking them off on her free hand. "One, I'm hardly likely to fall in love with anyone."

"Why not? You shouldn't allow one bad—"

"Two, I work too hard—you say so yourself." Her middle finger unfurled, as she continued to count out reasons he didn't want to hear. "Which leads me to the next point. Three, I don't have time to date...to meet men."

Jay started to panic. "But you don't want to meet men, do you?"

"Doesn't every woman want to find The One?" She raised an eyebrow. "Someone to love."

The One?

Jay lowered both his eyebrows in response.

"What?" She stared back at him. A fine wisp of silver hair blew across her eyes. She pushed it away, hooking it behind her ear. "Isn't that supposed to be every woman's dream?"

"I never thought it was yours."

"Jay!" She actually looked offended.

Holy crap! How had he misread her so badly? He'd listened so carefully to her no-romance protests that he'd missed the yearning hidden deep below.

"You haven't looked at a man in the two years I've worked with you."

She didn't look pleased with his observation.

"So maybe it's just as well Kingston's come up with this plan. I get the chance to marry someone I'll have business in common with—and I don't need to go through the drama of dating."

"You don't need to marry Fordyce to avoid that fate. You could marry me instead of settling for second best." He grinned, partly to irritate her, but mostly to give himself an out lest she realize how deadly serious he was. "We've got plenty in common."

She gave a snort. "Like what?"

For starters, they both spent most of their waking hours at Kingdom, but Jay decided she might not appreciate that reminder right now. He needed to proceed with care—and humor. He stuck out his thumb, mimicking her actions from moments before. "You like arguing with me—"

"*You* argue with *me*!"

"Two." He flicked out his index finger. "You think my opinions are fantastic—"

"I do not!" Then she relented. "Okay, maybe as far as Kingdom goes—I'll concede that."

"Three," he said, counting the point with his middle finger. "You adore my sense of humor."

She rolled her eyes skyward. "Can't you ever be serious, Jay? This is exactly why I would never marry you."

Ouch!

Before he could react, she blurted out, "Anyway, I'd hate for you to sacrifice yourself."

"But it's okay for you to sacrifice yourself?" he retorted.

She set her jaw in a way that he recognized only too well. "That's different. I'll be marrying Adam Fordyce to get what I want."

Even the wind stopped gusting in the taut silence that followed.

"All you ever think about is Kingdom," he said quietly.

She didn't say a word. Instead, she drained her coffee and carefully set the empty cup down on the sunlit bench between them.

"Georgia, I know you were hurt by Rid—"

She didn't allow him to finish. "Kingdom will never betray me."

This time, her smile turned his guts inside out.

Never betray her? What the hell did she think was happening? What did she think her father was doing?

"And marriage to Fordyce wouldn't be a betrayal?"

"Betrayal of what?" She sounded genuinely confounded.

Of yourself.

Jay suppressed the urge to yell it at her—he didn't dare show the terror that now churned inside him.

"You don't want to do this," he said, the calmness of his voice surprising him. "It would be a massive mistake."

Her careless shrug rattled him further. "Plenty of marriages have worked with less—"

"And plenty have ended in bitterness and acrimony," Jay interrupted her. "Don't you want more out of life than a billion-dollar divorce settlement?"

Georgia glared at him. "You don't understand what it's like to be a Kinnear."

It was his turn to shrug. "Not very different from being a Black, I'd imagine."

"Don't be silly!" Her lips curved up into a smile that held no trace of any real amusement. "You couldn't possibly understand."

"Try me." Jay bared his teeth in a feral grin.

"My life was mapped out long before my birth. From my father's perspective, it went wrong from the moment I was born." She paused. "I was supposed to be a boy."

"George." Jay supplied the name.

"You know?" The bruised look he'd hoped never to see again was back in her eyes. "He told you?"

Jay hesitated, debating with himself how to respond. He let his gaze drift around the landscaped garden. The nurses had vanished. Aside from the squabbling sparrows, he and Georgia were the only ones left.

Slowly, he shook his head. "It's not hard to figure out."

"Father was so sure I'd be a boy. He wasn't interested in hearing some medical technicians' determination of what my sex would be. Because he knew. He even had the christening invitations printed, inviting everyone to 'celebrate the birth of my son, George.'" Her face wore a strange expression. "Funny, huh?"

Even on the second telling, Jay found little amusement in Kingston's arrogant certainty that he could preorder his firstborn's sex. Even less did he like the notion that her father had made his disappointment so evident to Georgia from the day she was born.

"You want to please your father." He knew he had to proceed with caution. "You want his approval—but you don't need to go along with this...this—" *Insanity.*

"You don't understand. You asked what I want. Well, here's what I want. I want to be the President and CEO of Kingdom. I want it for me—not for my father. I want it because I've worked for it all my life. I want it because it's mine by right, my birthright. I want it because I deserve it."

The words were a death knell.

Hell, he'd known it...but he'd never understood how deep her desire went—nor how far she'd go to secure it.

But he couldn't walk away. He was fighting for her life—and his own.

"So you think by marrying Fordyce you can convince him to let you take charge?" The glitter in her eyes warned him he was on treacherous ground. "Fordyce is an ambitious bastard. What makes you think he'll step aside and let his wife be boss?"

Her chin went up. "I'll persuade him."

God!

Imagining what form her persuasion might take made him go hot...then very, very cold. Jay tugged at the knot of his suddenly too-tight tie. An icy knifepoint of fear cut deep into his heart.

"You deserve more!"

His anger burned a white-hot streak through him. Anger at Kingston for his callous indifference to his daughters. Anger at Georgia for her blind certainty that her father would honor her efforts. Anger at himself for his foolish hopes.

To give himself time to cool off before he blurted out anything he'd later regret, Jay raised his cup and downed the coffee in two gulps.

The heat scalded the back of his throat.

He set the empty cup down on the bench beside hers.

"I love Kingdom… It's everything," she said quietly.

The vulnerability in her eyes took away his breath, evaporating the sermon he'd been about to deliver. At last, he said flatly, "It's only a corporation, Georgia."

She was shaking her head. "Oh, no. It's much more than that. It's all I have. It's my heritage. My family. My life. My legacy. If I have to marry Adam Fordyce to keep that, I will."

"You shouldn't allow your father to dictate who you should marry." He drew a deep breath. "It wasn't successful last time—why the hell would it work this time?"

She went white. "You know nothing about what happened before!"

Jay winced.

He hated, *hated* to see her hurting. Guilt ate like hot acid at his gut.

But he couldn't keep silent…not anymore.

"Georgia, that night that you…that Ridley—"

"I don't want to talk about it," she cut him off. "And certainly not to you. It's none of your business, Jay."

The words were a punch in his chest.

But it was his business…

He wanted to look away, before she saw into his soul and read the truth that blazed there in ten-foot-tall letters of gold fire.

That she'd changed his life.

That after they'd met, he'd flown home and set the wheels in motion. That ten days later, he'd called Kingdom International looking for her. Only to learn that she'd been through surgery and was recovering from a head injury. He'd been on the next plane to New York. His first stop had been the Kingdom headquarters. Georgia had still been away on sick leave. There'd been little chance of convincing her staff to give him her contact details. But he'd caught a break. The busy receptionist had assumed he was there for an interview. And in that instant, Jay had taken brazen advantage of the woman's mistake and he'd made his next life-changing decision. It hadn't been difficult to smooth talk his way into Ridley's job.

If he told her the truth now, he'd drive her straight into Fordyce's arms—she was halfway there already. Then he'd lose all chance to win her back. Forever.

"I'd hate to see someone so smart and brave trapped in a miserable marriage," he finally managed. "I'm concerned about you, that's all."

Desperate, seeking to lighten the moment—hell, looking for any distraction—he bent forward, intending to kiss the tip of her nose in an amusing comic fashion.

But it didn't turn out that way.

Instead of brushing her nose, his lips planted themselves on hers. The jolt of the brief impact rocked through him. It wasn't a particularly sexy kiss, as far as kisses went. But his lips lingered longer than he'd intended, refusing to obey his command to back off. Now. Before he blew it all to kingdom come…

Yet, surprisingly, she didn't shove him away.

Her lips were soft beneath his. Then—more surprisingly— her mouth moved slightly, her lips parting a little—probably because she was in shock.

She tasted of strong hot espresso and a sweetness that was all Georgia.

Jay didn't dare press the advantage, nor did he deepen the kiss. Too much lay unspoken between them.

He shouldn't be touching her!

So he retreated, and gave an unsteady laugh, while silently cursing himself.

"Speaking of mistakes, that was a mistake," she said, much too quickly.

Who was she trying to convince?

Him?

Or herself?

But he didn't risk challenging her. His heart was thundering so loudly he was sure she would hear it reverberating around the empty garden.

Her hands came out, warding him off. "Don't move—stay there—I have to work with you tomorrow."

Picking up the empty cups, Jay rose and swung away almost treading on a trio of sparrows bickering amidst a swirl of fallen leaves. He retreated to the trash can nearby and tossed the cups in with barely restrained force. Then, fighting to keep his face from revealing anything of his feelings, he stalked back.

He refused to think of that sweet, gentle kiss as a mistake.

He came to a halt in front of her.

"You don't love Fordyce. It will ruin your life," he said softly, and shoved his hands into his pockets.

She said nothing.

"You'd marry a man you've never met, a man your father picked out for his ability to run Kingdom? *Why?*"

She raised her chin in that maddeningly familiar gesture. "I'll make it work."

Or die trying.

That was his Georgia. The blind tenacity. The pig-headed drive. Everything that made her the most maddening, most fascinating woman he'd ever met.

His eyes locked with hers.

"They call him Mr. Ice," he warned.

Cool, rational logic always worked better. Or provocation. Except, right now, in his desperation, he couldn't summon either...

"Don't give in." He was begging, dammit!

She must have sensed something of his black emotional maelstrom because she tipped her head to one side and considered him with eyes that had cooled to a clear light blue, so disturbingly similar to her father's that Jay was filled with a flood of dread.

"Jay, I'm not giving in. I'm compromising."

"You're damn right, you're compromising. You're compromising who you are."

This was her life—his life—she was talking about. He wanted to shake sense into her. But he kept his hands thrust deep in his pockets and watched the color leach out of her eyes and the wall go up.

Damn Kingston!

So he gentled his tone. "It's your father's loss that he doesn't appreciate you for who you are."

The smile she gave him was brilliant…and utterly fake.

"You're lucky," she said. "You were born the right sex. I'm sure your father is incredibly proud of you, his eldest son—and of your achievements. You've had freedom to carve your own life."

"I suppose you could see it like that," agreed Jay with little humor.

"I've always been expected to work for the family company. I can't leave."

"Do you want to leave?" Tension vibrated through him.

"No, of course not! Haven't you heard a word I've said? Kingdom is my life."

Kingdom.

That was all that mattered to her. All she wanted. What could he offer to match that? Except the freedom to carve out her own life.

The desperate determination in her eyes warned him that it was pointless to even try to negotiate.

Pivoting away, Jay drew a deep steadying breath.

It was perfectly clear. Pressure would only make Georgia dig her toes in further and push her faster toward the altar. The hell-bent desire to fill Kingston Kinnear's shoes consumed her. She would do anything to be President and CEO of the company she'd been raised to revere.

Even prostitute herself to a man of her father's choosing.

Six

Georgia had intended for her first meeting with the man who she was contemplating marrying to be in private—even if it was in the back seat of a limousine.

Instead, it was taking place in a marble-tiled lobby on New York's museum row in the midst of a high society affair.

Her father's driver, Bruno, had arrived on time to take Georgia to the benefit. But there'd been no sign of Adam Fordyce, apart from the exquisitely packaged corsage on the back seat with a handwritten note from Adam that he looked forward to meeting her at the party.

Now Adam Fordyce's narrow mouth barely moved as he said to Georgia, "I see you received my flowers."

"They're beautiful—thank you." She carefully touched the corsage on her wrist and silently reminded herself not to rub her eyes any time soon.

"Would you—"

"Should we—"

They both spoke at once, and Georgia laughed awkwardly and felt herself color. This had to be worse than being a teenager on a first date. Tonight had to go well. She couldn't afford to screw this up…

Then she sneezed. And worse, her eyes started to burn. Of all the bad luck!

Georgia set her cocktail glass down on a nearby pedestal and sent a prayer to the beauty goddesses that her expensive waterproof mascara would hold up.

"I'm so sorry," she sputtered, her vision blurring. She fumbled with the clip of her sequined clutch and dug frantically around inside for a tissue. Her eyes pricked and two more sneezes followed in rapid succession.

"Good evening, Georgia."

Jay.

He thrust a soft linen handkerchief into her hand.

She blew her nose and dabbed at her streaming eyes while Jay and Adam greeted one another. Then she opened her eyes and, to her relief, the world slowly realigned as the noisy chatter echoed around them.

Jay stood before her, immaculate in a black tuxedo and a startlingly white shirt. A black bowtie completed the ensemble. He looked fantastic. The bidding on him tonight was going to be insane.

For some reason, that did not delight her.

"Thank you." She grimaced. "This is becoming a habit." Fluttering his handkerchief between her fingers, she made a mental note to get both handkerchiefs she now possessed laundered and returned ASAP.

"It's the baby's breath," said Jay.

"What?" She squinted up at him.

He raised an eyebrow. "Those little white flowers in the corsage that make you sneeze."

"You're allergic?" Adam was all concern.

"Yes." Once again, Georgia felt awkward, her stomach knotting up. She could kill Jay for drawing attention to her weakness—even if he was right about the allergy. "It's the single-flowered version that's the problem. I'm fine with the double-flowered hybrid." The orchid in the arrangement would be fine—but it would be too difficult to separate it from the baby's breath.

"Here, let me remove it," said Adam.

"I'll do it." Jay moved in between her and Adam, blocking her date from view. His fingers were cool against her skin as he gently removed the corsage from her wrist. This close, his clean-shaven jaw was level with her eyes and she could smell his aftershave—that subtle fresh blend of greenery and wood—as he concentrated on her wrist.

"How did you know I'm allergic to baby's breath?" she murmured to Jay alone.

His head tipped up and his darkening gaze tangled with hers. Instantly, the memory of the last time he'd been this close flashed into her mind.

He'd kissed her.

It had been dizzying, disorienting. She worked with the man... She didn't want to be thinking of how safe, how comforted she'd felt when he'd brushed his lips across hers. Yet, there'd also been a prickle of high-voltage tension... something that had nothing to do with comfort...or safety. And she certainly didn't want to think about—

"I'm observant," Jay said flatly.

Georgia searched her plundered memory bank for an occasion when she'd had an allergic reaction that he might have witnessed and came up blank. But that meant little. There were so many holes where certainty had once existed. The knots in her stomach grew tighter, and she looked away deliberately, and tried to refocus on her date.

She caught Adam studying them.

"Let me fetch you a glass of water," he offered.

"I'll be fine."

The last thing Georgia wanted was for Adam to think she was some kind of freak. But he was unreadable. His dark remote face contrasted so sharply with the pale eyes that revealed no emotion at all. It was easy to see how he'd been nicknamed Mr. Ice.

"Is there anything else I can get you to drink?" Adam's voice interrupted her thoughts. "Another cosmopolitan, perhaps?"

Coffee…

Jay would have offered her coffee. Even on this rarefied occasion, he would've conjured up a paper cup of steaming black gold, and she wouldn't have needed to ask.

She almost smiled—and only just stopped herself from sneaking Jay a sideways conspiratorial glance.

Adam was still waiting for her response. Feeling guilty at the headspace Jay was occupying, she over-compensated with a thousand-watt smile. "Maybe a lime and soda?"

"Done."

She watched Adam disappear into the throng.

"So you're going ahead with this crazy plan to marry Fordyce?"

Georgia's heart sank. Since their confrontation in the hospital gardens, his accusation that she was giving in— and the implication that she was taking the easy way out— had gnawed at her. There was nothing easy about what she was doing. But she couldn't expect Jay to understand. How could he? He'd never been in her position…

She tipped her chin up. "The more I consider it, the less crazy it sounds."

"I've instructed Charis to bid on me if I fail to make the reserve."

"She's here?" The information came as a relief.

"Yes, I ran into her in the lobby—she'll be joining you at the table Kingdom sponsored."

All Georgia's bubbling questions dried up as she gave Jay a slow once-over. He'd make the reserve for sure. The formal evening clothes made him look breathtakingly gorgeous—and his slightly wayward hair only added to the appeal. Working with Jay every day, she'd never even thought of him as handsome.

Where the hell had her eyes been?

"We have a decent budget for this event." Georgia certainly wasn't going to feed his ego. "Charis will make sure you go for a respectable figure. Don't forget to talk up the raffle of the Kingdom trolley bag we're doing tonight. Make sure to slip in mention of the Kingdom brand as many times as you can so that we get some decent media attention. And get some photos with whoever makes the highest bid."

"Thank you!"

Was that a hint of irony she detected?

Before she could call him on it, she spotted the event organizer making frantic hand signals in her peripheral vision. She nudged Jay. "I think that's your cue—and I need to find the cloakroom to fix my makeup."

"The moment of truth—let's see what I'm worth." Jay's smile didn't reach his eyes as he took her in, from her hair styled in an updo to the dark sapphire dress and the diamond drop earrings she wore. "You look beautiful."

The mirror in the ladies' room lounge revealed that Jay had been delusional in his assessment.

After salvaging her eye makeup and repairing the damage caused by her sneezing bout, Georgia went back out and found Adam in the lobby, holding their drinks. Once she joined him, he made short shrift of the rich and famous glitterati crowd that surrounded him.

There was no sign of Jay.

To Georgia's irritation, there was little opportunity for the social let's-get-to-know-each-other-better chatter she craved with Adam amid waiters circling with platters piled high with canapés, the constant greetings from acquaintances and a never-ending stream of interruptions by Adam's business connections.

Finally, much to her relief, a bell sounded, summoning the crowd to a large triple-height gallery that had been set up for the benefit auction. Adam revealed flawless manners as he seated her at the table sponsored by Kingdom close to the stage, before taking his seat beside her.

Good. Finally they would get a chance to get to know each other.

Georgia smiled a greeting at the others at the table. Roberta was already there, accompanied by a heart-stoppingly handsome man. Then Georgia recognized him.

"Blake. Blake John Williams." She laughed as he rose to his feet. "How long it's been!"

He came from one of New York's wealthiest families. Was he the reason for her sister's recent surge in texting activity?

Marcia Hall was sandwiched between Roberta and Charis, who had—surprisingly—come alone. Charis looked amazing in a traffic-stopping dress covered with a riot of beaded flowers. It was nothing like the elegant garments Charis usually wore. Georgia had never seen anything like it. It definitely wasn't her sister's work. But Charis had discovered some exciting new talent. Once photos got out, the unsuspecting designer was going to be mobbed with orders.

Two other couples filled out their numbers at the table.

As the meal progressed, the conversation predictably turned to fashion. Adam was exchanging small talk with Roberta's date. Georgia's gaze strayed to the table where the bachelors were sitting. Jay was seated at the farthest end, head tipped to the side in a pose Georgia knew so well. Another of the bachelors leaned across and said something that made Jay smile, and he laughed as a third chipped in.

Georgia felt her own mood lighten.

When Jay laughed, he was utterly, irresistibly wicked.

If he laughed like that when his turn came to be auctioned, he would have no problem winning a more than desirable figure.

Her glance flicked across to Charis. How far would Charis need to go? But her sister was staring fixedly at the floral arrangement in front of her. Whatever Charis was thinking about wasn't making her happy. Georgia's own heart ached in response. Their father's rejection must be killing her sister.

For the first time in years, Georgia wished she and Charis were closer.

"A glass of champagne?" Adam offered.

It reminded her of Jay's joke about sharing a bottle if she bid on him—and won—him tonight.

Georgia came back to earth.

"Yes, please." She smiled, and the wine waiter at her elbow filled her glass.

"Excuse me for a moment." Adam pushed his chair back. "There's someone I must talk to—I'll be back shortly."

As he left, Georgia glanced back to where Jay sat to one side of the stage. He was chuckling at the antics of the first bachelor getting ready to be auctioned off.

As though he felt the pressure of her stare, Jay turned his head and met her gaze. His laughter froze.

A sharp pang pierced her chest, causing Georgia to draw a quick breath. What was this? She couldn't be jealous of the woman who'd win him...

How ridiculous.

Jay was her rival. A perpetual thorn in her side.

Their relationship was...complicated. Confusing.

But he made her laugh.

And in those unguarded moments, she forgot about her fears. She even forgot about the terror of not being enough.

But Jay wasn't laughing now. His gaze was boring into hers. He alone knew the stakes that faced her tonight, and the magnitude of the decision she'd made. Tomorrow, her world would be different. She'd have Adam.

She'd no longer be alone.

And after tonight's benefit auction, some other woman would be sharing a dinner date and laughing with Jay.

Georgia acknowledged the truth: she envied the mystery woman that carefree, frivolous experience.

One of the other bachelors tapped his shoulder, and Jay's fierce focus shifted, breaking the bond between them. He got up and headed for the stage.

When Jay leaped up the stairs two at a time, and sauntered into the spotlight, Georgia found herself tracking his long strides. He finally stopped and turned to face the crowded gallery, dimples slashing his cheeks as he grinned and adopted a pose so typical of Jay: legs spread apart, hands on his hips, head tilted back. Confident. Arrogant.

Of course, it only served to show off the superb cut of his tuxedo—and the lean body beneath. A charge pulsed through the crowd as the female half of the audience swooned.

The opening bid came quickly from Georgia's left.

Xia. A top fashion blogger. She and Jay had dated a while back. The relationship had fizzled out, but it had led to some fantastic product exposure for Kingdom on Xia's blog. Roberta still raved about the Xia Factor.

"Come, ladies, get out those checkbooks." The auctioneer was extolling Jay's virtues. Cameras flashed.

This was Charis's cue.

Georgia glanced across the table—but the chair Charis had occupied only minutes before was empty. Roberta was no help, either—she was conversing with her date, their heads close together. Quickly, Georgia scanned the gallery. There was no sign of Charis's stunning dress anywhere. Where had her sister gone?

From the lofty height of the stage, Jay's gaze met hers. His eyes were narrowed in challenge.

Of its own volition, her hand lifted.

"Is that a bid?" the auctioneer asked.

Georgia nodded.

Somewhere at a table behind Georgia, a woman whooped with excitement. Her girlfriends giggled, urging her on. Georgia turned in her chair and watched as a gorgeous platinum blonde, poured into a glittering red dress and sporting heavily mascaraed lashes that were too long to possibly be real, raised her hand to place a bid.

An unfamiliar tension curled through Georgia.

She narrowed her eyes. The woman didn't look like Jay's type—too glamorous. Too blond. Then it struck her: as much as she and Jay snarked and argued, she didn't really know what Jay's type was. Xia was beautiful in an exotic kind of way. Then there'd been a willowy fashion model: Dominique, if she remembered correctly. And there'd been a couple of others who had lasted little more than a couple of months. Nic and Carrie. Georgia couldn't believe she remembered their names.

Jay's girlfriends never seemed to last long.

There were no photos of any women in his office. Come to think of it, there were no photos of any description.

She told herself that Jay deserved better. She told herself that Kingdom contributed to the Bachelors for a Better Future Benefit Auction every year. She told herself a lot of things. And she even told herself that it was irrelevant how much fun it might be to call a truce on their rivalry and to spend a carefree evening enjoying laughter and a little champagne.

All the while, Jay's grin taunted her, daring her to do it.

She'd make it quick. Georgia drew a deep breath. "Ten thousand dollars."

Satisfaction filled her at the sudden silence that followed.

Xia was undeterred. "Eleven thousand."

"Twelve thousand." The glamorous blonde in the too-tight dress.

"Twelve and a half." Xia again.

"Thirteen." Glam sounded smug.

Xia shrugged, graciously giving in. Glam grinned, certain of her win.

"Bids?" The auctioneer called. "Ladies! Spoil yourself. You owe it to yourself to have a great evening for a good cause with this fine specimen of manhood here."

Sounds blurred around her. Lights flashed. Adam rejoined the table, sinking back into the chair beside her, and she only spared him one glance—glimpsing his dark frowning face—before swinging her attention back to the stage. Jay was worth blowing the whole budget on. After all, it was for a good cause.

"Fifteen thousand." Her voice rang out, loud to her own ears.

"Sixteen," Glam came back instantly.

Fifteen thousand was the agreed budget. Georgia barely hesitated. She didn't want that woman winning Jay for the night.

"Twenty thousand."

On the stage, Jay stopped grinning, and his eyes locked with hers.

"Twenty-two."

Glam wasn't giving up.

"Twenty-five thousand dollars," Georgia said with grim finality.

"That's more than we allocated from the marketing budget for tonight's event," Roberta chided from across the table as the auctioneer crowed, "Gone."

Georgia didn't spare her sister a glance; she was too busy trying to read the unfathomable expression on Jay's face. Was that a hint of satisfaction? Or a fresh challenge? But she replied, without needing to think too much, "It will be worth it—and it should make a splash in the fashion magazines and the wider media. There are enough cameras here tonight—plus it's tax deductible."

"It will need a fair amount of press coverage," Adam broke in, "to recoup that kind of expenditure."

"Leave it to me." Roberta was grinning. "I'll make sure I organize photos of Jay and Georgia wearing plenty of Kingdom loot in an A-list dining location that will get us the best kind of exposure."

Before Georgia could respond, Adam said, "Georgia, I'd like a word with you. Alone."

Seven

Georgia was conscious of Jay's eyes boring into the back of her head as she picked up her clutch, slung its delicate silver chain over her shoulder and rose from the table. Adam's hand rested on the base of her spine, and a commanding pressure guided her forward.

A set of doors led to a glass-enclosed balcony that ran along the length of the gallery. Georgia knew that once she stepped over that threshold, her relationship with Adam would change forever.

But she told herself this was what she wanted. She could salvage what she'd worked so hard to attain by marrying Adam. She would be President and CEO of Kingdom one day.

Why should she allow Jay's cautions to spoil her vision of the future?

Drawing a deep breath, Georgia stepped forward.

Beyond the glass walls, the cityscape glittered.

Adam's hand slid down her bare arm and came to rest against her hand. His fingers were cool, his touch curiously impersonal, despite the skin-to-skin contact.

Mr. Ice.

Unbidden, Jay's description of Adam leaped into her

mind. Georgia fought to block it out. *Not now.* Not when she needed to focus on Adam, focus on building a rapport with the man.

They were going to be partners. Intimate partners. In business. In marriage. In everything…

"What a beautiful night," she said.

Adam got straight to the point. "Your father has spoken to you—you know why we're here."

She nodded mutely.

This was it, the moment when her life changed. Georgia half expected the earth to move.

"What exactly is your relationship with Jay Black?"

What? She goggled at him. "Jay and I work together."

Adam arched his eyebrow in response.

"We're colleagues. We… We're responsible for a lot of Kingdom's strategic planning," she found herself stuttering. The antagonism and secret rivalry between her and Jay was something she didn't care to share, but Adam needed to understand that Jay was central to Kingdom's success. "And he's my father's right-hand man."

"Women don't bid twenty-five thousand dollars on a colleague."

"You heard Roberta. It was nothing more than a PR stunt."

Except it had felt way more personal than that…

Before she could marshal her scattered thoughts, Adam was already reaching into the pocket of his dinner jacket.

"I've got something for you."

"Oh?"

He drew a small square box from the pocket of his suit jacket. "I think you'll like it." He flipped the box open. "It has all three *c*'s—cut, clarity and color. Four, if you add carat. It's as good an investment as a diamond can be."

Investment. The ring sparkled up at her.

"Try it on."

Georgia slowly took the ring from the box.

"It's impressive." Then, in case that sounded too clinical, she added, "It's magnificent."

The ring was magnificent…in an icy classic kind of way. Was this how Adam perceived her? Flawless and glittering? The perfect trophy wife?

As good of an investment as a woman could be?

And why not? Her father measured her worth in the same terms.

"We will be married next June."

A summer wedding…

But instead of a warm wave of pleasure, Georgia felt flustered at his haste. He was talking of wedding arrangements already. What had happened to courtship? To getting to know each other? He'd taken her assent for granted. Was that her father's doing? Had he assured Adam she would not object?

Anger started to smolder deep within her heart. *Fine!* She'd let Adam find out who she was through negotiations—nothing new to her about that.

"We'll need to hammer out a prenup first." She spoke carefully, giving herself time to think and get her emotions under control.

"Sure." He shrugged. "But we already have an agreement in principle."

He stepped forward and his hands slid around her shoulders. He was tall—well over six feet. And solid. His chest rose like a fortress in front of her.

Reaching out a hand, she placed it on the wall of hard muscle that blocked out the light around her. Adam tensed. Panic crushed her. For an awful moment, Georgia felt… trapped.

She fought the suffocating claustrophobia that had come out of nowhere.

Deep breaths, she cautioned herself. It was okay. She

was okay. Or she would be, as soon as she pulled herself together.

Adam was going to kiss her...

She couldn't afford to screw this up. It had to work. And it was up to her to make sure it did.

She turned her face up and closed her eyes, dreading what was coming.

When his lips landed, they were firm...and cool. Adam Fordyce kissed with technique. That, at least, was a relief.

Yet, instead of being swept away by lust, as she should have been, Georgia found herself waiting...

And waiting.

For what, she wasn't sure. Whatever it was didn't happen.

He slid his hands along her back and pressed her closer. Out of nowhere came a stab of stark terror. She went as stiff as a board.

He raised his head.

"Nice," she choked out.

Made of ice, she found herself thinking.

Damn Jay! And why was she thinking of Jay, anyway? Or the coffee-flavored kiss full of care and tenderness he'd bestowed on her yesterday...?

The memory of their too-short moments of warmth and comfort in the garden's pale sunshine contrasted with the darkness that surrounded Adam. She pulled away a little more.

"Yes."

It took Georgia a scattered moment to realize that Adam was agreeing with her assessment of that cold kiss as *nice*.

In the dim light, she couldn't read his expression. It might've helped ease the tension in her stomach, the thunder in her head. She drew a slow steadying breath.

Nice.

She'd lied.

And the earth hadn't moved.

Beyond the glass walls, the buildings dominating the skyline stood glittering and silent. Nothing had changed.

Only the hammering of her heart.

She immediately grew impatient with her own reaction. Why should the earth have moved? She wasn't some teen princess with grandiose expectations anymore. She was a grown-up woman, with a hotshot position on the executive team at an iconic fashion house. Hey, she knew that the earth didn't move because of a kiss. That fireworks and glass slippers and golden rings forever were nothing more than fantasy. She understood reality. Adam was a real man—not a fairy tale prince.

She and Adam shared a common vision: commercial success.

It was a start—they would build on it.

She couldn't afford to think about the urge to flee; she wouldn't think about Ridley…and she wouldn't think of Jay. She had to think of Kingdom.

"Very nice," she amended, trying harder. *Throw more heart in, Georgia.* They would both have to work on this. She'd do more than her bit. Like she always did.

Georgia tried to forget that moment of panic when he'd taken her into his arms, that sensation of being trapped and crushed, that terrifying spike of adrenaline. It had come out of the blackness at the bottom of her brain… It had happened before, when she thought of Ridley, of that moment she'd walked into the hotel suite and found him with a sales assistant on the bed. While the woman had struggled to get her dress back on, Ridley had lit into Georgia, telling her it was her fault. She didn't have what it took to hold a man.

And after that, a big dark blank…

Not now. Please not now.

So she filled her lungs with air, and tried to smile at Adam.

If she tried a little harder, if she invested some more enthusiasm, it might ignite some magic. But searching for the positive side was hard work.

Especially when she longed for Jay. For the barbs and banter that had become so familiar. At least she knew where she stood with him. Most of the time. She longed to use him as a sounding board to clear this confusion that kissing Adam had evoked. To clear the sudden doubt she was experiencing...

Grow up, Georgia.

This is your life. Nothing to do with Jay...

Another thought struck her. Had Adam's cold kiss been intended to seal the execution of an agreement? Had it been that calculated?

She was a person, dammit. Someone with emotions and dreams, who possessed a heart, as well as a brain.

"There are some..." *terms* was too unromantic a word, Georgia decided "...things we need to discuss before I agree."

"Things?"

She shrugged, feeling unaccountably foolish. *Negotiate.* She gritted her teeth. "How this marriage is going to work."

"It'll work like any other marriage."

From nowhere, Jay's voice flashed into her head. *And plenty have ended in bitterness and acrimony. Don't you want more out of life than a billion-dollar divorce settlement?*

"Really?" She arched her eyebrows. "Most people don't marry for the reasons we will be marrying." *Most couples are in love, actually.* But of course, she didn't say that.

"So what things do you want to discuss?"

Now she felt even more idiotic. But Jay's sweet kiss of comfort in the hospital garden yesterday had let a whole lot of emotions out of the box. What with her father's dramas, and now this.... Boy, over the past few days, she'd discovered emotions she hadn't even known existed.

"Uh…how we will communicate—"

She broke off. Adam was staring at her as though she were crazy.

"How we will communicate?" he repeated. "Like most people do, I should think."

She could feel herself flushing. She tried again, "I'm talking about…"

Sex.

Adam's face darkened.

For a moment, she thought he understood.

But then he swung away from her, presenting her with a broad shoulder. Half his face was in shadow. The ring she still clutched mocked her. She caught a flash of cold fire and glanced quickly away, reluctant to fit it on her finger yet.

Turning back to face her, he spoke again. "You're aware of my relationship with Charis?"

Georgia sighed a small sigh of relief. It was too soon to be discussing intimate details—his change of subject was a good idea. Rapidly, she reviewed which of Charis's current projects Adam might be involved with. She drew a blank. "I didn't know you and Charis had any business dealings."

"My relationship with Charis has nothing to do with business." There was a husky undertone to his voice, a smoky heat in his eyes that belied his nickname.

That caught Georgia's attention. On rewind, her sister's silence this evening played through her mind, and understanding dawned in a flash. "Oh, my God. You're talking about a personal relationship, aren't you?"

Adam stared back at her, unblinking.

There was an instant of disbelief.

Then the outrageous idea coalesced into certainty. "You're lovers!"

The silence stretched as she waited—in vain—for a denial that never came. Tightness bubbled at the back of her throat as she thought about the kiss he'd given her while her sister sat inside the ballroom.

"Uh...the relationship is over?"

Of course, it must be. She couldn't believe she was even asking.

Otherwise—

His silence took on the quality of cold forged steel.

Otherwise...how could he possibly propose to her? Or kiss her? Her stomach twisted, a sick sensation filling it as the silence grew colder.

Georgia held up the glittering diamond engagement ring he'd given her like a talisman. "It's over as of now. Right?"

Adam's head jerked back. "That ring changes nothing. You need to understand that our marriage will not change my relationship with Charis—that's non-negotiable."

"You mean...you're going to..." she broke off, seeking a sanitized way of uttering the unspeakable "...you're going to keep..." *sleeping with* "...seeing...my sister while you're married to me?"

"I'm glad you understand."

Understand? Georgia stared at him. Had she gone completely crazy? Or was he crazy?

"So," she drawled, her brain working overtime to catch up, "you've discussed this with my sister? She knows you'll be married to me, even while you sleep with her?"

He gazed at her through slitted eyes, his face an iron mask. "Charis will do exactly as I want."

What he wanted was to marry Georgia and sleep with her sister. Have his cake and eat it. Bile rose at the back of her throat. Georgia's heart ached. For Charis...and for herself. The situation was ghastly beyond anything she'd ever contemplated.

Finally, she said, "So I guess our marriage will be in name only."

Adam didn't reply.

A numbing emptiness invaded her. Was this what she wanted? A marriage that was nothing more than a business arrangement? Marriage to a man who was sleeping with her sister?

You deserve more...

Jay was right. This travesty wasn't what she wanted.

"I want children," she said at last. The thought uncurled out of the secret mists of her mind. It was something she'd never contemplated, but which had always been there. Except she hadn't known it existed.

Adam was saying something. She hadn't heard a word of it.

"What?"

He spoke again, slowly, as though she were simple. "A child is no problem."

"No problem?" She tried to grasp what he meant by that. "You mean IVF, right?"

"There are easier solutions." His voice dropped, each word softly clipped.

Her whole being rocked as the words sunk in.

"Easier solutions?" she echoed the heresy he'd uttered and stared at him, shocked. He didn't just mean to marry her and sleep with Charis—he meant to sleep with them both! "But…"

How would her sister feel about that?

Certainty settled in fast. Jay was right. Adam Fordyce truly was made of ice. There was no humanity in the man who stood before her, his eyes so dead. Nothing. Jay might be maddening and infuriating. But at least he still had feelings. Emotions. This man had none.

Amoral asshat!

Poor Charis.

No wonder her sister had looked so miserable.

But Georgia knew how she felt about it. And that made her decision easy.

She handed the ring back to him.

Damn. Jay had been right. Again.

"I can't marry you, Adam. I'm sorry."

Why was she apologizing?

"Your father—"

Georgia shook her head. "No. Not even for my father."

He stared icily down his long straight nose at her. "Sleep on it."

Nausea rose in her throat at his phrasing.

"Keep the ring." His confidence was staggering.

She shook her head and thrust it back at him.

"At least take the weekend to think it over. Once you've had a chance to think about it, you'll realize there's no point throwing away everything we'll have together." He smiled. But the thin smile didn't reach his remote colorless eyes. "Call me on Monday morning—we'll talk some more. This is going to work."

Georgia knew she was going to be sick.

"Shall we go back in?"

Unable to speak, Georgia nodded. She hitched the chain of her clutch higher up on her shoulder. His hand rested lightly on her hip as he escorted her toward the gallery filled with chatter and laughter.

A sideways glance revealed that he was smiling, a hard savage smile.

"I need to go to the cloakroom." And then she needed to find Jay. He was the one person she could rely on to help her.

Without a backward glance, she left Mr. Ice standing alone on the threshold of the crowded room.

Georgia slunk into the ladies' room. Beyond tall urns overflowing with fragrant lilies and a velvet-covered chaise, she spotted a familiar exquisitely beaded gown.

Charis.

Her sister had seen her enter and was watching her in an ornately framed gilded mirror.

Despite her inner upheaval, Georgia flicked her a quick awkward smile. But Charis didn't smile back.

"Your lipstick is smudged." Her sister's face was pale and tight.

"Oh." Georgia flushed, and humiliation crawled through her. Damn Adam for putting her in this situation! She extracted Jay's crumpled handkerchief from the clutch slung over her shoulder and rubbed frantically at her mouth.

"It's fine now." Charis's voice was flat.

Nothing was fine. God, this was awkward. "We need to talk."

Charis's gaze shifted to her own reflection. She pursed her lips into a moue. "Come hell or high water, I'm going to finish the spring collection if it kills me."

"Father doesn't want you in the build—"

"He doesn't need to know!"

Georgia started to argue, then thought better of it.

"Why didn't you say you were dating Adam Fordyce when Kingston made his announcement?"

"I don't want to talk about it."

"Charis—" Georgia broke off, searching for an easy way to say this. "Listen, I'm not going to marry him—"

"Have you told that to our dear father?"

"No." Georgia's stomach seized up at the thought. "But I will."

"Good luck with that." Charis tossed the soiled towel in the disposal slot.

Then, for the first time since Georgia had entered the cloakroom, her sister swung around to face her.

"He won't let you back out."

She wasn't sure whether her sister meant their father or Adam Fordyce.

Tonelessly, Charis added, "You're welcome to Adam."

Georgia said in a rush, "I don't want him. Adam Fordyce makes me sick!"

"Then that makes two of us." There was such savagery in Charis's voice that Georgia recoiled.

Jay's provocative question rang in her head. *You'd marry a man you've never met, a man your father picked out for his ability to run Kingdom? Why?*

It had seemed so clear-cut, so logical.

Until Adam had kissed her…and then, to her appalled shame, her body had taken over…and the reaction had not been good. She'd found herself thinking of Jay…

So she'd turned Adam down. For the first time in her life, she'd gone against her father's wishes.

Once Kingston found out…

Georgia shuddered with dread.

But her father didn't know what she'd done. Not yet.

She felt a flare of hope. There had to be a solution. A way to keep her father happy…and keep her position safe. An overwhelming desire to talk to Jay filled her. Jay always gave her perspective. He had the ability to ask questions that made the solutions to whatever was bothering her so obvious.

She glanced at Charis. Her sister was blotting her lips with a tissue. She looked composed…but ghostly pale.

"Are you okay?"

Charis's eyes were dark and distant. "Why wouldn't I be? I have a collection to finish. I'm going to make it the biggest success Kingdom has ever seen. Then I'm going to live my life—without all the never-ending drama that comes attached to Kingdom."

Georgia wanted to argue—to convince Charis that Kingdom was what kept them together. Kept them family. She ached for what might've been. For all the years that had been lost. But Charis was clearly in no mood for a heart-to-heart.

She touched Charis's arm. "I don't suppose you know where Jay is?"

Charis shook her off. "He went home."

"Home?" Georgia realized she didn't even know where Jay lived. No matter. Bruno would know.

"He's flying out on vacation." Her sister opened the cloakroom door.

"No he's not!"

Georgia grabbed her clutch. Jay wasn't going anywhere. Not until he'd helped her sort this mess out.

Eight

It was already after midnight.

Jay had just finished packing the last white profession-ally pressed T-shirt into his bag and was about to zip it shut in readiness for his early morning flight when the doorbell chimed. Before he had a chance to react, it sounded again.

"Hold your horses!" He strode through the apartment and yanked open the front door.

Georgia stood in front of him.

To catch his breath, Jay leaned against the doorjamb and folded his arms across his chest. Even as he examined her, he prayed she wouldn't detect the sudden drumroll in his chest.

Jay didn't bother to ask how she'd gotten past the door-man; Georgia on a mission could achieve anything she set her mind to.

Under her evening coat, she was still wearing the midnight blue couture slip dress she'd worn to the benefit auction—and she clung to the silver-sequined Kingdom clutch that Jay had recognized from last fall's collection. Her silver-blond hair was still drawn off her face in a stylish knot although sev-eral tendrils had escaped, adding to her air of fragility. The stark simplicity of the look was broken only by the stunning pair of art deco diamond drop earrings he knew were her sole legacy from her mother…and a stain of red on her lips.

His gaze narrowed. Her lipstick was slightly smudged around the edges, showing signs of hasty repair. Her lips were full, ripe. Kissed.

Jay suppressed the surge of raw emotion that shook him. He might not know where she'd been, but he had a damned good idea who she'd been with…

"What do you want, Georgia?"

"May I come in?"

Cocking his wrist, he glanced at his watch. "It's late."

"You promised to share a bottle of champagne with me if I bid on you—so here I am."

Too late for champagne now, too late for the intimate tête-à-tête he'd planned to soften her outrage. He thought of all the great intentions he'd had to tell Georgia the truth.

But now it was too late to confess that he'd lied from the outset. That he'd never been recruited to fill the position Ridley—her errant fiancé—had left vacant at Kingdom. While she'd been recovering from a car crash that had sheared away a portion of her memory, he'd taken advantage of being in the right place at the right time so that he could have second chance to get to know her better.

He risked another glance at her tempting strawberry-red lips as the dreams that had sustained him for two years turned to dust.

He should've told her the truth, instead of being such a damned coward.

But he hadn't—and now it was too goddamned late.

There was no point in discussing the night they'd first met—a night she'd long since forgotten. Why open an old wound that held so much trauma for her? There was no point in convincing her to give him a chance to start over. Georgia was lost to him.

She'd followed her father's orders.

Yet, still, Jay found himself unable to resist the inexorable force that caused him to step back, allowing her space to pass and enter his apartment, even though the tightness in his lower gut warned him this was a dumb idea. Despite an urge to slam it, he shut the door with a dull click.

She shrugged off her coat, and he hung it up on one of the coat hooks that lined the hall alcove.

He flat-handed a control panel on the wall as he passed by, and the apartment exploded into bright light. Now was not the time for dim mood lighting. He waved her into the living space ahead of him. At the island of Carrara marble that functioned as a dining table and divided the streamlined butler-style kitchen from the lounge, he stopped, keeping the slab between them.

He didn't want her anywhere near him—not now, looking so well-kissed by another man.

A man she intended marry...for Kingdom's sake.

"You want a drink?" He sure needed one. "Tequila?"

Her shoulders hunched. "Not tequila!"

Stop being an ass, Black!

"What about a glass of that champagne you offered earlier?" Her brightness sounded forced.

He was in no mood to celebrate. Instead, he said, "How about coffee?"

"Much as I'd love a cup, the caffeine will keep me awake."

Jay clawed a bottle of whiskey out of the liquor cabinet and poured two stiff fingers of amber liquid into a tumbler. The time had come for him to cut his losses. To leave Kingdom, the cold corporation that had chained Georgia's soul. To find some distant place to lick his wounds in peace—preferably across a wide stretch of ocean.

London. Paris. Sydney.

Whatever. He certainly had no intention of dancing at Georgia's high society New York wedding.

For the first time, he was grateful that he'd be out of town for the next couple of weeks.

The tumbler thudded against the marble. He reached for a second glass, poured in a shot and pushed it across the slab to her. "Why did you come here?"

She set her glitzy clutch down and faced him across the sleek black-veined slab, her eyes unexpectedly shadowed. "I need…advice."

"Has something happened?" Giving a silent snort of derision, he picked up his glass and swirled the whiskey around the glass when she didn't answer.

Dammit, he could see what had happened. It didn't take a genius to work it out.

Genius? He was an ass!

He contemplated her over the lip of his glass. "It's Fordyce, isn't it?"

She nodded. "He asked—or, should I say, expected—me to marry him."

No surprise there.

"Congratulations." Jay took a slug of whiskey, set the half-empty glass down and wiped the back of his hand across his mouth to stop himself from swearing violently.

His pain would go away. Someday. On his deathbed.

Georgia leaned toward him and spread her hands out on the marble countertop. "Do you see a ring?"

He stared at her fourth finger.

It was bare.

The breath left his lungs, and his gaze skittered across the marble before rising to her face. "You turned him down?"

"Stone cold."

Stepping around the cold sleek slab, all he could see was the fullness of her bottom lip. "But you kissed him."

"*He* kissed *me*."

Under the stain of strawberry-red lipstick, her mouth

was trembling. The tip of her tongue slid along the inside of her lip, and he wrenched his eyes away.

"I couldn't go through with it."

She was pale, her eyes stricken. What the hell had caused her to look so wounded? Instead of a surge of triumph, Jay quelled an overpowering desire to go and hunt Adam Fordyce down. To pummel the tycoon to a pulp with his bare fists. Leashing his rage, he asked levelly, "What happened?"

Georgia wrapped her arms around herself and rubbed her palms over her bare shoulders. "You say he's made of ice. You're wrong—he's colder than ice."

Jay clenched his hands into fists at his sides. There wasn't a trace of ice within him. Only a raging molten heat.

"What did he do?"

"Nothing. He didn't hurt me—at least not physically." She shivered and goose bumps rose on her arms. "Sticks and stones—it's not true."

What the hell?

"Tell me!" Jay insisted.

She shook her head and winced. Uncrossing her arms, she smoothed her hands over her face, over her hair, coming to a stop as she encountered the topknot. "My head hurts too much."

Restraining his impatience to know what Fordyce had said to rattle her so deeply, Jay murmured, "Your hair is tied too tight. Take out those pins."

He moved so close that he could see the flecks of silver in her bewildered eyes. His fingers were already unclenching to help her. Her hair came down in a swath of soft silk. Jay's fingers tangled in the silver mass, threading through it, combing it until it fell around her face.

"Better?" he asked as gently as he could.

She nodded. "Jay, I'm so glad you were home."

Unexpectedly, she leaned forward to rest her forehead against his chest.

Jay went rigid with shock. He forced his hands down to his sides. She nestled against him, tucked against the white fabric of his dress shirt, while his heart rattled an erratic tattoo beneath. It was hard to remember that Georgia never liked being touched, that she held herself separate, distant. But not now. Not tonight.

If he bent his head, his lips would touch the fine silver hair—

Fool!

One. Breathe in.

Two. Out.

All Georgia wanted was a confidant. A little comfort. She'd had one hell of a week. He needed to keep reminding himself of that simple fact, until his moronic body got the message.

She lifted her face. "Can I ask you something?"

His hands wrapped into fists to stop himself from touching her.

"You can ask," he said warily.

"Is…is—" she stammered. "This is harder than I thought it would be."

Uh-huh. "What?"

"Um—"

"Spit it out!"

She bit her lip, and a pink flush warmed her cheeks. "Do you have a dream woman?"

He felt himself flush in turn. Saw her eyes register his discomfort.

"Oh," she said.

He felt awkward and exposed. "What nonsense is this?"

"Charis is your dream woman?" she asked.

"Charis?" It was the last thing he'd expected her to say.

"My sister."

"I know who Charis is," he growled.

Jay held back a curse. The woman he wanted was far from a dream. She was real. Flesh and blood. And she was cuddled up against him. Yet he didn't trust himself to touch her.

"Jay?"

There was a strange expression in Georgia's eyes. Was that yearning he read there? Or was he indulging in another futile fantasy?

"No," he finally said, "Charis is not my dream woman."

"I'm so glad to hear that."

His heart thumped in his chest, and he silently cursed the leap of hope. "What's this about?"

"So there's no chance that you might want to marry Charis?"

"I've answered that before." He knew he sounded terse. "Why all these questions?"

"Adam and Charis are lovers." She dropped her head down, and her voice was muffled by his shirtfront again. "I didn't want you to get hurt…if you felt something for Charis."

Jay almost laughed. Jesus…what a royal screwup Kingston had made.

"Did Fordyce tell you that?"

"It was obvious—and he didn't deny it when I blurted it out. It gets worse." She sucked in a deep shuddering breath. "I thought he was telling me their affair was over. He'd just proposed to me—if one could call it that. Whatever it was, he'd given me a ring. Stupid me." Her whole frame shook against him. "God, I was wrong. So wrong." Another shiver went through her, and she buried her face deeper against him. "Adam told me he would continue to sleep with my sister…that it wouldn't interfere with our marriage."

Damn Fordyce!

"I didn't even know Charis was seeing him."

Georgia's hurt and bewilderment hung between them, and Jay couldn't think of a single platitude that might ease her pain. Finally, he allowed his fists to uncurl and let his arms steal up around her. Bowing his head over hers, Jay couldn't escape the soft feminine scent of her. To his horror, blood rushed to his groin.

"How did you respond?" His voice was husky.

Georgia's head came up so quickly that his lips brushed across her forehead. She pulled back a little, putting space between them, and his arms fell away.

Had she felt his arousal? God, he hoped not.

"What do you think I did? I told him I couldn't marry him." Her chin came up. "I told him I needed the bathroom—I felt sick."

Jay forgot his own dilemma. He snorted. "You actually told him that? That he made you sick?"

"Not quite." For the first time, a spark of her familiar feistiness showed through her anguish. "Trust me, there was nothing funny about it."

"I'm not laughing." But he felt a rush of very male satisfaction. In all their barbed exchanges, he might have annoyed her, frustrated her, but he'd never made Georgia sick...

"I ran into Charis in the ladies' room." Her words tripped over each other. "I don't understand her. I don't think I ever have."

The pain that underpinned her confession made Jay swallow. God help Fordyce when he found the man...

"She told me she intends to be part of the launch of the spring collection—and to hell with whether Kingston lets her or not."

"Well, I suppose that's one bit of good news."

His response didn't help.

"It's not! I don't think she intends to stay at Kingdom. She didn't even want to talk to me. She's always been as stubborn as a mule. She even told me I was welcome to Adam—and then she picked up her purse and walked out." Georgia gulped in a deep breath. "I couldn't bring myself to go back into the ballroom, but Adam was waiting for me in the lobby. That's when I got really scared because he looked so terrifying. He said I had to marry him, it was all arranged—" She broke off.

The wild despair in her eyes tore his heart out.

Under his intense scrutiny, Georgia colored. "So I ran."

"To me."

"It was run to you…or throw up that five-hundred-dollar-a-plate dinner onto his highly polished handmade shoes."

That was his Georgia!

Something like euphoria made him feel as high as a kite. He stepped forward and took her into his arms. It felt…right.

"You don't have to do anything you don't want."

She sighed. "Just hold me, Jay. Please?"

God.

Torn between the need to give her the comfort she craved and his fear of what might happen next, Jay shuddered. There was no way he could disguise the effect her closeness was having on his body. But there was no chance that he'd resist her request.

Even if it cost him his peace of mind.

When his phone buzzed in his pocket, Jay cursed silently at the sudden tensing of Georgia's body.

"Is it Kingston?" she whispered, her fear tangible. "Charis?"

The spell was broken.

Jay moved away and pulled his phone out.

"It's my mother."

"Answer it—something may be wrong."

He bit down on a tide of four-letter words. Against his better judgment, Jay accepted the call.

His mom was loud and enthusiastic. He made himself wink at Georgia as he waited for his mother to run out of steam, and as soon as she slowed down, he said, "Mom, I'll call you back later. I'm in the middle of something."

"You work too hard, Jay. You should consider coming home. Permanently."

He didn't intend to have that discussion right now—not with Georgia watching, and a hard-on to end all hard-ons filling his pants. "Mom—"

"It would make your father so happy. And Suzie is looking forward to seeing you again. We all are. You've been gone too long."

He was relieved to hear that Suzie actually wanted to see him again. Georgia shifted from one high-heel clad foot to the other in obvious discomfort. Before he could smile at her, she drifted farther into his apartment, clearly intent on giving him some privacy.

"Mom, I have to go. I have someone with me." He cut off her rush of questions. "I'll see you tomorrow."

Jay killed the call and went in pursuit of Georgia.

Through an open door, Georgia spotted what had to be Jay's bedroom.

The enormous windows on the opposite wall framed the brightly lit city skyline.

Wow!

Fascination drove her into the room. It was decorated in shades of navy and dull gold brightened with an ivory knit throw draped across the bed. Over the headboard hung an abstract canvas full of stormy movement, dominated by midnight blues and inky grays, a narrow shaft of light piercing the dark turmoil.

Then she spotted the open steamer bag beside the bed. The sight drove all other thoughts out of her head.

She heard footsteps behind her.

Without taking her eyes off the bag, she asked, "When exactly do you leave?"

"First thing in the morning."

Georgia wished she could escape like Jay. Fly away. Go home to a family where everything was simple and uncomplicated. Before she could stop herself, she found herself saying, "Can I come with you?"

"What?"

Trying not to feel foolish, she considered pretending she'd been joking—as Jay had been when he'd invited her to marry him. But the impulsive idea wouldn't go away…

In a rush, she said, "I could check online and see if there are still seats available…" Her voice trailed away when she got no response. Maybe it was a stupid idea. "We don't even need to sit together."

"Why?"

At last, she turned to him.

He stood a couple of feet behind her. The dark intensity in his eyes unsettled her.

"Why don't we need to sit together?" By deliberately misunderstanding his question, she tried to inject some humor into an exchange that had grown astonishingly awkward.

For the first time, she became aware that it was well past midnight…that she was standing in his bedroom…that several buttons of his rumpled shirt were undone, revealing the chest she'd buried her head against. And his feet were bare. It was intimate. They were asking for trouble.

Yet, she wasn't the least bit afraid.

This was Jay…

Although she had to admit, after the auction earlier tonight, she was seeing him in a different light. He was a very attractive man. It would be all too easy to fall for him.

But Jay had never had any interest in her. She simply wasn't his type.

Jay still hadn't smiled. "Why would you want to come with me?"

"I need a break."

God, she hoped she didn't sound like she was begging, but she was at the end of her tether.

"You want to avoid your father," he said slowly.

"No," she denied too fiercely. She looked down, away from that penetrating gaze. "I just need to leave." Escape. Her father was going to kill her when he found out she'd turned Adam down.

The air vibrated with her desperation.

Jay blew out a breath in an explosive gust that sounded loud to her ears. "Georgia, you have to tell your father that you're not going to marry Adam."

"I know. I know. I will." *Someday.* "Just not yet."

Jay went silent again. From under her eyelashes, Georgia watched him, trying to read his thoughts. He must be thinking she was the biggest coward on earth.

As the seconds passed, the mounting tension started to get to her. Even taunts and rivalry were better than his silence.

Well, she'd better get used to it. Jay was going to be gone for two weeks.

It would mean two weeks without his heckling. Without his laughter and lame jokes. Without that crooked smile at her office door each morning...and two take-out coffees in his hands. Without someone to argue with and bounce her ideas off—and share the triumph of success with. The place was going to be dead without him.

She swallowed, stunned at how forlorn she felt.

Somehow, Jay Black had become so much more than

a threatening rival. More than a colleague to collaborate with.

An astonishing realization struck her.

Jay had become a friend.

A friend she could turn to for support…and comfort. She remembered the electric brush of his lips against hers. That had been something more than friendship…

No!

She couldn't afford any disturbing thoughts about Jay. He was her friend. Better to have him as a friend than a lover who would betray her at the first opportunity.

She gazed at him, silently imploring.

Jay thrust his hands through his hair, causing the espresso-brown strands to stand up untidily. "Georgia, it's my parents' wedding anniversary—"

"You're right. I'd be party-crashing." Embarrassment seared her.

"It's nothing like that." He gave her a long look. "But you'd be better off facing up to your father."

Watching Jay cross the room and hunker down to zip the steamer bag shut, she tried to imagine his parents' home in some pretty, small town. It would be modest. With a white picket fence. No doubt, his mother and father loved Jay to death. She seemed to remember that his family had visited him over the past couple of years. Jay had taken them to shows on Broadway, done family stuff. Not that she'd given it much thought; she'd been focused on work. Now she wished she'd paid more attention…even asked to meet his family. She thought of how fondly he'd smiled a few minutes ago while he'd spoken to his mom. A wave of something close to envy swept her.

It had been a long time since she'd had a mom.

Only a dad. Her mom had driven away one day and she'd never come back. It had been left up to Kingston to tell them weeks later about the helicopter crash that had claimed the life of their cheating mom and the boyfriend she'd loved more than her daughters.

What would it be like to have grown up in a safe, secure environment like Jay's family? To be loved for oneself? To have no expectations placed on you from the moment of birth? To have a mom—and a dad—who loved you?

To her surprise, Georgia discovered she wanted to find out. She wanted to feel what it was like to live in the warm surroundings of a normal family.

If only for a week…

Except she had to be back at work by Monday. Kingston would be there—supposedly taking it easy.

But if she could escape for the weekend…

"Jay?"

He looked up, his eyes unfathomable.

Hauling in a deep breath, she said with raw honesty, "I haven't taken a vacation in years. I'm not coping well with the decisions I've had to make this week. Going away for a couple days will give me a chance to get some perspective. Please, may I come?" Laying herself open like this was hard. She tried to smile but her bottom lip trembled. "I won't stay long—only until, say, Sunday night."

"What about your father?"

She fought the claustrophobic fear of her father's displeasure when he learned she'd left without a word. Even worse would be his rage when he learned she'd turned Adam down. She couldn't face him. Not yet. He'd steamroll her to change her mind, to go prostrate herself to Adam.

"I'll make sure Marcia and Roberta take care of him until Monday."

"You know that's not what I mean." Jay's eyes didn't leave hers.

Beneath her apprehension about telling her father that she'd turned Adam down lay the haunting terror that her father was going to disown her. Abandon her. Just like he'd done to Charis…

Without Kingdom, she had no family.

No future…

"Putting it off never makes it any easier. Trust me on that." Jay's smile was crooked. "I speak from experience."

"I know. I know. I'll do it. I won't put it off indefinitely. I'll do it on Monday."

"You don't want Fordyce telling him first—"

"Adam's so sure I'm going to change my mind that he told me to take the weekend to reconsider. He won't say anything to my father. Please, Jay. I need this time away to think about how I'm going to handle Kingston's reaction when I tell him that I've turned Adam Fordyce down." Just thinking about confronting her father caused her stomach to churn anxiously.

Jay's face softened, and her frantic fear eased a little.

Finally, he rose to his feet and placed his hands on his hips. He studied her in a way that was a little too calculating.

"What?" she demanded.

"Okay, if there's a seat, you can come."

She gave a squeal of relief and delight and rushed toward him to throw her arms around him.

"Wait!" He warded her off with one hand, and gave her a ghastly grin. "There's one condition."

"Anything!"

"You should know better than to agree before hearing the terms." His grin grew feral. "Haven't you learned that much this week?"

"Better the devil I know," she teased, back on familiar territory. "What do you want?"

There was an abrupt shift in his expression, and he stopped grinning. "You'll come along as my fiancée."

"What?" She hesitated, uncertain now. "What do you mean, your fiancée?"

"Don't worry. It won't be the real deal."

Were his parents really so conservative? "Uh, surely you can tell your parents we work together…that we're colleagues? We don't need to be engaged to spend a week-end together."

Jay's expression lightened as he gave a chuckle. "My parents haven't spent the past couple of decades buried in the woods. But they're hoping to persuade me to return for good. A fiancée with a career and a family in New York would convince them that's not going to happen."

Georgia was so relieved she would've promised any-thing. Besides, she couldn't wait to meet Jay's small-town family.

"Oh, I can do that. And I can tell them how indispens-able you are to Kingdom, how much Kingston relies on you and what a great future you have ahead of you. They'll be even more proud of you when they find out what a hotshot you are in the Big Apple."

She gave him a smile full of eternal gratitude.

"Thank you, Jay. You're the best—the very best friend I could ever have!"

Nine

Aspen, Colorado.

Jay had collected a sporty black SUV rental at the airport, and now, as they drove through the town bustling with Saturday morning activity, Georgia looked about with interest. Last night, when Georgia had begged Jay to take her home with him, she certainly hadn't expected their destination to be one of the premier ski resorts in the country.

She'd never been to Aspen—clearly, a big mistake. There certainly weren't many towns that boasted Louis Vuitton and Prada stores—Kingdom ought to have had store presence here, too. Georgia made a mental note to follow that up as they left the heart of the town behind, and Jay swung through a roundabout onto the picturesquely named Castle Creek Road. She wondered how far away from Aspen his parents lived. She'd love to come back for a look around the town.

"I thought you might like to see some famous Aspen Gold," said Jay, tossing her a quick grin.

They passed under a bridge, and the road opened out ahead. Georgia bit back a torrent of questions and sat back to enjoy the ride.

The road snaked upward as the dark blue-green mountains rose steeply around them. In the distance ahead, snow-capped peaks jutted out against the Colorado blue sky. The beauty was breathtaking. Her heart soared as they sped into a tunnel of ghostly silver-white trees topped with clouds of golden foliage. Too soon, they emerged on the other side. Seconds later, they swept through a bend, and the next flurry of slim silver-and-gold aspens flashed by. Georgia smiled in delight.

About ten minutes later, Jay slowed and pulled over.

"Why are we stopping?" she asked, turning away from the awe-inspiring landscape.

Jay killed the engine and swiveled to face her. "You'll need an engagement ring."

That brought her swiftly back to reality.

"It's not necessary—it's not a real engagement."

"It is for this weekend. My parents will never believe our engagement is real without a ring." Jay's eyes glimmered. "They'll be annoyed enough that I didn't let them know before."

"But they know I'm coming?"

He shook his head. "It'll be their anniversary surprise."

"You didn't call ahead to let them know you were bringing a guest?"

"You worry too much."

He leaned toward her and she caught a whiff of the delicious woody notes of his aftershave as he reached for his shearling jacket in the back seat. From one of the pockets, Jay extracted a small velvet-covered box and flipped it open.

The ring inside made her gasp.

A gorgeous round art deco diamond—the biggest blue-white she'd ever seen—blinked up at her. Set in white gold, with four diamond-studded petals folded back down the sides, it looked like a flower smiling up at her.

Georgia's heart sank. "My God. What if I lose it?"

"In one weekend?" Jay lifted a brow. "Unlikely. Anyhow, it's insured. Do you like it?"

I love it.

She controlled her impulsive response, but honesty compelled her to say, "It's the most beautiful ring I've ever seen."

Part of her was horrified. Jay earned a very good salary, but he wasn't wealthy…at least, not compared to her family. What he must've spent on that ring wasn't worth a one-weekend charade—unless he had it on loan. But even then, the insurance premiums would be horrific. A ring like this hadn't come from a last-minute foray into one of the airport shops. By some magic, Jay must've pulled strings to have it couriered to him this morning.

His attention to detail left her gasping.

Georgia's lips parted, but when Jay took her hand, all her questions scattered.

"Here, let me put it on." Cradling her hand between both of his, he stroked the length of her fingers. Her skin started to tingle. Then he slipped the ring onto her finger.

A perfect fit.

Adam had never even gotten his as-good-an-investment-as-any-diamond-can-be ring onto her finger. The memory of another engagement ring—Ridley's—crowded in. Shuddering, she blacked out those disastrous associations.

Thank God, this time it was only a pretense.

Because she truly wasn't any good at this engagement stuff…

Jay's ring winked up at her. She thought of her mother's art deco earrings, which were all she had of the woman who had walked away from her three young daughters. She stared at the exquisite ring for a long moment, wishing, wishing… For what? She gave up trying to figure out what she yearned for, and lifted her gaze from the most beautiful ring she'd ever seen to the man beside her.

"Jay, it feels like it's never going to come off."

He was smiling at her, his hazel eyes warm and amused.

Georgia took in his features. The firm chin and angled jaw, dark with rough stubble. The good-natured curve of his mouth. Her gaze lingered. Why had she never noticed until recently the deep slashes beside his mouth that gave his face such rugged masculine appeal? Or the spark of bright green in his eyes? Like moss in the depths of a dark pine forest.

She worked with the man every day and all she'd ever allowed herself to focus on was their rivalry. For good reason. Every secret, silent SWOT analysis she'd ever done had convinced her that Jay was her biggest threat.

Yet, when offered the chance to usurp her place in her father's life, he'd turned it down.

He did her head in.

"Good," he said easily. "I'm glad it fits. Now you don't need to worry about losing it."

Unexpectedly, he lifted her hand and brushed his lips across the backs of her fingers.

Her heart bumped in her chest as the moment stretched between them, oddly intimate...and so very sweet.

It was friendship, Georgia told herself firmly. That's what the warm glimmer in his eyes signified. No point making more out of it.

So, instead of leaning across the space between the seats and seeking the shelter of his arms as she had last night, she simply smiled at him. "Thank you, Jay."

She was thanking him for the surprising comfort she'd discovered in their friendship—and the opportunity he'd offered for her to be part of a loving family for a brief time, giving her time to heal, to become whole again. It was friendship. She needed to keep reminding herself of that. Because there were other unfamiliar yearnings beneath the warmth of gratitude, yearnings that felt nothing like friendship.

As she studied him, his expression grew serious. "There's something we need to talk about."

The sudden intensity in his eyes caused her to still. "What is it?"

Georgia might not be aware of it, but she wanted him to kiss her.

The dewiness in her eyes, the lush, ripe fullness of her pink mouth told Jay all he needed to know.

Even as hope fired up within him, he suppressed it. He understood her hunger. That desperate desire to seal lip against lip. But he could no longer be satisfied by kisses. He wanted more. Much more. Just for starters, he wanted to slip his hands under the soft sweater she wore, strip it away and touch her skin. He wanted to shuck off his clothes. He wanted her naked against him.

But he had no right to any of those things.

The moment he'd put the ring he'd inherited from his grandmother on her finger, he knew that he couldn't leave any unspoken deceit between them. He had to face his fear…and tell her the truth.

Even though it meant he risked losing her.

Forever.

So don't screw it up this time, Black.

Jay hauled in a deep breath to steel himself against the terror.

Cupping his hand under her jaw, he tipped her face up to his. Looking into dark-lashed eyes, he said in a rush, "What if I told you that we'd met before?"

As always, the beauty of her eyes, clearer than Colorado summer skies, enthralled him. Right now, they glistened softly.

"This is going to sound…weird. Sometimes I feel I've

known you all my life, Jay." Her throat bobbed. "You understand me—almost better than I understand myself."

"That's not exactly what I mean."

She blinked rapidly. "Then I don't understand."

Jay decided to sidestep the thorny issue of that powerful sense of connection he, too, knew so well. It had hit him the very first time he'd seen her in the hotel bar. Bam! Between the eyes. He hadn't understood it, either. So, for now, he was sticking to what could actually be explained.

"I'm talking about two years ago," he said softly, his heart pounding against his ribs.

"Two years ago?" she repeated slowly, her eyes never leaving his.

Jay nodded, watching her, his chest tight. Georgia—of all people—wouldn't have missed the significance of the timing. "Before I came to Kingdom."

"No!" She pulled back and laced her fingers together. His hand fell away. "I don't believe you. I would've remembered meeting you."

The interior of the SUV closed in on him.

To escape the sudden claustrophobia, Jay thrust the car door open.

"Let's walk," he commanded gruffly. Without waiting for an answer, he climbed out, dragging his jacket with him.

He led her down a short track between the quivering aspens to the edge of the bubbling creek. The wind blew off the distant peaks with a snow-chilled edge so typical of the Rockies, and Jay slung his jacket around her shoulders to block out the worst of it. The jacket was long enough for Georgia to sit down without getting her jeans damp. She did so, and then he settled himself on a tussock beside her.

A splash in the water caused her to jump.

"Trout. Brown trout," he told her.

Her profile was etched against the silver tree trunks that surrounded them.

"Where?"

Jay didn't pretend to misunderstand. She wasn't asking about the trout, and he knew he'd run out of time... and distractions.

"Las Vegas. I was attending a conference—you were there, too. With your fiancé." *Good-riddance Ridley.*

Georgia went very, very still.

The creek babbled busily in front of them as he waited for her response.

An aspen leaf drifted past on the surface. The current swept it between two rocks and it spun into the eddies below and down toward the deep rocky overhang where he knew lazy fish loved to lurk. All the courage he'd summoned threatened to drown along with the golden leaf.

She pushed her hair—paler than the silver bark of the aspen trees—off her face, and finally she looked across at him.

"When, exactly, did we meet?"

"On the Friday night." He waited.

There was an explosive silence as she absorbed that.

"I don't remember."

Jay had to ask. "How much do you remember about that night?"

"I don't want to talk about Ridley." Her tone was flat. There was no emotion in the words. He'd heard far more enthusiasm in her voice about the rising costs of Italian leather for next season's totes.

Tipping his head back, Jay stared at the blue sky visible between the gold leaves above. Hell, she never ever talked about the damned man. Why had he thought she would now?

Her eyes were bright with accusation when he glanced back at her. "You should've told me we'd met."

"I...tried."

He told himself he had. When she'd returned to work

on crutches, her broken ankle encased in a moon boot, she hadn't shown any hint of recognition. That had been when he'd learned what hell was. It had been blisteringly clear that Georgia didn't remember him. The concussion she'd suffered in the car crash had wiped out several days afterward…and parts of the time just before. Jay hadn't realized how much he'd been banking on her favorable reaction to finding him in the office next door. She'd refused to discuss the car accident, her injuries, any loss of memory and her ex-fiancé. And Jay hadn't wanted to rub her nose in whatever she remembered of her humiliation.

"Not hard enough!"

At her stony expression, the ache in his chest swelled.

He hesitated, loath to confess that he'd been afraid. Afraid of exposing himself to her ridicule as their relationship settled into habitual snark and rivalry. He was still afraid. But now, at least the past was out in the open—she knew they'd met before.

"I thought it would be better if you remembered by yourself."

"What do you know that I don't?" She shook her head and her hair swirled around her shoulders. "Dammit, Jay. You kept this from me, every day. For two years."

Anger and distrust cooled her eyes; he'd expected that. Hell, he deserved every bit of it.

"I'm sorry," he said.

"You're sorry?" She glared at him. "You think that's enough?"

"I know it can never be enough, but I'm very sorry—I shouldn't have kept it from you."

What he badly wanted was her forgiveness. Day after day, he'd held stubbornly on to the hope that she would remember. One day. How could she not? The bond that had linked them from the moment they'd met had blown him away. She had to remember it.

So each morning, he'd resolved that he would tell her the truth, while secretly hoping she would remember him. Each morning, he'd brought her a cup of coffee.

Each day, she'd greeted him with a wide smile, a clever quip and suspicious eyes filled with fear that he was trying to edge her out of Kingdom.

And each day, it had nearly killed him. And he'd put it off for another day.

Two years of his life—and hers—had ticked by. He'd hidden his desires by playing the fool. He'd made her laugh. He'd driven her crazy. But he'd also worked to help her chase the dream she wanted—a dream of a future that every day took her further away from him.

But Jay wanted more than a dream woman. He wanted Georgia. He loved her mind. He loved her spirit. And he wanted his ring to stay on her finger.

More than anything, he wanted her love.

A wave of self-disgust at his own impatience swept him. He was pressing her too hard. He'd harbored a selfish hope that telling her that they'd met before might jog her memory. It hadn't happened. And it was probably for the best. While she might get to remember him—the first time he'd held her, comforted her—on the flip side, she'd also get to remember everything else about good-riddance Ridley that she'd so carefully blocked out.

He sucked in a deep breath. "Do you want to call this off? Do you want to go back?"

"Back?" Her eyes were dazed.

"Back to New York."

Georgia stared at Jay. His normally smiling lips were pressed into a grim line and there was no laughter visible in his eyes.

"No, I want to stay!" Despite the shock he'd delivered, she wasn't ready to face her father. At least not until she'd decided how she was going to appease him without giving in to his wretched demand.

Jay gave her a long considering look and got to his feet. He stretched out a hand to help her up, but she ignored it, brushed past him and marched back up the trail. All too soon, they were back in the SUV. He restarted the vehicle and spun it around to head back the way they'd come— back to Aspen.

Thoughts tumbled through her head as she tried to make sense of what Jay had told her, what it meant for her. For them. For their working relationship.

Jay had lied to her.

Turning her head away, she looked out the window. Around them, imposing mountains dominated the vast landscape. But this time, instead of driving through the town, Jay headed into the surrounding hills. She caught a couple of the road names as they climbed higher and higher through the switchbacks and the homes became increasingly more exclusive.

Hunter Creek Road.

Red Mountain Road.

When a pair of stone gateposts set with heavy black wrought-iron gates came into sight, Jay slowed. He pressed a code into a keypad beside the gate, and the heavy gates swung swiftly and silently open.

As the SUV purred along a driveway lined with aspens that shimmered in the sunlight, she realized her assumptions about Jay's family might have been a little off. The driveway ended in a spectacular sweep in front of a house.

No, not a house. Forget that. A luxurious Colorado lodge rose out of Red Mountain to a haphazard height of at least four stories. Not even the warm rays of the morning sun could soften the craggy lines of the stone structure that had been built to withstand storms and snowfall in the harshest of winters.

Georgia stared. "*This* is where your family live?"

So much for a white picket fence…

And what about the party tomorrow?

Any chance that it would be a low-key family affair went out the window. She thought frantically about the casual selection of garments she'd tossed into her Kingdom carry-on for a small-town family visit. She'd deliberately dialed it back, not wanting to arrive with a mountain of luggage looking like some super-spoiled big-city fashionista.

Aside from the French blue jeans and turtleneck sweater that she was wearing with a pair of flats, and her Kingdom coat with its distinctive crown-pattern lining on the back seat, there wasn't much in her carry-on.

Mentally, she listed the contents. Fawn riding-style pants that never creased. A white shirt—not silk, because she'd foolishly decided silk would be too over-the-top. A plain wool cardigan—not cashmere. A white long-sleeved T-shirt. Apart from her Kingdom coat, her favorite pair of well-worn Chelsea JJB boots was the only recognizable brand she'd packed. One pair of modest heels—nothing like the sublime skyscraper works of art she wore most days to work. One dress. God. The dress! It was an ode to understated mediocrity.

Her confusion and shock crystallized into anger.

She could kill Jay for not warning her!

Before she could give voice to it—or the million questions bubbling in her head—a small crowd spilled out of the lodge's enormous wooden front door and tumbled down the stone stairway.

Later, she promised herself. She would kill Jay later. He'd die a slow death. A very slow death…

She was out of the vehicle before he could come around and open the door. More shaken than she would ever have admitted by the discovery that Jay didn't come from some average small-town home, Georgia hovered beside the SUV

as a woman wearing Western-style jeans, a pale pink cashmere sweater and a pair of black suede Jimmy Choo boots
rushed down the stairs to fling her arms around Jay and
kiss him soundly.

A moment later, the woman turned to Georgia and examined her. She had Jay's hazel eyes. It was his mother.
There was no doubt about those eyes.

Georgia smiled hesitantly at Jay's family.

The people who loved him. The people to whom she
and Jay were about to pretend they loved each other and
intended to marry…and live happily ever after.

For the first time, the stark reality of the deception they
were about to enact struck Georgia. If there was one thing
she was worse at than engagements, it was telling lies.

Unlike Jay…

How would she convince anyone that she was a besot-
ted bride-to-be? Aside from that fiasco with Ridley, she'd
never had much practice.

Her palms grew clammy.

There were two more women and a man behind Jay's
mother. The younger woman was more casually dressed
than Jay's mother in a pair of JJB boots—newer than those
Georgia had packed—along with black jeans and an oversized white linen shirt. Once again, Georgia thought of the
sorry contents of her overnight bag.

Jay moved closer. When he took her clammy hand in
his, it eased her fluttering nerves. The sense of relief she
felt further confounded her.

He gave her hand a gentle squeeze. "Mom, Dad, Jennifer, Betty…meet Georgia Kinnear. My fiancée."

Everyone appeared to freeze.

"Did you say fiancée?"

As Jay might have expected, his mother was the first

to speak, even as his father's face grew tight-lipped with disapproval.

"Kinnear? Isn't that the name of that man you work for?" His father's dark brown eyes bored into him.

Here we go, Jay thought. His father knew the industry inside out. J.J. knew exactly whom Jay worked for. This was simply the next salvo in a long running battle. Their relationship had gotten no easier with absence.

Georgia was smiling at his father, a careful, charming little smile. Jay noticed she hadn't offered her hand. Clearly, she feared his curmudgeonly parent might choose to ignore it. He rather suspected she'd read the situation correctly. Sometimes, she could be the most astute woman he'd ever known—yet, at other times, she remained as blind as a newborn mouse.

"I'm Kingston Kinnear's eldest daughter, Georgia." She was still smiling. "Nice to meet you."

Her hand had gone cold in his. Jay gave it another gentle squeeze.

"Georgia, this is my family. My parents, J.J. and Nancy, my sister, Jennifer…and Betty, who has looked after our family for decades. You'll meet more of the extended family and plenty of friends at the anniversary celebration tomorrow." Turning his attention to his family, he said, "I'm fortunate that Georgia has agreed to marry me." Jay raised the hand he held and kissed it.

He heard her breath catch. He froze, too. The slanting sun caught the ring on her finger, causing it to glitter with fierce blue fire. He felt Georgia jerk, and looked up.

Their eyes caught…tangled…held.

He forgot everything. His family receded. His whole awareness centered on the pair of clear sky blue eyes.

The moment shattered as a furry body barreled into his legs.

A golden Labrador grinned up at him, and he heard Georgia laugh.

"I see I forgot to introduce Zeus," he said ruefully.

She rubbed the dog's head.

Jay looked up. Everyone appeared to be transfixed at the sight of the ring on Georgia's hand as she caressed Zeus's ears. No one could have missed what he'd known the moment he met Georgia: the ring was perfect. The blue of the diamond reflected the brightness of her eyes, while the silver setting glittering with pavé diamonds matched her hair. With his grandmother's ring on her finger, Jay had sent a message: he expected his family—every one of them—to honor his choice.

"Don't let Zeus jump up—his feet are all muddy."

His mother was the first to step forward, gently kneeing Zeus out of the way. She kissed Georgia, first on one cheek, then on the other.

"This is such happy news," she said, her voice thick with emotion.

Thank you, Mom. A wave of love for his mother filled Jay.

His sister hadn't moved. She stood beside his father, a question in her eyes. Jay read it as easily as though his sister had yelled it at him.

What about Suzie?

Dammit!

The old guilt stirred deep in his gut. He pushed it away. He'd deal with Suzie later. Tomorrow. She'd be at the anniversary celebration. Unlike the old man, Jennifer would reserve judgment—even though her loyalties would be torn.

Jay headed back to the SUV. It only took a moment to heft their bags out of the trunk. Georgia, thank God, had traveled light. He retrieved their coats from the back seat. His mother had finally released his brand-new fiancée, who looked a little dazed as he dropped her coat over her shoulders.

"Let's go inside," Jay said brusquely. For now, she had endured enough. There was more to come—her weekend escape was the beginning of his purgatory. There was little hope of forgiveness: he'd left it too late for that.

"Give me one minute. I need a word with Betty to sort out a few last-minute details." Nancy Black touched her husband's arm and fixed him with a look that Georgia guessed held a warning. "Darling, prepare Jay and Georgia something refreshing to drink—I'm sure they're parched after the trip."

"I'll get Zeus cleaned up." Jay's sister grabbed the Labrador by the collar.

Georgia's desire to murder Jay escalated another level.

He hadn't been joking. He'd given his unsuspecting family no warning that he was bringing a guest—much less a fiancée. His mother's need for time to consult with the housekeeper revealed that much. Not that Nancy had made her feel like an interloper; to the contrary, Nancy's welcome had been the warmest of all.

Nor had Jay been joking when he'd said his parents would expect her to be wearing an engagement ring, although she hadn't anticipated that they would be quite so riveted by the sight of the ring on her finger.

This was far from the modest, ordinary family she'd expected.

Jay's mother exhibited the easy style of a woman comfortable with wealth, while his father wore jeans, a Western jacket and, once again, the ubiquitous JJB boots—although his were the scuffed cowboy kind.

And then there was the house…

Once inside the heavy front door, Georgia found herself standing in a double-height—or was it triple-height?—

foyer. Never-ending living spaces unfolded before her, with fabulous mountain vistas visible through the surrounding windows. In the distance, a curved staircase in black wrought iron with a carved wooden bannister rose to the upper floors. From the marble-tiled lobby, two steps led down to a spacious living area arranged around a stone fireplace. Wooden floors—walnut, she suspected—were scattered with large handwoven rugs. On the far side of the fireplace, Georgia glimpsed a dining space surrounded with vast floor-to-ceiling windows that framed more spectacular views.

She wanted nothing more than to get Jay alone. To demand some answers. Why had he never said a word about his family's wealth? In all the time she'd known him, all the time she'd worked head-to-head with him, he'd never discussed it. He'd mentioned parents and a sister in passing. But nothing had prepared her for this—this—

Words failed her.

Murder might not be enough…

As she and Jay trooped down the two stairs behind J.J., Georgia tried to fathom the family dynamics that were swirling around them. There was clearly a bond of deep affection—love—between Jay's parents. But the relationship between Jay and his father was not as easy to decipher. Jay gestured to a leather sofa. Once she sat down, Georgia glanced around with interest, taking in the pewter chandelier overhead and the pair of bronze elk statues beside the hearth. But when Jay settled beside her, his thigh close to her own, any curiosity instantly evaporated.

All she could focus on was the pressure of Jay's thigh against hers.

"So, you want to marry my son?" J.J. had taken the leather armchair directly across from where she and Jay sat.

Before she could respond, Jay spoke from beside her. "I proposed—I want to marry Georgia."

But J.J. appeared deaf to the warning note in Jay's voice as his bitter brown eyes drilled into Georgia.

J.J.

The name nagged at her. Jay's father looked vaguely familiar. But she'd swear they'd never met. Georgia took her time studying him. The broad shoulders and head of gray hair. The heavy brows over measuring eyes. He was the picture of a successful, wealthy man comfortable in his skin right down to the scuffed Western boots he wore. JJB boots. Like hers.

J.J. Black?

As in JJB Boots? Iconic Western boots. She and Roberta both loved them. She'd had a vague idea that the company was based out west. In Colorado?

Oh, my God!

Jay was one of *those* Blacks.

And he'd never told her?

JJB Boots!

Deep inside, something twisted painfully at that thought. Despite all their skirmishes, despite her fears that Jay was after her dream job, she'd always known he shared many of her own visions and values. She'd spoken the truth down beside the creek: Jay understood her better than anyone she'd ever met, and that only intensified the hurt she was feeling. He'd confessed to lying to her about the past. Now she'd discovered he'd chosen to tell her nothing about his family business—yet he knew everything there was to know about Kingdom.

How had he come to work for Kingdom? How had he learned about the post Ridley had vacated?

Jay had risen to his feet. A dark wood unit opened to reveal a liquor cabinet and a fridge. "What would you like to drink, Georgia?"

A destructive impulse to demand a triple tequila before noon overtook her. Georgia stifled it. Jay might be amused, but she doubted J.J. would appreciate it. Getting off on the wrong foot with the man would only make what was starting to look like a challenging weekend more difficult.

"May I have some water, no ice, please?"

"Sure." Jay took a bottle of mineral water out of the concealed bar fridge, then twisted the top off and poured it into a tall glass.

Georgia felt ridiculously obtuse. Part of it was Jay's fault—he'd never given her any hint. How could she have guessed? It wasn't as if Kingdom ever had any business dealings with JJB Boots.

Although that wasn't such a bad idea...

"—and I'll cut down on my working hours once you're back. Your mother will be pleased."

What? Ripped out of her thoughts, Georgia's sudden movement caused the ring on her finger to flash blue fire. All at once it no longer mattered how or why he'd come to work for Kingdom.

Her gaze meshed with Jay's.

"You're planning to leave Kingdom?" she whispered.

"Of course, he's going to leave!"

She blocked out J.J.'s loud voice and kept her eyes on the man who had become her rock. Jay's expression was unfathomable. It had been bad enough to think about him leaving her for a vacation, but for Jay to leave Kingdom forever...?

"My son was never going to stay at a New York luxury label when he has the solid family tradition of JJB Boots waiting for him back home."

There. If she'd needed confirmation, she had it in J.J.'s contempt. Anger, hurt, a raw pain contracted her chest.

But Jay's eyes remained steady on hers. "My fiancée would be the first to know if I were considering such a drastic step."

Fiancée. His warning was clear: she'd better not give the game away.

Even as he handed her the soda and sat down beside her, a frantic desire to slip into the bracing chill outside overcame her. Anything to get away from the suddenly oppressive mood in the room and to clear her thoughts.

Jay was part of JJB Boots. He had a career—a life—waiting for him here. A life he'd said he didn't want to be pressured into going back to. But someday, he would realize the value his family and the JJB Boots brand held.

Someday, he would leave Kingdom.

All Georgia's anger at Jay evaporated as a greater dread set in.

They made a great team. How often, during the worst moments of her day, when she was bogged down with stress and deadlines, would Jay arrive brandishing a cup of coffee just as she liked it and flash that lazy grin, his eyes glinting with devilry. Tension would seep out of her. Life would instantly become simpler, more fun for a few moments. Solutions to all the problems plaguing her would fall into place.

What would she do when Jay decided to leave?

A shocking realization struck her: she didn't want him to leave. Ever.

Really rattled now, Georgia couldn't hide her relief when light footsteps sounded, and Nancy reappeared.

"Ah, good. J.J., I see you got Georgia a drink." No one disabused her of the notion. "Everything is sorted out, Jay. The guest suite is ready for both of you."

The guest suite is ready...for both of you?

Georgia blinked. Twice. Her lips parted. "Um—"

"Thanks, Mom." Jay was already on his feet. "I'll take our bags up."

Georgia was left with no choice. Flashing a polite, vacant smile in the direction of her hosts, she abandoned her untouched drink and dashed after him. He took the wooden stairs two at time, his black boots thudding against the wooden stairs.

Black leather boots…

JJB Boots.

How could she have been so blind? She could've screamed. Had Jay been laughing at her all the time that he'd had her fooled?

"Wait," she called out as he reached the top.

"We're just through here." Without slowing, Jay vanished through a stone arch.

Ten

"You have some explaining—"

Georgia came to an abrupt stop under the arch. Through the rustic doorway, she could see Jay setting their bags down on an antique blanket chest at the foot of the bed.

She did a double take as she took in the size of the sleigh bed that dominated the guest suite. It was ginormous.

"—to do." Her voice fizzled out.

And just like that, Jay's relationship to JJB Boots became the least of her worries.

One bed… Two people.

And not another bed in sight. Tension gripped her belly. Refusing to acknowledge it, she reminded herself that she and Jay were colleagues.

No, they were friends.

Only friends. Nothing more…

She thought of the skimpy lace and satin pajamas in her trolley bag and drew her brows together.

"I am not sleeping here, Jay." She fought to keep her voice from rising. "Not in one bed."

"And if there were two beds? Would that make a difference?"

Georgia narrowed her gaze. She was starting to suspect

that the lazy mocking smile, the good-humored teasing masked a more intense, far more complex man. This Jay was all too familiar. Maddening. Provocative. Engaging. Amusing. But not even an invitation to debate the matter was going to distract her. Not this time.

"That hardly solves the problem," she said firmly.

The corners of his mouth kicked up into a crooked smile. Oh, she knew that smile...

Except this time, her reaction was different. More complicated. For once, she didn't rise to the bait. Instead, her eyes flickered to the undone top button at the neckline of his white shirt and the sliver of bare skin revealed at his throat, then quickly away...back to his face.

From the light in his eyes, she knew he'd recognized the heat she'd felt.

"We don't even have to sleep, you know." He followed that smile up with a wicked growl. "Not if you're so dead set against it. That should solve the problem, right?"

She swallowed hard.

Suddenly, she was finding it hard to breathe.

While that magnificent maple bed behind her was simply waiting...

Georgia's heart started a slow thud in her chest.

He was coming closer. The wickedness in his widening smile caused her throat to tighten further and her skin began to tingle.

How had she never noticed the sensual ease with which he moved...or the sexy slant of his cheekbones? The catalog of her oversights was growing longer by the hour.

"Hey." She struggled to laugh.

Too late. Way too late. It came out breathy and expectant, and the awful sound hung between them.

Nice work, Georgia!

Warmth flooded her face. Striving for firmness, she

channeled her most businesslike boardroom voice. "Don't tease, Jay."

His smile was all teeth, and his eyes gleamed.

"Whatever makes you think I'm teasing?"

At the low husky note, a pang of yearning—just short of pain—stabbed at her heart. A memory of that instant she'd uttered the reckless bid that had won her Jay at the Bachelors for a Better Future Benefit Auction swept over her. His stunned expression and the surge of triumph that had seized her in that moment came sharply back into focus.

When his gaze dropped to her mouth, the tingle flared into heat, shocking her with its intensity. Georgia resisted the urge to run the tip of her tongue over lips gone suddenly dry.

But she couldn't stop her heart from slamming against her ribs.

"Stop it!" she croaked.

"Okay." He looked up from her mouth and met her gaze full-on. "So what do you want?"

That huskiness in his voice—her heart recognized it. Even though she could've sworn she'd never heard it from Jay before. She backed up a couple of steps. The drumbeat against her ribs grew heavier.

"Your parents will be wondering where we are." Desperation called for desperate measures.

"My mother knows we'll be taking time to freshen up a little."

She took another step back. The big bed banged into the back of her legs, and she stilled in surprise.

"So, you never did answer my question."

She was aware of his intent gaze, of his lean strength, of the heat of his body in front of her. *Oh, dear heaven.*

"What question?" She shuddered inwardly at the squeakiness of her voice.

"What do you want?"

Her heart jolted. His closeness—

The rustle of denim, the smell of suede and the fresh mossy, woodsy scent of his aftershave filled her senses.

"Georgia…"

At last, she lifted her gaze. The final traces of a smile still lingered. But as their eyes connected, it vanished. The diamond hard-edged intensity in his expression caused her heart to splinter painfully.

Jay wanted her.

In the absence of his teasing smile, the hard slash of his cheekbones and the tight line of his mouth were a revelation. Again, that Alice-down-a-rabbit-hole sense of not knowing, not seeing the real Jay filled her.

Her breath caught in the back of her throat. She placed her hands on his forearms, the suede jarringly rough beneath her touch. "I don't think we should—"

"Don't think," he ordered.

His head came down.

"Feel," he whispered against her mouth.

Her heartbeat went through the roof.

Excitement tore through her. This kiss was nothing like the sweet, chaste kiss of friendship they'd shared in the hospital courtyard. This time, there were no preliminaries. His mouth was hard and hungry. His tongue lashed into her mouth, tasting her…scorching her.

Digging her fingertips into the thickness of his jacket, Georgia made a little sound in the back of her throat.

It was part surprise. Part something…darker, far more frightening.

Then she released her grip on him to edge her hands down around his hips. As he groaned and pushed closer, she clutched at his jeans, the ridge of the pocket edges rough against her fingers. Beneath the denim, she felt the tight butt she'd so covertly admired on the stairs only minutes before, and arched up against him.

He felt hard and unmistakably male against her.

Panting, she tore her mouth from his. Instantly, he eased back so that her hands slid from his buttocks to his hips.

Her hands tightened on the waistband of Jay's jeans.

Did he know what he was doing to her? Did he know about the desire that pulsed through her veins? She flipped him a quick upward glance from under her lashes. He was watching her, disconcertingly composed, his gaze steady. No glint of mockery in sight.

"Are you okay?" he asked, utterly serious for once.

"Of course!" She tried to smile.

But was this a good idea? They worked together. She was terrible at romance. And worse at reading men's intentions. Now was the time to tell him that the only thing they had in common was business. The fashion industry. Work. Kingdom.

Only…

That wasn't true. Not anymore. Something had changed. *She* had changed.

And Jay had changed, too.

He desired her.

Despite his level gaze and apparent calm, the evidence she'd felt pressed against her had been unmistakable.

Maybe she had it all wrong…

Maybe she *was* his type. Maybe he really did want her, Georgia, the woman she was under the Kinnear veneer.

Beneath the churning uncertainty and confusion, it was as if a dam wall had broken and a torrent of emotion had been released. For the first time in years, she no longer felt shamed by what she felt. By what she wanted.

Or by doing something about getting it.

So what did *she* want?

Right now, she wanted to be kissed by Jay…

A real kiss, not some sweet innocent kiss between friends. A real rip-my-heart out kiss, wherever that led.

"Oh." The sound burst from her in frustration.

Releasing his hips, she brought her hands up, sliding them over the rough suede past the buttoned edges until they closed on the lapels of his jacket. His eyes blazed as she gave a little tug. Then he laughed and twisted around, leaving her holding the abandoned jacket. She flung it onto the bed behind her.

His hands came down on her arms as she plunged forward, grasping a fistful of his shirtfront.

He steadied her. "Slowly, sweetheart."

"Don't you dare laugh!"

He didn't want her. The heat of all-too-familiar doubt rose through her. The fear of humiliation, of making a fool of herself all over again seized her gut. She swallowed.

Jay's hazel eyes were unexpectedly serious as they searched hers.

"Do I look like I'm laughing?"

His mouth was at eye-level. It was a beautiful mouth. It spoke to her in ways her heart understood. And it wasn't laughing.

Georgia wanted to sob with frustration, even as her grip on his shirt tightened, her emotions seesawing wildly between desire and betrayal. She twisted her hand. A button threatened to pop.

She didn't want it to be like this.

Forcing herself to look away from that mouth that was driving her crazy, Georgia released her grip on his shirt, and smoothed down the creased fabric.

The hurt that had been festering since she'd put two and two together about JJB Boots spilled over.

"Why didn't you tell me, Jay? About JJB Boots? Why the secrecy?"

Lifting his hands away, he speared them through his hair. She felt bereft at the loss of his touch.

"It was always on my résumé."

Which she'd never seen because she'd been convalescing when Jay had been hired. And why bother when every frenetic day, Jay's actions spoke louder than any testimony ever could? He'd proven himself an excellent hire. "You never talk about your family."

"You never ask," he countered.

Silently, Georgia acknowledged her blinkered absorption in all things Kingdom.

"I told you a couple of times that my mom and sister were visiting New York. You didn't show interest in hearing more."

"Your dad didn't come?"

His mouth tightened. "No." He ran his hands through his hair again and hunched his shoulders. "Who my family is doesn't change who I am. JJB Boots—and J.J. Black for that matter—do not define who I am." He looked up, his gaze direct. "I'm sorry. I screwed up. I hurt you."

His hair stood up in spikes where his fingers had mauled it. Without laughter, he looked older, resolute, disturbingly serious.

The maddening rival was nothing like the man who faced her now. He'd withheld so much of himself. She couldn't dismiss that. But the man hidden behind the mocking mask was so much more. Her apprehension lifted, causing her to blurt out, "You're my rock, Jay. I never want to lose that."

"You won't. I promise."

It was enough.

"What do I want?" She tipped her head. "More than anything, I want you to kiss me again."

The fingers that brushed against her chin, cupping her cheek, shook a little. His free hand came up to her shoulder. With a jerk, he drew her closer.

Caught in his embrace, held against him, despite everything she'd discovered about him today, despite everything he'd withheld, Georgia felt safe. She leaned into him and his arms tightened fiercely around her. He nuzzled her, and his breath warmed her neck. She needed that warmth. *His* warmth.

Then his lips were on hers, her lips parted and he sank in.

His leg shifted forward, sliding between her thighs. One hand closed on her breast, and his fingers stroked. Slowly, deliberately, he caressed the tightening peak under her sweater, causing bursts of arousal. Georgia's knees almost gave way again.

She closed her eyes, lost in the fresh flare of desire.

A little gasp escaped against his mouth.

A loud knock shattered the hot daze, and the bedroom door flew open.

"Georgia, we don't dress up fo—" Nancy stood in the doorway, her mouth a perfect *O* of surprise. "I'm sorry. I thought you might need some towels."

Flushing wildly, conscious of his hand on her breast and the solidness of the big bed behind her knees, Georgia tried to extricate herself from Jay's hold. But he held her close, refusing to let her go, his body shielding her from his mother's view.

Over Jay's shoulder, Georgia could see Nancy clutching a pile of towels.

Jay's mother cleared her throat. "Uh. Dinner will be ready in less than half an hour—we don't dress up. Please join us for a drink."

"Thanks. And, Mom…" Jay said as his mother paused "…wait a little longer after you knock next time, okay?"

Nancy's eyes were wide with shock. She dropped the towels on the tallboy just inside the door, nodded and fled.

Eleven

Jay's frustration knew no bounds.

After retreating to take a shower so cold that his skin still stung, there was no relief to be found back in the bedroom where Georgia stood in front of the dresser, brushing her hair. He pretended not to watch—all the while itching to run his hands through the soft silver strands as he had last night.

Hell, he'd need another cold shower if this carried on.

She'd swapped the sweater she'd been wearing earlier for a snowy white shirt tucked into her jeans and a wide woven belt. She didn't spare him a glance as she secured her hair in a loose knot at the nape of her neck. He wanted to rip the pins out.

"Are you ready?" His voice was husky.

She nodded and moved to the door.

Jay slung an arm across her shoulders once they exited the guest suite. Downstairs in the dining room, his mother and Betty had their heads bent over a piece of paper on the dining table, while Jennifer watched them approach from across the table.

"That's the final list?" he asked the women.

"The final-final list." His mother peered at him over

her reading glasses, revealing no sign of the awkward moment in the guest room as she smiled at Georgia. He loved his mom!

"More like the final-final-final list." Jennifer grimaced. "Between Mom and Betty, tomorrow is going to run like clockwork."

"They're a pair of dynamos—they wear the rest of us out." Jay tipped his head toward Georgia, allowing himself the surreptitious pleasure of inhaling her perfume. He pulled out the chair at the table for her.

"We kept it small," his mom was saying to Georgia. "Only a hundred and eighty guests. That way, we can enjoy ourselves."

"Is there anything I can do to help?" asked Georgia.

"Yes, you can help with all the last-minute details after dinner. Jennifer, I'll need you, too, please."

"With pleasure." Georgia sounded a little more relaxed.

He could tell that his mother already liked Georgia. How could she not? Jay felt a swelling of warmth in his chest as he sat down beside Georgia.

"So long as I'm excused from the flower arranging." His father's gruff voice interrupted his thoughts. The last to arrive, J.J. took his customary place at the head of the table.

Jay didn't register his mom's response because Georgia chose that moment to turn her head and give him a small smile, slashing his guts to ribbons. He slowly smiled back, and instantly the sizzle of awareness reignited between them. Then color rose in her cheeks and her gaze fell away, breaking the connection.

The meal passed in a blur.

"That was delicious." Georgia's knife and fork clinked together as she set them down on the plate.

"Betty is a marvel," his mother responded with pride in her voice. "What do you say, Jay?"

"The fish was good," he managed, scrambling to remember what he'd eaten. He'd been too conscious of Georgia's denim-clad thigh beside his own, his shoulder brushing against hers as he reached for the salt, her scent drifting across, intoxicating him.

"Of course, it is. Freshly caught by your father." His mother caught his eye and smiled.

Jay felt himself reddening—something he couldn't remember happening since he was a teenager. Was his enthrallment with Georgia so obvious?

"You used to come with me, Jay. Remember the bighorns in the high country pastures? The water holes where we'd find fish under ledges no one else knew about?" His father grimaced. "But these days, you have more important fish to fry."

"Jay and Georgia could visit over the winter. We could all go skiing." His mom looked hopeful. "And Georgia might even want to tag along next time you and Jay go out fly fishing."

"What would a New York fashion plate know about tying a fly?"

Jay winced at his father's rudeness, even as Georgia flinched beside him.

Georgia spoke before he got a chance, her chin rising a notch. "I can get by on a pair of skis—and I can certainly learn to fly fish."

His father snorted. "You'd get wet."

All Jay's muscles went rigid. His father was spoiling for a fight. With barely concealed anger, he said, "Dad, there's no need for—"

A chair scraped as his mom rose hurriedly to her feet. "Betty is sorting the cutlery and linen for tomorrow's party. I need to check on the apple pie and make sure it's not burning. J.J., you can come and help me."

His father clambered to his feet, pointedly ignoring Georgia.

Jay opened his mouth to blast his father, but was stalled by the touch of Georgia's hand on his thigh.

"Let it go," she murmured so only he heard.

"Suzie makes some of the best flies in Colorado." J.J.'s truculence sliced through the distance between them. "You should be marrying her."

"J.J.!" His mother's voice was sharp. "Now!"

"Uh, I think I might go help, too." Jennifer shot to her feet.

The moment his family disappeared, Georgia swiveled her head and Jay received a hard stare.

"Suzie?"

She began to remove her hand from his leg. He brought his hand down, enfolding hers, forestalling her withdrawal. He rubbed the back of her hand, luxuriating in her soft skin under his palm. "I apologize for my father's rudeness."

She didn't acknowledge his apology. "Is there something else you've forgotten to tell me?"

Jay didn't want to talk about Suzie. Not with his parents and sister about to return at any moment. "Let's discuss this later."

"I think you need to fill me in now."

The tilt of Georgia's jaw warned him that she was not about to be deterred.

"Who is Suzie? Your girlfriend?" she persisted, picking up the paper napkin laid across her lap and tearing it in half.

"Ex," he muttered.

Georgia narrowed her eyes until the flash of blue through the cracks of her black lashes glittered brighter than the diamond on her finger. "How ex?"

"I haven't seen her in years."

Georgia's look of relief caused the oppressive weight in his chest to lift a little.

Crumpling the shredded napkin into a ball, she dropped it onto the table. "Well, I suppose I should be thankful you haven't put me in the unsavory position of being the other woman."

Jay winced.

The sound of his mother's raised voice chastising his father wafted from the direction of the kitchen.

Georgia drew a breath. "My presence here is causing friction."

Damn the old man! "This friction between my father and me is nothing new."

"I feel so guilty for misleading your family. Your mother is so lovely. She believes I'll be back to visit with you. She's already including me in future skiing trips. I can even understand your father's hostility—he resents me because he believes I'm keeping you away. I shouldn't be here."

It was all his fault that Georgia felt like an outsider. By convincing her to agree to a sham engagement, he'd created this situation—not his father.

But the alternative was to lay his heart on the line...and have her stomp all over it. Because of his own male pride, he'd made it harder for her, not easier.

Tightening his hand around hers, he said, "The truth is, my father finds it hard to accept I'm a man, not a boy any longer. I'm not coming back. He knows that—but he refuses to accept it."

"He wants you to take over the legacy he's built," she said softly. "It's his dream."

The irony of that wasn't lost on Jay. Georgia craved most what she thought Jay had walked away from. Families could be hell.

He drew a deep breath and said, "But it's not my dream."

"He loves you, Jay." The sparkle in Georgia's eyes had gentled. She turned her hand over, threading her fingers through his, and Jay's heart contracted. "He wants what's best for you."

Jay shook his head. "No, it's not what's best for me that he wants. It's what's best for him. And that's not love."

"You need to talk to him." There was concern in her eyes.

Her compassion loosened a tightness deep within him. But he concealed his vulnerability by arching his eyebrows and saying with pointed irony, "*I* need to talk to *my* father?"

Georgia shifted in her seat, her cheeks reddening. "I'll talk to Kingston on Monday. Honestly, I will."

Instantly, Jay felt bad. Georgia's relationship with her father was far more complex than his with J.J.

He squeezed her hand, then released it and rose to his feet. "Okay, I'll go talk to J.J."

"Be gentle," she murmured so softly he had to strain to hear the words. "For both your sakes."

From the doorway of the den, Jay shook his head and smiled at the sight of Zeus sprawled across the leather chesterfield, snoring.

Wooden bookshelves packed with books on fishing, business management and the craft of boot-making lined the walls. A box-frame filled with the first flies that Jay had tied under his father's tutelage still held pride of place, and the almost-buried memory of that long ago time tugged at Jay.

"So the prodigal son has returned."

His father rolled the leather executive chair away from the window and set his whiskey glass down on the antique walnut desk next to a box of carefully crafted flies. The eyes that inspected Jay were filled with a critical glint that was all too familiar.

"About time, my boy."

Jay shoved Zeus to one side to make space on the couch. Settling himself beside the snoring dog, he crossed an ankle over his knee and strove for calm.

"Dad, we need to talk."

"This nonsense about an engagement must end." Already, his father was hijacking a conversation that hadn't yet begun. "I want you back home."

Slowly, Jay shook his head. He allowed a slight smile to tilt his mouth as he rocked his boot-clad foot back and forth.

"I'm not coming back."

His avoidance of the word home was deliberate.

Home was where the heart was, and his heart had taken up residence elsewhere.

"Of course, you are!" His father gave an impatient snort. "You've had enough time away. It's time for you to come back and marry Suzie."

Once again, his father was treating him like a boy, rather than the man he'd become. Keeping his voice steady, Jay said, "I'm not going to marry Suzie."

There was only one woman he planned to marry.

"You're engaged—"

"That's over. You know that, and Suzie knows that."

"Suzie still wants to marry you—she'll jump at the chance."

Jay doubted it.

Some of the residual guilt about his old friend stirred. He forced it down. Guilt was the last thing Suzie—or he—deserved. "What Suzie really wants is to be a permanent part of JJB Boots—marrying me would've secured that."

"That's not the point. Suzie needs you—she needs a husband," his father insisted. When Jay refused to respond, J.J.'s hands balled into fists. "The business needs you, too, Jay."

They'd finally gotten to the crux of what his father really wanted.

The old tightness was back in Jay's gut, winched tighter by the steel chain binding him to dreams that had never been his.

This time, when he shook his head, it was with finality. "You're looking at the wrong Black."

"What the hell is that supposed to mean?"

His father's bull-headedness was as frustrating as always. Colorado would never be big enough to hold them both. Jay felt his hard-won calm slip. "You know what it means, Dad. Open your eyes to what's in front of you. Jennifer—"

"Jennifer has done her best to help hold things together while you've been gallivanting around New York. You've gotten the qualifications we decided you needed, and I've given you enough time to gain the necessary industry experience to run our business."

Jay steeled himself not to react. Zeus pressed up against Jay's thigh. Absently, he scratched the dog behind his ears.

"I need you here running JJB Boots! Jennifer will get married someday—"

Jay's hand stilled as he cut his father off. "I'll be married first."

"It's not the same, Jay."

If Georgia had been here, she would've have accused him of being deliberately provocative. She would have probably been right. But his father's stance would have infuriated her, too. J.J. was almost as bad as Kingston.

Dinosaurs, both of them.

Zeus's nose nudged at his hand. Jay recommended rubbing the soft feathery ears and the dog settled his muzzle onto his paws.

"The world has changed, Dad. There is life after marriage. Jennifer and Suzie will make fine business partners in JJB Boots—even if both of them decide to get married someday."

"Don't be flippant, boy! You're my son. My successor. Your place is at the head of JJB Boots."

Jay didn't allow his rising annoyance to show. "I'm not coming back. It's not what I want."

They lapsed into uncomfortable silence.

He'd promised Georgia that he would be gentle, so he searched for words to soften the blow. "Dad, I'm a man, not a boy anymore. I will visit you and Mom. And I hope you take time out to come to New York next time Mom visits." But Jay wasn't holding his breath. It hadn't happened in two years.

With a violent kick of his foot, his father swung his chair away to stare out the window into the darkness that had settled over the jagged peaks. "I will cut off your allowance."

At his father's raised voice, Zeus whimpered. Stroking the dog's head in reassurance, Jay almost smiled. J.J. was using the same tactics Kingston had used so successfully on Georgia. But it was an impotent threat—and J.J. was enough of a realist to know it.

"You will find I haven't touched that for years." It had been longer than five years since Jay had spent a cent of the quarterly allowance he received from the trust fund set up by his grandfather. Nor had he touched the parcel of stocks his grandfather had left to him—as the sole grandson. "I'm quite capable of fending for myself."

"And what of your fiancée?" The chair spun back. His father's mouth was clenched as tight as a trap.

His fiancée…

A vision leaped into his mind. Of Georgia grabbing his shirtfront, pressing up against him, careless of his clothes or hers. Of the wild kiss that had followed. Of her hot little gasps against his mouth…

Whoa! He had to crawl into bed beside Georgia tonight…and sleep. He'd be awake all night if he started to think about the wild little sounds she'd made in the back of her throat.

"I wouldn't be so sure that little lady agrees with your

high moral stance, my boy. She's accustomed to the best in life. Luxury labels. High heels and charity balls. Not hiking boots and wading in mountain streams. That high society lifestyle, it doesn't come cheap. Will you be able to fend for her and keep her happy?"

His father had no idea what would make Georgia happy. But Jay rather suspected he might. If only she gave him the chance.

"I think I'll be able to keep my fiancée happy."

"Don't be so sure. Her father will expect—"

"Now that brings me to what I came in here to talk to you about." Jay's voice lowered as he lifted his foot from where it rested across his other ankle and set it firmly down on the rug. He sat forward on the chesterfield. "Why don't you tell me about the mission you've been on to buy up stocks in Kingdom?"

Twelve

With the heady scent of gardenia soap clinging to her, Georgia stepped out from beneath the shower and quickly wrapped herself in one of the soft luxurious bath towels that Jay's mom had left. The last thing she wanted was for Jay to walk in and catch her naked.

It was absurd to feel so nerve-rackingly aware of him.

They'd worked together in adjacent offices for years. But that was before that sizzling kiss. And now, the treacherous tingle that prickled along her skin refused to be doused by the rough rub of the towel.

Clothes, she needed clothes.

Back in the bedroom, she shimmied into her pajamas, covering up her shower-dampened body. Catching sight of her reflection in the armoire mirror, Georgia quivered. Pale aqua satin clung revealingly to her hips and bottom. The V-neckline of the flagrantly feminine cami top gaped wide, while lace side panels revealed still more skin. It looked like she was doing her best to stage a deliberate seduction.

What she needed was body armor, Georgia decided grimly. The corporate kind. A smart no-nonsense big-name jet-black designer pantsuit would work just fine. But she was stuck with what she'd packed.

She rolled her eyes. Of course, there was an alternative!

Ever conscious that Jay might stroll in at any instant, she sped to the armoire and emerged—triumphant—with a long-sleeved white T-shirt. She whipped it over the cami, and then scrutinized her image critically.

Not quite boardroom armor, but an enormous improvement.

Deciding that the chairs grouped by the glass door presented a better option than waiting in the bed, she made her way across the room. The damned satin pajama bottoms whispered against her sensitized skin with every step. Perching on one of the straight-backed slipper chairs, Georgia picked a fashion magazine off the coffee table. Her fingers trembled as she flicked through the glossy pages. Not even an interview by one of her favorite fashion feature writers could hold her attention as her stomach twisted into convoluted knots.

So much had happened today. The ring. Jay's confession that they'd met before he'd come to Kingdom—and she didn't remember. Meeting Jay's parents—and finding out that they owned the iconic JJB Boots brand. Then there'd been the discovery that his family expected Jay to marry another woman.

And the cherry on top: the shock that Jay actually desired her.

Restlessly, Georgia shut the magazine with a snap and shoved it aside. Once on her feet, she started to pace.

Jay wasn't engaged to Suzie; he was free to kiss whomever he pleased.

Georgia chewed her lip. Did it matter that he hadn't told her about his family's business? The JJB Boots brand held no threat to Kingdom. Did it even matter that Jay had never mentioned the first time they'd met? He'd done her a favor. It was a day she never talked about—she didn't even remember most of it. The little she did remember, she'd worked hard to forget.

If there was one thing her experience with Ridley had proved conclusively, it was that she was useless at relationships. She certainly wasn't expecting love and commitment from Jay. But she wouldn't mind another one of those knee-weakening kisses.

Shock caused her to stop in her tracks. She wanted—
Even more than kisses, she wanted to sleep with Jay.
She closed her eyes.
What was she thinking?

God, it was hard to admit. She wanted pleasure. The kind of mind-blowing pleasure that kiss earlier had promised. Opening her eyes, she stared blindly at the carpet. They were two consenting adults with no reason not to indulge in a no-strings fantasy for a night.

Maybe even two nights…

She could change her flight—and fly back early Monday morning. Excitement and nerves churned in her stomach.

Even as she considered the possibility, footfalls sounded on the wooden stairs and the door handle rattled. Her heart jolted, and the tension inside ratcheted up another notch. Georgia hesitated for only for a fraction of a second before diving into the big bed, sinking into the indulgently soft linen as the door swung open.

Jay had arrived.

The wooden door shut behind him with a heavy clang, causing the drapes that framed the glass doors leading to the terrace to flutter. Georgia's pulse rocketed from zero to a hundred when Jay strode in. Determined not to let the sudden intimacy rattle her nerves, she drew a deep breath to ask him how the talk with J.J. had gone.

But as he strolled forward and began to unbutton the tiny buttons at the cuffs of his shirt, the unspoken words dried up.

After shaking the cuffs loose, Jay started on the buttons down the front. Georgia could only stare as the shirt's edges parted to reveal an impressively muscled chest and a washboard stomach, both of which confirmed he was no stranger to a sweaty workout.

Georgia's fingers played frantically with the corner of the sheet as she watched him shrug off his shirt. With his hair mussed and his shirt billowing, he looked deliciously disheveled.

She tingled as acres of male skin were laid bare.

How had she missed that he was simply gorgeous for so long? Was she completely blind?

"You were right that I needed to talk to J.J." Jay fished into his pocket and dropped his wallet on the nightstand.

Then, to her relief, he walked across the room, giving her plenty of opportunity to admire the surprisingly well-developed laterals sloping to a narrow waist. With a flick of his wrist, he tossed the shirt over one of the chairs beside the glass doors.

He headed for the armoire. "Plenty of positives came out of it."

Jay lifted an arm, and Georgia couldn't help noticing the rounded peak of the bicep and, below, the bulge of his triceps as he rubbed his hand back and forth over the back of his neck. Somehow, he'd found time in his awful work schedule to do a fair amount of serious curls. A flush of warmth came with the discovery that the man who walked in and out of her office every day had a body worth lusting after—had she been given to lusting.

The sound of a zipper severed the sudden silence. Then he kicked off his boots and shucked off his jeans, and her brain stopped working.

Georgia tried—unsuccessfully—not to gawk at the muscled ridges on his chest. The taut, tight abs. Was she the only one who had never noticed? He'd certainly aroused enough feminine interest at the benefit auction. She discovered she didn't care for the memory. She didn't like the idea of Jay being pursued by every Dom, Nic and Carrie. She didn't like the idea of his being engaged to another woman—any woman!

Except her.

She was jealous.

Even as the realization dawned, her stomach clenched. After a final wide-eyed gawk, she forced her gaze away from his lean, taut body and bare muscled thighs, his snug-fitting black briefs—all that kept him decent—and fought to concentrate.

But she had to ask. "Your family clearly regard Suzie as much more than an ex-girlfriend."

He shot her a quizzical look. "Suzie and I had an understanding."

"Understanding?"

The word was jarring. It reminded her of her father, and that terrible, distasteful confrontation with Adam which, in truth, she hadn't understood at all. Dread weighed down her stomach.

"Exactly what kind of understanding?" she prodded.

"Suzie wanted children—and so did I. One day." He shrugged one beautiful bared shoulder. "Neither of us had found anyone better. We'd been friends—and work colleagues for years—she was Jen's best friend. There was no good reason why marriage between us shouldn't work," he said, his voice growing muffled as he bent down to pull off his socks. "It was convenient."

Jay disappeared into the bathroom, closing the door with a click.

As she stared at the closed door, Georgia wrestled with the uncomfortable emotions coursing through her. Jay wasn't in love with Suzie. He wasn't in love with anyone. He'd told her himself he had no dream woman. She slowly let out her breath and felt her tension ease. Her jealousy was unfounded...and simply silly.

By the time Jay reappeared a few minutes later, his hair damp and his jaw smooth, with a thick white towel slung low across his hips, Georgia had recovered her composure.

Raking a hand through his hair, he came toward the bed.

He sat down on her side of the bed, and the towel slipped a little lower.

Georgia sneakily side-eyed Jay's mouth to see if he was grinning. Only to discover that his lips were firmly pressed together, the bottom one full and surprisingly sensual.

"What Suzie and I shared...wasn't enough. Something was missing." He planted one hand one either side of her shoulders and leaned toward her, the fresh tang of soap mixed with the woodsy smell of him surrounding her. "There wasn't any chemistry," he murmured.

Excitement started to spiral in the pit of her stomach. She ached to touch the rough dark stubble on his jawline, to run a finger over that unexpected bump on his otherwise straight nose.

"I wanted more," he whispered, his eyes smoldering like molten embers. "I wanted this."

He cupped her cheek, his fingers gentle, and her heart contracted. And then he kissed her.

The hunger of it seared her.

This was hot and burning. This was a flame igniting potassium. She saw flashes of lilac. White. Silver. Burning.

A frightening emotion shifted deep in her chest. A new shivery, painfully raw pleasure. If this was chemistry, well, she couldn't get enough of it.

Drawn by the unnamed need, she confessed, "I've never felt anything like this before."

Summoning all her courage, she wound her arms around his neck and tugged him close, closing the gap between them. Maybe Jay was right. Maybe chemistry was worth everything.

"Do you want to do this?" he asked against her lips.

"Oh, yes!"

He moved his hips. "Are you sure?"

Georgia moaned and arched against him. "Very."

She wanted to see if she could lose all sense of time and place like that again or whether she'd imagined it. She wanted to experience the excitement, the rightness of his mouth against hers. For a moment, she thought about where they were, in his parents' home, then discovered she didn't give a damn.

Her breath caught, freezing in her throat.

She'd always worried about doing the right thing, about what people thought, about the consequences. But she wanted this more. Much more. She wanted Jay.

All of him.

Body. Heart. And soul.

She reached up and stroked her index finger along the blade of his nose, curiously exploring the jagged ridge where he must've have broken it at some stage. He'd gone very still, watching her.

His pupils flared. In retaliation, he trailed a fingertip along the sensitive skin of her neck, along her jawline. Her head fell back, her lips parting.

Then he touched her mouth.

"You have a beautiful mouth. Made for kisses." His voice held a dark deep edge, as one finger outlined her lips.

They felt full and swollen. His face was at an angle, throwing his cheekbones into sharp relief. No vestige of humor remained in his intent eyes. Only heat.

"So kiss me," she invited.

With a hoarse groan, Jay hauled her closer and licked her open mouth. His mouth sealed hers shut and their legs tangled, the satin of her pants slippery between them.

"How have I managed to resist you?" he murmured.

She didn't think she'd ever get enough of touching him. Her arms crept up around his broad shoulders. She reveled in his skin, sleek and supple, beneath her fingertips.

His hand smoothed over her shoulder and traveled down until it rested, strong and steady, on the curve of her breast. His fingers stroked, and she gasped.

He kissed with fierce intensity, and Georgia responded kiss for kiss. When his hand edged under the T-shirt, she aided him, lifting, twisting, breaking the kiss, impatient to get the garment off, craving the caress of his hands on her bare skin.

When he touched her, she transformed into someone else.

Someone more than Georgia Kinnear, daughter of Kingston Kinnear, gifted student and hotshot executive. Jay made her feel like the most amazing, tempting woman in the world. Sexy. Desirable. Special.

He was nothing like any other man she'd ever known. Her father. Ridley. Adam.

He made them all look like greedy, controlling jerks.

No wonder she loved him.

She *loved* Jay?

Georgia's breath caught, freezing in her throat.

But he allowed her no time to ponder the discovery. He ran two fingertips along the lacy neckline of her camisole, his lips following the invisible tracks he'd traced. Then the camisole, too, was stripped away.

He tasted her. The soft hollow at the base of her neck. The valley that lay between her breasts. And finally, when she thought she might go mad, he tasted her taut nipples.

Then he returned to her lips and kissed her with a passionate intensity born of desperation.

They only had tonight. Or maybe, if she got very lucky, two nights…

When he shifted again, and his hands sought the waist-band of her pajama bottoms, she was quick to help him, dying to feel her bare body against his.

His fingers stroked. Heat scorched her. Her breath hooked in the back of her throat, then hissed slowly out as his fingers retreated. A heartbeat later, they slid forward again, teasing her nub with sure purpose. Her hips twisted. She bit her lip to stop the squeak that threatened to erupt.

She'd never considered herself vocal. Jay had discovered a side of her she hadn't even known existed.

Two—God, she thought it was two—fingers slid into her. Deep. She arched off the bed and her breath caught on a sob.

"Jay!" It wasn't a protest.

"What do you want?"

She cast around for words. Polite words. Words that wouldn't make her blush. "I want you. There. In me."

Jay seemed to know exactly what her jumbled words meant. He shifted to rummage on the nightstand. Then he was back. He moved over her, above her, resting his weight on his elbows as he nuzzled her neck. Then his hardness found her.

Georgia gasped at the tightness.

There was a moment when she thought it would be impossible. Then he slid a little deeper. The tightness expanded into a painful tautness. She tensed.

"Relax," he whispered.

The sensual tickle of his tongue against the sweet groove beneath her ear caused her to shiver, then convulse into giggles. And the tension drained out of her.

When Jay moved again, her arms closed around him, pulling him deeper. She walked her fingers down his back, adoring the way his body stiffened, and dug her fingers into the mound of muscle on either side of his spine. He groaned. Her fingers crept lower…lower…

"Don't touch," he managed to say. "Or I will come."

The threat—if that was what it was—caused her to raise her hips a couple of inches off the bed, arching against him, then sinking down onto the mattress again. It was Jay's turn to gasp as the friction notched a turn tighter.

"Do. Not. Move."

"Yes, Jay."

She whispered the obedient words against the curl of his ear. Then her own tongue snuck out and she experimentally licked the edge. He hissed.

The friction of his body quickened against hers. Georgia felt the edge of tension rising. Hot and tight. Her feet came off the bedding, her knees hugging his hips, deepening the pleasure. Her eyes shut tight and she focused blindly on the driving desire. Then, unexpectedly, she came apart.

Georgia gasped.

Sheer delight rippled through her.

His body jerked. Once. Twice.

Then he fell forward, and buried his face in the crevice where her neck met her jaw. With a groan, he murmured, "Georgia, you are the most unforgettable joy of my life."

Thirteen

Jay stared down at the woman asleep in the bed.

She lay on her side, knees bent, her cheek resting on her palmed hands. The diamond he'd placed on her fourth finger winked at him. Jay wanted nothing more than their engagement to be real. For the ring that Georgia said fit so perfectly to stay on her finger. Permanently. With another simpler gold band beside it.

And he was determined to make her happier than she'd ever been.

Dark eyelashes lay peacefully against cheeks flushed with sleep. Unable to resist, he bent down and brushed his lips across hers.

She opened her eyes, stretched languorously. Then her eyes widened.

"Jay?"

"Good morning." He set two cups down on the night-stand. "I brought you some coffee."

"You must've read my mind."

He gave her a slow smile.

Leaning forward, he kissed her again. This time, she was fully awake and her lips parted beneath his. Placing his hands on either side of her, Jay braced himself against the onslaught of desire that rushed through him.

Lifting his head, he groaned. "We can't afford to get distracted. It's almost time for the party."

Georgia wound her arms around his neck. "Thank you for my coffee."

"Any time."

The mood in the room was imbued with an intimacy and sense of promise, filling Jay with a surge of renewed hope. Yesterday, he'd come clean with Georgia. And last night had been incredible. Now he simply had to convince her they belonged together.

Forever.

Then her phone rang.

Where had she put her purse last night?

Catching a glimpse of it buried under Jay's shirt on one of the chairs by the window, Georgia slung her legs out of bed, remembering too late that she was naked.

Flushing, not daring to look at Jay, she grabbed a throw off the bed and pulled it around herself. When she reached the chair by the window, she clutched at the throw and clumsily dug the now-silent phone out of her purse, glancing at the screen.

Roberta...

Panic instantly had her wide awake.

She frantically hit the redial button and stared blindly out over the private terrace to the mountains beyond, counting the rings and silently urging Roberta to answer.

When, at last, she heard her sister's voice, she said, "Please tell me Kingston is okay."

"He's fine." Roberta sounded loud and comfortingly familiar. "Breathe, sister. Be very grateful that you're not here. He's making everyone's life miserable."

"Oh." Georgia shut her eyes as the waves of panic subsided. "I'm so glad."

"Glad that we're suffering?"

Georgia stifled a sob of laughter. "Glad that he's back to his normal self. Glad he hasn't had a relapse."

"I'm still not sure there was much wrong with him to start with," Roberta said tartly. "But the stock price at markets' close on Friday? Now that's a different story."

Hunched over her cell phone, Georgia felt the familiar anxiety rise. "What do you mean?"

"Someone is buying up Kingdom stock." Roberta's voice took on a hard edge. "And that is enough to give our beloved father a real heart attack."

Georgia's grip on her phone tightened. "I'll fly home immediately."

"Don't bother to reschedule." Roberta's sigh came loud and clear over the miles that separated them. "There's nothing you can do—certainly not until Monday. But I called to tell you…" Roberta's voice trailed away.

"What?"

There was a pause, then Roberta said, "I just wanted to remind you that I'm not in the office for the next few days. You're flying back tonight, right?"

Georgia hadn't gotten around to changing her flight to the morning. "At this stage, yes."

"The sooner, the better. With the weather closing in, the airports may close."

So it was done. There would be no second night with Jay. The disappointment was crushing.

Georgia ended the call and turned to find Jay watching her from the bed, his arms linked behind his head.

How would she react when he breezed into her office bearing cups of coffee after he finally returned from vacation? She froze. Would she ever forget how he'd kissed her, licked her, loved her last night?

Would they be adult and pretend it had never happened? Or would they revert to the snarky, energetic rivalry they'd shared before? Would they still be able to work together? Or would awkwardness take over?

Georgia faced the reality of loving Jay. She wasn't dumb enough to pretend to herself that Jay felt the same about her. He wanted her. Sure. He liked her—she was pretty sure about that, too. They had their shared work ethic in common. She simply had to keep her emotions under control. It shouldn't be difficult; she'd had enough practice.

"Is everything okay?" he asked.

She slipped her phone back into her purse. "Kingston is giving everyone hell, the weather's terrible in New York and Roberta reminded me that she won't be in the office tomorrow."

"Sounds like business as usual."

About to tell him about Roberta's concerns about the stock price, she hesitated. There was nothing Jay could do about it until tomorrow. For now, she was going to enjoy the rest of her escape with Jay. Tomorrow, she'd be back in New York—and back to reality.

She flashed a smile at him. "Time for us to party."

The celebration was in full swing.

Tall stands of exquisite flowers and masses of colorful balloons filled the airy space. A quartet played, and there was a roaring fire in the fireplace.

Everyone had been so welcoming, so pleased to meet Jay's fiancée. In addition to family friends, plenty of Aspen's well-heeled crowd were present. Georgia had taken the opportunity to add several valuable contacts to her network.

Yet, with Jay's arm hugging her to his side, the feeling of being a total fraud swamped Georgia.

"This is awful," she whispered to him after the dozenth time his mom had excitedly dragged another of her friends over to introduce her only son's fiancée. "Your family doesn't deserve this, Jay."

Jay tilted his head closer. "Let's talk about this later—"

"That was your mom's best friend—your mom told her I'm her new daughter. I can't do this, Jay. We need to tell your parents the truth."

"Okay. But after the party. I'm not going to ruin this occasion for my mother. There's not long left, people will start leaving soon."

"Sorry to interrupt you lovebirds." Betty's arch tone caused Georgia to start. "Jay, can you give me a hand moving some of the anniversary gifts into the den? They're almost spilling out the front door."

"Of course." He shot Georgia a brooding look. "I won't be long."

He wound his way through the crowd with the housekeeper bustling behind him. Georgia watched him pause to respond to a greeting from a multimillionaire who'd made his fortune in retail. Then Jay turned to kiss a renowned actress on the cheek, before shaking hands with another couple. Georgia watched how the faces of men and women alike lit up. Jay was well-respected, and an easy authority radiated from him.

How had she ever missed that authority?

Shifting from one foot to another, casting little glances in the direction where Jay had disappeared, Georgia felt like a teenager in the throes of a crush, hyper-aware of Jay's every move.

She slipped outside.

On the covered terrace that faced the majestic Rockies, the guests had broken up into groups. Some stood clutching tall glasses bubbling with the best champagne, and others congregated on built-in seating around the edges of the terrace, while waiters circulated with trays still piled high with food.

Jennifer was chatting with a group of beautifully dressed women.

As Georgia approached, Jay's sister rose to her feet and came toward her. In a low voice she said, "That's Suzie in the red dress."

Georgia glanced past Jay's sister. A jolt of shock caused her to catch her breath.

"But she's—"

"Yes. And, in case you didn't know, Suzie also worked with Jay and me at JJB Boots." Jennifer bent her head closer and lowered her voice. "Mom had already consulted with a wedding planner. The caterers had been booked. The dress and the bridesmaid's dresses had been ordered when Jay dumped her for you."

"Jay jilted her?" Georgia knew she was gaping. How could Jay have done that to Suzie?

"You didn't know?"

She shook her head. "No."

"Don't feel sorry for Suzie—she'd hate it. I was so pleased they were getting married—my best friend and my big brother. Everyone was thrilled. We all knew it was only a matter of time before Dad retired and Jay stepped into his, uh, boots."

Despite the joke, there was real anxiety in the other woman's face. Jennifer honestly believed that Georgia had been the cause of her brother's breakup with her best friend.

"Jay had never done anything unexpected in his life. Sure, he and Dad fought, but we all knew they'd hammer their differences out eventually. But then he met you and broke off his engagement to Suzie. He walked away from JJB Boots and he hasn't been back since. Dad wants him in the business…but Mom and I would settle for having him come home from time to time. We hope you'll persuade him to visit—even to spend Christmas."

"You think Jay will do what I want?" breathed Georgia. The idea was so preposterous she almost laughed out loud. Only Jennifer's set expression stopped her mirth from spilling over.

"My brother is so in love with you that if you asked him to mortgage his soul to buy Kingdom International for you, he would."

In love with *her*?

Georgia nearly admitted that Jay didn't love her at all, that this engagement was one big sham. But she came to her senses just in time. Of course, Jennifer believed Jay loved her—after all, they were engaged, and she had a great big glittering rock on her finger to prove it.

Georgia curled up a little more in shame at the charade she and Jay were perpetrating on his family. It needed to end. And she needed to leave. She didn't belong here.

She itched to reassure Jennifer, to tell her that she was no threat, that she would never keep him from his family…that she didn't have the power to break his heart. She wanted to tell her that she and Jay were only friends.

But that, too, had become a lie.

She realized Jennifer was still waiting for a response.

"I'll talk to him," she said lamely.

"You'd better come and meet Suzie—you'll be seeing plenty of her when the two of you visit."

There was no way out.

Suppressing her own discomfort, Georgia approached the pretty blonde in the red dress. An uncomfortable silence fell as they reached the group. After the introductions, Suzie gave her a sweet smile. Georgia could only admire her.

To break the ice, she smiled back. "I understand you work with Jennifer at JJB Boots."

Suzie's eyes lit up. For the next few minutes, Georgia forgot her discomfort and listened with interest to Jennifer and Suzie kidding around. When a break came in the conversation, Suzie glanced around and said easily, "Ladies, why don't you give Georgia and me a chance to get acquainted?"

The women in the tight-knit group looked at each other and then rose to their feet in unison.

"Come, sit." Suzie patted the cushion beside her.

Georgia sat, smoothing the skirt of her simple pink knit dress around her knees.

Suzie touched her hand. "Don't worry. J.J. is not going to get his way. Jay finds working with him stifling—they fight like bears. J.J can be quite something and he's never understood what makes Jay tick. But he's never worried me. I love it here. By taking over JJB Boots and marrying me, Jay would've done what he considered his duty. But then he met you. If we'd gotten married, it would have ended in divorce at some stage. Jay did us both a favor."

Georgia stared.

How could the other woman not have been in love with Jay?

But then relief surged through her. Under different circumstances, she would have liked to have been friends with Suzie. A pang stabbed her heart. Deep down, she knew that when this charade was over, she would never return to Colorado.

How on earth was she ever going to be able to face Jay every day at work?

"J.J. believes that the end always justifies the means. That's why he's blackmailing Jay."

Suzie's words jerked her back to the present. "Blackmailing Jay?"

"Manipulating is probably a better word. Jay hasn't told you?"

Slowly, Georgia shook her head.

Suzie rolled her eyes. "Jay's always been protective. J.J.'s not going to get anywhere, but Jay should have told you. You're a big girl—and he can't play the knight in shining armor forever. Honestly. Men!"

"I'm sure Jay will tell me," Georgia defended Jay, despite an inner twinge of unease.

Suzie's gaze moved to a point behind Georgia. "Speak of the devil."

Jay guided Georgia down a set of steep stone stairs to the pool deck below. Inside the stone pool house, the distant chatter of the guests dimmed and all that could be heard was the tap of her heels.

"The water is heated—my parents swim most days," he said, leading her to a pair of oversized wrought-iron chairs with plump overstuffed cushions set amidst a forest of greenery.

But Georgia didn't take the time to study her surroundings—or to sit down. Instead, she impaled him with suspicious eyes. "Jennifer tells me you jilted Suzie practically at the altar."

Jay winced.

"Is J.J. blackmailing you?"

"Who told you that?" he demanded.

"Suzie."

Jay drew a deep breath and sat down. "My father has been buying up stock in Kingdom—"

"J.J.'s behind the erratic stock prices?" Georgia interrupted him. "How long have you known?"

"I noticed the shifts in the stock a few months ago—"

"A few months?" She frowned down at him. "When did you plan to enlighten me?"

"At first, the movements were irregular…with no obvious pattern. It could have been a variety of factors. Last week, an earlier sequence of patterns was repeated. I confronted my father. He admitted he was responsible. I've dealt with him." His father had miscalculated—and he would not be doing so again.

"You've dealt with him?" Georgia still hadn't sat down. "You should've told me."

"I only spoke to Dad last night, after dinner." Jay knew he was on thin ice. He'd intended to tell her last night...but once he'd gotten to the bedroom and found Georgia in his bed, all good intentions had flown out the window. He'd abandoned his strategy of playful patience...and given in to desire.

"You've been keeping me in the dark. You're supposed to be my—"

"What? Colleague?" He raised an eyebrow, suddenly tired of watchful caution. "Friend?"

"No! Yes. You're both of those. But you're more." Her expression shifted.

Jay held his breath, waiting.

"You're my lover." At last, she answered his silent question.

Somewhere deep in Jay's chest, a warm glow ignited.

"Georgia—" He reached forward and snagged her fingers between his. "I'd never let my father harm you. Believe that."

She resisted. "I need to call Roberta—"

Jay tightened his grip on her fingers, restraining her. "Listen to me. I've sorted it out."

He yanked her hand; she lost her balance, toppled over and landed sprawled across his lap. Her blue eyes blazed up at him. He pulled her close, securing her in his hold. However much he stood to lose, there would be no secrets between them. Never again. "Hear me out. My father has sold the stock he purchased to me."

"To you?" She stared up at him, emotion shifting in her eyes. "Why would you want to own Kingdom stock?"

Why indeed?

He'd been asking himself the same question.

"I don't," he said tersely. "I did it—" He broke off.

For you.

But Georgia was frowning. She was adding up the limited pieces of information she had at her disposal and coming to God only knew what conclusion. In his arms, he could already feel her stiffening. She moved restlessly in his lap and against his will, his body reacted to her abrupt movements.

"Sit still," he growled.

"The takeover—"

"Listen," he said roughly, determined not to be distracted by the dictates of his body. It was imperative for them to talk. "My father has no ambitions to stage a hostile takeover."

"How can you say that?"

"Dad had some mad scheme of using his newly-acquired stake in Kingdom to force me to do what he wanted—return to JJB Boots."

Her frown had deepened. "He thought that would work?"

He shrugged. "He thought if he had a decent block of Kingdom stock, he could lean on the Kingdom board to fire me."

"Why did you resign from JJB Boots?"

Jay hesitated. "When I went to that fashion trade show I was seeking…something. I thought I was looking for a new challenge…but I couldn't crystallize what I needed. All I knew was that I no longer knew where my life was headed—or what I wanted." There was no harm in admitting any of that. "I was in danger of becoming one of those sad sons who can never make a decision without running it past Dad's master plan first. One of those men who never stand on their own two feet, and live out their lives as sad shadows of the men they might have become."

Georgia shifted. "Sometimes it's easier just to be swept along with the current."

"But it's harder, too." Jay wanted her to understand. "You lose yourself—and finding that inner certainty again takes strength."

"And Kingdom offered a bigger and better challenge?" Her voice was as brittle as glass. "One that would make you strong again?"

He didn't respond as she wriggled in his lap, and he loosened his grip so that she could sit up to face him.

Pulling the hem of her pink dress straight across her knees, she said, "Was that first meeting that Friday night really a fortunate coincidence, Jay? Or did you—and J.J.— plan that, too?"

"My father had nothing to do with it. Our meeting was nothing I'd ever planned for." But it wasn't the whole truth. There was more. "I didn't come to Kingdom to apply for a job. I came looking for you."

"Oh, God." Georgia stiffened in his arms. "Let me go."

Let her go? Anything but that!

But she was so tense in his hold, so rigid, it was clear she didn't want to be anywhere near him. The battle inside him was fierce, and the familiar fear was consuming. If he let her go…he was going to lose her. Forever.

But he was out of alternatives. He had no choice but to release her. So Jay opened his arms, and she scrambled off his lap.

Her chest rising as she drew a breath, Georgia pushed her hair off her face and finally looked at him.

"That Friday night did we…?" Her throat bobbed. "Did I know you were engaged?"

"No."

There was a sudden spark in her eyes. "Did you take advantage of the situation…? Did you take me to bed?"

"What do you take me for?" The ache in his chest deepened. "I was engaged… You were in a state of distress. We didn't sleep together—at least not in the way you're asking."

The tough, determined set to her jaw was one Jay knew all too well.

"What's that's supposed to mean?" she demanded.

"In the interests of full disclosure, you should know that we stayed together that night. You shared my room. And I held you—until you fell asleep."

Her hands came up to cover her eyes. "Oh, my God."

"You didn't want to go back to your room because your fiancé and his—"

Georgia's voice cracked. "You know about that?"

Her hands dropped away from her face, and she stared at him, flushed deep, deep red with a humiliation that made him want to draw her into his arms.

"That you caught your rat-shit fiancé in bed with another woman? Yes, I know about that. You told me."

"*I* told you?"

He nodded.

"So you thought it might be a good idea to take me back to your—"

"There were no other rooms available. The hotel—and the adjacent hotels—were jammed to the rafters with conference goers. You were distressed. You had nowhere to go. You slept in the bed. And once you were asleep, I moved to the couch. A very uncomfortable two-seater couch, I might add, but I'll forgive you for not thanking me for my gallantry."

A little of the tension went out of her. "Well, thank God for that."

"I'm not that much of a bastard. You were very shaken after breaking up with Ridley."

"How I wish my memory about him had been blanked out." She stared at Jay bleakly. "That…incident…has replayed in my mind over and over, thousands of times."

He'd been so sure the traumatic memory had been suppressed that he'd never dared bring it up to her. "Georgia, none of it was your fault."

Her expression didn't change. "My father doesn't agree. He blamed me. Ridley was the perfect son-in-law as far as he was concerned."

Jay gave a snort of disgust. "Then you had a lucky escape."

He was tempted to tell her that Fordyce would've been a far worse mistake, but managed to bite the barb back.

He'd never given up hope that Georgia would remember him. But she never had, not even now when he'd filled in the gaps she deserved to know.

"What is it, Jay? What's wrong?"

"You were gone when I woke up on the Saturday morning," he told her.

Slowly, she shook her head. "I don't remember. Days… that entire weekend…is simply gone."

"I know. I tried to contact you—only to learn that you'd crashed the rental on the way to the airport. You'd been hospitalized. I was worried." Nothing as mundane as worry. When he'd heard that she'd been in an accident and was awaiting surgery…he'd been truly terrified. He'd sweated bullets. "I wanted to see for myself that you were okay."

"I was fine."

The sound he made was not pretty. "I got to see you several weeks later, and you were not fine! You returned to work far too soon, hopping around on crutches—"

She shrugged. "Kingdom needed me. Besides, I'd heard Ridley's position had been filled, and I was eager to meet his replacement."

Jay knew she'd been worried her place in her father's

life…in Kingdom…might be usurped. The day she'd met him, she'd been bristling with suspicion.

Even though he doubted Georgia would ever admit it, the period after her accident had been one of crisis. Her faith in herself must've been badly shaken by her memory loss, by Ridley's betrayal and her father's angry disappointment. Hardly surprising that she'd turned, as always, to work.

Kingdom had always come first, and Jay knew it always would. The company pulled at her…even as her father pushed her away. And it saddened him to see how hard she worked to try to gain her father's approval and love.

"You should've been resting, keeping your ankle elevated." He didn't want to nag, but he couldn't help himself. "That's what non-load bearing means."

"Well, you certainly reminded me of that often enough."

He had. He'd tried his best not to hector her, and had taken refuge in the taunting rivalry that had grown between them.

"And you brought me coffee…" her voice softened at the memory "…whenever I needed it."

But bringing her coffee was never going to be enough.

For him.

Or for her.

Despite everything, he couldn't help her attain what he knew she really wanted: to prove herself by getting the top job at Kingdom and winning her father's love. And Jay was in danger of doing what his father had done to him: smothering her with protection and expectations.

If he loved her, he had to give her the freedom she needed.

Even if that meant losing her forever.

Fourteen

Fake.

Their engagement was fake. She was an imposter…a fake. She, who worshipped at the altar of honesty, had lied. To Jay. To herself.

She'd been so scared of becoming lovers with Jay, so fearful of jeopardizing their working relationship, so terrified of risking the tentative friendship between them, that she'd been blind to the fact that she was falling in love with him.

Forget blind. She'd been asleep.

For years!

What if she took a chance and told him how she was starting to feel?

As Georgia stared at Jay, a vision of all the possibilities filled her mind. They were dynamite together. She wanted to share her slice of Kingdom with him…the plans and projects and shining success she'd plotted for years.

But before she could get up her courage, he spoke. "Do you ever think about what you want? Deep down?"

She was shaking inside when she said, "I want to be someone people respect and—"

"People? Or your father?"

Jay's interruption jolted her.

"Are you sure that's what you want?" He tipped his head to one side, studying her. "What you really want most?"

She wanted more than one night... She wanted a future with Jay.

Georgia drew up her shoulders and let them drop. "There are other things I want."

"Like what?"

The impossibility of Jay falling in love with her made her hesitate...

Her mind veered away and she thought of her weariness. "Well, a vacation would be nice." Not running away or avoiding, but simply a time to relax and reflect.

"What else?"

"I've been meaning to spend more time with Roberta. I missed her when she lived in Europe. Yet, since she's returned to New York, we haven't spent much time together." All they seemed to do was work.

"You two are close." His voice had dropped.

"Very. It's quite strange because when we were children, she was much closer to Charis."

"Did you resent that?"

"No. I don't know. Maybe."

"Perhaps much of the tension between you and Charis comes from your father's dominance and manipulation?"

"What's this? Psychoanalysis 101?" But she had to admit that her father had always made it clear that Charis was his favorite—even when she pretty much killed herself to be everything he'd ever wanted from the son he'd never had.

"No. I have no desire to fix you—you are perfect the way you are."

She blinked in disbelief. Had she heard right? Had Jay actually told her she was perfect? With no gleam of mockery in his eyes...eyes that were already glancing away at the watch on his cocked wrist.

"What time is your flight?"

Her heart contracted. She told him, even as she tried to fathom what he was thinking.

But his face gave away nothing.

"The guests will be leaving soon, and then I'll give you a ride to the airport."

She'd half expected him to ask her to stay.

But he hadn't. Something inside her withered.

"I suppose you've got what you want all figured out?" She flung the words at him, feeling curiously defenseless.

If it hadn't been for his stillness, and the slight narrowing of his eyes, she would've thought he was quite at ease.

"Yes, I know exactly what I want." His lips curved up, but his eyes remained watchful. "Two years certainly gave me plenty of opportunity to work that out."

The fears that had always been so much a part of her everyday life bubbled up. She hesitated, and then said in a rush, "Is Kingdom part of it?"

"If you have to ask that, you don't know me at all." He took a few steps away, making her feel more alone than ever. "Come, we need to go back to the house."

What did Jay really want? There were so many more questions she wanted to ask, but Jay was waiting, his body tense.

So, she would be leaving…

There was the confrontation with her father that lay ahead. Her heart plummeted. She was dreading it. But she couldn't prevaricate anymore; she had to tell her father the truth that she'd turned Adam's down proposal. But she was not going to allow him to banish her from Kingdom as he had Charis. And before she left Jay's parents' home, she owed them an apology for the sham engagement. She wasn't much looking forward to that, either; but at least then her conscience would be clean. She wanted Jay's parents to remember her as someone with integrity. Even though there was no reason she would meet them ever again.

"Come on." Jay had paused on the stone stairs. He held out a hand to her. "Let's go say goodbye."

All the guests had finally left, and the anniversary party had been a stunning success.

While Georgia packed her bag, Jay had disappeared to check his email and make a couple of calls. Once she was all packed up, conscious that she would be leaving very soon and that she still had to undo some of the damage she'd done this weekend, she made her way downstairs.

In the den, J.J. was at his desk and Nancy sat on a couch with Zeus asleep at her feet. J.J. narrowed his eyes over the top of his spectacles as Georgia entered.

Once again, the shame about lying to Jay's parents washed through her. So much for her high principles. "I've come to say goodbye," Georgia announced.

"No doubt we will be seeing more of you, for those skiing trips at the very least." Nancy rose to her feet. "The snow will be here soon."

J.J. removed his spectacles and set them down on the desk. "You do know that Jay is only marrying you because you're your father's right-hand man, don't you?" He paused. "Jay has always wanted to call the shots."

"Stop it, J.J."

Georgia gave Jay's mom a grateful smile, before turning her attention back to J.J. "Jay could've taken over JJB Boots, if that's all he wanted, and he would've gotten total control far more easily." Suzie was right. J.J. had no idea what motivated his son. "But that's immaterial, and you have no need to worry about me keeping Jay away, because I won't be marrying him. Our engagement was a facade. Fake."

There was a gasp. Then Jay's mother was at her side. "What's this nonsense about a fake engagement? The two of you are perfect for each other. We—I—would welcome you with open arms."

Bemused, Georgia stared at Jay's mother. For the first time in years, the yearning for a mother flared. Then she threw her arms around Nancy and hugged her. A real warm hug. Tears pricked at the back of her throat. "I'm so sorry for deceiving you. Thank you for being so welcoming. Whoever gets to be your daughter-in-law is a very lucky woman."

Nancy hugged her back. "Georgia—"

From behind her, she heard a curse.

Georgia let go of Nancy and spun around. Jay stood in the doorway, her trolley bag at his feet. Now that it was finally time for her to leave, Georgia felt a lump in her throat.

It was time to finish what she'd started.

She hurried to Jay's side.

"This belongs to you." She tried to wrest the beautiful ring from her finger, but it refused to budge.

"Don't," said Jay, his jaw tight.

"I've already told your parents that our engagement is not real—and that I'd never stop you coming back."

"I'm not coming back to JJB Boots. My father knows that."

J.J. muttered something Georgia decided it was better not to hear.

"Your father can come along to New York next time Jennifer and I visit," Nancy said quickly.

This time J.J.'s muttering was louder.

Nancy rounded on her husband, her hands on her hips, her eyes flashing. "It's time we traveled together. Why, I was speaking to Joyce earlier, she and Bill have been wanting to go on a cruise for years, but they've never gotten around to it. She invited us to go along."

"Wait a minute." J.J. looked concerned. "I can't simply leave our business—"

Nancy tossed her head. "If you want, you can stay here and run JJB Boots, but I'm going on a cruise."

"You can't expect me to leave the company for months—"

"One month, that's all." Nancy brandished her index finger at J.J. "I intend to go once a year. While I certainly don't expect you to do anything you don't want, I've been dreaming about this for a long time. Now I'm going to do it."

"Go, Mom!" Jennifer's voice rang out from the doorway. "Make your dreams happen."

"Dad, you could always leave JJB Boots in Jennifer and Suzie's more-than-capable hands." Jay's suggestion broke into the cacophony. "Who knows? You might even find they do an outstanding job."

It was the baffled expression of blank shock on J.J.'s face that caused Georgia to interject, "Don't make the mistake my father made two decades ago. He was married to his business. He put Kingdom ahead of my mother's needs. He drove my mother into another man's arms. And then she died—they both died—and she never came back."

And her father was still putting Kingdom ahead of his daughters…

She thought about Jay's reasons for walking away from JJB Boots. He'd said something about needing to become his own man…not a boy in the shadow of his father. Was she in danger of having her growth stifled by her father?

She'd always held her father up as an ideal—a role model. He worked hard, he'd built a successful brand, he struck fear and awe into the hearts of everyone who knew him. She'd long ago decided that the only way to gain his respect was to rise to the top in the family business.

J.J.'s astonishment had turned to real horror, bringing Georgia back to the present. "Nancy would never leave me. I doubt she'll even go through with this cruise nonsense, either."

"Oh, I'm going through with it. I'm booking that trip first thing tomorrow. I'm going to have fun!"

Jay crossed to hug his mother. "Way to go, Mom!" Then

he straightened, and said to his father, "Georgia's right. You should think about having some fun, too. Before it's too late." Then he added, "Now, Georgia has a plane to catch."

"Don't let her get away," his mother called from behind them. "Keep that ring on her finger."

In the doorway, Jay paused, and said over his shoulder, "I have no intention of letting her get away."

The SUV swept down Red Mountain, and Georgia felt like part of her heart would remain behind. This was the place where she had first realized how deep her feelings for Jay went…how much she loved him. This was where they had first made love.

Her thoughts were interrupted by the vibration of her phone.

"Leave it!"

Irritated by Jay's peremptory tone, she ignored him and hauled the phone out of her purse to check the screen.

"Oh, no! My flight's been canceled. I'm going to have to call the airline to rebook." Another thought struck her. "I'll have to book myself into a hotel, too."

"You're welcome to stay with my parents."

"I don't think so—not after dropping that bomb that we're not really engaged."

Jay steered the SUV toward the town center and threw her a mischievous look. "Maybe we can finally share that bottle of champagne I promised you if you bid on me."

"Never mind a bottle of champagne…. You still owe me the fantasy date I won." Then she had second thoughts. "We'd better not do that today. Roberta would go nuts. She'll want to leverage every PR angle. She'll make sure our *date* takes place in some A-list restaurant and that we're appropriately dressed in all things Kingdom with a photographer of her choice on hand to document it."

"God help us both." Jay gave a theatrical shudder that

had her laughing, even as he pulled the SUV into the fore-court of one of Aspen's luxurious hotels. Within minutes, they were ensconced on a terrace with the mountains looming all around.

Once the sommelier departed after a lively discussion with Jay, he turned to face her. "There's something I need to discuss with you," he said quietly.

The energy that came off him in waves made Georgia feel decidedly on edge. "What's wrong?"

"I've resigned from Kingdom, Georgia."

"Resigned?" The bottom dropped out of her stomach. This was worse than anything she could have anticipated.

A mix of emotions swamped her. Complex feelings of bewilderment, betrayal and a sense of being utterly abandoned when she'd least expected it. Her worst fears had come to pass. She'd known this would happen. Now it had.

She was losing Jay…

"Does Kingston know yet?"

"I emailed him my resignation before we left my parents' home."

Then on the heels of her inner turmoil, she said, "Does that mean you're going back to JJB Boots?"

He shook his head. "I think you know better than that. JJB Boots does not—"

"Define you? Own you?"

He nodded. "It took a while to break those bonds."

"Was it worth it?"

He nodded, his eyes intent. "I will never regret it."

"Will you stay in New York?" She asked the question, though she dreaded the answer.

"I don't know yet."

Georgia had never considered leaving New York, never considered leaving Kingdom. But if Jay was not there…

Something inside her shriveled up.

Raising her chin a notch so that he wouldn't see how

devastated she was, she asked, "So what's next? Another journey? Where to this time?"

He gave her a smile that was all too familiar…and more than a little wicked. "Now, that rather depends on you."

"On me?"

He nodded. "A couple of hours ago, you asked if I knew what I wanted. I do. I want you, Georgia. I would like to ask you to marry me—to spend your life with me. That's what I most want."

Her throat closed. She had to choose between Jay…and Kingdom. She couldn't have both.

"You don't need to give me an answer right now. Take all the time you need."

"I have to go back to New York—"

There was a slight change in his expression, a tension in his body. Did he think she was trying to escape?

"I have to tell my father I can't marry Adam," she said.

Jay hadn't asked her to choose, of course. But she knew she had to be clear in her own mind about what she wanted. She didn't ever want to feel regret. Or to feel she'd been co-erced into making a choice she wasn't ready to commit to.

Could she do it?

She didn't even have to weigh up the pros and the cons.

Because she wanted Jay more than she wanted Kingdom. The contentment, the laughter, the feeling of being valued that Jay brought to her life.

It was a shock to acknowledge. And it had happened slowly, so slowly that she'd never even noticed he had become more important to her than her very reason for being.

The sommelier came back, bearing a bottle of champagne and two flutes. He filled their glasses with a flourish before retreating.

Jay lifted his glass to her. "Here's to you, Georgia."

"And you." Her glass chinked against his. "I—"

Her phone rang. She set her glass down to pick it up and glanced at the screen.

"Bingo." She glanced across at Jay as illumination struck. "It's my father. Do you want to guess why he's calling?"

She didn't wait for an answer but pressed receive.

Her father's voice was loud in her ear. "Jay has resigned."

"I know," she said.

"You know?"

"I'm with him right now. And Kingston, there's something I need to tell—"

"So what are you doing about it?"

The look she shot Jay said it all.

"Kingston—"

"Roberta says you've been in Aspen. What kind of crazy, irresponsible move is that?"

She rolled her eyes at the interruptions. "Think of it as business."

"Business? What do you mean?"

"We should open a store here."

For the first time, there was a pause.

"Do a cost analysis," her father commanded.

Georgia remembered saying something similar that first day they'd driven through the town. It made her feel distinctly uneasy. She was nothing like her father.

"Kingston, I'm not going to marry Adam Fordyce."

"I'll hire someone first-rate to manage—" There was an abrupt pause. "What did you say?"

"I'm not going to marry Adam."

Her father actually snorted. "Of course, you are—we've agreed to it."

"*I* haven't agreed. And as the bride, I'd say I have some choice in who I marry."

"Don't be silly now, Georgia."

He was still treating her like a child. But then she had

never fully stepped out of that role. She'd kept him on a pedestal as a way to avoid having to create an intimate relationship. She was no longer a girl, it was time to become her own woman.

"I'm not being silly at all. I'm perfectly sane. Probably for the first time in my life. And I'm going to marry Jay."

At that, Kingston exploded. Georgia held the phone away from her ear.

There was a wild joy in Jay's face. He threw his head back and laughed, then raised his glass to her in acknowledgement.

Finally, when her father paused to draw a breath, she said into the phone, "My mind is made up. And I'm taking a week's vacation—maybe even two weeks."

She shot a look at Jay to assess his reaction.

He just grinned.

She was done arguing with her father. "Disinherit me if you like—I'll only quit. Then you won't have as much time to play golf."

Georgia's heart was pounding in her chest as she killed the call and smiled across at Jay. "That was far easier than I thought it would be. He needs to face reality. He can't run my life anymore—because I'll be spending it with you."

Jay raised his champagne flute, his face alight with admiration. "To you, Georgia. My fiancée."

But he hadn't finished yet.

Leaning forward he brushed his mouth against hers and murmured, "I knew from the moment I met you that there was no one else like you. How I love you."

There was so much pride in his voice that her heart melted like honey in the sun. She wished she could remember that first moment they'd met. But it didn't matter, because she'd grown to love the man who challenged her more than any other, who understood her, who matched her. He was her future.

Epilogue

It had been an hour since the crash of the phone hitting the desk told Marcia Hall the call had come to an end. It had been awfully silent in the massive adjoining corner office since then. Marcia was starting to feel a little concerned about her boss.

From the parts she'd overheard, the call had not gone well.

She rose to her feet and made her way to the water-cooler beside the group of sofas across from her work-space. Through the wall of glass windows, the predicted storm clouds were closing in, darkening the sky outside. She was a little worried about Roberta and Georgia flying in these awful conditions. She poured a glass of water—chilled to the exact temperature her boss demanded—and made her way through the adjoining door into his office. It was more than an office. It was the archive of his life. The photos on the walls documented his meetings with stars and fashion icons.

He sat there, staring at the blotter. His gaze lifted as she stopped before the desk.

"That stupid girl turned Adam down!"

When he spoke of any of his daughters like that, it upset

her. "Don't work yourself up, Kingston. We don't want another trip to the hospital."

"Bah."

She set the glass down on the leather mat in front of him. "Here, have a sip of water."

He glared at the glass.

"She's taking a vacation." He looked dumbfounded. "She's not coming back to New York tomorrow. She doesn't even know how long she intends to be gone."

Marcia suppressed a smile of glee at the news that Georgia wouldn't be flying in this weather. "Kingdom is not a prison. She's allowed time off."

Kingston let out a growl. "Her refusal to marry Fordyce puts me in a goddamned uncomfortable predicament."

Marcia couldn't have stopped the smile that split her face if her job had depended it.

Had Georgia finally realized what had been there in front of her all this time? She hoped so. No point telling her boss that his predicament was one of his own making. Instead, she said, "Kingston, she's a grown woman. Let her go... Let her make her own decisions."

"I need her here. With me. With Kingdom."

"If you don't let them go, you may have no Kingdom." Nor any family, either.

He laid his head back. "Marcia, this isn't how my plan plays out."

"Sometimes life has a way of upsetting those rigid plans." Then more softly, she said, "You need to learn to let go, Kingston."

His eyes were closed, and he gave no sign that he'd heard her.

"What the hell am I supposed to tell Fordyce? How will I ever face the man over the negotiating table again?"

So, this was about loss of face rather than about the loss of another daughter. "I'm sure you'll find a way."

From the outer office came the sound of a ringing phone. She glanced toward the door, and then back at the man she'd worked with for almost three decades. The man she knew better than anyone else in the world. He was as deaf to reason as he was blind to the truth.

Marcia Hall shook her head and went to answer the phone that wouldn't stop ringing.

The show must go on.

* * * * *

COMING SOON!

We really hope you enjoyed reading this book. If you're looking for more romance, be sure to head to the shops when new books are available on

Thursday 11th July

To see which titles are coming soon, please visit

millsandboon.co.uk/nextmonth